STELLA GIBBONS

Starlight

VINTAGE BOOKS
London

Published by Vintage 2011

4 6 8 10 9 7 5 3

Copyright © Stella Gibbons 1967

Stella Gibbons has asserted her right under the Copyright,
Designs and Patents Act 1988 to be identified as the author
of this work

First published in Great Britain by Hodder and Stoughton Ltd

Vintage
Random House, 20 Vauxhall Bridge Road,
London SW1V 2SA

www.vintage-classics.info

Addresses for companies within The Random House Group Limited
can be found at: www.randomhouse.co.uk/offices.htm

The Random House Group Limited Reg. No. 954009

A CIP catalogue record for this book
is available from the British Library

ISBN 9780099528692

The Random House Group Limited supports The Forest Stewardship
Council (FSC®), the leading international forest certification organisation.
Our books carrying the FSC label are printed on FSC® certified paper.
FSC is the only forest certification scheme endorsed by the leading
environmental organisations, including Greenpeace. Our
paper procurement policy can be found at
www.randomhouse.co.uk/environment

Typeset in Bembo by Palimpsest Book Production Limited,
Falkirk, Stirlingshire

Printed and bound in Great Britain by Clays Ltd, St Ives PLC

To
A. C. B. W.
in
perpetual love

The fated people – the worshippers and poets, the magicians and lovers – who live by the light of the stars

1

'Well, what's he like? Hurry up, can't you? Lord knows it's miserable enough, stuck here all evening . . . I been looking for you since the church went seven.'

Gladys Barnes did not hurry up. She just glanced through the open door into the bedroom she shared with her sister, who was sitting up in their big double bed. Annie was wearing two thickish old coats, and a woollen balaclava helmet shrouded her untidy silvery head; her eyes glared with eagerness through her glasses.

'I'm putting my slippers on, should think you could see,' Gladys's tone was repressive, but less hurried, less nervous, than usual; this was always so, after her Sunday evening church-going.

She unlaced her shoes without haste, and put them side by side under the table. She untied a scarf from her head and folded it and laid it in a drawer, and slipped on a large wool cardigan and settled it about her. Then, and only then, did she look again at her sister.

'For 'eaven's *sake*, Glad,' said Annie, in a voice suggesting the control, with difficulty, of seething impatience.

'S'pose I can take me things off, can't I?' Gladys advanced into the bedroom with an unhurried step, unlike her usual blundering bustle. 'Pillows all upside down again,' she observed, whisking away the warm untidy nest they made and shaking them, in spite of protest, into coolness and plumpness.

'You can't half be unkind, Glad,' Annie said resentfully, 'you know I don't never get out not to see anyone nor hear a bit of news.'

'If I don't,' Gladys said awfully, 'I ought to, by this time.' She sat down in an old Windsor chair, which she pulled out so that she was beside her sister. Then stooped, with difficulty for she was stout, and picked a thread off the worn rug.

''Ave everything comfortable, then we can enjoy ourselves,' she observed.

'Oh do get on, Glad, you aren't half a trial.'

Gladys leant back, with folded hands. 'Like a cup of tea? I could do with one.'

'I don't *want* no tea, I want to hear what he's like and what the vicar said and everything . . . I don't know though, p'raps it would be nice. You can tell me while you're making it.'

Gladys's desire to tease, concealed beneath all this picking up of bits of cotton and plumping of pillows, had apparently died away. But she did not move.

'I'll just 'ave a bit of a sit down. My legs don't half pay me,' she observed.

'Tisn't all that far.' Annie was now leaning comfortably back against the pillows, and the glare from behind her glasses had subsided.

'I don't know, must be half a mile. More like three-quarters.'

'Three-quarters! You and your three-quarters, it's not more than half, if that. I used to run along there in no time. I remember one Christmas Eve I was late for that service they always have, what's it called, the one with the candles. They have the church all dark, and walk round it singing, lovely it used to be, and then they light it up again −'

2

'Pascal candle.'

'No that's Easter, Glad. Something – something – I shall forget my own name next.'

'It's on the tip of my tongue, too.' There was a pause, while both sisters gave quiet attention to the matter.

The room was small and low. It was lit by a central light, weakly shining from the middle of a ceiling dark brown with age, under a torn shade equally grimed, and furnished with pieces frail with age and the battering of many moves, spread over the seventy-odd years of the sisters' joint life. The wall-paper's pattern was almost indistinguishable, and older; even older. Gladys and Annie alleged that it was bunches of pink roses tied with blue ribbons. The bed and its shiny blue coverlet was just, but only just, clean.

Dust, grease, dimness. Yet the room was cosy. Thin red curtains kept out the foggy night at the square window, and Gladys, the one who went out to work every day, knew that, from outside, they made a faint but heartening ruby glow; the little, old, broken gas-fire burned with an opulent roasting flame. It ate shillings, fair ate them, was the sisters' verdict, but what could you do?

On the mantelpiece there was one of the pink roses given away with a detergent packet; Gladys had put it into a green glass vase. Annie liked a bit of green; always had. The sisters had been born in the country.

Gladys shook her head at last.

'It's no use. It's clean gone.'

'I can't remember, neither. Put the kettle on, Glad, and let's have our tea.'

The new curate appeared to have been forgotten. But not so. When the tea had been measured into a brown pot just big enough for the two, and they had suggested having a bite to

3

eat, and said that they really oughtn't to, and reminded each other that it was only Sunday, there was the week to get through, and then given way as they usually did and set out the sliced bread and the margarine, the subject was reintroduced.

'Go on, Glad, tell us. What's he like?'

'Young,' pronounced Gladys, a pleased light in her big blue-grey eyes, as if at something remembered. 'Around about twenty-six, I'd say. And ever so . . . severe.'

'Severe! But nice-looking, is he, Glad? The Reverend – Gerald – Corliss. Posh name.' Annie's quick, babbling voice hurried out the words.

'I wouldn't say nice-looking. No, not to say nice-looking. He's ever so thin.'

'Well that's not his fault. They have to be.'

'No they don't not in our church, that's Roming Catholics.'

'They do *fast*, Glad, I used to hear Mr Fleming tell us, when I used to go.'

'Course I know some people do. Tisn't the same.'

Here there was an interruption to the talk.

It was so faint that ears less accustomed to being on the alert for the tiniest sound that hinted and threatened an invasion of privacy might have overlooked it. But Gladys and Annie both heard the slow footsteps padding across the floor of the attic above, and both paused, Annie with her bread and margarine and Gladys with her cup, suspended. They exchanged significant nods.

'First time to-day,' whispered Annie. 'Asleep, I expect. Didn't do so well last week, can't have. I never smelt no fish and chips last night.'

'Think we ought to run up and see?'

'Nar!' Annie's sudden violent outward sweep of her hand in rejection of the suggestion, and the harmless shout in her voice,

4

hinted at a girlhood spent in a younger, rougher, yet more innocent London. 'He likes to keep himself to himself. You know that.'

'I know he's very funny, you have to admit it.'

'No more mental than what you are,' Annie said obstinately. 'On his own, no-one to look after him . . .'

'A lot's done for people that didn't used to be, Annie. For mental people and old folks . . . and homes and that . . .'

Gladys's voice trailed away and her sister, glancing quickly at her, said, as loudly as her weak voice permitted:

'It's all that Jean calling him Old Mental. Like her sauce. He's an educated man. Used to be a teacher, I shouldn't wonder, and come down in the world.'

'Ought to know better than going out begging, then.'

'It isn't begging, not downright it isn't. He works,' Annie protested.

'Work! Bits of dolls made of straw – who wants them?'

'Go on about the curate,' Annie said.

Gladys began on a rambling and roundabout account of the new curate's first Evensong at Saint James's, interrupted by questions from her sister about who was there, and what everybody was wearing. This evening, there was also a young girl and her boy to be described, whose banns had been published.

The other room belonging to the sisters was both living-room and kitchen: the furniture was as battered and the rugs as worn but there was one pretty thing in it: a piano with pleated silk, once green, behind its rosewood rack, and bronze candlesticks blackened with age: in front of the grate were two unbelievably shabby armchairs. Sometimes, Gladys would help Annie to creep out and sit in one: the window in this room looked clear out across the roofs to the Heath and the rampart of Kenwood's trees, and she could see the Fields, as they called them; 'up the Fields'.

Outside on 'their' landing was a tap above a slate sink, and under it their rubbish bucket and another, empty now, which would later contain coals. A third bucket, handleless, rusty, but neatly lined with newspaper and containing a few branches of wood with their leaves still adhering stood by the other two, but at a distance. The stairs, narrow and hardly covered in a black shrouding of bare, ancient carpet, went down into a dimness faintly haunted by the smell of cats.

There was a family on the ground floor, a young woman and her husband and two children and another coming. Gladys took a great interest in Mr and Mrs Simms, while dismissing all their casual attempts at neighbourliness, and unfailingly describing their inquiries as to her health and welfare as 'nosiness'. This, however, she confided to her sister alone, keeping up with the Simmses a series of hearty, daily, meaningless exclamations and smiles.

This small house was one of a pair, standing side by side and detached from the others in a row of tall brown brick ones, in a *cul-de-sac*. To get to Rose Walk, a way must be found through a maze of broad roads lit by the baleful glare of lamps that poured down thin orange light, and then along side turnings where the softer glow of the old lamps shone on small hardware stores, and grocery–dairies that still carried the faintest flavour of the little Welsh–owned milk and butter shops that had kept a cow in the yard at the back fifty years ago: drapery shops selling knitting wool and nylon stockings and an occasional gay cotton dress; newsagents with windows full of pornographic paperbacks and cigarettes – and then the street curved unexpectedly and you faced an upward slope paved with big old slabs of stone. Impersonality was given to the scene by a big block of Council flats opposite, and then, as the eye wandered over the dim sheds and slopes of choked, tortured grass and the general desolation of some railway tracks, it was caught by Rose Walk, tucked away on the left.

It was a double row of brown-brick houses, half of them bombed and boarded up, and not a whole window in one. At the end stood these two small stout cottages, painted white; thick little places, solid and secretive, with a bearded, coarsely-moulded face looking mockingly down from the wall exactly where the two were joined. The Barnes sisters lived in the far one of the two. Surprisingly, it had a name; it was called Rose Cottage. The other, equally surprisingly, was Lily Cottage, and had been unoccupied for years; even in these times, it was in such bad repair as to be uninhabitable, and this street was not on the Camden Council's priority list for demolition.

And all around the pair of cottages, for mile after confused mile, far as the wearied eye could reach, the lights smouldered through the foggy night and the cars crept throbbing along the over-lit roads. The poisoned air stands for thousands of feet above the city: the Wen, the great Wen, that never sleeps.

2

Just after the church clock had chimed, footsteps ran smartly up the stairs and paused outside the door of the outer room. A woman's voice called, 'Anybody home?' Then someone knocked.

As if suddenly pricked with a pin, Gladys sat upright, frowning, all her good-nature gone, while Annie pulled her coats closer and seemed to retreat within the balaclava. A litany of whispers began.

'It's that Jean.'

'What does she want?'

'Banging up 'ere. No peace.'

'Don't take no notice.'

'Glad. Glad! It's me – Jean – are you asleep?' and more knocking.

'Better go, I suppose.' Gladys shuffled into her slippers, which she had discarded in the cosiness of Sunday evening, 'Won't get no peace till I do.'

'Make it sharp, Glad – don't let 'er come in here, I don't want no Jeans round me.'

Gladys said, 'No fear,' nodded reassuringly, and went out through the dark outer room to the door.

''Ullo – what's up?' she demanded.

'Oh there you are, I thought you must be asleep or sunnick.' Mrs Simms stood in the doorway, the light from the inner room shining dimly on her tower of yellow hair and sharp young face. '*She* was round just after tea. Told me to tell you. She's sold the 'ouse.'

She seemed to launch the sentence into the dusk, without preparation, cruelly.

Gladys actually lurched forwards, as if the words had been a blow on her back, clutching at her cardigan, dragging it round herself. She gave a great gasp, but instantly checked her breath, with a wild backward glance towards the inner room. She shook her head frantically, jerking her thumb towards it, and Mrs Simms significantly nodded. Gladys turned back, blundering across the room, and shut the door, mouthing something re-assuring to her sister, then drew the visitor into the living-room, switching on the light. Its weak rays shone on her face, pale as lard, sweaty, fallen with terror.

'She never 'as, Jean! She can't 'ave – oh God 'ave mercy, Lord help us, what'll I do?'

She sank into one of the armchairs and sat there staring wildly up at the young woman. Mrs Simms stood staring back with mixed curiosity and a kind of gloating pity.

'She 'as, though. Told me herself. Said would I tell you and your sister and Old Mental.' She nodded, jerking her head at the ceiling.

'Oh, Jean, isn't it terrible – oh God, be merciful to Annie and me and that poor old gentleman –'

''Ere, who's a gentleman? Selling dollies round people's places, he ought to be put away. Well, that's what she said. All fixed up, it is. She said you'd better go down to the Town 'All about it, the men'll be coming in any time now to paint the place, she said, and do it up. Not before it was time, neither – Christ, if I'd known the kind of dump Ted was going to land me up in, I'd never 'ave married 'im, baby or no baby.'

At another time this remark, which confirmed, from her own lips, suspicions as to the age of Mrs Simms's eldest compared with the time she had been married, would have filled Gladys with a detective's triumph. Now, she merely uttered a kind of moan and said faintly, as if trying to escape the torture of her thoughts:

'What'll you do, then – with those two little children – oh, isn't it awful –'

'Not to worry about us. We got a Council flat. 'Eard last night. Down Hampstead Road, it is, nearer my work. Move in end of the month. Suits me. Near the shops, plenty of company, I can walk to work – no more one and six a day touch on fares.'

'I'm . . . glad. I really am glad for you, Jean.'

'Ta and all that.' Mrs Simms looked uneasily away then went on, 'She'll be coming round to 'ave a natter with you, she said.'

'I don't want to see 'er! She's let us down – swore to me not six months ago – yes, six months it was, just the six months, I remember because I'd been just six months working with Kyperiou's – swore she wouldn't never sell the place. *Swore* it.'

Mrs Simms shrugged. 'She's gettin' old. Wants to retire to the country – she can 'ave it, for me. Old folks, they're always changing their minds, Ted's mum does, she gets me down.'

Gladys was pressing her lips restlessly together and twisting her hands as if trying to gain courage to ask a question, and at last she almost whispered:

'Jean – tell us, dear – did she say 'oo's bought it?'

She waited, her large frightened eyes fixed on the other's face. Mrs Simms stared back, spite, pity, all her former expressions replaced by a solemn one that made her suddenly look even younger.

'That's just it, Glad,' she said, half under her breath, 'it's one of these here rackmans. A real bad type.'

Gladys made a kind of terrified lowing sound, her eyes fixed, wider and wider.

'But he's got plenty of money. 'Eaps of money, she said, and he offered 'er a good price and his money's as good as anyone else's.' She shrugged again. 'So she's sold it. And next door, and all the row's gone, too, she said.'

There was a silence. Into it, from the next room, there came faintly a voice calling, 'Glad! Glad – what's it all about? Glad!'

Gladys stirred in her chair. 'I'll 'ave to tell her,' she said fearfully, 'it's no use. She'll 'ave to know . . . did Mrs Adams say when she'd be round? . . . not that it'll do any good, if 'e's – 'e's that sort . . . we'll be out before you can say Jack Robinson.'

'Oh don't be so soft, pull yourself together, can't you?' Mrs Simms suddenly almost shouted, 'his kind's not all that popular nowadays, you go down to the Town Hall and moan a bit, they'll do something for you – you're a pensioner and God knows what, aren't you, I'm damned if I'd take it like you are.'

'You're young, Jean.'

It was unanswerable. Mrs Simms shrugged, and put her fingers up to the tower of hair above her peaky white face. She hung for a moment, as if uncertain what to say, then said sharply, 'We got some ice cream. The kids didn't want it – care to finish it?'

'Thanks, Jean. Annie would like it, I expect,' Gladys said dully. Mrs Simms shrugged again, and after another glance at the doughy, downward-gazing face, down which tears were now running, went out of the room.

In a little while, Gladys forced herself to get out of the chair. She straightened her cardigan, which was a bright turquoise blue and looked as if it had formerly belonged to an even larger wearer than herself, and uselessly fingered her hair, hanging in curls round her face, while staring unseeingly at herself in the dusty looking-glass over the mantelpiece. Then she turned out the light and marched across to the bedroom door.

'Well!' Annie observed, as it opened and her sister stood there in dramatic silence, 'what in 'eaven's name was all that about? I thought you was never coming.' She peered closer. 'You been crying?'

Gladys had intended to be brave. But the sight of the familiar room, with the teapot and loaf on the table and her sister sitting up thin and birdlike in their bed, broke all her bravery down. She gave a great kind of howl, and fell across the shiny blue coverlet, weeping out that Mrs Adams had sold the house to one of those awful rackmans who was going to turn them out into the street. The gas-fire, with that meticulous sense of the fitting sometimes shown by domestic objects assumed to be insentient, chose this moment to go out. Gladys heard its expiring groan, and cried the louder.

'Well,' said Annie, temporarily stunned by all this, looking down bewildered at her sister's grey-streaked head, 'crying won't 'elp. Do get up, Glad, 'ere, 'ave this – and tell us all about it.' 'This' was a paper handkerchief.

Some natures find relief in telling, and hearing, all about it, and Gladys's was one of them. Already, too, her dramatic, colour-loving spirit was relishing the drama of their situation . . . and though it was awful, shocking, terrible, they were not out on the street yet, and Annie, amid her cries of amazement and indignation at the baseness of Mrs Adams, and her shudders at the hints of their new landlord's nature, managed to remember there was a shilling in a pocket of one of her old coats.

Under her directions, Gladys first dried her eyes, then hunted, still whimpering, through the row hanging behind their curtain, found the coin, and put it into the meter. Then, as the gas began its heartless but cosy roaring again, another cup of tea was suggested, and made, and in twenty minutes from the breaking of the unbelievable news, the Barnes sisters were discussing it, and trying to work out a plan. The arrival of a saucerful of melting ice cream, delivered safely by a staggering toddler, cheered them further.

Gladys's attendance at Saint James's Church, which was fairly regular, had given her a sense of relying upon 'God and Jesus Christ', in the larger problems of their lives. She went to church because one of the ladies for whom she had worked encouraged her to keep up the custom. Annie's mysterious bed-ridden habits, it was taken for granted, prohibited church-going for her.

Gladys now began to think that some of 'them up at the church' might help.

'They're educated, Annie. They know what to do. I'll go round and see someone there first thing to-morrow.'

'You don't hardly know no-one there, Glad.' Annie, at first the calmer of the two, was now looking more frightened and desolate than her sister. That's Glad all over, she was thinking. Creates like anything and properly upsets you and then all up in the air and everything's going to be lovely, and you can get on with it.

'I do know him. He always shakes hands with me and says "Good-evening, Miss Barnes",' Gladys said with some indignation.

'Not to know him intimate, Glad.'

'I don't want to know him intimate. He'd only be on at me to go up there every day or something. I just want a bit of help.'

13

'Well if I was you I'd go to the Town 'All. You don't 'ave to know them.'

'Nor I don't 'ave to know the Vicar. All I want's a bit of help. That's his work, isn't it? Living for others. Loving thy neighbour.'

'We ain't his neighbours. You can't call living up 'ere right on the top of the Archway Road neighbours.'

'Top of the Archway Road! It's a good mile.'

'That it isn't. I could walk down there in a few minutes in the old days. I remember –'

'Oh well you always was one for flying along. Couldn't never keep up with you. All I know is, it takes me a good twenty minutes getting down to Kyperiou's.'

'You're stout,' Annie said flatly.

Her anxiety and fear would have its outlet, and it flashed out in the comment. If that wasn't just like Glad – start talking about something important and off she'd go, like some old cow in a field, wandering – but it wasn't nice to think of your sister as a cow, and Annie inwardly scolded herself.

'I am not!' Gladys exploded, large eyes indignant and sad behind her glasses, 'I'm slimming – you know that.'

'Oh yes, you're always slimming. Show you a doughnut and where's your slimming then?'

Gladys suddenly laughed. 'Can't say "no", can I? Don't let's 'ave words, Annie.'

'I'm sorry, Glad. I didn't mean to be spiteful.'

Annie re-emerged from the balaclava, into which remorse had sent her as a tortoise into its shell.

'Forgiven and forgotten, ducks. Then I'll go down first thing and 'ave a word with 'im.'

'With 'oo?' The dartings and short-cuts taken by Gladys's

mind often left her sister three or four stages behind in what, for want of a better word, must be called their discussions.

'The *Vicar*, of course,' impatiently.

'Well I'm sure I don't know what good 'e can do and if it was me I'd go down to the Town 'All like you say Jean said – the Vicar ain't supposed to know about the 'ousing problems.'

'It's all Christianity,' was Gladys's final contribution; a cavernous yawn, immediately infecting Annie, warning them both that it was after ten, and they were exhausted with talking and terror and blown out with four cups of tea apiece.

By mutual though silent consent, they said no more about the threat; awful, to them, as that of any looming hydrogen holocaust. The lengthy preparations for Annie's going to sleep began: the drawing of water from the tap on the landing, the warming of it, the modest washing, while she slowly and pain- fully stretched her arms to bathe neck and face, and even managed, at the cost of an actual, though brief, agony, to wash her feet. Nurse came twice a week to bath her but she liked her wash every night.

She would never allow her sister to help her unless she was too ill – 'like that time I had the pewmonia' – to move. A country cleanliness, though overlaid by sixty years of life in London, still chirped feebly in her spirit.

When she was ready for sleep, the usual exchange took place.

'Glad? Coming?'

An absent answer from the next room, where already a faint air of festival prevailed; a mouth full of biscuits, a chair drawn nearer to the flaring gas-fire, and Gladys sprawling in it with a copy of that week's *Reveille*.

'Shan't be a sec. Just having a read of "Revel".'

'That means twelve o'clock,' her sister observed, 'wasting the gas.'

A biscuit-y mutter, then silence.

'Glad! I'm ready.'

Gladys got up, without a shade of irritation on her face, brushed away quite a lot of crumbs from her chin, and went into the next room and bent over her sister, as she lay, small and muffled in many nightclothes, on her side of the bed.

''Night, Annie. Don't you worry, old dear.'

''Night, Glad.' They exchanged the brief dry kiss of age.

'Oh, Glad – isn't it awful, isn't it awful?' Annie suddenly wailed, raising herself on her elbow, 'what shall we do? There ain't *no-body*, there ain't *no-body*.'

'Then we'll 'ave to 'elp ourselves, won't we?' said Gladys, giving her a second, warmer kiss. 'Now you go to sleep.' She gently pressed the trembling body back into the bed.

Soon there was silence in the darkened room. Gladys sat on, studying the jocular pages of *Reveille* with eyes that could read perhaps two-thirds of the joke-captions and snippets of information and news.

But she could not enjoy it, as she usually did, for Jean's news hung and gloomed at the back of her mind, darkening every picture she looked at and every thought that came into her head. At last (and it was twelve o'clock, as Annie had foretold; the wind was their way and she just heard the bell of Saint Barnabas's, across the Archway Road, striking the hour) she scattered *Reveille* all over the floor with a despairing gesture and turned off the light. She had decided nothing, but that she would go to-morrow to see the Vicar.

3

Whenever Gladys walked across the small churchyard of Saint James's towards its hospitably open door, she felt as if she were in the country. There were so many trees about, and the Fields were near at hand.

The Vicarage was an enormous house, built of dark-grey brick, standing in a large garden beside the church; comfortable, dignified, even secluded. The hell of the traffic pouring ceaselessly up and down the hill was separated from it by only a few yards, but the garden was laid out with the Victorian lavishness in the use of land, and its thick laurels and its bushes of bay whose rich green was dimmed with soot did create a privacy: threatened, perpetually broken by noise, but nevertheless a prevailing privacy.

Gladys had not reckoned with having to march up to the door of the Vicarage; she had had some vague idea of a chat with the Vicar at the door of the church, where their encounters always took place.

But she was not intimidated by the house. Before the 1914 war, she had been in service in a mansion in Belsize Park, and again, between the wars, had worked as daily help in two good places in Hampstead, and she knew what the inside of a big house was like.

But she had not been prepared for the new curate opening the front door.

17

Tall and grave, and looking even more severe than at church on the previous evening, he stood, seeming seven feet tall in his long black cassock, and said, 'Good-morning.'

And no more. Behind him, cavernous passages and closed doors and high pale arches receded into the dusk lurking in a dark old house on a November morning. A very faint scent of distant coffee did something to relieve the generally forbidding air but, though Gladys's senses welcomed it, neither by any sudden cheery reference to it from the curate, nor of its own accord, did it approach any nearer.

Still – 'good-morning'. Polite, anyway.

'I want to see the Vicar,' she said, peering up at him through her glasses. These, suddenly to her dismay, grew misty; a blush of embarrassment had come up into her face.

She must have heard the Vicar's name over and over again but it had never clung to her memory – where, indeed, there was little room for facts. She always thought of him as the Vicar. But you could not call anyone Vicar when you spoke to them. Not polite. At Belsize House, she had always been called Barnes. Housemaid. Not tall enough for parlourmaid . . .

'The Vicar is out.' Pause. Gladys could think of nothing but coffee. The steam slowly dried from her glasses while they stood staring at one another. Then the curate said:

'Perhaps . . . what did you want to see him about. Er . . . perhaps I can help you?'

More likely to frighten me, thought Gladys, with that long face – and he can't be thirty yet. Give me a nice fat face like Georgie's, any time.

'Well it's like this,' she began, but broke off the comfortable easy beginning to ask doubtfully, 'When'll he be back?'

'To luncheon, at one o'clock.' As he spoke, the church clock struck eleven: Gladys had never been one for early rising unless compelled, and she did not go to the Cypriot café where she worked as cleaner until the afternoon. Sudden despair overcame her, and she was so hungry!

'Oh I can't never wait all that time,' she almost wailed, 'it's ever so urgent and serious.'

'You had better come in,' Gerald Corliss said, and stood aside to let her pass.

'I am a parisher.' The mutter just caught his ear as he strode swirlingly ahead of her down the stone-paved passage.

'What?' he said, half-turning.

Manners, thought Gladys, *what*, indeed. She repeated her avowal in another form. 'I mean, I go to Church regular. I was there last evening. Eveningsong. I saw you,' she added, hoping to defrost the atmosphere a little.

'Well, you could hardly avoid that, could you? I was not so fortunate. The congregation, *small though it was*, just looked to me like so many hats and faces.'

He led the way into a room that looked like an office, darkened by the shrubs that grew closely about its small ogive window, and seated himself at a large old desk, covered in faded green leather and with many drawers and pigeonholes. He waved her to a hard chair opposite, and she sat down. The scanty light fell full on his bloodless young face as they confronted each other.

'Now.' He folded thin hands together. 'What is . . . the . . . trouble?' He sounded as if he were searching for words.

Gladys replied by starting up in her chair and crying, 'The milk! The milk!'

Mr Corliss also started, as well he might.

'The milk?' he repeated, looking dazed.

'The milk for your coffee. It's boiled over. I can smell it. We'd better go and see to it.'

19

And she bounded away, following the reek that led her unhesitatingly down another gloomy stone-paved corridor and through more than one crypto-scullery into a huge mournful cave of a kitchen, where, on an electric cooker of the newest design, a small saucepan was bubbling hysterically in a white froth.

Gladys, charging across the kitchen, grasped the handle and shrieked. Mr Corliss, gliding rapidly up behind her, took it from her and said, not mildly, as he set it in a place of safety:

'It isn't hot. They can't get hot. It's a patent handle.'

'No more it isn't. Silly of me,' said Gladys. She glanced about her. 'Now, where's the cups?'

Mr Corliss, now looking unmistakably irresolute, silently indicated the giant's dresser, where six of them, among a scanty collection of other china, hung forlorn. Gladys quickly had two down.

'That was . . . my mistake,' he said suddenly. 'I had just put . . . the saucepan . . . on when . . . the doorbell rang.' The words seemed to come out in sharp little bites.

'Just like me, butting in at the wrong moment,' his parishioner said sunnily. 'Sugar? In the cupboard, is it?' She darted at a Brobdingnagian door.

In a few minutes the Reverend Gerald Corliss was returning to the Vicar's study with a laden tray. On it were the coffee pot, two cups and a plate of biscuits. His visitor marched behind with the jug of hot milk.

This was certainly better, thought Gladys, eating and drinking and looking around her. Cheered you up.

'Go on, aren't you having any?' she said gaily, waving a biscuit at the grave figure seated opposite.

He muttered something and poured out a scant black cupful.

'Can't think how you can drink it like that and no sugar neither . . . biscuit . . . no? Oh come on – treat yourself.'

Angry colour rose in his face. He felt young, inexperienced; he detested people, he detested the world, he was rotted through with spiritual pride, and it was the deadliest sin on the list, and why had he been cursed with a temperament, background, upbringing and education that made him unable to stomach, even after prayer and concentration, creatures like the fat blowsy woman sitting opposite? God forgive him, he hated her kind and her.

'Perhaps you had better tell me what the trouble is,' he said, and dislike made his musical Public School voice even colder than usual.

Thus sparsely encouraged, Gladys gave the following account.

'Mrs Adams, got two houses up Archway Road way, well, I say houses, a row it is really, let out to all these men, a lot of railway workers, nasty dirty work, she slaved for him, years, it was, not really married they weren't, excuse me mentioning such a thing but we're all 'uman aren't we, I said to her, slaving for him all those years well she didn't get her reward. Left it to that Elsie. All of them. And the men wouldn't stand the place going down. So off they went in the car. Brighton, it was, and owns our house too, and swore to me on the Bible only six months ago Gladys Barnes, she said, your home is as safe as mine and then leaves Jean, that's the young woman in my house, you would have thought he'd have left it to her after all those years, and she's very nervy, and said she wouldn't marry him, not if he was hung with diamonds, and I suppose that led her up to sell it.'

Mr Corliss seized the pause, when Gladys broke off to refresh herself with more coffee, to say rather faintly, with a now gentle coldness:

'Er . . . I'm afraid . . . it isn't quite clear . . . a friend of yours is in trouble?' He took a hold of himself, fighting off distaste. 'She . . . isn't married, I understand?'

'Hasn't been for years,' Gladys said robustly, taking another biscuit. 'No, it's my home. She sold it.' Her eyes, wide with suddenly remembered distress, stared at him grey-bluely through her glasses. 'It's me and my sister. She's got this trouble, they don't know what it is. In bed all day but Nurse comes twice a week, don't like her much I must say, always on about something, and Jean said go to the Town 'All but I don't trust them.' She stopped abruptly, took off her glasses, and wiped her eyes on a piece of rag.

At least it was not something ugly. Mr Corliss's distaste receded, and was replaced by a faint concern for his visitor. She was apparently threatened with losing her home. A picture of his own ancient home, set in the midst of humpy Wiltshire hills and their scarves of dark woods, rose before his inward eye:

> *Ah, shall I ever in after-time behold*
> *My native bounds — see many a harvest hence*
> *With ravished eyes the lowly turf-roofed cot*
> *Where I was king?*

he thought. O Virgil, serene master . . .

He read his newspapers, as a part of his training to be a priest in the modern world, and he had at least learned how serious, nowadays, was the loss of a home.

'And she's threatened to turn you out?' he asked.

'Never said a word,' retorted Gladys, 'told Jean to tell us and the old gentleman what lives up in our attic, well I say gentleman, though he does make these little straw dolls and totes them round, little figures and that, nothing but begging really but she needn't be personal, worst of it is, she says he's the rackman kind. You know, a really bad man.'

The last words, in their simplicity, set so many echoes ringing in a head not so long ago down from a theological college that again Mr Corliss had to pull himself together.

'You mean . . . your new landlord is a thoroughly bad type?'

'That's what I'm saying, aren't I?' Gladys's tone was impatient; she had lost her awe of Mr Corliss and was rapidly forming a low opinion of his intelligence. He didn't seem to understand what she said.

The despised one was, in fact, silently praying for help. Even at twenty-seven, there were many humiliating years of self-knowledge behind him, and the briefest of prayers, launched with a kind of calm desperation, was a tried resource.

It seemed to him that this one was answered. He leant towards her.

'Do nothing at all,' he said firmly. 'Just go home, and wait until you hear something more either from your old landlady or this new . . . chap . . . who has bought the house, and then decide what you will do. Er . . . how . . . about . . . er . . . funds?'

'Eh? Money, do you mean?'

He nodded. 'Yes. Are you . . . er . . . in immediate . . . want?'

'Not immedit. I got my pension, see, and Annie has hers, and we get a bit off of the Assistants. And I got me cleaning work. Not that that's much,' she added hastily fearing to scare away any funds that might be available, 'no, not immedit.'

'Because I dare say we could . . . if you were . . .'

'Now don't you worry about me,' said Gladys, fortified by coffee and biscuits and comforted by having been told to do exactly what she wanted to, namely, nothing at all, 'I'll be all right. Trust in One Above,' she added, feeling it was high time something about God came into it; after all he was the curate.

'Yes, exactly,' he answered almost inaudibly, 'if . . . that's where . . . He is . . . but certainly . . . trust.'

Well that's a nice thing to say to one of his own parishers, thought Gladys, marching away from the front door to which he had scrupulously escorted her. *If that's where He is, indeed.* Where else should He be? and she glanced up at the heavy sky louring over the Fields. And never told me to come again or anything. Oh well. Better write him off, as they say. A washout. She went off towards the bus stop.

'There was a caller for you this morning,' Mr Corliss said to the Vicar over their lunch, 'a Miss . . . Barnes.'

The Vicar, an elderly widower, shook his head. 'Don't know her. Is she a regular?'

'Apparently. She said she was . . . a parishioner.' He decided his ears must have misled him about Gladys's version; there wasn't such a word.

'What did she want? Money? Was she collecting? or did she just drop in for a chat?' Mr Geddes glanced, as if in search of something or someone, round the vast dining-room. 'Some of them do do that. Margery – my wife used to keep them at bay. Everyone, or almost everyone's, so lonely, that's the trouble nowadays.'

'She said she was threatened with eviction. Or so I gathered. She . . . her account was rather confused.'

'Eviction – oh dear. Unless it's very bad, young children and so forth, I don't think we'd better get ourselves mixed up in that. The local Press would be better – or the Town Hall best of all. If there were young children I would consider letting them come here, the parents too, just until they were settled somewhere, there are those bedrooms standing empty upstairs and very much on my conscience. But an elderly woman – you did say she was elderly?'

'Between sixty and seventy, I should say . . . only . . . it's so difficult to judge. Unusually talkative,' Gerald added, hoping his distaste did not sound in his voice.

'Barnes – oh, Gladys *Barnes*. Of course I know Miss *Barnes*. Yes, she is unusually talkative. I don't know her well, she's a rather irregular attendant, has a sister with some mysterious ailment – nervous, I should think – that keeps her bedridden, so our Miss Barnes can't always get away. Threatened with eviction, eh?'

'So I . . . gathered. But it . . . wasn't very clear.'

Mr Geddes laughed shortly and observed that he imagined it wasn't. 'Did she leave an address?' he asked.

'Yes, she did as a matter of fact. Rose Cottage, Rose Walk, N.W.5. I remembered it because . . . an unexpectedly charming name.'

If Mr Geddes thought this hardly the right reason for remembering a parishioner's address, he said no more than a dry 'H'm – it doesn't look very charming,' as they went out of the room. Mrs Hemmings, who came in every day allegedly to care for the comforts of the elderly widower and the young bachelor, was hovering, wanting to clear the table.

'I'll get along there to-morrow, if I can make time,' the Vicar promised, as he went into his study. 'I called there once, when I first came here, I remember now.'

But he was thinking more of how much he disliked poor Mrs Hemmings's cooking and her sour face. Would it be shockingly selfish to bring his mother down from Harrogate to look after him? She had only been released from the tyranny of many stone-floored, rambling, draughty, mousey vicarages three years ago, and the hotel was warm, pretty and comfortable.

Dammit, he thought suddenly, of course I'll ask her. Don't we both know, bless her, that she's only dying to come?

4

It was well after dusk, the next evening, as he climbed determinedly up the short flight of stairs that led to the Barnes sisters' rooms.

As usual, he had had a long day; up for the six forty-five; then another service at ten for those too old or frail to attend the earlier service; the tasteless lunch (a minor comfort now, with others oh how unbearably greater, lost to him, had been his wife's cooking), hospital visiting, perhaps the dreariest task that falls to a parish priest, all the afternoon; then Evensong, read through with the curate in the dim, empty church; and now the visit to Miss Barnes. It was to be followed by the meeting of the Men's Group, at eight, at the Vicarage.

At the top of the stairs he was confronted by darkness made just less impenetrable by a dim glow falling through a skylight. There was the musical dripping of a tap somewhere. He thought he could make out another flight of stairs, presumably leading to an attic. He was confronted by a shut door, with a dim light shining under it. He tapped.

A gaping child had opened the front door to him and nodded when he said 'Miss Barnes?' He had carefully moved aside the chair on which it had climbed to turn the latch, and had distinguished a murmur about 'Glad'. He had smiled at it – pale, trousered, sticky and apparently hermaphrodite – and realised that, from this moment, he was on his own.

He repeated the tap.

At once came a distant squeak. 'I'm all right, Jean, I don't want nothing, Glad'll be back any minute.' The tone was full of quite unequivocal rejection. Mr Geddes cleared his throat.

'It's the Vicar, Mr Geddes. The Vicar. From Saint James's Church.'

Stunned silence followed. Then – 'I'm in bed. Bedridden. Can't 'ardly move.'

'I wanted to see the Miss Barnes who comes to Saint James's,' he called, feeling the strain on a sixty-year-old throat.

'I can't get out of bed. Very weak. It's my sister you want. She's just popped out.'

'Now don't disturb yourself,' patiently bawled Mr Geddes through the twilight. 'You stay comfortable, and I'll wait here until she gets back. I don't expect she'll be long, will she?'

'Just popped out. Ran out of bread. It's only round the corner. Joneses.'

Silence fell. Mr Geddes wondered if he might venture to sit on the stairs. Better not, perhaps. He sighed.

'Did I hear a male voice?'

Mr Geddes jumped nearly out of his skin. It was the hoarsest of near-whispers and it seemed to float down from the ceiling. Glancing rather wildly upwards he could make out a glow, of a faintness to match the eerie sound of the question, at the top of the attic stairs.

'It's Mr Geddes, the Reverend Robert Geddes. I've come to see Miss Barnes but she's out.' He launched his explanation hopefully into the gloom, upwards.

'Ah . . .' breathed the voice, as if satisfied. 'I'll come down.' At the same instant there was a courteous squeak from Miss

Barnes's hidden sister. 'If you'll just open the door, sir, and come into the front room, you'd be more comfortable waiting there. You could switch the light on. It is just by the door.'

'Thank you – I will. Thank you.' The mild nightmare showed signs of dissolving.

But now slow, slapping footsteps were descending the attic stairs, with an effect of caution, as if the person coming down were feeling their way; old footsteps, conveying weakness, as had the bodiless voice.

Mr Geddes, not a romantic or imaginative type, had had enough. He was also hungry.

He opened Miss Barnes's door with a jerk, fumbled against the wall, and crisply switched on the light. The room's cosy poverty was revealed and also the further room, with Annie, sitting up muffled in some of the coats, nothing of her visible but her eyes, glaring out of the balaclava. She uttered an un-intelligible sound conveying welcome, and Mr Geddes lowered himself thankfully into an armchair.

He turned his eyes towards the door.

Another moment and a little old man crept up and stood framed in it as if he were a picture, looking mildly in.

He wore clothes faded to barely distinguishable shades of dim brown, sage and stone colour, all toned down to one overriding hue; it was as if he were dressed in dead leaves. His long-nosed face suggested the mask of a horse or sheep. Intelligence, of a kind, looked out through milky-brown eyes.

'When I heard you were a priest, I thought – an educated man,' he observed, 'and it's many weeks since I talked with an educated man. There's,' the eyes moved to Annie and he inter-rupted himself to give a little bow and say, 'Good-evening, Miss Annie,' then went on in a lowered tone – 'There's so many women about, so very many, and none of them you might call educated.'

His voice sank to a confidential murmur, '. . . one educated man to another,' he ended.

All Mr Geddes could find to say was, 'Good-evening.'

He judged that the visitor must be nearer ninety than eighty; skin, hair, eyes, teeth, stance, voice all thinly proclaimed great age. He wore bedroom slippers worn almost down to their supporting sock on his little feet, embroidered in orange and flame and ruby but all faded to a near-whiteness.

'My name this month is Lancelot Andrewes,' he remarked, shuffling into the room, 'I make a habit of taking a different name every month, sometimes that of a writer, sometimes a thinker, sometimes a prophet or a philosopher.'

'But what's your own name? The one your mother called you by?' Mr Geddes asked, wondering, but not about that.

'Ah. My real name. It really is Lancelot. Lancelot Fisher. I expect you have read Malory?'

'Not since I was at Oxford.'

'You were at Oxford. A great privilege. I never went to any University, my father was poor, very poor, poorer than what I am, you may say, because I have chosen to be poor, but he didn't have no choice. That is the 'ardest way of being poor. It was my mother gave me the name, she used to read, poor soul. Poor soul.'

Mr Geddes was beginning to find the conversation soporific. Thoughts of the brief interlude due to him in his armchair, with the evening paper, would intrude, and he turned in relief to loud, stumbling, bumping sounds, accompanied by a voice offering excuses and explanations, which were now coming up the stairs. Lancelot Fisher advanced into the room and sat down collectedly in the other armchair, and also looked towards the door.

'Well, fancy!' cried Gladys, floundering in and flinging a sliced loaf on to the table, 'sorry I was out, we just ran out, that Joneses they never 'ave any after six, you'd think there was another war, Jean's, that's the young woman downstairs, her Melinda, spoiled little madam she is, told me you was up here, and Mr Fisher too – what's your name this evening, Mr Fisher? – ever so nice of you to come round,' to the Vicar, with a flush rising to mist her glasses as she realized she still did not know his name, 'I expect your curate told you I come but you was out.'

She began unwrapping cardigans, scarves and a thick coat from herself, the while glancing distractedly towards a cupboard on which stood a tea canister, with a portrait of Her Majesty on it smiling out across the room. 'I'm sure you could drink a cup of tea. And you could, couldn't you, Mr Fisher? Never say no to a cup of tea, do you?'

'It's very kind of you but I won't, thank you,' said Mr Geddes. 'I just –'

'Oh but you must,' screamed Gladys, scrabbling on a shelf for the milk, 'can't let you go without a cup of tea, and you coming all this way, wonder you didn't get lost –'

'I will have a cup of tea; thank you,' observed Mr Fisher, raising his eyes from his study of the carpet.

'Oh we all know *you* never say no, Annie, we're out of biscuits again –'

How long this struggle between disinclination and hospitality would have gone on Mr Geddes never knew, for at that moment a woman's voice called urgently up the stairs – 'Glad! Quick! 'E's 'ere – the rackman. In a car!'

Silence fell, and, instantly, every eye was fixed upon Mr Geddes, as if he – the one who had been to college, the one who knew how things worked – would know what to do, while on every face there was an expression of terror. In another moment, the young woman's eager face appeared at the door.

'It's 'im, Glad . . . 'ere . . . let's . . .'

She pushed without apology past the seated men and, followed by the muttering and trembling Gladys, hurried into the bedroom and over to the window. She cautiously moved aside the curtain. Mr Geddes, forgetting everything but human curiosity, got up and followed, and next was made aware, by a sensation of moth-like pressure and eld, that Mr Fisher was at his side. Even Annie was leaning awkwardly sideways from her bed to stare down.

The street was only a short way below. Its paving, heaved into irregularities by the bombing of twenty years ago, gleamed greasily in the faint light of its one lamp, and, down at the end of the dark, boarded-up, double row of houses they saw the great car, its insolent snout pointing down the Walk as if threatening it.

'Consul. Does 'imself well,' breathed Jean Simms. 'Shuvver, too – see 'im, Glad?' But no-one answered her.

A man was standing there, hands in his pockets, a little beyond the rays of the lamp, staring up at the cottages. He was stout, and wore a soft hat, and that was all they could see of him.

'Someone in the car . . .' whispered Gladys, and instantly all their eyes turned to it.

They could just distinguish a figure sitting in the back, with head swathed in a voluminous, spirit-like whiteness that might be a scarf.

Transfixed, they stared. His inspection did not last longer than a few minutes but there was something chilling, something impersonal yet intent about it, that was frightening. The chauffeur did not move; the woman-like shape in the back of the car was leaning slightly forward as if to see the house, too, but it also was motionless.

All at once, the picture broke up. The man stirred, and pushed his hat on to the back of his head, and walked back to the car.

He got in beside the white shrouded shape, and the car backed, edging its way into the narrow entrance and then turned the corner and went out of sight.

'Well,' Mr Geddes was the first to speak, '*he* doesn't look very alarming, does he?'

His strongest impulse was to take that look off their faces.

The young woman suddenly exclaimed, 'My God, the kettle, and young Melinda's in the kitchen,' and sped away. Annie, emerging from her retreat, said tremulously, 'What's 'e like, Glad? I couldn't make much out. My eyes are ever so bad to-night. I can't hardly see. Muss be the fog.'

''Orrible,' Gladys said with relish, 'great fat thing, coming 'ere after dark like that, why couldn't he come daytime like anybody else? It just shows you.'

'Probably he was on his way to somewhere else and just stopped by to have a look at his new property,' said Mr Geddes comfortingly, though he had in fact been disagreeably affected by the little scene, especially by the glimpse of the white muffled figure in the car.

'That's 'er,' said Jean Simms, reappearing with surprising speed and Melinda clamped on to one hip, ''is wife.'

'Is 'e married, then? It said in the paper that sort always has – you-knows,' said Gladys.

'He's married all right. Crazy about her, too. Mrs A. told me. Said 'e'd only bought the 'ouses because she used to live round 'ere.'

'Jean! I'm ready for my tea,' shouted a young man's tired voice up the stairs. Interrupting herself long enough to bawl – 'Oh shut yer face – give us a minute, can't you?' over her shoulder, Mrs Simms went on, 'Yes. That's what she told me. *Likes the neighbourhood* – she's an invalid or sunnick. She can *'ave* the neighbourhood. Night, all,' and, clutching the staring child, she hurried away.

Mr Geddes had returned to the living-room. Mr Fisher had resumed his seat and his downward contemplation of the carpet. The Vicar thought that he must be going – the easy chair and the evening paper were not for him, this evening – and not a thing had been said yet about the cause of his visit. He cleared his throat and addressed himself decidedly to Gladys, now fussing with the teapot:

'I understand that this man has bought the house from your old landlady, Miss Barnes, and that she told you he has a bad reputation as a property-owner?'

'A regular rackman, she said, you might say if 'e's all that bad why did she let him 'ave it but his money's as good as anyone's I s'pose.'

'What do you suppose will happen now?' asked Mr Geddes, knowing from experience that it was sometimes necessary to distress people by making them come to the point – and, really, he must not stay a moment longer, he would be late for the Men's Group as it was: Gerald would have to begin without him; well, that would be excellent experience for the young man, it would teach him that vicars sometimes missed trains or fell down staircases or caught influenza.

'Gawd knows and He won't split,' retorted Gladys, anxiety, alarm, and the duties of hostess causing her to forget whom she was addressing, 'she said he wanted quire property in this distric' –'

'Choir property?' repeated Mr Geddes, bewildered. He was not the first listener to wish he had an interpreter while Gladys was explaining something. 'Oh, to acquire property, I see, yes?'

'She said he hasn't got no property here yet, all over Islington way, he is, and he wants to make a start here. He's bought the row, all the 'ouses in the Walk, she said, got them cheap, they

33

did say they was coming down but that was years ago – Annie, when did we hear they was all coming down along here?'

Annie, who had got her tea first and was luxuriously sipping, moved the balaclava in an unhelpful gesture.

A power cut now added to the evening's excitement. There was much exclamation, and a slow departure on the part of Mr Fisher in search of candles. When the room was once more, if faintly, lit, Mr Geddes said firmly, addressing Gladys:

'Now I want you to know, Miss Barnes, that if anything really serious happens we at Saint James's are your friends, and, if things get serious, you can come to us and we will do what we can. Nothing serious has happened yet, has it, now? I know you must all feel shocked and *upset*' – he included Mr Fisher in what had grown, during the last hour, to have for him the atmosphere of some family party – 'but nothing has *happened*. And it may not. Always remember that, and keep cheerful.'

'They're going to do up the place first thing, Jean said so,' Annie put in, still swallowing tea, 'upsetting us. Painting, and that.'

'But surely . . .' Mr Geddes just refrained from an eloquent glance around him, 'fresh paint, new wallpaper . . .'

'Paint. Stinking the place out,' said Annie, with rustic frankness and Mr Geddes gave it up.

The proverb about angels being able to do no more than their best occurred to him as he made his way down the stairs, escorted by Gladys's recital of the things that could happen to all at Rose Cottage, beginning with trebling everyone's rent and ending with eviction.

Mr Fisher lit them down with the candle, which he had crept up to his own domain to fetch.

'Got thousands of them up there,' Gladys had whispered during his lengthy absence, 'doesn't want the electric. 'Oards them.

I don't let *her* know,' indicating her invisible sister with a nod, 'she wouldn't sleep a wink, afraid of fire. Mind you, the electric don't go up there. But they could 'ave run a wire, she isn't so bad, I was telling your curate, except for that Elsie, won't hear a word for *her*, not a word, and you can't blame her.'

They were in the hall now, a broad little place, with rich mouldings of smoky plaster roses and clustered leaves banding its ceiling. Mr Fisher was coming slowly down to them, extinguishing his candle as they entered the weak glare of the suddenly restored electric light, and slipping it, still smoking, into his pocket ('I'm always telling him,' said Gladys, aside).

Mr Geddes, confused by the cascade of her farewells, was surprised to find, on shutting the front door on them, that the old man was outside it. He had put on a cap and a thick old overcoat of the same colourlessness as all his clothes and wore stout boots with an indescribable air of belonging to the earlier years of the century about them. He now held out his hand to Mr Geddes, under the mocking blind eyes of the mask that hung between the two cottages. A mile away in Archway Road the traffic kept up its dreary roaring; here, there was near darkness, and a silence.

'Good-night. A privilege, meeting an educated man,' his remote voice said thinly.

'Going out . . . Mr Fisher? It's not a pleasant night for walking,' Mr Geddes said, concerned for him, and taking the small hand in a worn thick glove.

'I makes a habit of walking on the Heath in all weathers. Don't be afraid for me . . . The moon will rise at eight o'clock. I always takes a note of when. Our ways don't lie together, but I 'ope we meet again.'

He drifted away, shuffling past the boarded houses, down to the end of the Walk, and Mr Geddes, feeling dismissed, let him go.

5

Gladys did not confide her anxieties, in the week that followed, to the Cypriot family in whose café she worked.

Her instinct to tell everybody everything, at length, struggled with her instinct to mistrust all foreigners. Her mistrust was general; and hardly applied to her employers, who were kind enough, called her 'Glad', and were lavish with leftovers. She explained her liking for *them* by saying that they were 'different'.

But – 'Those dark eyes! I never trust 'em,' she would usually say, and some dim notion that the rackman was a foreigner linking up with her general mistrust, together with the popular rumour that foreigners were great snappers-up of property, kept her silent.

However, while sluicing water over the linoleum patterned to look like mosaic, she would sometimes pause, and stare pensively down into the pail. The proprietor's wife, wiping down a table or returning from taking a tray of pastry covered in wisps of coconut to a customer, would drop a 'What up, Glad? you lost somesing?' in passing, and Gladys would start awake. Mrs Kyperiou was a peasant, with a peasant's feelings about work: unless it were siesta-time, you did not stop working, much less stare into your pail, in the middle of washing the floor.

But, although Gladys told them nothing, an occasional sigh

or shake of the head which she could not resist, hinted at anxieties.

The Simmses left on Wednesday, their few shiny cheap pieces in a van belonging to a friend, and the two hermaphrodite children, pale and sticky as usual, smilingly riding in the middle of the furniture.

The sisters had a hasty farewell visit from young Mrs Simms, who bestowed on them an ashtray with an Alsatian dog curled round it and the tip of his tail broken off. She was in a great hurry, having delayed this ceremony until a few minutes before the van left, and her farewells were confined to hasty waves and the laying of the ashtray on Annie's bed.

'Well, good riddance to bad rubbish,' observed Gladys, standing at the window and looking down into the street, where the last pieces were being loaded into the van, 'and *that* can go in the bucket,' glancing disdainfully at the Alsatian. 'There's Nicky and Alexander, Annie. Now why aren't they at school?'

'Jean said their baby's got the measles. S'pose *they'll* be getting the push any time now,' Annie said sadly.

The two little Jamaican boys belonged to the one family left in the most habitable of the boarded-up houses. Smiling and numerous, respectable and tidy, they felt themselves lucky to be living in it.

'Poor little devils,' said Gladys ominously, not meaning the measles, 'I pity them.'

'Oh don't remind of it, Glad,' and Annie retreated: she meant the probable eviction of Nicky and Alexander.

'I like that. 'Oo started on about it?'

It was a morning of thin, fine November air and brilliant sun; every shade of rusty red and faded blue on door or railing glowed through the genial light.

'Bye-bye! Bye-bye, Melinda, bye-bye, John, bye-bye!' shrieked Gladys, leaning out of the window to wave. 'Got a nice morning for it, anyway. I'm not 'alf glad to see the back of her. Get a bit of peace now, p'raps. And that Melinda, spoiled little madam.'

'It'll be a bit lonely for me, Glad. Stuck 'ere all day, not a soul to speak to.'

The van and its load turned the corner and was gone.

'P'raps he'll let the downstairs to someone nice, now. Respectable. Not like her. That hair! looked like that Awful Tower in Paris.' Young Mrs Simms's hair, in Gladys's mind, condemned her more than the baby born four months after marriage; the baby at least, Gladys would say, was natural.

Now that the van had driven away, the Walk was quiet except for the little coloured boys, playing some unobtrusive game with marbles on the ridge of concrete outside their front garden, from which the iron railings had been taken to make fighter-bombers long, long before they had been born. Occasionally, a passer-by or a car went along the road at the end of the Walk. Gladys stretched, and folded her arms comfortably.

'Well –' she was beginning, and Annie was anticipating a favourite observation about the baby and its problematical new frock, when her sister exclaimed – 'Ullo!'

'What's up now?'

'Young woman, smartish, looks like a foreigner.' Gladys instantly let the curtain fall and remained rigid behind its concealment, staring.

But it was too late. A dark head was tilted back, dark eyes that had caught the curtain's movement lazily surveyed the window, the sauntering footsteps slowed to a stop, and a voice called up leisurely:

'Hullo?'

'Cheek,' muttered Gladys, 'who does she think she is?'

'Miss Barnes?' called the voice. 'I want to see you.'

'Knows my name,' hissed Gladys, with a lightning turn to the bed, where Annie was painfully divided between curiosity and some new threat from the rackman and had not quite decided whether to retreat.

'That's me,' announced Gladys, suddenly opening the window and leaning out. 'What is it that's wanted, please?'

'I want to see you. It's about the house being done up. It belongs to my mother now,' the girl said. She did not exactly smile: her expression suggested sunlight behind clouds on a close, hushed day.

'Oh. I'll come down.' Gladys shut the window, with trembling limbs and banging heart.

Pausing only long enough to hiss quite a lot of information and comment to the cowering Annie, and to cast a swift glance over the parlour – yes, not too bad – and to dab fiercely at her hair, Gladys marched down the stairs and flung open the front door.

My lady was on the doorstep.

'Good-morning,' Gladys said, with meaning. This low calling up out of the street between total strangers would get no encouragement from her.

The concealed smile just broadened, like heat coming through the clouds.

'Oh . . . hullo. My name's Peggy Pearson. My mother wants me to look over the place and see about getting it done up.'

'Well . . .' Gladys began doubtfully, but before she could say any more, Peggy Pearson had stepped inside and was looking indolently about her; up at the plasterwork of the ceiling, the generous proportions of the stairs, the decent squareness of the hall.

'Very dirty, isn't it?' she remarked at length.

Gladys, encouraged by a manner that seemed to show neither greed nor severity, was trying to summon courage to ask the questions never absent, now, from her mind and Annie's; whether they were also haunting the mysterious tracts of Mr Fisher's, she could not have said. But, momentarily, indignation at Peggy Pearson's comment drove the questions from her mind.

'She's had a lot of trouble, slaving herself into the grave for him these ten years and all those men, never satisfied, a nice cook she is, up all hours on the Railways and then leaving it all to that Elsie, well, I said, I for one don't blame you, and expecting to live comferable in her old age no wonder she sold it, always meaning to do it up though I don't like the smell myself, turns me up, well it would anybody, wouldn't it, you'd better see her. I don't know nothing.'

'That's all right,' said Peggy Pearson, still looking round, and Gladys was sure that she had not been listening. 'What's upstairs?'

'My sister's bedridden,' said Gladys instantly.

'All right. I shan't eat her.'

Gladys led the way upstairs, the questions unasked.

'It's quite small,' said the girl, having glanced into the recent home of the Simmses on the second floor, 'it *is* dirty. But pretty, really . . . That your flat?' glancing up the stairs.

'It's two rooms. We share the toilet. There's no bath,' said Gladys, raising her voice as she toiled up before the visitor so that Annie, now no doubt in full retreat, might realize the incredible fact that the rackman's representative would any minute be upon her.

'Oh, my mother'll put one in. That little cupboard-place at the back would do. They could put in a new door.'

Plenty of money here, thought Gladys. Talking about putting in baths like you might buy a box of matches.

She opened the living-room door. Sunlight was streaming

through the window and the distant fields, beyond the two miles of roofs, looked green as green. Peggy Pearson glanced round indifferently. Then her eye went to the farther room, where, half out of the balaclava, her two coats neatly buttoned and the *Mirror* spread before her, Annie looked up long enough to give a hospitalized smile. Miss Pearson returned it with a casual wave of one gloved hand and, after a glance about the room, turned away.

Gladys's relief at seeing Annie undemoralized took the form of a slightly more cordial attitude towards their visitor. Tea might provide an interval in which *the questions* could be asked, and she was also anxious to keep the rackman's daughter − if she was his daughter − from questions about the attic. Mr Fisher wouldn't be able to stand up to shocks of this kind as stoutly as she, Gladys Barnes, had.

'How about a cup of tea?' she asked. 'After all those stairs?'

'Not so many,' Peggy Pearson said. 'All right.' She sat down in one of the armchairs and began to take off her gloves. 'Thanks.'

While she bustled about, Gladys began on the questions. It was no use: she had to know; and Annie and Mr Fisher must be thought of; the answers meant as fearfully much to them as they did to her.

'Your mother thinking of making many changes here?' she asked, with her back to the visitor while she elaborately hunted for biscuits which were staring up into her face.

'Depends what you mean by changes.' The voice held just a note − so slight that Gladys could wonder if it was there at all − of teasing.

'Well' − she suddenly turned to face her, with the biscuits; a bit of a girl, not even the owner, couldn't be more than in her early twenties, she was not afraid of her, and would show

41

it – 'Rents, and that. She going to put them up?' Gladys could find clear speech, when fear and desperation drove her.

Miss Pearson shook a dark head; small, the hair centre-parted and hanging like a nymph's about small ears. She yawned behind a muscular hand.

'Not . . . thinking . . . me and my sister was wondering . . . not . . . eviction?'

Trembling, she spilled some water as she poured it from the kettle into the pot.

The dreaded word was out, and Gladys stood staring, dismayed. Suppose it 'put the idea into the daughter's head' and she suggested it to this unknown 'mother' – (could she be the white-swathed ghost in the rackman's car?) – then she, Gladys would have brought it on them all.

'My mother said you aren't to be frightened. Is that mine? Thanks.' She held out her hand for the cup. For once robbed of words, Gladys stood staring and for a moment did not pass it to her.

'Who's frightened?' she demanded at last. Miss Pearson shrugged. 'I don't know. That's what she said, though. Tell them they aren't to be frightened.'

'I'm not frightened. Nothing to be frightened about, far's I can see.'

'All right. She just said I was to tell you.' Peggy Pearson bent her head over her cup and took an indifferent sip.

Gladys carried a cup through to Annie, whose eyes glared up at her with a hundred questions and all of them alarmed.

She had heard every word. Of course they were frightened, all of them, she and Glad and Mr Fisher – with him you couldn't be certain, but he must be – but it wasn't nice to hear it said right out. Oh, if the girl would only go away and leave Glad and her to talk it over! Why did Glad have to go and offer her tea? She was always wasting tea on people. *Frightened?*

'All right.' Miss Pearson stood up, looking round for somewhere in the cluttered room to put down her cup. 'I'm off. I'll tell mother and she'll send someone in.'

'When'll that be, then? We got to have some idea – my sister's bedridden and I go out to work – I can't go shifting stuff ready for the men and them not coming, I know what they are . . .'

'These'll come. They're people my father knows. Some time early next week. You can move into those rooms downstairs, if you like, while they're here, my mother said.'

Gladys stared. High-handed, but after all the girl's mother did own the place. And was anything going to be done about those two rooms on the ground floor with their ceilings all down? Empty, they'd been, for years.

'She said *he'd* bought it,' she muttered.

'Who said?' Miss Pearson was pulling on the gloves that matched her suède coat.

'Jean, she had the flat below us, only moved out this morning, she said she told her –'

'Who told who? I can't bother with all this . . . my father bought the place and he's given it to my mother and she's coming to live here and someone's coming in to do it up and she told me to tell you all you aren't to be frightened. That's absolutely all I know. I've got to go now. 'Bye.' She waved, without looking at her, towards Annie.

'Coming to *live* 'ere?' Gladys repeated eagerly, leading the way across the landing where the tap lacking a washer dripped musically. 'P'raps the men'll see to that tap then?'

'I dare say. Or someone will. My mother doesn't like irritating noises, her nerves are bad.'

Gladys, inwardly raging to get back and discuss every detail of what had been said with her sister, now took a reckless plunge.

'There's a very old gentleman, educated he is, name of Fisher, well, it isn't always he changes it every month, I mean, that's his real name but he makes believe, he can do for himself, lives up in the attic, earns a bit showing off fancy dolls, do you think she'd let him stay on? He's not really what you'd call mental.'

They were on the doorstep now and the door stood open to the bright November morning. This time Peggy Pearson laughed, shortly but outright, showing teeth small, white, and pointed as those of a young fox.

'I expect so. She likes what you'd call mental people. 'Bye!'
She walked away, leaving Gladys staring after her.

6

The Reverend Gerald Corliss associated the season of Advent with the scent of violets.

This was the hour before the dawn of the Church's year, when the end of the nave was in darkness by four o'clock, and Evensong was said under a night sky. To him, it always seemed darker, more patient, and more a time of waiting than the three days following Good Friday.

Born and brought up in the country, he knew well that English violets did not appear until the spring, but the flowers that haunted this season for him were not country ones; they belonged to London, and were sold in bunches made up with an alien leaf; sometimes at street corners, but most often in expensive flower-shops, and their faint scent was blent with that of the London smoke.

He thought of this idea about violets as a weakness in himself, and faced it resignedly. Nevertheless, he always bought a bunch of violets in the first week in December and put them in his room.

It was all petty; the association, the tiny self-indulgence, and the introspection. He did not need telling that, in 'a world bursting with misery', he should have felt ashamed; and he was ashamed. He had read somewhere that among the crosses bestowed by God temperament might be included, and the clerical essayist had added, almost casually, that it could be one of the heaviest.

There was no doubt about the nature of Father Gerald Corliss's cross, and it weighed several ton.

A coffee-party was always held in the church hall at Saint James's after Evensong in the first week in December. The Vicar, whose cross was not in his temperament, felt that the month was a gloomy one; and with the exhausting business of commercialized Christmas only three weeks away, to say nothing of the gloomier aspects of the Advent message looming over his congregation (although few of them took *that* seriously), he did feel that a little social intercourse sweetened with coffee and biscuits would lighten the atmosphere. On Sunday evening, December the third, therefore, some seventy people had gathered in Saint James's Parish Hall.

Coffee was being served by three Youth Club members, and two seasoned elderly ladies, both the latter included in Mr Geddes's list of 'stand-bys'. These stayed in the background, in the little room fitted with tap and sink, behind the bar with its correct height and curve and its brilliant striped awning. There, scarcely hampered by lack of room and ancient equipment, they washed up and boiled water with the casual speed of some force of Nature.

The Youth Club, in which the moving spirit was a darting kind of boy known as Disher, had collected for, and installed, the awning. Nothing strong to drink was served, but the awning did give a note of sophistication: I may be an old shed, I may suffer from draughts, but at least I know what's with it and what isn't, the Hall seemed to be saying.

The Vicar was sitting on a hard chair, cradling his coffee-cup and chatting with two or three of the men in the congregation, while a steady roar of conversation, broken by occasional squeals from the young group led by Disher, filled the gradually warming room.

Gerald Corliss was stalking in and out of the chatting groups, doing his utmost not to appear aloof and wishing guiltily that he were at home reading Teilhard de Chardin; pausing at decent intervals to ask someone how their leg was or had they managed to get rid of their cold, and quite unaware, amid his uncomfortable efforts, that no-one was thinking him intellectually arrogant or aloof but many were saying, 'Poor boy, it is a pity he's so shy.'

It was the last thing he ever thought himself; the Public School vocabulary omits the word.

It is not expressing it too strongly to say that horror came upon him when he saw, staring at him out of a small group, two large blue-grey eyes behind glasses, below a green beret set rakishly on greying curls. It was Miss Barnes; he could never forget *her* name; in fact he sympathized with Mary Tudor; he knew how she must have felt about Calais.

She was waving to him with a half-eaten biscuit.

He went up to her, and summoning every drop of mateyness in a most unmatey nature, said: 'Oh . . . good-evening, Miss Barnes. Nice to see you here . . .'

'I expect you're wondering, well, I said to myself, she can't come to no harm, got the Coloured Supplement and I'll be home by nine, be a bit later I expect but they can't knock you on the head if there's two of you though they're up to anything these days and Miss Gallagher, that's her in the scarf, she goes part of my way and now it's painted it don't seem so lonely somehow, I miss the children, though, that Melinda she was a spoilt little piece always after pennies, you got a penny Glad, she'd say as bold as you like and the men are working all hours not regular men they aren't, some friends of the rackman's I

47

expect, I said would he just put the kettle on and have one himself if he felt like it, and there's going to be a carpet. Grey and pink.'

Her breath seemed to run out, and she put her head down and gulped at her coffee, keeping her eyes fixed on him as if daring him to run away. Gerald had set himself to listen; now he was trying to interpret. It was the first time he had done so; usually he was trying so hard to be un-aloof that the meaning of his parishioners' remarks eluded him.

'Oh . . . you . . . your sister. Well, you . . . must have a . . . change sometimes . . . you know . . . The last time I saw you . . . you were rather . . . upset . . . some disreputable type had bought your home over your head, hadn't he?'

'Oh, I'm still there, I'm still there,' Gladys said earnestly, 'there's been a change for the better, she's got it now, he gave it to her, bought it for her for a present, she said, that girl, I mean, Peggy she calls herself, been several times, very smart, it's all painted down below and up as far as our landing, said they'd come up farther if I liked, well, I said, I'd welcome you for one but my sister said all that mess, Glad, and the smell of paint you can't sleep of a night, the carpet's come, down in the hall in a roll it is, pink and grey, I had a peep.'

Another pause, and this time a bite out of another biscuit which she had, as if absently snatched from a tray borne past at a run by Disher.

'Oh hullo, Miss Barnes, I was afraid you wouldn't be able to leave your sister, I'm glad you managed it.'

Mr Geddes had come up, smiling, cordial. That was the way it should be done. Gerald knew, none better, that it was the way. But his Vicar must have had nearly forty years of such situations.

Gladys, switching the eyes, began again about the Coloured

Supplement, and the rackmen's men but was effortlessly stopped in full spate.

'Now, how're things going? They haven't turned you out yet, *I'm* sure, you look very cheerful. Doesn't she?' to Gerald, who gave a bleak smile. How to explain to the Vicar or to anyone else that the cheerfulness was part of Miss Barnes's general incomprehensibility?

'Won't be no question of turning out so far as what I can see, neither, it 'asn't been mentioned *nor* putting up our rents, that Peggy she hasn't got much to say for herself but what I hear of her mother she don't seem so bad, an imbalid, and goes about after dark all the time, seems a bit funny but I s'p'se it's nerves, she hasn't been near the place not to see it 'cept that evening you was there if that was her in his car, and not a sign of him, the rackman, thank God, leaving it all to her, yes, I 'spose we must. Well I'll be saying good-bye and thank you for a pleasant evening, oh, coming to live in our 'ouse, I forgot to tell you, keep an eye on things, might be worse, at least she won't let the roof leak, oh, and knocked a hole right through into next door for a kitchen, four rooms weren't enough for her, so it's one house really now, yes, Vi must be off, I'm coming.'

The last remark was addressed to Miss Gallagher, a shyly smiling figure in old brown coat and headscarf who had drawn near, and was hovering expectantly during the monologue. Mr Geddes shook hands with them both, expressed his relief and pleasure at 'things going so well', and they made their way through the crowd to the door, which opened on to a dark little cobbled lane where damp trees dripped.

Gladys was not, in fact, as cheerful as she appeared.

As she and Miss Gallagher set off through the almost deserted orange-lit streets, where the only movement was that of big cars speeding impatiently on short journeys to the pub or the houses of family or friends, she began immediately to confide in her friend, who was well accustomed to her part as listener, and only put in a word occasionally to show that she was paying attention.

'Didn't tell him about what she said about don't be frightened, sauce! Who's frightened? I said to Annie all I'm frightened of is not having no new rent book nor contrac' or nothing, I never had none with Mrs A. but we'd known her since dad was alive, she used to come out over the Fields with me and Georgie when we was little, six years older than me . . .'

'Oh, have you heard from your nephew, then?'

'Not – for – these – eighteen – months!' cried Gladys, hurrying along faster than ever and speaking with immense drama and emphasis, 'vanished. Well as good as, said he was going to take this job at Orpington in a garage, got this bit of money put by, you must come down and see me, auntie, he says, and never another word, I wonder if it isn't a mystery –'

'It does seem a long time. Eighteen months.'

'Oh, we'll hear from him any day now I expect, he's like that, always was from a baby, what was I saying, it all seems a bit queer to me, Mrs P., I mean, never coming to the house, still it's better than the rackman, well, here's the parting of the ways as they say, nighty-night and thanks for your company.'

'Bye-bye and thanks for yours. See you next Sunday.'

'See you!' shouted Gladys, and charged away down the darker streets, past the little shops where occasionally some proprietor was displaying his goods in a quiet, lit window. A cat darted across the road, and a distant diesel train blared impersonally. The dun clouds of the London night pressed down low on the roofs; kept at bay by the orange glare in the better-lit streets, they now took possession once more.

She came round the corner into Rose Walk – and there was

the car again! drawn up just outside the house, this time; she could see the girl, Peggy, and another woman. A man was sitting at the wheel, staring at nothing in particular.

Used to wrap themselves up like that when they had the face-ache, was Gladys's reflection upon the white scarf that was folded about the other woman's head, as she drew near to the car. But the next moment most of her sturdy good sense was scattered, as the head turned quickly, and she saw such a face as to strike even her thoughts dumb, and fill her with awe.

It had been very pretty; pretty in the way of a rose on a summer morning; a dewy way; a girl's way, and above all an English way. It could not have been the face of any but an Englishwoman, and it was a sick face, transparently white, with eyes so large in their hollow sockets as to be haunting, unnatural, like the cavities in a skull. The mouth drooped mournfully, the marvellous, shaped, curling gold hair visible beneath the gauze scarf hung to the shoulders of a rich fur coat.

But there was something more than sickness and whiteness and the abnormal size of the very bright eyes. Gladys felt it from her first stare at Mrs Pearson, but had no word for it; she felt only the overruling sensation of a most unfamiliar gravity and awe. The word *death* breathed chillingly from some cave in a mind so stuffed with cosy things that there was barely room for it. As she said afterwards to her sister, 'That was what she put me in mind of – death. Poor soul, I thought.' Yet – it was not only death.

'Hullo – here's Gladys,' said the girl Peggy, who was standing beside the car and seemed to have been arguing with her mother about something through the half-opened window. 'My mother was wondering if she would go in and look at the house. How've they been getting on?'

'Well, I said to Annie, I'm sure they're foreigners, the way they work isn't natural, always at it, don't even stop for a cup of tea, I never saw anything like it, they've finished except for just below our landing. Pleased to meet you,' she ended in a mutter, in the general direction of that face. Her sensation of awe had dissipated itself in an indignant conclusion that such a one ought to be looking up from the pillows in a hospital bed.

'Later on, perhaps you'll let me do up your rooms for you,' Mrs Pearson said, in a voice so soft that it was difficult to hear, in spite of the absolute stillness in the dim street. 'They do need it, Peggy tells me . . . I like everything to be pretty all round me. Light colours. Pink's my favourite.' The words came whisperingly out of the dimness.

'Well that's ever so kind of you Mrs Pearson but it's my sister, she's such a one for the smell of paint, it always has upset her, she's the one who's really set her face against it, I'd be only too glad, I don't mind telling you she was always promising to have them done up, promises are like piecrust I used to tell her and now it's too late –'

'Oh don't say that!' It was almost a cry, and Gladys gaped at her. 'It's never too late. I'll talk to your sister and I'll have it all made pretty for you. And isn't there – Peggy' – she glanced timidly at the silent, graceful figure standing beside the window – 'Peggy said there's someone living up in the attic – an old man. What about him? Wouldn't he like his room done up? and the electric light up there? The men told Mr Pearson it doesn't go up that far.'

In spite of the kindness of the speech, Gladys felt her usual impulse to defend Mr Fisher from intrusion, however well-meant, and exclaimed sharply:

'I couldn't answer for him, no I couldn't, he don't never let anyone up there, he likes it kep' private, I been up there sometimes to inquire like but he keeps the door half shut, he's got his home up there, see, all his bits of things it's only natural, been there years now, it's only natural, his home.'

'But surely – electric light . . .' The voice died away. The huge eyes stared.

'Someone's coming now,' Peggy interrupted. 'Is this him?'

Gladys peered down the street in the direction of the light advancing footsteps. It undeniably was Mr Fisher, and the knowledge that it was now December, and he would therefore be appearing under a new name, occurred to her, together with the irritated conviction that another jawing-set-out would now keep her out here in the cold for goodness knew how long, and Annie thinking she was hit on the head.

The problem of these names was embarrassing. She did not want Mrs Pearson to think Mr Fisher was mental. Yet it certainly did *sound* mental – giving yourself a new name every month. She plunged into explanations even as the footsteps drew level with them.

'Likes his little joke,' she gabbled, 'sounds funny I know but he calls himself something different every month, wonder what it'll be this evening? Hullo, Mr Fisher!' she called, when he was upon them, 'what's your name this evening? Here's Mrs Pearson wants to put the electric light up your room and do it up for you – nice Christmas surprise for you, innit?'

The old man had been going past the car and the group gathered about it without a glance, and this increased his champion's annoyance. No point in upsetting people. Rude, too. No harm in just saying 'good-evening'.

However, he paused, and turned round. About his neck, slung from a piece of thick string, he carried a small tray woven of some kind of shining straw, and on it were grouped three or four little dolls, made of the same material, and decorated with gilt braid and coloured beads. He looked solemnly into the car, and leisurely too, as if considering its occupants, then said, turning to Gladys:

'Good-evening, Miss Gladys.' At the same time, he made a silent bow in the direction of Peggy, then a second more ceremonious one to the window of the car. But to the question he did not reply.

'What's your name this month, Mr Fisher?' repeated Gladys. 'I was just telling Mrs Pearson . . . This here lady is Mrs Pearson, you know, our new landlady.'

'Thomas Browne, this month. During December this year, I am Thomas Browne. He wrote a beautiful book, very grandly written it was – *A Physician's Faith*.'

Gladys glanced at the audience, pleased that he should be showing himself in character.

'Oh don't talk about names –' Mrs Pearson had fallen again into inexplicable agitation. 'You must never play about with your name like that – names are . . . it's very dangerous – you don't understand –' A torrent of near whispers poured out, in the dimness.

'Mother, are you going in to see the house?' Peggy interrupted, 'because, if you aren't, I must get over to Hampstead, she's expecting me at nine.'

'What, lovey?' Mrs Pearson broke off, thrusting her face forward, 'Oh . . . yes . . . of course . . . Mrs Corbett . . . I'd forgotten. Er' – timidly to the chauffeur – 'may we go to Hampstead, now, please . . . MacLeod House, Heathwood Avenue . . . no, Peggy, I won't come in now, I'll see it when it's finished . . . have you seen my stair-carpet?' to Gladys, 'it's so pretty. Pink and grey.'

'Well I did just have a peep couldn't resist it, ever so sweet, rolled up in the hall, I said to Annie I hope it don't come up to our landing, what with our coal bucket and that tap, soon spoil it.'

'But you'll like to see it when it's on the stairs, won't you? I'm having your stairs done, too, you know, in your house as well.' And then Mrs Pearson fully smiled. A girl of seventeen was suddenly looking out through the window. Or was it that Gladys had grown a little more accustomed to the unforgettable face?

'I s'pose you'll be letting those rooms on the ground floor, then?' she blurted, on an impulse to relieve the anxiety she and Annie felt on this point.

'Oh no . . . Peggy says the ceilings are down, and that must be put right of course. But I shan't let them. Mr Pearson wants to use those rooms for store-rooms.'

Her smile faded, and was replaced by an expression of gravity, as if, now, the talk had touched on a matter that was not a smiling one. Mr Pearson, and what he stored in the rooms, was important. 'And in Lily Cottage . . . such a sweet name! . . . I'm going to have a bathroom . . . a good big one . . . and then' – a luxurious small sigh – 'my bedroom will be that room overlooking the yard at the back. It's nice and quiet there, Peggy says.'

While this talk was going on, Mr Fisher had turned away, with two more silent bows and a tiny lift of his ancient cap, and, having groped under layers of coats and waistcoat, produced from a hidden pocket a large old-fashioned key. He mounted the steps of Rose Cottage and inserted it in the door.

'Mr Fisher! Mr Fisher! Don't lock me out! Wait for me – if I haven't forgotten my key again!' Gladys lamented, having been occupied, during her conversation with Mrs Pearson, in a similar search among her own cardigans and scarves.

The old man gently pushed open the door to its fullest

extent, so that it rested against the inner wall, and, leaving it so, marched silently up the stairs just visible in the weak glow of the electric light. But that glow was brighter than it had been; it was thrown back, now, from walls of a dreamy rose-pink. The plaster whorls on the ceiling suggested the icing on some giant's birthday cake.

'Oh, how pretty!' cried Mrs Pearson, peering out. 'It really is a lovely colour, isn't it, Peggy?'

'I suppose so. Mother, we really must go.'

'All right, dear. Please, George . . .' to the driver.

'Night, Mrs Pearson, night Peggy, night all!' called Gladys, as the car began to move, then, recollecting some half-dozen questions, she began an interrogatory scream that died away as the car gathered speed and turned the corner.

The Walk looked so dim, so lonely and deserted after it had gone, that she made haste to shut the front door and hurry up the stairs to the comfort of their own rooms, and Annie's re-assured cry. For she had, as usual, and certainly with more reason than she would have had twenty years ago, been anticipating murder.

7

'Because I may as well do that as anything else.'

Peggy spoke in a controlled tone, keeping her eyes fixed on the shop-lined streets going by.

'I don't know why you won't *live* with your old mum, dear,' Mrs Pearson went on timidly, keeping her eyes on her daughter's profile. 'You can have anything you want, come and go when you please, be as free as air. I know it isn't what most people call a *nice* neighbourhood but it's a quiet street, very quiet, for London, and the house is going to be lovely. Why won't you, dear?'

In Peggy's short lifetime, she had found no weapon stronger or more successful than silence: the simplest, easiest weapon and, usually the most neglected. She did not use it now, however, preferring to keep it for a more dangerous occasion:

'It's quieter up there – more like the country,' she said.

'Well, lovey, if you're so fond of the country why did you ever leave Rattray's?'

'I was sick of it,' said Peggy hardly, 'dead sick.'

'Well, then, dear –' Mrs Pearson stopped, paused, and tried again. 'It seems so funny, going off to live with some old lady you met on the front at Hove, instead of at home with your own mother.'

'I'm . . . fond of the dogs. And she's an old fool but she'll let me do what I like.'

'We all have to do that, it seems to me,' Mrs Pearson said, sighing again; she had allowed the folds of the white scarf to slip from her head, and now looked more like any mother arguing with an unsatisfactory, much-loved daughter.

The car had left the poor streets, and was climbing towards Hampstead. The lights of London below were hidden, but they threw up such a rich glare that the thick haze was rusty with it. Leaving shops and houses behind, the car sped along the highest part of the ridge, between dark leafless trees sunk on either side in the valleys. It swerved left, towards Branch Hill.

'I only hope it works, dear, that's all, and Dad and I won't have you grumbling. Is there a riding-school on the Heath, love? You'd like to go on with your riding, wouldn't you?' Mrs Pearson breathed, keeping her eyes fixed on the long black eye-lashes, curved like scimitars, that lay on the olive cheek. 'Peggy – there was someone there, wasn't there? Tell me, darling. I know there was something that happened. I can feel it, and see the horses – beautiful wild things, so fierce! – but I want to hear all about it. I am your mother. Please, Peggy?'

Now Peggy used her weapon. She neither moved nor spoke, keeping her eyes fixed on the road down which the car was running. It swung again to the left and stopped before a pair of tall wrought-iron gates standing open in a long barrier of glossy laurel and rhododendrons that shut away the outside world. All around were similar walls of foliage, silence, mist, and big leafless trees.

'Right up to the door?' the chauffeur suddenly demanded, in an outraged voice, half turning and looking at the women contemptuously through the window.

'Please, George . . . Mr Pearson did say . . . he wanted . . .' said Mrs Pearson, and the man, muttering something, turned the car in at the gates.

The shrubbery ended in a circular sweep of gravel before a handsome old house built of red brick, with a flight of steps leading up to the white pillars of a porch and a glass door. The most conspicuous feature of the place was a room built out over a lawn to the left, whose windows, through a screen of trees, overlooked the surprisingly abrupt drop of a near-by valley. It was filled with the motionless lights of a long main road, the moving ones of a procession of cars, and the house lights of a large, scattered suburb.

The chauffeur stopped the engine and Peggy, alighting, grasped two large and heavy cases and lifted them without apparent effort.

'Isn't that heavy for you?' Mrs Pearson almost whispered, and Peggy shook her head impatiently, as she opened the door of the car. The chauffeur merely sat, ignoring them both. Peggy set the cases down, shut the door and put her head in at the window.

'Good-bye, mother – *au revoir*, rather. I'll write in a day or two. When do you move in?'

'Oh, soon. Soon, I expect. I don't know – Dad will see to everything. Good-bye, my lovey, take care of yourself.'

'Bye-bye,' said Peggy, making a little face that was teasing and almost affectionate, then turned away.

Mrs Pearson sat still for a moment, watching her walk easily up the steps, with a case in each hand, towards the glass door between the pillars. Then, starting, as if out of some painful dream, she leant forward and said to the chauffeur, 'Could we go home now, George, please?' and at the timid request he started the engine and drove away.

Peggy put down the cases, and rang the bell.

The freshness of the white paint and the soft brilliance of MacLeod House's brass pleased her.

She did not usually look for such things, liking, as she did, the open air and solitary places above all else, but the atmosphere of solid comfort backed by a considerable amount of money, was soothing. She felt that in MacLeod House an absorbing grief could be indulged without any interruptions from the world outside; the tears could burn themselves dry in sullen peace.

The door opened, and a small old man in a white jacket looked out at her inimically.

'I'm Miss Pearson. Good-evening,' said Peggy, whose first encounter with a houseman this was. She did not smile and neither did Hobbs.

'Good-evening, miss. Mrs Corbett is expecting you. Will you come this way, please.'

She followed him across a hall that was in fact a large and lofty room, panelled in white, carpeted with old rugs in soft blues and browns and pinks, and having, under an arch and some white fretted wood vaguely Oriental in suggestion, a staircase leading up to a gallery running round the interior of the house. Peggy's eye lingered on the carpets. Yes; they were the real thing. She could remember having seen, as a child, that particular kind of rug being woven – 'in the sloms of Tashkent', she thought.

'Miss Pearson,' said the houseman, opening a door.

The room seemed as large as Saint James's Parish Hall, it was the one built out over the great lawn, the one overlooking Hendon in its valley; and the warm scented air struck Peggy's face, already too hot, with that sensation of deliberate insult that most people experience on feeling a draught.

Two people were islanded in the midst of its splendours of green walls and tasselled cushions and paintings of flowers; a stout old white-haired woman in a black dress, and a middle-aged man who was standing by the mantelpiece. He had an air of wanting to rest his arm along it, had not the procession of dogs, modelled in china and of every breed, that walked along it, prevented him. The two were watching television.

Four black pugs, all, at the first glance identical, sprang up at Peggy's entrance, and began to leap about, bark and caress her, sniffing at her ankles and jumping against her skirt.

'There you are, my dear,' said Mrs Corbett, smiling and pleased, 'punctual to the minute (Arnold, turn that thing off, please). Down, boys, down; you know Peggy, now. Don't make a fuss.'

Peggy dropped composedly on one knee and began to caress the pugs, keeping her eyes on Mrs Corbett.

'It's lovely to see them again,' she said, and then her glance just moved, with the smallest effect, to the man.

'Oh yes, of course – you don't know my son – that was the fortnight you were in New York, Arnold, you remember – while I was at Hove, I mean, staying with Vera – my son, Arnold, Miss Pearson. Get Peggy a drink, Arnold. Peggy, what will you have, dear?'

Slight smiles and inclinations of the two heads, the sleek dark one and the one that was balding. He studied her with a morose look that was just short of rudeness, as she knelt beside the dogs, and, having heard her clear little 'Cinzano, please,' busied himself with filling a glass.

'How did you come?' Mrs Corbett went on comfortably while her blue eyes fixed themselves eagerly on Peggy's face, 'you did say you haven't a car, didn't you? and we're so cut off here, if you've no car . . .'

'It was quite easy. I hired one.'

'So much more reliable than taxis . . . very sensible . . . Now

61

do *lie down*, boys,' to the dogs, 'we don't want you fidgeting about.'

Three of them flopped back and resumed their doze, but the fourth remained on his hind legs, paws resting on Peggy's arm and eyes fixed steadily on her face.

'What is it, then, Dee?' she asked him, letting the caressing note sound in her voice that came as rarely as her smile. She made a tiny grimace at his haughty black mask, then looked across at Mrs Corbett and briefly laughed. Dee turned away his head, hurt.

'You remember which is which!' her employer cried, delighted, 'do you know, Arnold, I got chatting to Peggy on the front at Hove – you remember, I told you – and she could tell which of our boys was which the second time we met! You know,' to Peggy, 'that was what really decided me to ask you to come here – that, and your being a dog-lover like myself. I knew you understood them, you see. It's no use . . . I can teach these foreign girls everything, but I *cannot* teach them to look after the dogs properly. They won't *love* them. I always say it takes an *English* person to *love* a dog.'

'You don't look English, though, somehow,' Arnold said clumsily, 'so . . . dark.'

'Well, I am,' Peggy said equably.

The pause that followed was so tiny that it escaped notice by the mother and son. He'll be easy, Peggy thought.

'Did your driver know the way up here? Some of those chaps haven't a clue, especially in the newer firms . . . who did you go to?' Arnold Corbett asked.

'Some firm near Euston, I forget its name,' Peggy lied. 'Yes, he was very good. No trouble at all.'

'It's quite dicey, mind you,' Arnold went on, warming to his interesting subject, 'I've known even experienced taxi-merchants drive round here for ten minutes or more looking for the place, and of course you can never get one if you should happen to want one. If my car's out of order I know what to expect. Ages on the phone and then nothing doing . . . you may be lucky between theatre-time and midnight, of course, but . . . over-population's the trouble, everywhere,' he ended gloomily.

'Where is your nearest rank . . . just in case I want one on my "evening out" – if I'm to have an evening out?' Peggy asked, half-turning, with serpentine grace, to Mrs Corbett, knowing how her profile must be silhouetted against the long pale sweep of the curtains.

'Of course you will, dear – what an idea! (Arnold, did you hear that?) I shall just mention it a few days beforehand if I *should* happen to want your company in the evenings . . . and there is the dogs' run, of course, but Arnold often does that. We dine at seven,' Mrs Corbett went on, 'because the servants like a long evening –'

'I'll say they do,' her son put in.

'Now you mustn't give Peggy a wrong impression, Arnold. I know the poor old dears can be trying . . .'

'Why you don't get three or four foreigners over I don't know. You'd have no difficulty.'

'I know that. It isn't that and you know it.' She turned to Peggy. 'All of them – the cook and my parlourmaid and the houseman, and the chauffeur, even my "daily", have been with me since my husband's time. They are all getting old, now (like me) but that's no reason why I should turn them out, and have a lot of Italians in the house. They were all with us in the old days.'

Her eyes turned towards the handsome curve of the bay window, curtained from pelmet to shining floor with fawn satin embroidered in wreaths of flowers. 'Nearly fifty years ago.

Hendon was famous for its flying-fields then, and Golders Green
– that was a village. The Garden City was just being built.'

'Beastly hole.' Arnold held out his cigarette case to Peggy,
who smiled and shook her head.

'It was pretty in those days – all the little new houses, and
artistic young people just starting life. Of course, our friends
were different; they were in the flying set, but just beginning
too. Oh, I can't *tell* you how *exciting* it all was,' she ended,
with an animation in her voice which, to her, conveyed all
the glamour lingering in her mind's eye and in her heart:
while the feeble sounds, muted by age, conveyed to Peggy
just nothing.

She kept her luminous and long-shaped eyes, wherein two
stars always burned, fixed upon her employer's face as if she were
interested, while behind them a long yawn stretched itself out.

'One evening a week or so I have friends to dinner. Bridge
most afternoons, with my three old pals from down the road
(you'll meet them). Most evenings after dinner we watch television. Bed by half-past ten, usually.'

'A thrilling programme,' muttered Arnold, 'so now you know
the worst, Miss Pearson.'

'I like a quiet life,' Peggy answered in the same unruffled
tone. 'I've lived mostly in the country, you know.'

'Bores me stiff, the country, I must say. Give me town every
time.' Arnold's dull blue eyes were fixed on her face.

'He's a naughty boy, isn't he, doggies? He likes the bright
lights,' said Mrs Corbett cheerfully, touching the nearest plump
back with the toe of her black velvet shoe, 'a naughty, naughty,
naughty boy.' Bee, disturbed, moved pettishly away. 'Well now,'
Mrs Corbett went on to Peggy, 'I'm sure you'd like to see your
room, wouldn't you.' She began to struggle from her chair. 'Oh
dear – can you give me an arm, please. I get so stiff.'

Peggy complied, with considerable inward dislike of the contact with soft old fat, black georgette, and gilt jewellery.

'I had it done over for you,' Mrs Corbett confided, as all three slowly mounted the stairs. 'The last companion I had stuck religious pictures all over the walls (I'm funny in that way, I cannot bear churchy people) and it used to depress me so much . . . when she left, I thought, aha, new wallpaper! No, boys,' to the dogs, who had followed them, '*not* in Peggy's room.'

'I'll say good-night, mother, if you'll excuse me,' said Arnold, pausing surrounded by dogs, on the threshold, 'there's something I want to watch on ITV – good-night, Miss Pearson,' and, instructing the dogs to leave him alone, he went off down the corridor.

'He has his own, in his den,' Mrs Corbett said, opening a door on a perfect specimen of a hotel bedroom, characterless even to incredibility in brown and beige, 'then if there's something on BBC 2 or ITV he wants to watch, he can watch it while I have *my* little party with BBC 1 in the drawing-room. Are you a keen looker-in?'

'I like the animal programmes,' Peggy answered, this time without lying.

'Oh – *dear* Michaela and Armand – so do I.'

Peggy did not think it necessary to add that this was not what she meant.

'I hope you'll like the pictures.' Mrs Corbett moved with her waddling walk across the room. 'I chose them myself when I had the room re-done. At Harrods. (They have a lovely picture gallery there, I expect you know it?) I'm afraid I'm not at all artistic. (My husband, bless him, used to say, "Cora's a fool but she is good-tempered.") But I flatter myself I *do* know what I like.'

They had paused in front of a boat rushing along over a foaming summer sea. There was enough in the idealized scene to move Peggy's heart with a sudden agony of desire: the over-heated room's walls seemed to fall apart, and all the splendour and smell of the ocean drove in.

'I . . . that's . . .' She could not bring the words out, and stood in silence, trembling with longing, and with rage at herself.

Mrs Corbett, as was usual with Mrs Corbett, had noticed nothing.

'And this,' she said, before some white Irish cottages under a violet mountain, 'I love that, don't you?'

'I . . . don't know which I like best. They're both . . . I like this one, too.' It was a path leading through autumn woods, hung with those leaves that suggest golden coins. Peggy would not let herself shut her eyes on a memory of Sussex downs.

'There! they'll remind you of the country.' Mrs Corbett, after a last pleased glance round, retreated to the door. 'It's so nice to have you here, dear, and I'm sure we shall all get on well together . . . no, boys, you mustn't stay here, come with Mother. Dee! *Not* on beddies, you know that's not allowed.'

'Let them stay, please, I don't mind. If you like, I'll come down when I've unpacked and take them for their run, shall I?'

'Will you really? Aren't you tired? But I don't expect you are, you're so young. One forgets . . . How old are you, my dear?'

'Twenty-two.'

'Are you really? Only twenty-two. Well, it's a long time since I was twenty-two . . . I'll leave them with you, then. The lead is hanging in the hall, by the front door.' Mrs Corbett at last got herself out of the room. Peggy's first action was to cross the room and jerk apart the curtains veiling the windows. She pushed the casements back and, gasping, leaned out into the night.

A slight damp wind blew into her face, bringing the scent of dead leaves and wet bark. From the dark screen of trees, behind which the valley lights glittered, an owl hooted on a soft wavering note. She shuddered, shut the windows quickly and dragged the curtains across them. Then she turned to her unpacking.

When she ran downstairs half an hour later, she wore a white raincoat, and on her head one of the scarves, usually made of cotton printed in some brilliant uncommon design, which she affected in the winter. Her suits and her greatcoat had been, for some years, of a dark tweed, flecked with violet or yellow. She gave out an impression of dark skies and winter starlight.

She put her head round the door of the great drawing-room with a grand-daughterly air; Mrs Corbett was watching the television lackadaisically.

'I'm going to take them for their run now,' Peggy called, interrupting the noises and actions on the little blue screen that presumably were occupying her employer's attention.

'Oh all right, dear, thank you.' Mrs Corbett glanced round and smiled and yawned, 'Really, this isn't very thrilling, I think I shall go to bed.'

A man smashed his fist into another's face, there was a brisk outbreak of screams from an ugly girl, and Peggy shut the door on the entertainment.

The dogs ran joyfully along the road under the quiet trees. No footfall but her own, no droning rush of any car; the lamps burned like veiled crystals in the mist, drops fell heavily from the iron-coloured branches as if the trees wept for their brothers in the country's menaced woodlands. It was not country, but it was better than shops and streets. Peggy thought that a few months at MacLeod House would 'do'.

8

The 'home' to which Mrs Pearson had begged, rather than ordered, the driver to return was a tall, seedy old private hotel in the neighbourhood of Euston, whose back premises overlooked a vast area of demolition and rebuilding. It was kept by the man and his wife, acquaintances of Thomas Pearson's in the secretive, hidden underworld of petty crime in which the latter had lived for years; the removal of the brick and mortar screens protecting the proprietors from the public eye had filled them with an uneasiness expressing itself in a surly manner, and they were talking of selling out and taking themselves off to a similar place in Brighton.

Having parked the car, the man George stalked ahead of Mrs Pearson across the pavement to the hotel entrance, leaving her to push her way through the swing door unaided.

'All right, are you, dear? You look all in,' said Mrs George, a stout woman wearing a short black dress glittering with gilt threads, coming out of the reception desk as Mrs Pearson slowly approached.

'I'm tired, Marie, and so cold. I nearly die every time I have to say good-bye to Peggy.'

'Now don't be like that, Nora, she's only gone to Hampstead,' Mrs George soothed.

'It's four or five miles away,' Mrs Pearson said dolefully.

'Well, what's that! Really Nora, be your age . . . now come

on upstairs, I've got a gorgeous fire for you and you need a drink.'

She steered her friend's drooping form up the stairs; carefully, but with a manner that suggested that of one who humours a mental case rather than affection.

The room she led her into had a superb coal fire blazing illegally and royally in the bow-shaped grate, below a wide marble mantel-piece yellowed by smoke and marked by many deep stains from cigarette butts. Thick red curtains shut away the desolation outside, with its suggestion of lunar craters and civilization's collapse.

The man George was already seated by the fire, on a giant sofa. Beside him, but at its far end, sat another man; short, dark, leaning back and listening in silence to a stream of complaint the other was uttering. He gave the impression of being farther away from his companion than the few feet between them, and he was smiling.

He sat up, as the two women entered, saying, 'Nora, you're late, and you look cold, you're frozen, come here, sit down, warm yourself, for God's sake.' Rising, he bustled about, settling her nearest the fire and arranging cushions at her back. The Georges exchanged a sneering furtive smile.

Mrs Pearson crouched forward to the blaze, holding out hands of a skeletal fragility, with nails painted rose colour, to the flames. She kept her eyes fixed dreamily on their red and yellow dance, what was going on in the room appearing to drift past her unheeded.

'Christ!' exclaimed George, who had been sipping from one of the glasses filled by his wife at a table in the corner, 'what's in this, for God's sake?'

'Something Tom here dreamed up,' she said, 'I don't know . . . he mixed it just before you came in . . . what is in it, Tom?' turning to the dark man.

'Powder. A very strong powder. Not like you usually get. Special, from an Indian friend of mine who keeps a little shop,' said Thomas Pearson, smiling.

'One of your little shops, I s'pose.' George was still sipping, with an expression of gross satisfaction growing on his face. 'There's a bit more than the old curry powder in *this*, I bet.' He laughed, looking sideways at his tormentor and master. The hope of escaping, somehow, from the load of debt that bound him to Pearson and of in some way destroying the knowledge that Pearson had of his past life, grew fainter with every day that passed.

'You do talk a lot of bloody rubbish, George,' his wife put in uneasily, 'here, Nora, do you good.' She held out a steaming glass.

Thomas Pearson caught his wife's wrist gently before she could take it. 'Not for you, Nora, too strong. I mix you a special.' He went across to the table.

He had begun to put on flesh young, and now his small features were sunk in fat and he carried a belly. But his eyes were beautiful, dark and almond-shaped like those of his daughter and having in them a sparkle resembling the reflection of a star in dark water. His nose and mouth were finely curved and hinted at voluptuousness and one could feel in him the strength of a rib of steel. But one also felt that this was a man who could be made weak, and destroyed, by one passion.

'Here,' he said, holding out a glass of the drink he had prepared, and, smiling, he added a word or two in another language than English, at which his wife smiled back as she took the glass.

'That's what you always say.' Mrs George, emboldened by drink, put in curiously. 'What's it mean, anyhow?'

'Between Nora and myself, that,' Pearson said indifferently, without turning to look at the questioner.

'Why've you still got that accent, too?' Mrs George, who was becoming drunk, went on aggressively. 'You been over here long enough. You talk like some foreigner.'

'I suppose,' he paused, then went on with a faint smile, 'I remember I was born in the sloms of Tashkent. My mother was a "lady" there. She made me take her name, not my father's. She was a priest's daughter.'

'Go on. Tell us something true for a change,' Mrs George dared to sneer.

'It is true. A Scottish priest. And there was a man in the old quarter – farther down, even, than we lived, who was Scottish too.'

He paused again. Through her increasing drunkenness, Mrs George's curiosity was alive and eager: her first impression of Thomas Pearson, when they had met him in Brighton a year or so ago, had been of what she called *a nasty customer* and she had long wanted to know more about him. Her curiosity even conquered her real fear of him.

'He'd been a soldier. Fought at Egeram or one of those places in the First World War, perhaps, and I believe he had a still down there, where he lived. A deserter, I am sure. My mother used to get whisky from him and it kept me alive in the winters. They are – were – very cold, our winters. She made me . . .' he broke off, turned quickly, looked across the room and saw two avid masks turned towards him, lit with the pure essence of curiosity and hardly drawing their breath. He smiled contemptuously.

'So. Perhaps my blood remembers the sloms of Tashkent and that's why I speak with a foreign accent,' he ended, and turned back to his contemplation of the great fire.

'You do talk a lot of bloody rot, Tom,' Mrs George said stupidly, again, after a pause. 'Like George. You men.'

'Perhaps. Now come along, Nora, you're tired,' rousing himself.

'Yes, you get her off to bed quick or she'll have one of her turns, and I can't stand that, it gives me the horrors. So get out, both of you,' Mrs George almost shouted, with a distorted face.

He turned and glanced at her once, and she drew in her breath on a renewed half-shout, and was instantly silent. Pearson put his arm about his wife and helped her from the room.

There was an eiderdown that covered the entire expanse of their double bed, and slippers trimmed with fronds of feathers, a delicate nightgown, a rosy ribbon to band her heavy, magnificent hair; and he helped her to undress and at last lay down beside her. Their quiet talk about the house that was being prepared for her passed gradually into silence, then to tender kisses, and at last into passionate love-making. The god's presence is not to be mistaken, and he was there.

Every few days, Peggy would slip out of the house, usually in the late afternoon while Mrs Corbett was playing bridge with her three old friends – and make her way down, past trees and open water, to the hotel amidst the desolation lying around Warren Street.

The dogs had become devoted to her. They would hear her step in the hall, scratch at the door of the room where the bridge game was going on, eager to follow.

'No, no, Cee, it's only Peggy. She's going O-U-T,' Mrs Corbett would explain to the three sagging, painted faces round the table, the six hands whose rings winked above the cards. 'Be quiet, A., lie down.'

'Working out all right, is she, Cora?'

'Oh, very well.' Mrs Corbett would study her cards. 'She's a sly little thing, though. I was surprised.'

'Shy? *I* wouldn't have said shy.'

'I said SLY, Dorry, not shy. You really ought to wear your aid, dear, you're getting worse and worse.'

'I don't notice it getting any worse. Cis, do you notice my hearing's any worse? I hate that thing, it cost me seventy guineas and I'm always so conscious of it.'

'I was saying only the other day to Madge, I thought it was worse. I think it's worse since you had that thing.'

'She doesn't wear it half the time. Naughty.' Mrs Corbett glanced at the crystal and gilt clock. 'Nearly tea-time – shall we be devils, girls, and have crumpets today?'

'You always tempt us. I put on six ounces last week. Oh well – perhaps just this once.'

'Six ounces! You'll have to "watch out", as they say.'

'I don't know why you all bother about it, fussing over ounces. Harry likes me well-covered.'

Three of the old women said nothing. The one they called Madge was the last of them whose husband was alive, and she was full of triumph because of the simple fact. Every incident, every detail concerned with her hair-dressing, her clothes, her shoes, her make-up, was referred to it.

Two of her old friends confided to one another their contempt for her boasting: only Mrs Corbett, of the three, found in it a cause for wistful envy. 'Ah . . . she's lucky,' she would sigh, 'she doesn't realize how lucky. Poor Madge – she's got it all to go through – but she has got those lovely grandchildren.' A heavier sigh.

The front door would shut on the overheated rooms, the forced flowers, the harmless stuffy silence. Peggy would move forward into the open air, with the light step that years of riding had made no clumsier, under the great trees now stripped and iron-coloured against the soft bloom of the winter sunset; she would drift like one of their blowing leaves down the dim road.

Sometimes, Arnold Corbett's car would draw up as she left the house, bringing him back from his afternoon's golf.

'Hullo' – he would quickly let the window down and lean out – 'getting away from it all for a few hours?'

Peggy would smile, or perhaps, let the effect of a smile come through the mask of her face, but she would barely stop.

'Care for me to run you down?'

'No, thanks all the same.'

'You surely don't want to hang round waiting for that bloody bus?'

'I'm walking.'

'Walking?'

'Over the Heath.' She would drift away from him, with a backward, faintly-smiling valedictory glance.

'You're a glutton for punishment, aren't you?'

He would smile after her, not troubling, in those early days, to watch her disappear in the dusk. He took it for granted that she was going to meet a man in these damp, gloomy, hemmed-in meadows lying at the end of the avenue, beyond the great soot-marred beeches.

Women were always meeting men, and even he, sometimes, was one of the men a woman met.

He would drive the car in and put it away, and go up to his own sitting-room, his 'den' as his mother called it, and there pass the time until six o'clock with the evening paper and recalling the afternoon's game: at six, he would loaf downstairs to join his mother for their first drink. The old women were gone by then, each one gliding in her car a few hundred yards down the road to another comfortable great house. The Corbett house would begin to smell faintly of the coming dinner, and there would be a faint anticipatory stir within Arnold because of this, and because of the promise of relief from boredom in the voices from the television.

Peggy usually covered the miles between MacLeod House and the hotel in just under an hour; almost sixty minutes spent with moist grass under her feet, and untainted air moving coolly past, and the indistinct shapes of trees above her in the dusk; the tiny barbed or mailed insects in their winter sleep around her in their millions; the warm birds sweeping silently, or with a last lonely chirrup, over her head.

But during the hour she was never out of sight of London's lights on the valley, and though, by comparison with life in MacLeod House, this was freedom, to her it was only a wider cage.

She learned Mrs Corbett's language, during the next fortnight or so; setting herself to master it precisely as she would have done the sounds necessary for communicating with a horse or a bird. It was a simple language. Peggy thought the late A. J. Corbett had summed his wife up accurately when he had called her 'a fool, but good-tempered'.

One day at luncheon, she asked if it would be all right for her to go that afternoon to see her mother?

'Quite all right, if you can manage to be back by not later than six . . . there's this party. Not a real party as I said, but I shall want someone to help hand things,' explained Mrs Corbett. 'I daren't hire anyone, haven't for years, the servants get so upset . . . we'll have our real party on Christmas Eve, of course, as usual. How is your mother, dear?' pausing on her way to her afternoon rest. 'Better, I hope?' She stood, half-way up, looking down at the dark, slender, beautiful being in the hall below.

Yes, thank you, Peggy thought that she was better. She seemed pleased at the idea of having her own home again. Peggy smiled up at Mrs Corbett, all grand-daughterliness.

'Ah, yes.' Mrs Corbett glanced out through a window half-way up the stairs, at the busy suburb down behind the screening trees. 'There's nowhere like your own home, I always say.' She climbed ponderously on, and Peggy went off on her own affairs.

9

'You're looking better, Mum,' she said to her mother an hour later.

'Am I, dear?' Mrs Pearson smiled. 'I expect it's the idea of having a place of my own again, after all these years wandering about. You don't remember that little wooden house we had in Tashkent, do you?'

'"The sloms of Tashkent" – I've heard that one ever since I can remember.'

'That's your father . . . it *was* a slum, I s'pose, but it was pretty. Fancy having a house with a wooden staircase up to the front door because of the mud the river brought along! That's what I'll always remember about it – and how we were always laughing, Dad and I, and when the storks came that first spring and nested on our roof "I'm sure of having a baby now," I said, and your dad said, "Leave that to me." He could be very naughty, in those days. We were ever so happy,' she ended, in a wondering tone. 'We were young, of course,' she added, as a child repeats an excuse it has overheard used by adults, 'I was eighteen and your dad was twenty-two. Easterns grow up so quick.' She sighed.

Peggy tried to see the picture, the little wooden house, stork's nest, laughing young pair, through her mother's eyes for a moment. Her expression was touched by derision and a little disbelief.

No: it was useless. She could not see her young parents laughing in their happiness.

'I wish you'd tell me why things went wrong,' she said at last, lying back in the chair she had drawn up beside the bed, and put out her small hand, with its muscles made strong by handling horses, and gently covered her mother's skeletal one.

'How do you mean – wrong, dear?' Mrs Pearson turned away, groping uneasily for the cigarettes under the pillow; her face was almost hidden in trailing silky curls. One corner of her lips, white now, showed between the gold.

'Well, isn't something wrong? You aren't like most people's mothers, are you, for a start?'

'I've always been a good mother to you, Peggy, I've done my best, I've always put you first, I had such a struggle you wouldn't believe with your grandmother, she was so harsh with you . . .' Mrs Pearson dashed the curls aside, revealing her frightened face. 'You don't remember what it was like, you were too little –'

'It's all right, Mum, keep calm. I'm not complaining. I only wonder sometimes how your being ill started. That's all.'

'Your dad always saw to it you went to good schools,' Mrs Pearson went on wildly, keeping her head turned away.

'All right. All right. I hated them.' Peggy's voice was so calm that it seemed to quieten her mother. In a moment, Mrs Pearson tried to light a cigarette, then dropped it on to the eiderdown. 'Light it for me, there's a dear – ta.' She drew in smoke, then let it out in a gasp and went on more quietly, 'I had this power, you see . . .'

'You mean you believed you had it and a lot of fools believed it too,' Peggy said hardly.

'It isn't like that, dear.' Her mother looked at her in gentle surprise. 'I did have it. Some people do. I've been told I could be one of the great mediums.'

Peggy shrugged. 'It's all absolutely beyond me . . . but go on.'

'— and we were so poor, Peggy — your grannie, too. She put your dad out to work almost before he could walk properly. I've never forgiven her for that — herding sheep and running errands — and if she caught him begging or stealing because he was hungry she'd whip him. Whip him? — he was nothing but a baby. She'd always kept her self-respect, you see — read her Bible every day.'

'Look, Mum. I've heard all this before, or most of it. But you've never told me how you first got ill.'

Mrs Pearson did not answer for a moment. She lay on her side, the cigarette drooping between her lips and sending its delicate smoke upwards in one wavering grey column, while her beautiful eyes looked away; to somewhere or at something that was not in the room. She began to speak slowly, in a low, reminiscent tone.

'We were so poor, and I had this power, and I could see into the future, you see, I could touch a ring or a scarf, and know . . . and once, it was one very cold morning and you were crying because you were hungry and there was hardly a bit in the house. And your dad —' she paused, and her eyelids fell, covering her eyes. 'I'm not blaming him. He couldn't find work and we were almost desperate. And he was proud of me, too. He brought someone along.'

Her voice died away. The room was quiet. Peggy got up, and wandered over to the window and, pushing aside the curtain, stood looking out over the desolation of the great crater and its machines, and the full moon riding above them. She let the curtain drop and turned back to the room.

'Some man who wanted to know about some business speculation, and I told him.' Her mother was half-lying, half-sitting up on the bed, looking straight across at her, and nodding so that each beautifully-shaped curl clustering round her face nodded too. 'I used the power for that, you see, and after that . . . there were lots of them.'

'People wanting their fortunes told?'

'It seemed like hundreds. Every day. I got so tired, Peggy, and the power began to go. We got a lot of money. And your dad was so pleased! and so proud of me. He'd never had any money before, you see, dear, you mustn't blame him. He'd always done such shocking rough work.'

'It was overwork, in a way, then?' Peggy put the question, though she was now slightly bored with the subject, and turning in thought to her own inner world. She suspected that her mother's story did not . . . was not . . . there must be something . . . But time was drawing on, and she must be going, and she felt no strong interest.

'Oh I wish you wouldn't bother me!' Mrs Pearson burst out, pressing her hands against her head, 'I can't bear talking about it. Leave me alone, please dear, do leave me alone. I told lies sometimes. There, now you know. Earned money by lying, and making-up. Because my power had gone.'

'Now don't get upset,' Peggy went over to the bed and rearranged the blankets and eiderdown. 'It was nothing – heaps of people must have done it. And if the customers got their money's worth, what does it matter?'

Her manner was like a nurse's; detached and brisk.

'*You don't know what you're talking about.*' The voice, whining and quick and high, came out from the coverings she had drawn up to her mother's chin and made Peggy start. At the same instant, she caught an extraordinary kind of flash from the violet-blue eye visible in the sideways-turned cheek, seeming for an instant to change its colour.

'Mum?' She bent over her. 'Are you all right?'

'Of course, dearie, only a bit tired. And there's a lot I want to tell you one day about your grannie, now you're old enough to know. She made this marriage late in life, you see —' the voice sounded ordinary again.

'Do you want some tea?' Peggy interrupted, bored now.

'I will if you'll have it with me, lovey.'

'I can't, I must get back. She's got a party on, and she'll want me to hand things.'

'Peggy, I wish you'd stay. Won't you? Just till your dad gets back? It's so lonely here . . . and . . . I get thinking . . . and . . . besides . . .' Mrs Pearson whispered.

Here, after a knock at the door suggesting a ladylike hesitation about intruding, Mrs George came in with a tray.

'Here's your tea,' she said. 'Oh — hullo,' to Peggy. She set the tray down by the bed. 'My god, four o'clock and nearly dark. Makes you sick, doesn't it? Shall I pour out?'

'I'll do that — thanks.' Peggy set about it in silence. Mrs George hesitated, moving Mrs Pearson's collection of ornaments about on the mantelpiece and looking uncertainly from mother to daughter. She had suddenly become ravenous to know when the Pearsons would be going: Nora Pearson 'gave her the creeps'.

'Well, how's that place of yours getting along?' she demanded, accepting a cup from Peggy and sitting down by the electric fire, 'if you've got workmen like the lot that came in to repair our second-floor-back ceiling, I pity you, that's all.'

'They aren't a firm. It's some men Tom knows,' said Mrs Pearson, now revived by tea, and sitting up, 'they're to do with one of the shops — I don't know much about it really. But Peggy says they're working hard.'

'Any idea when it'll be ready?' asked Mrs George, trying to sound casual.

'By the twenty-third!' Mrs Pearson exclaimed, smiling. 'In three days' time I'm moving in. In the afternoon. This young girl, the German –'

'What German? You surely aren't having one of those *au pairs*, Nora? Never there when you want them and always getting pregnant? And a German! You must want your head ex –' She broke off, confused.

Nora was half-mental anyway, having these queer turns and saying she could tell the future and all that; she really did need her head examining.

'She's not sixteen yet. She's had a very hard life out there. She won't get into trouble,' Mrs Pearson answered, with that serenity she sometimes unexpectedly showed, which was so unlike her usual manner and which was accompanied as if by some celestial dancing-partner, with the sweetest of child-like smiles.

'How'd you manage about all the formalities? Papers and that?' Mrs George asked. 'There's no end of bother, getting these girls over here.'

'Oh Tom doesn't bother about papers and that kind of thing. You ought to know that by now, Marie. He knows someone who has a friend. It was easy, really,' Mrs Pearson almost laughed.

'You'll *have* to let the police know. It's the law, Nora – you'll *have* to,' said Mrs George warningly, driven to speak because she feared repercussions upon the family of George.

'Tom'll see to all that. It'll be all right.' Mrs Pearson leant back on the pillow, smiling still. 'I know it will. I've *seen*.'

'Mum, I really must go,' Peggy interrupted, pulling on her gloves.

'All right, if you must, dear.' Her mother looked up at her, and Peggy stooped, and just touched her forehead. She nodded at Mrs George. ''Bye.'

Mrs George saw no reason to give her more than a grimace and silence.

'Peggy!' Mrs Pearson sat up suddenly.

'What, Mum? I've simply got to fly,' irritably, and pausing at the door.

'You aren't walking back over the Heath, are you? Because there's danger there, and I can't protect you now. I could have, at one time, but now . . . it's so hard. I can try, try until I feel as if I'm leaving my –' she stopped, drawing in on a great gasp, her eyes fixed in a Medusa-stare.

'Don't fuss, Mum, you know I never take any notice of that kind of thing. Besides, I like danger. I'll be all right. See you.'

She shut the door.

Mrs George was beginning something about the papers, and readily supplying details of the most recent horror, with her thick legs held out to the warmth and her second cup of tea at her elbow.

'Don't, please, Marie. It isn't that kind of thing. But anywhere lonely, that's been spoiled – that's where *they* come.' She spoke in an undertone that Mrs George could hardly hear. She leant back on the pillows looking exhausted.

'Who come?' Mrs George asked curiously; then lowering her voice, 'I say – Nora. How about reading the tea-leaves?' Her eyes were avid and scornful and afraid.

Mrs Pearson shook her head without looking up. She had languidly reached for a women's magazine from the table beside the bed and was looking with pleasure at each bright, enticing illustration; seriously considering the merits of every advertisement.

'I can't do that, dear,' she said in a moment without glancing up, 'or rather – I could if I'd let myself. But I said I never would again, you know. Not deliberately. Not even for a friend.'

10

Peggy walked quickly northwards. By quiet roads and short cuts she came out at last on to the former meadows of Parliament Hill, and walked straight up them, crunching through grass now lightly whitened by frost. She passed one or two people taking their dogs for a run. Below, London began to arrange itself into a colossal shallow bowl, filled with sparkles and glints.

She stopped, once, to look down at the new skyscrapers in their fierce delicate beauty; they were squares, oblongs, towers, bastions, made of light without visible walls; palaces built for the god Mammon out of glittering shadowy silver and palest gold, insubstantial, chilling. Then she sped on. The air was very cold.

On the summit of a hill she paused again. Moonlight had come into its own, and the lights below seemed remote. The greyish expanses of Hampstead Heath now spread away towards a barrier of ancient forest. She went straight towards it, down into a valley where clusters of reeds looked brown against the pallid grass.

She glanced, indifferently, towards a shape that was moving erratically among the reeds; colourless as the tussocks around it: featureless, no more than a bundle of clothes that suggested humanity.

The figure stooped, retrieved something from the grass, and, retracing its steps to a pile of objects that glimmered at a distance, placed it on the heap. At the same moment, Peggy heard the sound of a motor-cycle engine, and saw a red light coming down a distant path.

She quickened her pace, and was soon at the top of the opposite slope and disappearing into the shadow of some large trees. She wanted no involvement with humanity.

The engine stopped, and the rider dismounted, revealing himself in the chill light as a policeman, and a young one. He advanced leisurely towards the figure, which had stood still at his approach, with uplifted face turned towards him.

'Busy?' he inquired, when he was within a few paces of what he now saw to be an old man – and a mental case, he judged.

'Isn't it time you were at home, Grandad?' he added, as it was borne in on upon him that here stood no ordinary old man but a true ancient, who must be nearer ninety than eighty.

The young policeman, whose name was Charley Mackray, had tried to make his voice at once authoritative and kindly; indeed, his disapproval was mild. But it was disapproval; ninety-year-olds should be safe at home on a frosty night in December, full moon or no full moon.

He had expected a whine about 'doing no harm' or a whine of some kind. But the voice that answered was no whine; it was weak, so worn by the use of almost a century that it barely carried across six feet of air, but it sounded sane, and it did not lack dignity.

'I am collecting the litter,' it said slowly. 'It is an outrage on these meadows, all what's left of the pools and streams where the monks once caught their Friday fish. On fine nights, this is what I do. I puts it into a heap. And I keeps the clean paper.'

Charley Mackray did not know what to do or say for a

moment, because he was so surprised. The reference to monks and fish and pools, too, had rather confused him: a number of other things and people seemed suddenly to have intruded themselves between the Law, represented by himself, and this grotesque figure.

'Well, that's nice of you, grandad, but there's keepers for that job, you know, paid by the Council. That's their work.'

'The 'Eath covers six hundred acres. They can't possibly collect all the litter scattered by all these ignorant people; there aren't enough of 'em,' was the retort.

'Well, neither can you, if it comes to that . . . and at your time of life you ought to be at home, not out here – miles from anywhere and . . . getting colder every minute.'

Charley here made a noise meant to playfully convey arctic chill, and stamped his feet on the path, which rang in satisfactory confirmation beneath their impact. 'Now how about you getting along home?'

'I'm not cold. I don't want to go, not yet. I haven't finished my work. You can leave me, officer. I shan't come to no 'arm.'

Charley looked at him, in growing irritation and helplessness. He was doing nothing wrong. But he was very old, he was plainly eccentric, and he ought to be somewhere safe, where people could keep an eye on him.

'Suppose you came over bad suddenly and fell down – you might freeze,' he almost pleaded, 'you go home, be reasonable, don't *be* like that,' he ended youthfully.

The old man, slowly stooping, showed signs of beginning to return to his task.

'I've had enough of this – you're loitering, that's what you're doing – what's your name?' Charley demanded with sudden official sternness. 'Come on now.'

'Lancelot Fisher,' was the answer, given instantly, while the small figure seemed to freeze into the stillness of a bird surprised by a hawk. The voice had suddenly become almost inaudible.

'Address?' Charley made as if to take out his notebook, with fingers in the edge of a pocket, while wondering what on earth to do next.

'Rose Cottage, Rose Walk, N.W.5.'

Even as he caught the nearly-whispered words, there sounded the shrill note of a bell and down upon them coasted a figure in a clerical hat, which stopped just short of Charley's machine and dismounted from a bicycle.

'Hullo, Mr Fisher – in trouble with the Law? I'm sure he can't have done anything very serious, he's an old friend of mine, I'm the Vicar of Saint James's, Highgate,' said the new arrival. 'I've been over seeing someone in Hampstead . . . what's he done?'

Charley was relieved to see that Mr Fisher had a respectable friend. Wild thoughts of having to carry the old man off to the station on the back of the bike had been passing through his mind.

'Nothing really, sir. Collecting litter or something. But I thought it was time he went home – on such a cold night. And I still do,' he ended severely. 'At his age.'

'Yes, yes, quite right. It *is* cold. I'll see him home – I'm going his way. You'll give me the pleasure of your company, won't you, Mr Fisher?'

This was received with a silent downward bend of the head. Mr Geddes's unusually keen sight had enabled him to recognize the old man at a distance of some hundred yards, and it now told him that Mr Fisher was trembling so violently that he seemed about to fall.

'I'll take him into the Vicarage and give him something hot to drink,' he said. 'I'll look after him – it's all right. (He's quite

87

sane – just – lives in a world of his own, that's all),' he added, in an undertone.

'All right, sir. We have to keep an eye on them, you know. I'll be off, then. Thank you. Good-night.'

Charley kept his face and voice rather stern to the last: he could not quite put his finger on the point where the Law had been deflected and cheated of doing its job, but he felt that it had. However, presumably the Church could be trusted to take over. With a gesture of farewell, which pointedly excluded Mr Fisher, he mounted his machine and rode off.

'There!' exclaimed Mr Geddes, 'he's gone. Now let's walk up this way and you can tell me all about it.'

Mr Fisher made an inarticulate sound, which Mr Geddes's patient and practised ear interpreted rightly.

'No, leave it for tonight. You've made a good-sized heap,' glancing towards the grisly collection, 'the keepers will come tomorrow and burn it. Come along – we'll soon be home.'

In fact, he did not think that they would.

Mr Fisher's gait, a cross between a shuffle and a totter, was not only slow, but instantly aroused the fear that he might at any minute fall down, and the path leading up from the valley towards the ponds, and thence off the Heath, was steep.

'An educated man,' Mr Fisher said feebly, beginning to move waveringly between the tussocks. 'We might 'ave some conversation – only I am rather tired. I don't mind admitting it, not to an educated man. But people will . . . I don't *like* people,' he ended suddenly, on a pettish note like a weary child.

Mr Geddes answered only by wheeling the bicycle nearer to him, and they moved into step together, beginning the long ascent. For some time they made their way in silence. Mr Geddes was occupied in steering his bicycle and keeping an eye on his companion in case he stumbled, and he also felt irritable, and tired, and strongly disinclined for talk following an afternoon with a tiresome former parishioner. He wished, increasingly, that she had ceased to keep in touch with him after she left the parish. So far as Mr Geddes could make out, she derived no benefit from their continuing relationship, while all he himself got from it was irritation.

But let *her*, for heaven's sake, be temporarily forgotten. He had better say something to the old man.

However, it was Mr Fisher who broke the silence.

'*I* was brought up,' he observed, 'to think every little 'elps.'

There was criticism implied here; of Charley Mackray and Mr Geddes, who had prevented the picking up of litter.

'"Little drops of water",' Mr Fisher continued severely, between small, stifled gasps, while the uncertainty of his gait perilously increased.

'Yes, of course.' Mr Geddes paused, steadying the bicycle. 'The lights look rather fine from here, through the trees, don't you think?'

'And "little grains of sand",' Mr Fisher paused, and looked outwards. 'No, I don't think they do look fine. Dreadful, they look to me, wicked, and not caring about the likes of us. "Make the mighty ocean, And the something land" (you would know. Being educated).'

He began to totter on again, restored by Mr Geddes's ruse, and muttering to himself as he went.

'. . . postage, that's the problem. One pair of 'ands can't manage it all, in London, but abroad . . . it's the postage . . . and I been thinking, what good could any of 'em do.' The breathless, muted voice was almost inaudible. 'Some millionaire, perhaps. But mostly that sort doesn't care.'

Mr Geddes, with fifty years' experience behind him in listening to the uneducated and the inarticulate, had the impression, as the whispers went on, that some scheme was being mulled over which should benefit humanity. He said nothing, however, wanting Mr Fisher to keep his breath for climbing the hill.

'I've worked – it all out, evenings. Oh, it's a task, a regular task, it is. A lifetime's task, you could say,' the old man muttered, looking down at the path under his straying feet.

They had now reached the brow of the hill and again Mr Geddes paused. Several paths leading down to the Ponds and Parliament Hill Fields sloped away before them, but it undeniably did look a long way.

'Sure you're up to walking?' he asked.

Mr Fisher answered by tottering to a near-by seat and collapsing on it, with a mutter about getting his breath, at the same time trustfully turning to his companion his long sheep's face, which in the moonlight looked as if he might well be dying. For a moment neither said anything, and the wind blew against them with the note that, even from a cloudless sky, hisses *snow*.

'Can you ride a bicycle?' suddenly demanded Mr Geddes, all his practical ability challenged.

'Used to. 'Aven't for years,' in a gasping whisper.

'Come on, then, I'll help you mount, and wheel you down the hill!' Mr Geddes exclaimed cheerfully, and was relieved to see the words have a reviving effect.

The old man got slowly up, and put out a small hand, which even through its glove struck cold and frail, into the one held out to him.

He mounted successfully, as if his muscles responded to the challenge of memory, and in a moment they were wheeling down the hill, Mr Geddes with a supporting arm around the light body balanced on the saddle, and Mr Fisher gripping the handles with what strength he had and even a faint smile of pleasure.

In ten minutes they were going along the path beside the Fields that look out over the main road, and a man out walking a couple of greyhounds glanced at them curiously.

'Better get down, p'raps,' observed Mr Fisher. 'People . . .'

'Yes, perhaps . . . can you manage?'

Mr Fisher replied by dismounting without mishap, and the final totter to the Vicarage began. It took nearly as long as their entire descent from the middle of the Heath.

As the large, gloomy house loomed before them, looking out over its be-shrubbed and tolerably wide carriage-sweep, Mr Geddes noted the dreary glow from his curate's uncurtained window. He thought, for the hundredth time, that he *must* arrange for his mother to come. Two unusually busy men, living alone and 'doing' for themselves, needed feminine support as well as eatable cooked food. Their present way of living was rapidly approaching the limit of discomfort. Discomfort didn't matter so much, but if it interfered with one's work . . .

Mr Fisher tottered with some briskness up to the pillared porch, then sat down abruptly on the step while Mr Geddes got out his key.

'Gerald!' shouted the Vicar, striding into the hall and standing at the foot of the broad staircase mounting into darkness, 'get us something hot to drink there's a good chap, will you? – I've got someone freezing down here . . .'

Reading Simone Weil, I suppose, he thought, as a faint distant shout replied. 'Come in, Mr Fisher, there'll be a hot drink in a minute – would you like a brandy?'

But Mr Fisher was too occupied with getting himself safely into the hall, and in shutting the door, to reply.

In a moment Gerald came down the stairs, pale, peering,

and giving a general impression of having stumbled through some theological palisade, leaving books collapsing in all directions behind him.

'Oh . . . hullo, Vicar . . . I was just working on my sermon . . . what'll you have . . . er . . . good . . .' in the direction of Mr Fisher, who had now collapsed into a very old armchair which had faithfully accompanied Mr Geddes all the way from Cambridge in 1919 to settle at last on the floor of Saint James's Vicarage.

'This is Mr Fisher, a friend of mine. We met on the Heath,' said Mr Geddes, firmly discouraging questions. 'Did you say brandy, Mr Fisher?'

'I don't touch spirits, never, as a rule. But it would be warming – thank you.' He inclined his head slowly and deeply towards Gerald, who was hesitating, rather appalled by the visitor's age and the colour of his skin. He made off towards the cavernous kitchen.

'Come along, Mr Fisher . . . Gerald, I hope the fire's in . . .' the Vicar called after him.

He led the way to the study.

Did him an injustice there, he thought, or perhaps he's getting sick of the woman; I hope so. ('The woman' was poor Simone Weil, whom Gerald was just discovering.)

The fire was in, if only just, and Mr Geddes recklessly piled on small logs, comfortably conscious that prunings from the Vicarage garden's too-abundant trees would provide plenty more. 'Come close to the fire, Mr Fisher – this is the best chair, I think – and I'll draw the curtains.' (Was it his curate's immersion in his inward world that caused him never to think of drawing curtains, however bleak and drear the night outside?) 'There, that's better.'

Mr Fisher was soon sitting, as upright as he could make

himself, almost on top of the fire, with a small glass of brandy in one trembling hand. He now slightly cleared his throat.

'Ah,' he began, 'there's nothing like a open fire. I always 'ave a open fire at 'ome. Wood. I collects it. On the Heath. I like to see the flames making their movements, and you can believe there's caves and that, in the red coals.'

'Yes . . .' Mr Geddes was hastening out of the room in search of something hot for himself, which he hoped was brewing in the kitchen. They took it in turns to perform such tasks, and past experience warned him that if Gerald and milk were involved, the latter would shortly be boiling over. But he stopped at the door.

'An open fire? Isn't that rather dangerous in that old house – and at your age, Mr Fisher?' He remembered Mr Fisher's habit, deplored by Gladys Barnes, of putting just-extinguished candles into his pockets.

Mr Fisher was staring into the fire. 'I am careful. I give you my word I am careful. And Miss Barnes kindly allows me to keep my wood on her landing, so there's no occasion for me to go down to the back yard. In this yere cold weather there is nothink like an open fire. For the beauty of it. And there's wood for the taking, over the 'Eath.'

'Well, I hope Miss Barnes keeps an eye on your fire for you while you're out?' Mr Geddes lingered.

'No, she don't. I don't like people in my place, especially I don't like womenfolk – throwing things away, and always putting in a word when you wants to be quiet. The ladies can keep themselves to themselves and I'll keep myself to myself.'

He turned back to his contemplation of the fire and Mr Geddes, stifling a laugh, made his way to the kitchen – to be met by the usual odour and the dismayed face of his curate.

'I only turned my back a second, I give you my word.'

'It comes up before you can see it,' Mr Geddes told him, pouring out milk from a fresh bottle which he opened by bursting the foil cap with his thumb. 'The drinking chocolate's come – oh good.' He snatched a tin from a half-unpacked box of groceries on the old wooden table. 'You having some?'

'No thank you, I don't . . . er . . . you hadn't forgotten the meeting at eight-fifteen?' said Gerald, absently watching the preparation of the brew.

'No – no, it's been at the back of my mind ever since I got in, I'll get rid of him the minute I can but I must just see him on his way,' Mr Geddes was now swallowing the almost boiling drink standing.

'There are quite a number of things on the Agenda . . . that draught at the back of the church . . .'

'Damn the draught,' said Mr Geddes impatiently, 'though of course I don't sit there . . . do *you* mind draughts, Gerald? (I must get back to him, he'll be falling into the fire).'

'Not really,' was the dreamy answer, 'I suppose if one's been to . . . our kind of school . . . one doesn't.'

'No, we do learn not to notice minor discomforts . . . gosh, if you could stand my *alma mater*, you can stand most things!'

He glanced at his wrist. 'It's after eight . . . can you go on, and tell them I'll be there in five minutes . . . you might get the prayer over for me, if you will?'

He hurried off, and Gerald, having scraped ineptly at the burnt milk crusted on the gas cooker with a cloth that should have been burned some months ago, put it on the draining-board, with the wondering reflection that in the late Mrs Geddes's time the kitchen might have been comfortable, even cosy. He went off to the Parochial Church Council Meeting.

Mr Fisher was asleep. Mr Geddes gently shook him by the shoulder, and the pale eyes slowly opened and stared at him.

'I have to go to a meeting now,' the Vicar told him, 'but you're welcome to stay if you like – I shall be some time, I'm afraid, but if you wait, I or my curate will see you home.'

'I will be getting on my way.' Mr Fisher began to get to his feet.

'Sure? We could run to a taxi, I think – you must be very tired – if you like to wait?'

'No, no, thank you. It has been a pleasure, talkin' to an educated man.'

'Then I really must go. Good-night, Mr Fisher – we'll be seeing one another. You can let yourself out, can't you?'

The old man's gesture of farewell, a solemn movement of the hand and a deep bend of his head, remained with Mr Geddes as he crossed the dark garden to the church, looming some fifty yards away.

The taxi fare would have come out of his own pocket: he thought he knew human nature well enough, after fifty years of bashing at it, to be sure that Mr Fisher would not steal anything on his way out. A strange old man. Oddly likeable.

The church clock struck the hour, high up in the windy moonlight. St. Thomas's Eve! Tomorrow would be the shortest day.

11

At Christmas, Gladys relied upon the arrival of two envelopes from ladies for whom she had formerly worked, and on the morning of the twenty-third she and Annie were awaiting the postman.

'Sure not to be here till round about eleven and then it'll be the van,' observed Gladys, stationed at the bedroom window overlooking the street.

'Oh I can't think about nothing else but them moving in. I do think it was too bad not to 'ave let us know – that Peggy – she's downright unkind.'

'Well let's hope they'll let us have Christmas Day in peace. Sure to, come to that. Whoever heard of anyone moving in on Christmas Day?'

'You don't know, Glad,' Annie said with dismal significance, 'that sort' – she meant the sort employed by Thomas Pearson – 'they don't work not like ordinary people.'

'Oh do for pity's sake cheer up – here's the van!'

Gladys ended on a joyful scream and ran across the room. She hurried down the stairs, surprising in their pink and grey new carpet after the dinginess of the sisters' landing, and dashed open the freshly painted front door.

If it had been a white postman, there would have been perhaps friendly exchanges about smartness, come into a fortune, won the Pools, or even 'about time, too', concerning the redecorating. But the two letters she almost snatched from a well-kept black hand were delivered without a smile, and intellectual eyes, behind glasses, looked at her gravely. 'Thanks ever so – just what I wanted!' she cried, beaming. There was no answering smile but an expression of benevolence replaced the gravity.

Educated student. Doing it for the money. Don't laugh, might crack something, decided Gladys, toiling up the stairs with the letters. 'Annie, Annie, it's all right – they've come!' she began to scream, as she reached the landing. 'Now we can enjoy ourselves.'

There followed a delightful half hour, while they examined the three pound notes sent by Mrs Harriman and the two sent by Mrs Lysaght, and discussed how they would spend them.

Mrs Lysaght was Mr Geddes's former parishioner who had moved to Hampstead. It was she who had persuaded Gladys to resume the church-going that Gladys, more from the delightful pressure of living than from indolence or disinclination, had allowed to lapse: and perhaps it was the only contribution towards leaving the world a better place than she found it that Mrs Lysaght had made.

Gladys did not have to leave for work until the afternoon, and she was just, with a pleasant sense of leisure, swathing herself in the cardigans and mufflers fitted to face the piercing wind while she 'popped round to Joneses'; and debating with Annie whether, in view of their Christmas box, she might not instead go up the Archway in search of some nice bargains in the way of food, when the bedroom door was roughly opened. Gladys screamed. Annie cowered into her wrappings.

'You Gladys Barnes?' demanded the dark man who stood there, unsmiling, with a hand on the door.

Gladys, open-mouthed, nodded.

'Mrs Pearson's moving in this afternoon,' he said. 'The men'll be here soon. You be here to let them in.'

'I – I –' Gladys was trembling so that the words would hardly come, but she found some courage. 'I can't, I got to go to work, 'meditely after lunch, they're expecting me. And it's the money –'

'Where do you work?' he interrupted, flashing a glance, terrifying to both sisters, on Annie, who had ventured to move from the strained position into which fear had flung her. She froze again, and Gladys said:

'Kyperiou's, it's a caff in Archway Road, but please don't go making trouble there, it's my job, see, nice people they are –'

'You do what I say and there won't be trouble.'

Gladys's terror was beginning to lessen; because, in her nature, hope and gaiety were always ready to pipe up like two irrepressible little birds. She actually thought, *You can see he's Peggy's father.* For she had known, from his first appalling appearance, who this was . . . the legendary, the horrific, the dreaded rackman in person.

'It's the money,' she said, indignation beginning to struggle out through fear, 'I was counting on it – must 'ave it. For Christmas.'

He took out a pocket-book bulging with red and green.

'Here.' He pulled out a note.

But Gladys now felt actually capable of standing up to the creature; the fact that he was so like his daughter had made her feel him less of a monster.

'It's one pound ten it'll be,' she said quickly, 'a pound for the two days, and then there's the staff box.'

'I shan't want you for two days, only for today.' He crumpled up the note and threw it at her feet. 'Here – do what I say.'

'It's not *right*,' burst out Gladys, crimsoning. 'It – it's not *right*, that's what it is.'

He shrugged. 'Ah, perhaps not. A lot of things aren't, in this world. What you have to remember is *facts*. It's a *fact* that I own this house, and the one next door, and the row up the street. It's a *fact* I could turn you out this minute. It's a *fact* you owe me a month's rent –'

'I got it,' Gladys dared to interrupt, 'and I got Mr Fisher's upstairs too – in case you came in unexpected. We was wondering –'

He held out a dark hand, impatiently twitching the fingers.

There followed some bustling and removal of dirty notes and silver from the depths of a handbag which had once been smart. Hesitatingly, her detestation and fear showing on her face, Gladys held them out.

He forced her to advance, step by step, until she had put them on his outstretched palm; flat, insolent, not even cupped to receive them.

He pocketed them and said again, 'You stay here today,' and was turning away.

Gladys made an effort that seemed to crack something in her spirit.

'You thinking of making any changes?' she blurted: and could hardly believe that the awful question which had been throbbing within her for so many days, had actually sounded out on the air; the question sometimes hinted timidly to Peggy, that Peggy had always ignored, and now put to the rackman himself.

He did not look round. 'What changes?' he said, half-way through the door.

'Rents . . . and that . . .' she faltered.

'You do what Mrs Pearson wants, you always do what Mrs Pearson wants. Then there won't be any changes.' He moved on, not looking round.

'And the old gentleman – him upstairs,' she gabbled, daring to follow, 'he's ever so old, earns a bit showing off his little dolls – pays regular –'

'He can stay. But tell him; always do what Mrs Pearson wants. Then there'll be no "changes", as you call them.'

He was gone.

As may be imagined, this left the sisters with conversation for the rest of the day, and had not even more interesting events begun to occur almost immediately, the topic would have lasted well into the next week.

Gladys was divided between terror lest her job should be lost to her through this intolerable piece of interference, and overwhelming relief that she had at last asked the cruel question and received reassurance.

Not that you could trust a rackman, of course. But for the time being . . . And, as she lived from minute to minute, and was acutely uncomfortable whenever facts compelled her to look a few days ahead, she felt that a load of worry had been rolled away.

The note was still lying, crumpled up, on the floor. Her first action was to pounce on it; when you live from minute to minute and are over seventy, with an invalid sister to support, you can't afford to leave notes lying at your feet, however insolently they may have arrived there.

'Ten shillins,' she announced to Annie, who had not uttered a sound since the appearance of their visitor, 'I'll go along tomorrow same as usual. Well!' relishingly, as her spirits soared, 'I'm glad I've seen him close to, they say they mostly never come near the places they buy (like murderers only the opposite), not that he's much to look at, come to that, those black eyes. I never do trust 'em, very like Peggy, isn't he, funny, it must be, having a rackman for your dad but I don't expect she minds, doesn't notice I expect, very wrapped up in herself she is, I've always said so, some man in her history I wouldn't be surprised, s'pose I may as well go and do the shopping seeing it's stopped snowing, hope I don't slip that's all, could you fancy a bit of boiling bacon, they had some round at Joneses for one and six, not all that fatty, you feeling all right, old dear?'

The last question was accompanied by a dart to the bed, where Annie had suddenly fallen back despairingly among the pillows.

'Oh Glad! That awful man – in our home!'

'Cheer up – he didn't do no harm. There's always the pleece –'

'The pleece! Oh Glad! In our home!'

'Oh shut up do – you give me the sick!' burst out Gladys, shaking the pillows as if they were Annie herself. 'It's all right, isn't it? We got ten shillins – better than nothing, and he said he ain't going to make no changes –'

'In our home! I can't get over it – 'ow can you take his wicked money?'

'Money's money,' pronounced Gladys with a last jerk of the bedclothes. 'Couldn't 'elp meself, could I? S'pose you'd of liked me to chuck it back at him?'

'Coming into our home and throwing his wicked money at us – money got out of little Nicky and Alexander I shouldn't wonder. You 'eard anywhere they might of gone?'

The coloured family living farther up the Walk had surprised the sisters by a sudden departure.

'Not a sound.' Gladys's tone was good-humoured again; she welcomed the change of subject. 'I'll ask that black what sweeps the road up Churchill Rise, he might know (if he isn't hiding up in that arch if it starts snowing, I'll bet that's where he'll be, and can you blame him, I often think, if we're cold what about them), could you fancy a bovvil before I go off?'

On Annie's giving a weak nod, the subject of Nicky and Alexander's problematical whereabouts was gone into at length, while Gladys half-filled a kettle from the tap on the landing, set it to boil on the rusty ancient cooker, and opened a new one-ounce bottle of Bovril.

The hours were long for Annie while her sister was at work, and they had been greatly brightened by the daily visits from Nicky and Alexander on their way home from school, invited in by Gladys after many commands, of a truly awesome impressiveness, Not to Touch and Not to Lark About and to Keep Out of That Mrs Simms's Way, while the pair silently listened; their four jetty eyes had widened and widened until they suggested dark jewels from some remote planet. Annie mourned and missed Nicky and Alexander, doubtless driven out, with their numerous relations, by the rackman.

'Make it strong, Glad. I feel that weak.'

'Don't I always? I hate dish-wash.'

'You don't 'ave to tell me. It's not me gives tea to 'alf the street if they pops in.' Annie reclined on her rearranged pillows, sighing at intervals, while Gladys spooned out the Bovril with a lavish hand. 'It's the shock,' she added.

Annie was still sipping, and Gladys was about to go out, when her sister exclaimed, 'Glad! You can't go. 'E said so.'

Gladys paused, staring, then sniffed.

'Like his sauce . . . but I s'pose . . . well, they'll be open till eight . . .'

She began to un-swathe. 'If they was to come and there wasn't no-one to let them in and they complained . . . but I don't like it, no I don't, but what can you do? . . . here, I'll have a bovvil too, I could do with it.'

The consumption of the Bovril spread over into lunch, for there was so much to talk about.

Gladys minced up the remains of the previous day's best-end-of-neck (New Zealand) in the clumsy forty-year-old mincer, and, with the addition of two potatoes, well salted and mashed with half a gill of milk left from their breakfast, produced a shepherd's pie that was just not quite enough for two.

But the Bovril had provided a passable foundation, and, with six staleish brussels sprouts added, there was in fact a lunch.

Gladys could cook. She loved her food, and she had a most un-English talent for making something tasty out of scraps that most women would have thrown away. It is not too much to say that she and Annie would have died years ago from some illness invited by malnutrition if they had not been carefully fed.

'Quite nice, these sprouts,' commented Annie, sitting up in bed with her lunch spread out on the old papier mâché tray with its spray of Japanese flowers. 'When did you get 'em, Glad?'

'Saturday – or was it Monday? I got a half. Pull the leaves off. Make 'em small, I hate those great lumps of sprouts. These're all right inside, even if they are old. Like me,' and Gladys went off into a great cackle, in which Annie more primly joined.

12

In the midst of their meal, there came a grinding of wheels outside, followed by a great bang on Lily Cottage's front door.

'"Dab-on-the-door-said-Daniel"!' cried Gladys, flying up with her mouth full, 'it's them! Lucky I never went out. Morning, I call this, not afternoon. Wonder they dare.'

'Lucky I stopped you, you mean.' Annie was sopping a piece of bread round her plate to make sure of the last drops of gravy. But her sister was already half-way down the stairs.

The moving van and its men employed by Thomas Pearson suggested his aura of silent lawlessness.

It was a small vehicle, dinted and unobtrusive, painted a dingy grey, and the men were dirty beyond the ordinary grime of a day's work and were almost in rags.

Gladys felt no surprise, after one glance at their faces, to learn from their mutters to one another that they were foreigners. This was how she expected foreigners to look.

One of them came up the steps and reached past her and thrust at the door she had only half opened, so that it swung back and crashed into the wall behind.

'Here, steady on!' exclaimed Gladys, 'mind our paint. And you can mind me while you're about it. Pushing like that.'

He did not trouble even to glance at her.

'Deaf, I s'pose,' observed Gladys to the surrounding air.

She withdrew into the back of the hall and stood watching. They carried up, in silence and with the greatest care, the new furniture and the mirrors and plump pink cushions: object after object conspicuous for bright colour and prettiness. It was a pleasure to watch, and a highly unusual sight in Rose Walk, and Gladys began to meditate getting Annie out of bed to share the treat.

'I s'pose you know where everything's got to go?' she said at last, as one of the three came up the front steps leading into Lily Cottage, 'because I don't. Open the door, he said, never a word about where to put the things.'

Without looking at her, he held out a dirty sheet of paper, on which she could see little squares, each one filled with small circles that were numbered; then tramped on his way.

'Oh . . . all right, so long as you know, before you come I was thinking how you might like a cup of tea but being deaf I s'pose you couldn't hear me if I asked.'

The remark might not have been uttered. Gladys began to feel that she was wasting her time; a sense of importance and involvement in Lily Cottage's fortunes that had crept into her feelings, despite her fear of the rackman and her resentment, was agreeable, but it was freezing cold with the door open. She was shivering.

'You nearly finished?' she called suddenly, and even as she spoke, one of the men slammed the back doors of the van. Evidently the little armchair, puffed and padded with rosy satin, had been the last of the load.

''Ave I got to sign a paper?' screamed Gladys, seeing unmistakable sign of imminent departure and feeling that her part in all this had been so slight that the rackman might well come down on her. 'Oh all right, it's all the same to me, funny thing all three of you being deaf, s'pose that's why you all work together, birds of a feather, as they say, well if anythink's wrong it's not my fault and I 'ope you'll tell him so, if you can talk, that is, dumb as well, p'haps, it's a great misfortune . . .'

The man who had given the orders and was evidently the leader turned slightly just before he climbed in beside the driver and gave her one look – coming up from such an inward furious preoccupation with God alone knew what pains and despairs that Gladys actually took a step back.

It was far more frightening than any look from the rackman himself during their recent interview, and it gave her a dreadful hint of what his powers could do to someone even more within his grasp than Annie and herself.

But she forgot it at once as she shut the door.

Unable to resist temptation, she hurried from cottage to cottage, darting through the arch in the hall and back, climbing up to marvel over the bedroom, all pink, with a curly gilt mirror above the fireplace of stepped artificial brickwork that had replaced the basket grate of a hundred years ago.

A gentle warmth, pervasive and soothing, floated night and day through Lily Cottage, the result of comings and goings by what Gladys thought of as 'the oil officials' some days ago. Central heating! But only in the cottage where Mrs Pearson would live.

The kitchen and another bedroom in Rose Cottage remained chilly and not luxuriously furnished; the kitchen, indeed, was an old-fashioned affair, so Gladys thought, with – could you believe it – two old rusty irons in a corner, and a rug made of old bits of rag and an old armchair and a wooden table. But there was a new electric cooker.

Mean, thought Gladys. All for Show, but Mean – oh my goodness, she inwardly shrieked, here's Nurse! and I never put the water on!

Nurse's knock was unmistakable; a rat-a-tat which managed to carry all the gay and sunshiny side of Ireland, and Nurse herself, standing on the doorstep in her dark blue, with her neat dark-blue car parked at the kerb, had the beautiful Irish skin and the sparkling Irish eye.

Large, solid and firm as some bonny Prize Show dahlia was Nurse, with a kind and interested manner which almost managed to conceal her daily preoccupation with the affairs of dozens and dozens of other patients.

'Hullo, dear. All ready for me?' cried Nurse, already across the hall because she knew from experience that Gladys Barnes was seldom all ready for her, and not a second must be wasted, 'and how's Annie today? New tenants moving in?'

'Not a drop of hot water have I got!' screamed Gladys, toiling up after the sturdy black-silk legs, 'I clean forgot – besides it's Tuesday, Nurse, it's Tuesday!'

'Coming today instead of Wednesday because of Christmas, I did tell you dear,' said Nurse over her shoulder, crossing the landing in three strides, 'never mind I'll just take a look at her. Or perhaps there's a drop hot next door. Very handy having that door in the hall – painted you up very smart, haven't they? Nice people? You run down and see if there is a drop. Well how's Annie today dear?' Nurse was now in the bedroom and holding Annie's wrist.

'I darsent, Nurse –' Gladys was beginning mysteriously.

'Oh go on with you, no-one would grudge a jug of hot water, God love you, and Christmas three days away,' interrupted Nurse, peeling off bedclothes.

'I *darsent*, Nurse, and that's a fact, the kitchen's downstairs, parlour and bedroom next door, another bedroom and kitchen downstairs, here.'

'Where's the bathroom, then?' interrupted Nurse, re-tucking

Annie, who was vainly trying to push in a word concerning her condition between their voices. 'I'll fetch it.'

'Next door. Came in this morning as bold as brass and threw ten shillings at me . . . I wouldn't if I was you, really I wouldn't, Nurse. He can be ever so nasty.'

'Well I'll just leave her for to-day, she's nice and clean like she always is,' pronounced Nurse with an approving pat on the quilt, 'and perhaps you could manage a wash down for her on Christmas Eve,' glancing at her watch and giving up the search for hot water with a philosophy taught her by years in her profession. 'How's the old gentleman these days?'

'Oh fine,' said Gladys instantly, with a lightning glance at Annie, 'out and about s'usual.'

'Well mind you let me know if he gets bad,' said Nurse, disappearing across the landing. 'The minute he complains you let me know. At his age you can't be too careful. Take care of yourselves. I'll let myself out. Merry Christmas!'

Her voice died away, and was followed by the slam of the front door.

'Annie!' exclaimed Gladys, clasping her hands, 'if you could see downstairs!'

'Nice, is it? I heard them carrying it all in and I did wish I could see . . .'

'It's fairyland!' nodding her head. 'That's what it is – fairyland! I wonder – could you possibly manage to come down?'

'I would love a peep. I get so dull up here all day on my own.'

'You had plenty of company to-day – more than what you want, I should think,' said her sister grimly. 'Oh well, better not, p'raps. Just supposing he *did* come in to see how things were going . . .'

'Oh don't! Shall I ever forget seeing him come round the

door! My heart's still going from it. I did try to tell Nurse, how it's going, but you was both jawing fit to burst yourselves –'

'Going on about hot water, she's always on about something, and the old gentleman, what business is it of hers, can't even die in peace nowadays –'

'Oh don't talk about dying. It's Christmas.'

'Well, seeing it's all in, I s'pose his lordship'd kindly give me permission, they'll be sold out, I wouldn't wonder and I 'aven't got a shilling only coppers, if it goes out while I'm gone you can keep warm can't you, shan't be a tick, it's starting to get dark already and not four yet, can you beat it, well I'm off.'

While she was speaking, Gladys had put on for the second time that day her mufflings and coverings and now marched out of the house.

The warmth from Lily Cottage came up faintly but agreeably to meet her as she went down the stairs, and, feeling the need for its comfort, she crossed under the arched doorway into the other house and went out by the other door.

Silent and warm, glowing in its gilt and rose, the witch's house stood in the falling dusk, waiting for the witch.

Gladys had not been gone five minutes before faint sounds became audible to her sister. Dismissing a first terrified thought that the rackman might be stealing up the stairs, she concluded that the maker of them was Mr Fisher. But she did not call out, because the years of their mutual tenancy had taught her that Mr Fisher did not welcome being hailed by those he called the ladies.

Presently there came a faint tap at the living-room door.

'Is that you, Mr Fisher?' called Annie, 'come in. You must excuse me being in bed, as usual.'

The door gently opened, and there stood the old man, so wrapped in his dead leaf-coloured clothes that he appeared shapeless, leaning against the jamb, with his face even more colourless than usual. He was breathing fast; he half raised a hand in greeting.

Annie looked at him in silence. She knew that he would want to be the first to speak.

'Good-evening,' he said at last, and she could hardly catch the words, 'I was wondering . . . could you and your sister be so very kind as to give me the loan of a scoop of tea? It isn't . . . quite . . . convenient for me to go out this evening.' The sentence ended on a gasp.

Annie, who had long had her own views about Gladys's social manner to Mr Fisher, was thankful that her sister was out. Here was the chance to deal with him in the way he would welcome.

'Of course. Please help yourself, the canister's on the sideboard. And please won't you make it down here? Then p'raps I could have a cup, too.'

Annie's simple code of manners hardly extended beyond the lavish sprinkling of her sentences with 'please'.

'Very kind of you,' said Mr Fisher, with a stiff inclination of his head, and he shuffled into the room in the faded silk slippers, 'If I may say so – neighbourly. But you . . . and Miss Gladys . . . always neighbourly . . .'

He began to fumble with the lid of the canister, in a way that would have set Gladys screaming offers of help.

But Annie was silent, and did not even watch, but kept her eyes fixed on the square window opposite her bed in the farther room.

The curtains were apart, and Gladys had refrained, from motives of economy, from putting on the light; behind them, the curve of Parliament Hill showed black against a sky of purple bloom and icy pink.

Mr Fisher had tottered between canister, tap and cooker for a full twenty minutes before the kettle lid began to rattle. Annie refrained from the shriek with which her sister would have greeted this event, and Mr Fisher, left unharried, dealt with it; very slowly but nevertheless safely.

At last the tea was made – and, even as the old man poured on the boiling water, the hissing of the gas-fire ceased, and the two rooms were plunged into half-darkness.

Annie did not cry out. She said gently – and she felt like talking quietly, the dusk was so silent, and the sky above the distant Heath so soft and cold – 'Could you please switch on the light, if you'd be that kind, Mr Fisher?' and he shuffled across the room.

But 'the electric' had joined the gas in what seemed a shaming conspiracy.

'Perhaps I might draw the curtain back a little?' he suggested.

'Yes, please,' Annie's tone was touched with mortification.

Followed more tottering, shuffling and fumbling, then the curtains were drawn, fully revealing the superb fading light, and letting it shine faintly through the room.

She had wondered whether he would take his cup of tea and retreat with it up to his attic. But he first handed her her own cup on a tray, which he found, undirected, on the side-board; then sat down in the armchair and began to sip, always in silence.

Annie considered apologizing for the behaviour of the gas and decided against it. Keep your poverty to yourself.

Darkness had fallen. Suddenly a shaft of silver light slid over the ceiling, and engines sighed to a stop outside. Annie started, to the peril of her tea.

'That's them – the rackman, I shouldn't wonder,' she quavered, and Mr Fisher, far from coming out with some manly and comforting remark, merely turned his gaze gravely towards the door, as if anticipating the monster's immediate entrance.

In a moment they heard the door of Lily Cottage open, and voices, together with sounds suggesting that suitcases were being carried upstairs.

A woman's voice, harsh and irritable, implored someone to take care for God's sake. The impression of noisy haste and impatience was disagreeable, coming up into the room where, in the unearthly light, they had been drinking their tea in companionable silence, and Mr Fisher put down his cup and began slowly to get up from his chair.

'Oh don't go, Mr Fisher . . . stay and keep me company . . . Glad'll be in any minute . . . I don't like the idea of them coming up here and me alone,' his hostess implored, and, with a reluctance expressed by the extreme hesitancy of his move- ment, the old man resumed his seat.

They sat in silence, Annie's eyes staring out through the gloom at Mr Fisher as if in search of human support, and Mr Fisher's wandering uneasily round the room.

The angry demand for care had been followed at once by a rich glare of light from below, so strong that it poured through the arch and illuminated the sisters' stairs, and their landing and even made objects dimly visible in the bedroom. Annie sniffed.

'Quite a saving, that'll be,' she muttered. 'Oh I wish Glad ud come in . . . s'pose they wanted something?' – and even as she spoke the familiar voice was heard below.

'Hullo Peggy, got here then, nice and warm, afternoon Mrs Pearson, I just popped out, there's always, well, I said, he did say stay while they brought them in but I thought to myself you never know when they're going to take it into their heads to close near Christmas making up for the rush pleased to meet you, Mrs George, yes, next door, we're neighbours, got the upstairs place and the old gentleman has the attic I don't expect you'll see much of him, keeps himself to himself, well I'll leave you to get on, those men I don't mean to tell tales but sulky, well, I said, dumb as well as deaf best to make a joke of it with that sort but brought the things in ever so careful I must say. Well seeing there's five of you I'll be toddling, there now! wouldn't that happen! Just what I said!'

The voice was getting nearer as Gladys climbed the short flight, and the last exclamation was uttered at the door, where she paused to take in the fact that her sister was in the near-dark with a visitor.

'I've got one here . . . shan't be a jiff . . . one for each.'

Followed rattling and jingling sounds and gas and electricity flew back into their cages. She hastened to put a match to the pettishly hissing fire, then, having nodded to Mr Fisher without enthusiasm, proceeded to unmuffle, accompanied by a report on what was going on downstairs.

13

Four handsome pigskin cases had been carried up by the man George. A fifth, made of the cheapest materials and with its handle fastened by string, had been dragged up with difficulty and panting breath by its owner, who went about her task with irritating slowness, and frequent glances about her, as if she found difficulty in realizing where she was. Lily Cottage echoed, in a muffled fashion, with the sounds that accompany resumed occupation.

Having without one word to anybody dumped his burden, George went out, slamming the door after him, and settled himself in the car with a newspaper, reading with an expression of fury that seemed dredged up from some burning private marl-pit.

Mrs Pearson had gone straight to her room, at the back of the house. She felt for the light near the door, switched it on, and looked about her, drawing a breath of satisfaction.

'Mm . . . pricey,' said Mrs George, who had followed. 'I like all your pink and gold.' But this was the most she could force herself to dredge up from the family pit. She stood looking round the room with envy unconcealed.

Mrs Pearson went to the bed and lay down, kicking off her shoes, sliding out of her fur coat, drawing the eiderdown over her shoulders.

'Peggy, love, get me a hot-water bottle. And my cigs. And the matches. In my bag.'

'You can do that.' Peggy jerked her head sideways at the other girl, who was kneeling beside one of the cases and attempting to open it. 'Cigarettes and matches. In her bag – look, over there.'

She turned exasperatedly to her mother. 'I thought she spoke some English?'

'So she does – don't you, Erika? I expect it all seems a bit strange.'

She glanced at the wizened creature, and a smile came over the pretty skull that was her face. 'But you must talk slowly. "I – want – cigarettes. In – my – bag."' She pointed, and Erika went across and opened it and fumbled within. She found the cigarettes and brought the packet across to her employer.

'Well – sooner you than me – Germans,' said Mrs George, not troubling to lower her voice.

'Sh-sh. We'll get on nicely, once we're settled.'

'She looks downright mental,' Mrs George went on. 'I hate anything like that round me.'

'S'sh,' Mrs Pearson said dreamily again, drawing in smoke. 'She's going to forget all that, now. Thanks, lovey,' as Peggy returned with the hot-water bottle, having found a boiling kettle in the kitchen, thoughtfully set on the cooker by Gladys. 'Oh, I like being here. I like it already. It's so quiet. Look at Tom's roses . . . Peggy, take Erika and show her her room. Take some roses for her, no, more – take six or seven.'

She watched contentedly while Peggy snatched the narrow pink and yellow buds from the vase, scattering water, and went quickly out of the room.

'Erika – you go with Peggy. See your room,' said Mrs Pearson, and Erika slowly moved towards the door.

'I'll have a look too,' said Mrs George, making to follow.

'No, you stay here,' said Mrs Pearson tranquilly. 'You scare her.'

'I'd scare her all right if she was working for me. Her sort needs keeping down – Germans.' But Mrs George stayed where she was.

'No, no, you've got it all wrong, she needs lifting up. You'd better go now, Marie, your light's all jagged. It's like that with people sometimes. They can't help it, but they'd best keep away from each other.'

'Oh if you're going to talk your nonsense I'm off,' Mrs George said, her eyes wandering uneasily away from the haggard, smiling face.

The back bedroom in Rose Cottage was small, and completely square, with a high ceiling and a small window; the lightest of primrose paint and green, leaf-scattered wallpaper could not remove a faint suggestion of a cell.

Erika, slowly pushing back hair from her eyes, stood looking around, while Peggy jammed the roses into a vase.

Erika's eyes moved to the ceiling, to the narrow window, through which shone a dreary orange glare behind dark roofs. She said nothing.

Peggy glanced at her. 'Go on, draw the curtains. Here . . .' she said, as Erika did not move. She went across and dragged them together. 'You'd better get yourself some English, quick, I can't be here all the time, and you'll have to look after my mother by yourself. Can you make tea?'

'*Kaffee*,' whispered Erika, shaking her head.

'*Oh* . . .' Peggy was quivering like some impatient filly, 'I suppose I'd better show you.'

'Mother,' she flung at Mrs Pearson, as she led Erika, stumbling and pushing at her hair, back into the bedroom. 'I hope you know what you've let yourself in for.'

Mrs Pearson gave a small indulgent laugh. 'She'll be all right.'

Mrs George, having put away silk and nylon underclothing in the drawers, was wandering round picking up the little glass grotesques which she had arranged on the dressing-table and mantelpiece, and putting them down again.

'Well – I'm off,' she said at last. 'If you'll be all right. I can't say I'd care to sleep here with *her*. She might turn funny.'

'She's all right, her light's faint but it's blue. She's had a bad time. Very bad. I don't know what I can do for her, but I'll try. I always wanted a daughter. Peggy's so independent, she'd never let me help her.' Mrs Pearson moved her heavy gold curls restlessly against the pillows. 'I can't get near Peggy. She's shut me out.'

Mrs George heard this without any show of interest. She said, 'Well –' again, made a gesture of farewell, and announced her intention of 'looking in again in a day or two'.

'Yes, do come again, Marie. Phone me.' Then Mrs George, picking up her coat, went off, as it happened, for ever.

With the shutting of the front door, a hush settled over the house. Mrs Pearson lay still, staring at the glow of the lamp beside her bed. She heard the car drive away; then it was so still that she could hear the distant voice of Peggy, instructing Erika in the kitchen in the next cottage, and certain trampings to and fro, overhead but outside her own ceiling, which she knew must be caused by her neighbour, the stout old woman who lived in Rose Cottage. She turned her face into the pillow and shut her eyes.

'Mum.' Peggy's voice broke the silence; there was no tender questioning note, only a flat repetition of the little name. 'Do you want anything to eat?' She was standing by the bed, accompanied by Erika holding a tray.

'What have you got for me? – thank you, lovey, that was thoughtful.'

'Cold stuff. This – *she* can't make tea,' indicating the silent figure with a motion of her hand.

'She'll learn, dear. I'll teach her.' Mrs Pearson sat up. She looked at Peggy wistfully, 'I suppose you want to be getting along now.'

'Yes. It's nearly seven and there's a film I want to see.'

'But just tell me you think it all looks pretty.'

'Oh yes, it looks pretty, all right. 'Bye.' With her clouded smile and her secret look, armoured in her silence, she went out, shutting the door behind her. Mrs Pearson was alone with her attendant in the rosy box of a room.

She turned to Erika, who had not moved from her place beside the bed. Standing with lowered head, hair falling over her eyes, the tray held stiffly in front of her, she did indeed justify Mrs George's comment. Her eyes were fixed on the food on the tray.

'*Schatz* –' Mrs Pearson said, and the dull little orbs came round to rest on her face. Mrs Pearson moved her head towards the tray. 'Help yourself. *Essen*. Here –' she stretched out her hand, 'I'll have a biscuit and my tea, first.'

When she had helped herself – 'Take it, go on, take it. *Essen – essen*.'

Erika slowly picked up the tray and went across to a table by the window and set it down. '*Dankë schön* –' she whispered, in a meagre voice which seemed the authentic note of her thin, flat body. She began slowly to eat.

'Go and sit by the fire, *schatz* –' said Mrs Pearson in a moment. Erika slowly lifted her head, her jaw suspended in the act of eating, and looked at her, then she recommenced her slow chewing.

There was a longish silence. The room's warmth and rosy light seemed to deepen; all sounds had ceased from the cottage next door; once the harsh note of a diesel engine blared from the railway running beyond the Council flats.

'Go and sit by the fire, *schatz*,' said Mrs Pearson presently, very softly; a piece of bread was falling from Erika's hand and her head was drooping. The murmur seemed to reach her, for without looking at Mrs Pearson she got up, and stumbled across to the fire, where she rearranged herself and resumed her consumption of the food. But her movements became slower and slower, her head fell forward, and gradually she slid down until she was lying in the full warmth, her scanty hair spread about her hidden face.

Mrs Pearson remained motionless, except for her slight movements as she lit cigarette after cigarette or pressed out a consumed one, her eyes fixed on the lamp. They did not close, their lids did not blink; they remained widely spread, with violet shadows beneath them, blue whites and ever-spreading, velvety black iris drawing all the life in her face into themselves; enormous; tranced, in the unchanging light.

There was no sound or movement in the room beyond those slight ones made by the burning of electricity, which give a false impression of life. The stirring of breath from the two human creatures was no more than the faintest flutter. But, when enough time had passed for the room to sink utterly into this silence, there came a change.

It was in Mrs Pearson's eyes. Something glanced out of them; drew back and vanished, then returned, as if with a pounce of satisfaction, and glared out avidly into the room. The eyes had the expression of a creature that feeds. They settled on every visible object; the sleeping girl, the expanse of pink carpet, each little glass animal on the dressing-table; sucking at them and caressing them, and moving slowly over them, as if what was looking out had been starved for a very long time.

14

A knock on the door sounded; subdued, as if someone meant to recognize the presence of invalidism.

The feeder in Mrs Pearson's eyes was no longer there. Flash – gone. They turned, in gentle inquiry, to the door. 'Who's that? Come in.'

'It's only me, thought I'd just look in see if you wanted anything. My, you do look cosy,' said Gladys, joyfully marching forward.

'It was sweet of you, thank you. Yes, I'm very cosy. My husband'll be here presently.'

'She dropped off?' Gladys looked with frankest curiosity at the girl sleeping beside the fire. 'Skinny, isn't she? Come from far?'

'Germany. She's been in one of those camps.'

Gladys's eyes grew wide in eager horror.

'What, one of them awful places! How in the wide world did she ever get out?'

'No – no, of course not. There aren't places like that any more – at least . . .' she paused, and when she spoke again, it was to draw the words out doubtfully, while her lowered eyes were fixed on the smoke of her cigarette, 'not . . . so that people can be kept there . . . they're . . . empty. At least, you couldn't see . . .' She broke off. 'No, she was in a camp for refugees. She wandered round with her grandad and grandmother; begging, I suppose, really, until they got to this camp. In West Germany.'

'Well I never,' said Gladys, wonder and pity, as well as curiosity, on her face. 'What's her real name, then?'

'Oh . . . it's Erika, all right – I don't know her other name – Mr Pearson knows. Mr Pearson managed it all. He had a friend and he knew someone . . . you know how it is.' Mrs Pearson laughed, like a mischievous girl.

'He got her away, anyhow, thanks to Mr Pearson's friend, and here she is. Her mum and dad were killed. They had a farm, but the Russians burnt it.'

'There's beasts for you,' said Gladys, but automatically; the story was too enthralling to invite a pause.

'Mr Pearson's friend's got the address where her grandparents are, and he'll write to them and tell them how she's getting on, and I'll bring her up. It'll be an interest for me.' She lit another cigarette. 'Her light's very faint, but it's blue.'

'What light?' Gladys demanded blankly.

'The light round her head, dear, her aura. We all have one. Yours is blue, too,' she added casually.

Gladys made a rudimentary movement of neck-twisting and eye-rolling as if trying to see above her head.

'Go on,' she remarked at last, doubtfully, looking sideways at her landlady. The room seemed less cosy suddenly.

'Oh you can't see it. You can never see your own. But it's there, and blue's the best colour to have.' Mrs Pearson smiled at her, and Gladys, after some hesitation, smiled back.

'Then I'm all right, aren't I?'

'Yes, dear. You're all right.'

Mental, Gladys was thinking. Well I never. But doesn't seem likely to get violent. They say they're often all right except for the one idea. Seems kind enough, though. Oh well, might be worse. But the room still did not feel quite so cosy.

Their voices, though quiet, had aroused Erika.

Her sleep had always been in places where the walls were thin and a ceaseless, restless murmur of sound vibrated, and her body kept an awareness of hunger even in a slumber as light and thin as itself. She sat up slowly. As she did so, the sound of a key in the front door, followed by its closing, sounded through the quiet of the house. Mrs Pearson, listening, smiled.

'There's my husband,' she said.

'I'll be off,' and Gladys started for the door, 'only looked in, sure you're all right, well, you'll have company now, ta-ta for the present.'

Nice company, she thought, hurrying down the stairs, and shrinking almost into the wall to avoid the dark figure (how dark he was, clothes and all, made you feel downright queer) coming up them; nice company, a rackman and a German what's been a beggar. Annie won't half be thrilled.

'Good-evening,' said Thomas Pearson.

'Oh – oh. Good-evening. Cold. Cold, isn't it. I was just . . .'

He went on without answering, and Gladys was left reflecting upon his tone. Sarcastic, she decided. Like his sauce.

Erika had two thoughts, as she stood by the fire (some dim instinct having impelled her to get up) and saw him come in. Were they going to eat? Would he hit her?

When he had held his wife in his arms for a while, moving his lips to and fro over her cheeks and brow in gentle caresses, he let her decline on to the pillows and, half lying beside her, stared across the room at Erika.

With his coming, something of the East had come, perhaps brought by the unmistakable shape and colour of his eyes, perhaps suggested by his attitude as he reclined; the sultan, with his favourite wife, summing up a new slave with cruel and melancholy stare.

'You'll frighten her, Tom,' Mrs Pearson said at last, putting a palm against his cheek and slightly pressing his head towards her, 'don't. She's all right. I can hardly make out her light, but it's there and it's blue.'

'I must tell her . . . You,' pointing one finger, that stood out dark and unmoving in the pink light towards Erika, 'do what Mrs Pearson says. If you don't there'll be trouble, bad trouble for you. I'll kick you back to where you came from. You'll starve. So remember.' He spoke in a pidgin-German.

After a moment, she nodded slowly.

'Get out, now. Go to bed.'

'*Gute nacht, schatz. Schlafe gut,*' Mrs Pearson said. 'Come here,' she coaxed, 'come and say good-night properly.'

Erika slowly approached, head hanging, eyes fixed uneasily on her face; when she stood close to the bed Mrs Pearson stretched up her face and kissed her. Erika stared, with unchanging expression; she made no movement to return the kiss.

'Get out,' said Thomas Pearson suddenly, and she turned and went slowly towards the door.

'Get yourself a bit of cake. In the kitchen,' Mrs Pearson called. 'Girls of her age can always manage a bit more.' She turned to her husband as the door closed. 'Growing,' she explained.

The kitchen in Rose Cottage, as Gladys had instantly decided, might have belonged to another house. The general pinkness and luxury stopped at its door; even the lighting was weak. Yet, while Erika slowly fumbled with the lid of an old cake tin that Peggy had crossly opened an hour or so ago, her eyes moved from one shabby object to another with a slightly livelier expression.

This was a real room. She had been in places like this before;

123

they were in houses. She believed that Mrs Pearson was lying on a bed in a shop window, such as she herself had stood outside, in the savage winter wind of some German town, looking at the splendour within and trying to catch its warmth. She liked this room best. The glory and comfort of the other had been too much: unreal; would, perhaps, be suddenly snatched away.

Eating, she crept up to the room that Peggy had showed her; Peggy's sharpness had not been noticed by someone to whom sharpness was the human being's usual manner. This room was like a shop window in the daytime; colder, but with the same splendour; she had not of course realized that it was her own.

She was standing there, slowly turning the pages of a magazine gorgeous with coloured advertisements of Western Germany's prosperity, and photographs of eupeptic beauties in furs, when with noiseless step, Thomas Pearson came suddenly upon her.

In silence, after snapping his fingers to attract her attention as if she were an animal, he knelt and demonstrated how to turn on and off the electric fire. 'Understand?' was the only word he threw at her.

When she nodded slowly, he looked at her for a minute, with a black expression. Another living creature. So many of them, so many, and all there only to demand that he withdraw his attention from Nora. But Nora had called this one *schatz*; treasure. He went quickly away, in silence as he had come.

Erika slowly lowered herself until she was crouching beside the warmth, and did not move, while heat gradually crept through the room and brought up burning patches on the unhealthy skin of her face.

She glanced through the magazine for a while; then riffled

the pages of an old volume, *The Pink Fairy Book*, lying on the table beside her bed.

More coloured pictures; men in cloaks and crowns; *zweigen*, and girls with hair to their knees. Deep within Erika, memory began to stir in its sleep and its bruised lips smiled. *Grössmutter* . . .

Her stomach was full, warmth had seeped through her unhealthy young flesh and rickety bones. Slowly, regally, fully awake now, Memory stalked out of its lair.

But, once outside, it did not present before Erika pictures of dwarf and goose-girl dwelling in the murmuring pine forests of the *Märchen* her grandmother had told her in her babyhood. Being a German's memory, it turned, instead, to the electric fire.

How did it work? What had the man done to it?

On and off, on and off, Erika made it go for twenty minutes, while she watched its alternately reddened and steely face. Then, at last, when she understood the mechanism, she undressed and got into bed.

15

On Christmas Eve, Peggy was in the drawing-room, tying to the Christmas tree, whose branches almost touched the ceiling, the balls of coloured plastic which have replaced the fairy-like spun glass of other days. She had laid out cigarettes, and seen that the forced pink and white hyacinths whose scent filled the room were well displayed.

The old woman who acted as parlourmaid had tottered in, followed by the older houseman with a tray of *canapés*, for whose safety Peggy could not refrain from apprehensive glances; these had been returned with spiteful ones by man and maid. They were very jealous of her.

'These won't work,' she observed, indicating the coloured bulbs that were to light the tree. 'Can you do anything, Hobbs?'

Her voice sounded young and harsh across the softly-coloured old room. Hobbs, thinking with secret satisfaction of his spasmodic, but often convenient, deafness, made no sign that he had heard, and old Doris darted at Peggy a look of mournful dislike. They continued to fiddle about in silence.

Peggy indulged in a shrug, and at that moment Mrs Corbett, accompanied by the prancing and excited dogs, came in.

'These won't work,' Peggy said, demonstrating again, 'I think the battery must have run out.'

'Oh what a nuisance: it was all right this morning. Hobbs,'

turning to the old man, who had just reappeared with a second tray, 'have we another battery?'

'I always keep one, madam. It's replaced every year, a few days before the tree is dressed,' said Hobbs, managing to sound insulted.

'Get it, will you, please – or perhaps Doris could?'

The matter lapsed. Hobbs, pursuing the private pattern of his life, went out to the hall and hovered cleverly, doing nothing at all, while Peggy and Mrs Corbett discussed final details.

'What about the dogs, Mrs Corbett? Will they be coming?'

'Oh they're coming. It's my turn this year. The girls and I take it in turn to bring our doggies. I wish they could all come, bless them, but that naughty Roddy will fight with my boys, he upsets everyone, doesn't he, A.? Isn't Roddy your worse enemy, Cee? (Look at his ears, Peggy – he knows the name, don't you? No, Roddy isn't coming, you needn't make that noise.) Aren't you slim, Peggy! That black makes you look even slimmer . . . oh dear, to think I was once as slim as you . . . oh there you are, Arnold, where *have* you been? Peggy's had such a fight with the lights.'

'Party at the club. Bit of a lush-up for Christmas Eve. I expect the battery's gone.'

Bringing the smell of an expensive after-shave lotion, he came up to the tinkling, glittering tree and solemnly inspected it. Peggy stood in silence, struggling with such a feeling of boredom and despair as seldom assailed even her. She could walk out of here to-morrow morning; nothing need stop her.

What was she doing in this hot room, with these fools, living their half-life?

Oh it was something to do – it passed the time – it made a break. The language of boredom and despair.

'I agree with you, it's a dog's life.'

The mutter came from the corner of Arnold Corbett's mouth, while his sad eyes turned to glance at her; his hands were busy with some wires in the tree. She was surprised into speech.

'I didn't say so, Mr Corbett.'

'Oh for God's sake make it Arnold, it is Christmas Eve. I know you didn't say anything, but you looked it . . . What's the matter? Boy-friend trouble?'

'No – just the feeling there's another year nearly gone,' she answered, paling.

'Here, here – you save that up for New Year's Eve – that's the time *that* really gets into its stride . . . no, seriously, Peggy –'

They were alone in the room; the four dogs dozing beside the fire. Mrs Corbett had gone off in pursuit of Hobbs, who had hovered himself out of sight.

'I've been wondering about you – attractive girl like you – not engaged or anything – you don't wear a ring – or do you?' He caught clumsily at her hand and held it.

She had made no attempt to withdraw it; only steadily increased the pressure of her own on the moist, hot one that clasped it, smiling into his face.

'Here, Peggy – that hurts . . .'

She suddenly relaxed the pressure, and he snatched his hand away, staring.

'I've never felt a girl's hand so strong – your muscles are like steel – where did you get muscles like that, in God's name?'

'Riding,' said Peggy; the word would come out, it came out quietly, to match her smile, but it was fatal; it carried for her an enormous load of pain and lost ecstasy, and tears rushed up into her throat. She turned away.

'I'm sorry, Peggy,' he said, following, 'here – don't – I'm sorry. Fact is, I'm a bit high . . .'

'I – don't like being touched. That's all,' she muttered, turning round.

'All right. I said I'm sorry and I said I'm a bit high. It is Christmas Eve. And I'd appreciate it if you don't go running to my mother. She wouldn't approve.'

'I shan't run to anyone. But just remember; I don't like being touched.'

'All right, Peggy. I – really am sorry. Get awfully lonely some-times . . . silly, isn't it?'

'Too bad,' she said, turning away.

'I wish you'd be a bit nice to me – oh all right. As you were. How about a drink on it? Oh blast,' as the bell of the front door sounded melodiously. 'Press on regardless.' He turned, straightening himself, to face the arrivals.

In a moment the first guests were in the room, ushered warmly by Mrs Corbett; a stout old woman tightly packaged in turquoise lamé, and her stout old husband.

Peggy was known to all the elderly pairs who followed; she had passed sandwiches to the wives at bridge parties and listened to desultory chat from the heavy old husbands. This evening everyone was slightly livelier than usual, because of married children and grandchildren flying in on their way to holidays abroad, visiting the old people for a few hours; letters were arriving from all over the world, sending love and photographs and news, even if the senders could not be there in person.

It was a sober, noticeably respectable group, offering little chance of adventure or change; the men were heads of companies, directors of wealthy firms or financiers who had retired from active speculation; and their wives were satisfied with lives padded at every angle by expensive comforts.

Peggy stopped for a minute's chat with Gwen Palmer (usually referred to by Mrs Corbett as 'poor Gwen Palmer'), who 'must have been' driving her little car round the broad shady local roads for some fifteen years, now, and with whom Peggy associated the idea that she would not mind marrying Arnold.

She had not heard anyone say so, and nothing in Miss Palmer's manner contributed to the theory, it was merely in the air, like a scent, and clung to everyone who entered its orbit; it was part of the general boredom, to Peggy.

Self-possessed and graceful, her dark eyes and their stars looking out between the short curtains of her black hair, she moved between these elderly people, seldom adding the low note of her voice to the babble.

Taking a drink for herself – Peggy was fond of drink – she stood in a corner, close to the window through which, in spite of heavy curtains, a whisper of cold air was blowing.

Her pleasures were not those of most girls.

Her long walks in the loneliest places that could be reached and returned from in one day, her solitary visits to films about war or exploration or savages; her occasional descents upon the Zoo, where she would stand, looking, before the cage of some wolf or puma that had paused in its terrible pacing to stare, unseeingly, out across the passive, affectionate crowd; her swift homeward walks across crammed and desperate London – these were her own. She had lied about them to Mrs Corbett, until she found that her employer did not find such recreations eccentric, merely dismissing her as 'a funny girl'.

'But I would never go to the Zoo,' Mrs Corbett would add. 'I could never bear it. Those poor creatures. How they must miss their freedom.'

Peggy was still too young to know that the true tragedy was their no longer missing their freedom.

Some weeks before Christmas, she had gone to the Royal

Smithfield Show: making her solitary way along with crowds of red-faced, solid men and their wives; crowds that she had hoped to avoid by paying the pound entrance fee of the first day's showing.

She had come to look at the Highland cattle.

The hall was so enormous, and the crowds so dense, the cacophony of voices and the brilliant lights were so complicated and overwhelming, in effect, that she climbed to the gallery which runs around the main hall, hoping to see from above the stalls where the cattle were kept, and then make her way there.

She leant on the rail and looked out over the scene, much as the puma or ceaselessly pacing wolf would look out across the heads of a crowd.

It was spread below; vast; extraordinary; frightening; a colossal pattern of the angular bright shapes of agricultural machinery, painted red or blue or yellow, and lifted slightly into the air, quivering with light and noise, on stand after stand. Peggy looked down at it inimically. What had this to do with cows wandering homeward through dewy fields?

She stood there for some time. Then her brooding stare caught, at the far end of the Brobdingnagian view, miniature reddish blurs that, in contrast to the immobility of the gaudily painted ones, were *moving*; something beside men and women was alive down there. She took her arms off the rail, and went slowly down into the organized confusion.

Presently, after a considerable walk, she found herself outside a square enclosure surrounded by tiers of seats, where the Highland steers were being judged, and went in.

She sat down, among people whose faces were not London faces and heard, just behind her, two men talking in Welsh. The few women seated near her had soft, alive faces; gently alight as they chatted, or watched in considering silence. Many in this crowd were laughing, but quietly, as if in the pleasure of a holiday that was too natural to create excitement. And then – drifting casually, moving along the heated air, as if it had nothing to do with the scene and had its own power and could ignore everything else – she caught the scent of hay.

She sat forward, watching, as the stubborn steers were pushed and tugged into line by the stockmen in their white coats.

There was one that attracted her attention, as he did everyone's.

His wild, stupid eye looked out through fringes of orange hair and his massive body resisted every step forward. Occasionally he moved sideways or backwards in a movement pettish yet charged with the strength never fully exerted. The audience, with none of the amused anticipation of trouble that would have been shown by a London one, observed him with a critical, yet detached interest: it was a steer that did not want to do what it was told, no more and no less, and the men and women from the Highlands and Cumberland and Denbighshire took in every point that the judges would consider in deciding their awards, commenting occasionally on some outstanding example; assessing the bulks of flesh paraded before them.

Peggy had no sentimental love for the row of thick bodies veiled in amber hair, but she *felt* for and with them; hers was the wild eye turning in useless rage, the horn helplessly slanted in a half-threat towards the stockman's white-coated breast, the hoofs spurning the sawdust, and she drew something from them too; strength from their thews and their thick fat, and their tufted sides and horns like dim, yellowy mother-of-pearl.

The conspicuous steer was in charge of a man nearer seventy than sixty, with a face long-nosed and deep-coloured; and stubborn as the beast's on which he was compelled to fix all his attention. At the end of the judging, this steer, as if maddened by four minutes of enforced stillness, suddenly jerked loose from the rope round its neck and made for the exit, followed by the man.

One or two people scattered. No woman screamed. A quiet grin played over the faces in the seats and those outside the exit, and there were some quick sideways jumps for safety as the beast and man swayed straining together from side to side, along the plank barrier. A thud sounded, unmistakable in origin to this crowd; it was a horn landing on wood; then two more stockmen came round the side of the pen and began to hustle the rebel into his quarters.

The stockman in charge growled out something in an unintelligible dialect, and they sheered off, grinning; Bob was as bad as Bhaddain for having his own way; best leave him to it.

Peggy sat on, looking broodingly at the re-formed line of thick bodies and glinting eyes and coarse fringes of hair, before which the judge, silent and grave in bowler hat and a dark suit suggesting an earlier day, walked with his notebook.

She was thinking, now, about her own situation: wondering, for the first time, why her strong pride was keeping her from the thing, the only thing, that she wanted to do in the world?

The thought recurred to her in the midst of the party this evening; the people were fools, and the room stifling, and she wanted only to be in the meadows with her lover, where she could never be again.

Glancing over the chattering groups, replenishing empty glasses, observing whose conversation was distracted by glances at a distant plate of *canapés*, drawing the servants' attention to lack of alcohol – so the time wore towards eight o'clock. She found herself near Arnold Corbett, who was standing by the Christmas tree, looking out heavily across the crowded room. As she passed, he made to catch at her arm, then checked himself.

'You're the one who doesn't like being touched, that's the drill, isn't it? Am I forgiven?'

Peggy moved her head in a way that meant nothing. She did not answer, and looked stony; she began to move away.

'I say – don't go. Stay and . . . you look simply lovely in that . . . you look simply lovely.' He was drunker than he had been earlier, but not embarrassingly so; she had to admit that he carried liquor well. 'Stay and talk to me, Peggy.'

'I hate talking.'

'Just a few minutes.'

'All right. Only keep it short.'

'You can be damned rude.'

'Can I?'

'What have I done? It's Christmas Eve, isn't it? Time for jollity and kissing under the blasted mistletoe and all that, isn't it?'

'I suppose so.'

'You know, you're a mystery girl. You puzzle me. You bother and bewilder me (I won't say bewitch – early days yet). What's your background? Why aren't you married or going to be? You don't look English. Remember I said so, that first evening you came?'

'I do remember, and I told you, I am English. My father has a chain of shops and property in London, and my mother's an invalid . . . I met your mother on the front at Hove and we got into conversation about the dogs and she took a fancy to me because they did, and here I am . . . any more you want to know?'

'Yes, a damn sight more . . . I want to know about *you*. Come for a run in the car to-morrow afternoon?'

'On Christmas Day? Be your age . . . I'm wanted here – and I hate motoring.'

'You hate a lot of things, don't you? . . . be a sport.'

'With twelve for dinner in the evening? . . . I'll have to ask your mother.'

'Why? We're both over sixteen.'

She turned and looked full at him.

'Look here. It suits me, being here. It's quiet, and no-one bothers me . . . so far. I'm not going to do anything that might get me sacked.'

He shrugged. 'Oh . . . all right. Have it your way. Fair enough.'

But as she walked off she turned her little head over her shoulder to say mockingly:

'I'm going to see my mother to-morrow. You can drive me over and bring me back, if you like.'

'I don't know that I particularly want to,' he said, looking sadly at her, yet sullenly too, out of his protuberant eyes.

'All right. As you'd say, fair enough,' she answered indifferently.

16

'But how will you manage about getting back, dear?' asked Mrs Corbett, sitting after lunch on Christmas Day in the warmth of the drawing-room, with the Christmas tree glittering and occasionally tinkling gently, in the background, and the dogs dozing around her feet. 'There are no buses or trains, and I doubt if you'll get a taxi.' She looked at Peggy with a trace of the annoyance that only came to her when her plans for entertaining were threatened. 'I shall want you here quite by six, you know. I'd forgotten the buses.'

Peggy ventured to smile. 'Mr Corbett has very kindly offered to bring me back . . . and to take me, too. I hope . . . is that all right?'

'Oh quite all right, dear – so long as you're both here by six, and it will do him good,' Mrs Corbett said. 'He's been stuck in that room of his all day smoking himself like a kipper and . . .' she checked herself; there was a bottle of whisky up there, too, but she was too old, and too tired, to think about the whisky . . . 'it'll do him good,' she ended.

They drove away about three. Peggy, who was wearing a black jacket and cap, carried a bunch of Christmas roses. He had not seen her clothes before, and commented on them.

'I like your fur.'

'It's new. I just bought it. It isn't fur, it's nylon.'

'Well it looks like fur . . . most of the girls I know wouldn't be seen dead in imitation fur. But I must say that looks all right.'

'Most of the girls you know aren't interested in what happens to wild animals, I suppose.'

'I'm damned sure they aren't . . . are you a crank, as well as a lot of other things, Peggy?'

'Probably.'

She turned aside and watched the empty grey roads going by. The cap she wore was shaped like a silky black bag and sloped away from her olive brow, giving her an Egyptian look. A scarf of Indian silk, purple and orange, was tucked into the neck of her jacket. The roses looked stiff and very white against the black coat. She smelt sweet.

Hers was not a charm of warmth or kindness. But it was a strong charm; he could think of, and feel, nothing else.

'Look out! You'd better let me drive, if you're going to sleep!' she exclaimed in a minute.

'*Better let you!* I should think so. It's your fault — I can't concentrate,' he said angrily.

Peggy laughed.

As they approached their destination, through meaner and meaner streets, Arnold's interest became stronger. He had been puzzled to 'place' her since his first sight of her; for she seemed one of the rare people who truly are classless; even her voice gave no clue to her background, and when the car, on her instructions, stopped at last outside the two cottages, side by side at the end of the street of silent, half-ruined houses, he frankly stared at her. Would she say anything about the neighbourhood in which her mother lived? He betted himself she would not.

'Thanks,' she said casually, preparing to get out.

'Wait a minute – I'll do that.'

She waited while he went round to open the door.

Rose Cottage and Lily Cottage had a festive appearance, for, as in every other house in the neighbourhood, their rooms had been decorated with paper-chains; and festoons of pink and yellow could be seen through their windows in a glow of light. A red paper crown had been fixed somehow on the head of the horned and bearded mask that smiled down between them.

Peggy went up the steps, and paused for a moment at the door, looking back at Arnold where he stood beside the car. Dusk was falling, the air was clear and still; the railway lines caught a faint sheen from the dying light. The windows of the Council flats across the gap glowed golden, filled with intricate patterns of red and green and blue.

'I'll come back for you – what time?' he called, hoping to see what kind of a someone opened the door. The house looked prosperous enough, incongruously so. But a lick of paint, he told himself, cost little and could do a lot.

'Oh – five-ish. Thanks.' She waved and turned away as the door was opened by Erika, who looked fearfully at her. Arnold, trying to see, but getting only an impression of youth and a coloured dress, backed the car and drove quickly away.

'Mrs Pear-son in zir living-room,' said Erika over her shoulder, painstakingly repeating what she had evidently been taught to say, and Peggy followed her.

She came upon a scene which continued the festive note struck outside. Three people were sitting on the rose-covered chairs drawn up to a bright fire; the fourth, Annie Barnes, was stretched, with an air of trying to take up as little room as possible, on the sofa. There was a table laden with bottles and glasses, an open box of sweets, a smell of roasting chestnuts, and Gladys Barnes, with a green paper cap over one eye, lifted a glass, crying 'Here's Peggy! Merry Christmas!' The only gentleman present, Mr Fisher, began to get slowly to his feet as she appeared, and totter into the curve of a formal bow.

'Dearie! I knew you were coming; I *saw* you!' Mrs Pearson cried, from her place close to the fire. 'We're having a party – come on, Erika, near the fire, *schatz* – I knew it was you, when I heard the knock. See who's here?' pointing with a skeletal finger at Annie. 'Isn't it grand?'

'Never thought to see Annie downstairs at a party again,' put in Gladys, as Annie, deprived of balaclava and coats, looked around for something to shrink into, 'ever so kind, well, I said, turkey and all, sent it up on a tray, doesn't speak hardly no English but means well, and Mr Fisher too – you all come, your mother said, not but what we hadn't got a bit of something for ourselves but that'll do over Boxing Day, I said, and came up, ever so kind, just said, you take my hand and try – you'll find it's much easier, and down she came.'

Gladys signed off with a flourish, finishing her glass of port.

'Got to get up again, though, mayn't be so easy,' put in Annie, in a warning pipe.

'Oh, you'll do it, you see,' Mrs Pearson assured her smilingly. 'Come to the fire, Peggy.'

'Mother, I can't stay long,' Peggy said. 'I just came to bring you these. She has twelve people for dinner to-night.' She put the roses into her mother's hand.

'Mercy it isn't thirteen!' said Gladys, re-filling Mr Fisher's glass. 'No more – no, Miss Gladys, I beg of you no more. This will have very serious results for me,' the old man protested, but Gladys imperiously filled it up to the brim, saying that she could always drink it if he didn't.

'Oh Peggy – Christmas Night! Can't you phone her?' Mrs Pearson cried.

'I said definitely I'd be back by just after five.'

'Well, have a drink with us then – you must have a drink. What'll you have? Whisky, port, gin?'

'Whisky – strong.'

Gladys, who seemed to have appointed herself Ganymede to the gathering, poured out a potion strong indeed and held it out to her.

'How's Erika getting on, Mother?' Peggy asked, taking it; she sounded bored, and was.

'She's getting along fine,' said Mrs Pearson, looking indulgently at the girl seated on a tuffet at her knee and slowly eating something. 'Doesn't her hair look pretty? I did it for her, this morning. And she's going to learn a new English sentence every day, aren't you, *schatz*?'

'Wood – yuh – lakyuh – tea?' said Erika with lowered head, looking up from under the yellow ribbon circlet that confined a tiny knob of hair, and Gladys broke into clapping.

'Bravo – that's the style – be chattering away nineteen to the dozen soon, won't you, Erika?' Mrs Pearson also clapped; lightly, as if two skeleton leaves rattled together in the wind, and Gladys glanced at the window. 'Getting dark, isn't it – brrr! glad I'm not outside – shall I draw the curtains?'

Mrs Pearson silently indicated that Erika would do it, and, when it was done and she had stumbled back to her place, Gladys, glowing with port and still pleasantly distended by a generous Christmas dinner which did not seem to have suffered by being confined in frozen packets, and glasses, and tins, almost shouted –

'Christmas Night! Christmas is the time for ghost-stories, always sit round the fire and tell ghost-stories at Christmas.

What say we put out the light?' and before anyone could speak or move, she had blundered up and across to the door and touched the switch. The room sank instantly into deep shadow and sumptuous red glow, in which every face became transformed into a mask of strong lines and cavernous darkness or blanched with ruby fire.

'That's better – nice and cosy,' said Gladys, as no-one else seemed inclined to speak. 'Now who'll begin? Mr Fisher, I bet you know some ghost-stories, don't you? At your age. Come on, don't be shy.'

But the room continued silent. Peggy leant back, nursing her glass and staring into the fire, and Annie's eyes were fixed doubtfully on her sister; Mr Fisher moved uneasily, muttering, under Gladys's exhortations.

'Oh come on now – ninety next birthday and don't know no ghost-stories –'

Mr Fisher either could not, or would not, find any words, but sat on the edge of Annie's sofa, nursing his glass and staring down at his barely visible slippers, and was mute. Annie felt sorry for him; Glad ought to know that he never had liked the ladies, and here he was, the only man among five women; enough to make anyone shy. He was moving his head from side to side in a movement that conveyed absolute refusal, discernible even through the dimness, and Gladys was compelled at last to give way.

'Oh all right then – some people can be very funny – what say I start, then –'

'Mother?' Peggy's voice came sharp and low across the good-natured one, 'are you all right?' She made a movement then checked herself, listening. They were all listening now.

'She's breathing funny,' Gladys said doubtfully, staring across the soft dim glare into the darkness where Mrs Pearson reclined. 'Here, I'll put on the light –'

'*No!*' Peggy whirled round on her, 'whatever you do – *no-one's to put on the light.*'

'She does sound funny – better go for the doctor, p'raps? Only they'll all be out probly – being Christmas Night –' Gladys shivered, suddenly and violently, 'You got the door open, anyone? There's an awful draught in here – cold as charity.' She glanced overhead; the paper chains were moving, with a faint rustling sound.

'You'd all better –' Peggy was beginning, when a high soft shrill sound began to waver up into the darkness. The room was bitterly cold now. No-one moved. The fire glowed wild but still, giving out light but no heat.

'. . . I . . . see . . .' keened a voice that might have been the wailing of a suddenly awakened evening wind, 'and people . . . red . . . red light . . . food in them . . . I . . . taste . . . taste . . . one, two three, four . . . kinds food . . . and smell . . . her tongue . . . her mouth . . .' And then . . . 'Go now. Coming back soon.'

Gladys uttered a moo of terror.

'She's gone mad – she's raving – get a doctor, quick –' and Annie began to struggle up from her couch, silently pushing her feet against the old man, who was sitting as if frozen, his eyes fixed on the dim corner whence the sounds were coming. Only Erika did not move from her place by Mrs Pearson's knee but crouched down to the floor, and slowly covered her face with both hands.

Peggy spoke, calmly and with authority.

'There's nothing to be frightened of. She'll be better in a minute. She gets these attacks sometimes, it'll pass. It's nerves.'

The voice was chanting, more faintly now.

'Go . . . so dim here . . . dim . . . can't see . . . but soon see with her eyes . . . ah – ah – ah only light on the tunnel . . . grass . . . so green . . . so . . . Can't go there you fool. Never go there. You fool.'

It ceased abruptly and there was complete silence. No-one moved until Annie dared to drag a hand across her face to wipe away her streaming tears of terror. Mr Fisher suddenly gave her feet a sharp push, freeing himself.

'Peggy?' said Mrs Pearson's voice faintly out of the dimness. 'I dropped off, I'm so sorry, everyone, I was dreaming.'

'Dreaming!' Gladys exclaimed, very ready to welcome this explanation. She was chilled, inwardly and outwardly, by the cold that had checked the fire's warmth and the uncanny breezes that had stirred the paper-chains. 'Of course you were – feeling bad, are you? or better for your forty winks? I shouldn't wonder if it wasn't that tinned pudding, say what you like it's not natural. Tinned pudding.' She gave a nervous laugh.

'Put the light on, Peggy dear,' Mrs Pearson went on tranquilly, 'you'll have to be going, you'll be late. Erika, *schatz*, wake up.'

Their eyes, fixed on the outline of her dim reclining shape, saw her hand steal out and rest on Erika's bent head, 'It's tea-time – "would-you-like-your-tea-now",' she coaxed softly. 'We've got a Christmas cake.'

Peggy suddenly flooded the room with light, and Erika went off docilely towards the kitchen.

The explanation offered by the familiar word *dreaming*, with its lifelong connotation for them all of nightmares and garbled speech, has soothed some of the party. Gladys felt a glow of anticipation, in spite of her distended person, at the mention of Christmas cake, and Annie, glancing at Mr Fisher, experienced a revival of the friendly feelings momentarily quenched by his abrupt movement.

Mr Fisher, however, did not seem restored. He was even paler than usual, and continued to gaze silently at the floor. In a moment, while preparations were being made for tea, he tottered slowly to his feet and made his way perilously and silently between chairs and coffee-table to where Mrs Pearson sat.

He began slowly to incline himself above her, performing a bow so deep that Gladys, idly watching, was on the verge of screaming, 'Watch out, Mr Fisher!' in anticipation of his over-balancing when he began tremulously to come up again.

'Thank you indeed, madam,' he said in his weak voice. 'A very pleasant party and a very agreeable occasion. Hospitality. Unfortune, I must be off now. My daily walk. Even Christmas I don't miss it so will say good-afternoon and many thanks. The dinner was much appreciated. Turkey. Many a year since turkey. Good-day, all.'

Turning, he tottered away, so slowly that Gladys had to resist a second impulse to grab him and arm him out of the room and into the hall, where they heard him, through the half-open door, slowly climbing the stairs.

'Just go and see what young Erika's up to,' announced Gladys; it was the first opportunity she had had for being alone with the interesting newcomer; 'shan't be not a tick. You and Peggy can keep Mrs Pearson company,' she added to Annie, who fixed a glare of the liveliest alarm on her hostess at the suggestion. Peggy slowly lit a cigarette, looking thoughtfully at her mother.

The kitchen looked less gloomy than usual, scattered as it was with the remains of the Christmas dinner and the various packets and cartons that had contained it. Erika was standing by the cooker, twisting her hands together and staring vacantly at the kettle on the hot plate.

She looked up not quite smiling as Gladys marched in. The past days had taught Erika something; in this house that was like a shop window people did not suddenly hit you, and although she understood perhaps a sixteenth of Gladys's Niagara of words, she felt dimly that they were *something* that was not directed adversely at herself: she had no concept or words to express *kind*.

'Just on the boil is it?' began Gladys. 'Don't like these 'lectric stoves, never did, you can't trust them, give me gas any day, you can see what it's up to, and takes all night and blow you up if you get water on it, she swore by it, had the latest kind, but I never could, I'll just put the cups on the tray, how many are we, you, me, Annie, and Mrs P. four, s'pose Peggy'll be off; the old gentleman's gone out, very arbitary, can't stop him if he makes up his mind, can you? You come from far off? Germany? Ger-ma-ny? Dootch?'

Glady's intention to act kindly by Erika did not affect a determination to find out everything possible about her.

Erika nodded. 'Germany, *ja*,' she almost whispered.

'All your family – people – dad and mum –' Gladys swerved hastily from *dead* and, instead, pointed upwards with a lightening assumption of solemnity. Erika stared, then slowly nodded.

'Sad,' said Gladys, swooping on the kettle, 'give us the tea – that's right – shan't be long now – Nana bring you up, then?'

Then, as this was met only by a stare – 'Nana – Nan – your grannie. She bring you up?'

Some memory stirred in Erika's skull of another conversation resembling this one; there had been someone who neither shouted nor threatened nor pushed her aside, who had asked her about *grössmutter* and *grössvater*, talking slowly to her in a quiet, clean room.

'*Grossmütter*,' she said, while she struggled with the cellophane wrappings round the cake, 'I – go – wiz – her *und grössvater*. *Heim*.' She shook her head. '*Nein*.'

'Then where's she now, then?' Gladys again sharply pointed upwards, 'Passed on?' Curiosity had temporarily driven the kindness from her face; her expression was all Must Know.

'*Altersheim*,' and as the unintelligible word came out Gladys saw, to her dismay, tears rise suddenly into the small eyes, while out came an unsteady sob.

'Here, here, cheer up' – Gladys seized the cake and tore off its wrappings with a hand contemptuous of modern packaging – 'if she's passed on she's all right, God'll be taking care of her. Had her life. Glad of a rest, I'll be bound.'

Erika could only shake her head, swallowing her numb grief, but an emotion that was not disagreeable overcame her as Gladys suddenly thrust a thick old arm about her shoulders, nearly overbalancing her, and bestowed what children once called 'a hug and a kiss'.

'There! Soon be better. Now you take the cake and I'll take the tray and off we go on the road to Zigazag.'

Erika, comforted, picked up the cake and followed her through the connecting door.

They met Mr Fisher shuffling down the stairs, and Gladys hailed him.

'You off out, Mr Fisher? Look what we got, you're missing something nice, won't you change your mind? Freezing outside and they say it's going to snow, I'm dreaming of a White Christmas, White Boxing Day it'll be instead, won't it, not that they're always right, beats me how they can guess it right at all.'

The old man shook his head. 'It's kind of you to suggest it, but you know I never miss my daily walk. I could never have kept my health, not if I hadn't 'ad my daily walk all these years.'

'Pitch dark and snowing,' cried Gladys dramatically, pausing with the tea-tray at the door, and Mr Fisher shook his head with the faintest of smiles.

'Not yet, Miss Gladys. It's a clear night.'

Gladys made a gesture implying 'wilful man must have his

146

way' as best she could, being hampered by her burden, and he went out.

But the thin grey clouds of the early evening had thickened and grown yellow and now hung low over the little houses with their brightly lit rooms, while innocent blasts of wind, born only of earth, stirred the paper-chains through ill-fitting window-frames. On the corner of Rose Walk the old man met a fierce blast, pure and icy and fanged – the herald of the snow, and, walking ever slower, by the time he had reached the corner where Saint James's Church stood, he was breathing painfully and his limbs were trembling.

The church was lit, its windows glowed dim rose and blue and gold and the door stood ajar. He hesitated for a moment, looking up at the spire soaring against the threatening sky. Then he began to shuffle at a creeping pace across the churchyard grass towards the open door.

17

The Rev. Gerald Corliss had some difficulty in preventing an exclamation of 'Good!' when the vicar warned him that Evensong, said instead of sung on Christmas Night, would probably take place in an empty church.

Mr Geddes had added, firmly, that he would not be present.

His plan for bringing his mother down from Yorkshire to keep house for himself and the curate had at last, and very suddenly, been put into action. She had arrived on the day before Christmas Eve; and Mr Geddes decided that he owed her a quiet time.

He was going to sit by the fire with her on Christmas Night and nibble something appropriate, and gossip. He did not add 'What is a curate for?' but Gerald sensed the remark poised on his tongue's tip.

So Gerald read the service to himself in the darkened church, the wind slapping and shaking sixty feet up in the dim curves of the roof and two lamps shining gently over the altar in the side chapel and its white flowers and evergreens.

In the pauses, when the congregation should have given responses, the silence seemed to him not empty but filled with the invisible presences whose company he so much preferred to that of human beings; and he listened to it, lingering over the words and over the unheard voices that answered

148

them. It was an hour of peace for him – delicious, he feared, was the word.

Though the light faded off into obscurity near the door, it nevertheless did not leave the far end of the church in complete darkness, and during one of his long dreaming stares towards this region he gradually became aware of a figure slumped in one of the pews. He felt not the slightest suggestion of its belonging to another world; indeed, something in its posture gave it the painful, weary stamp that belongs peculiarly to earth, and he supposed that it was one of Saint James's devout elderly ladies, who had crept out through the flaying wind to do her last Christmas duty that day.

Only – the ladies of Saint James's did not slump.

The last moments of Gerald's Christmas Day Evensong were not such pure delight as the first; he felt the presence of that figure, so different from the happy Unseens who had answered in the silence, and he also felt it would be his duty to go and say something to it.

The service over, and a prayer for patience and forgiveness offered up, he walked swiftly down the aisle towards the doors, peering, as he approached it, at the half-reclining figure.

In a moment, he recognized the old man brought to the Vicarage some weeks ago by Mr Geddes. He seemed to be asleep.

He gently touched the old boy's shoulder. It was irritating that he could not recall his name; he did remember Mr Geddes using one, but that was all.

'Er . . . wake up . . . er . . .' And then, as frustration and a little anxiety grew – 'er . . . hi . . .'

Leaving his task for a moment, he darted across to the switchboard near the door and flooded the church with light. How ugly it looked . . . *Oh damn. What use am I, Lord?*

In his absence, the old man had awakened. His faded eyes stared up solemnly and his lips moved uncertainly.

'Just dropped off . . . no 'arm done.'

'Of course not,' said Gerald heartily. His voice, pitched louder than usual because of presumed deafness, echoed desolately back from the lit emptiness. The next thing was to get the old chap out of here and on his way home – but how the wind was thundering overhead! The church seemed filled with the twelve sons of Aeolus now . . .

'It's a very cold night, I think snow's coming. Now how are you going to get home?'

'The name this month is Benjamin Jowett,' said Mr Fisher mildly, 'if you should wish to use a name. The real name is Lancelot Fisher. But you may take your choice.'

'Suppose we stick to the real name, it's easier. Now – about getting home. Look here, we're in luck – I've got the use of a friend's car, he's gone to France for Christmas, it's in the Vicarage garden – I can run you back. You come with me and I'll have you home in – where do you live? Near here?'

He felt that the interview was going rather well. He had banished the bewilderment aroused by Mr Fisher's assumption of the great classical scholar's name as firmly as he had banished the twelve sons of Aeolus, and there seemed a fair prospect of an act of human kindness getting done. But—

'Now I do 'appen to be here,' said Mr Fisher, slightly rearranging himself so as to present an appearance more suitable to his surroundings, 'there's somethink I would wish to take you into my confidence. Worrying – like.'

'Oh?' was all Gerald could find to answer. Had he been wearing boots, his heart would have made the familiar descent. 'Er . . . some trouble about . . . funds . . . money, is it?'

'No, it isn't funds. You must be surprised, sir, but that is *not* the worry. I got my pension and something from the Board of Assistance and . . . I make a bit every day by my handiwork. I don't suppose you seen my handiwork? Model figures and that?'

The curate shook his head. Patience, he told himself, and suddenly, wildly, wanted to laugh. The brightly-lit hollow in which they sat, thundering faintly with the threatening blast, the crowded silence all around them, and the old creature's half-dignified, half-pompous manner, and now the sudden intrusion of handiwork, had induced mild hysteria.

'I 'aven't none about me this evening or I would show you.'

'Another time, I hope . . . What is the trouble, then?'

Mr Fisher leant forward and spoke in a voice so lowered that Gerald had to lean forward as well to catch the words.

'Our house, where I live, that is, has recent been bought by one of them property speculators, what uneducated people call a rackman. (Because of that case in the papers. You will recall, being an educated young man.) Bought it for his wife, a Mrs Pearson. Very delicate, and goes about in 'er dressing-gown all day. Kind enough. 'Ad us all in the house down to a party this evening and sent us up a turkey dinner. Very enjoyable, it was.'

He paused; divided, Gerald thought, between recollections of the turkey dinner and an attempt to control wandering thoughts.

'Yes – well. That all sounds very nice,' he encouraged. 'This Mrs Pearson is your new landlady, then?'

'Presume-ably. Yes, presumably. But in very bad health. Looks like a walking corpse you would say, if you could see her –' (I'm sure I shouldn't, thought Gerald irrelevantly.) 'Kind enough, oh yes. Kind enough. But – *a lost soul, I would say, myself.*'

The words, almost sighed out and accompanied by a solemn and questioning glance from the pale old eyes, banished every trace of Gerald's desire to laugh.

A lost soul!

It must have been many years since the words had been spoken from the pulpit at the far end of the church or said in private conversation anywhere, or used without mockery in any novel or on any stage.

But to the priest of three months' standing they came home with their ancient force. Their power was such that it called out in him an authority he did not know he possessed. He said instantly:

'No soul is lost. You mustn't say that.'

Mr Fisher's solemn expression vanished – to be replaced by one of that obstinacy invariably associated with mules.

'Oh mustn't I?' he said, with as much tartness as his near-century-old voice could summon. 'I suppose I can have my own views, I suppose I'm entitled to them? It still being a free country.'

'I meant that the mercy of God is infinite. No soul is ever lost.'

'I don't believe in no God. I hates the brute.'

It took Gerald's breath. He could only stare. The gentleness of Mr Fisher's usual manner, combined with an aura of reasonableness that seemed to surround him, made the words astonishing – and Gerald had an instantaneous depressing conviction that, at ninety, no change of heart was likely. Before he was aware of what he was going to say, he heard his own voice, with the true priestly sharpness:

'It makes no difference whether you believe in Him or not. *He is* – and no soul is ever lost.'

'I should say different. In this case. If you was to see her you'd say different too. I know you're an educated man – and a parson – and you got to say what they teach you. But I got my right to my beliefs. Free-will,' Mr Fisher ended triumphantly. 'Same as you have.'

But he did not pause to let this sink in. He hurried on – 'And that isn't all. This afternoon, it's not two hours ago, we was all sitting round the fire. Down in her place. As natural and comferable as you like. And − off she went.' He nodded twice. 'Like *that*,' a feeble attempt at snapping fingers inside a thick woollen glove. 'What they call a trance.'

For the second time, Gerald stared.

'A kind of fit, do you mean?' He supposed that the old man was mis-using the word. But Mr Fisher shook his head in some impatience.

'Fit! No − I knows a fit when I sees one. My sister had fits. (Twelve of us, and five died, and one had fits.) This wasn't no fit. Mrs Pearson breathed funny and she talked funny. In another voice. This wasn't no fit. It was a trance.'

There was a pause. Mr Fisher appeared to sink into a reverie, staring down at the floor with his eyes half-shut, while Gerald studied him, in perplexity and irritation. All he wanted to do was to bundle the old creature into Paul's Mini-Minor and run him back to whatever den he lived in.

But the words *a lost soul* had sunk into his own soul. It might be only the dramatic language of the uneducated − but for him it possessed compulsion. He must learn more about this Mrs Pearson who spoke 'in another voice', and then − God give him wisdom − try to see her. It might merely be a case for psychiatric treatment. He stifled a sigh, and said:

'"Another voice", you say . . . what kind of a voice?'

Mr Fisher slowly raised his head. He looked very tired.

'Shrill − like,' he said, 'more like a kid's voice. Somethink about green − green grass in a tunnel. Very queer, it was. Quite uncanny. It properly upset one of the ladies in our 'ouse, Miss Barnes, Gladys Barnes. Almost crying, she was.'

'Miss Barnes? Do you live in the same house with Miss Barnes? She comes to church here.'

'She may do, for all I knows. It's a free country. She may do,' was the answer, given with dignified indifference. 'But she certingly lives in my house.'

Gerald was rebuking himself for feeling a sense of congratulation that at least two of his most trying parishioners were under one roof . . .

As the hour of seven at that moment sounded faintly, high amid the clouds and the trumpeting wind, he modelled his conduct on that of his Vicar and said decidedly:

'Well, thank you for telling me all this, Mr Fisher –'

'When I assumes a name every month, there's no harm in *calling* me by that name. I have no objection. Benjamin Jowett.'

Gerald ignored this. There were limits. 'I hope we may be able to help Mrs Pearson. The next thing will be for one of us to call on her – I am sure Mr Geddes would – and . . . talk to her. One of us will do that immediately after the holiday. And now – home, I think, don't you?'

As he led the way towards the vestry he felt a mingling of priestly fatherhood towards the obstinate soul dwelling in the ancient flesh shuffling beside him, mingled, in an odd way, with a sensation that was faintly filial.

Slowly they made their way, Mr Corliss leading and Mr Fisher following, down the nave sunk in shadows. The only light now shone by the altar, where the flowers and evergreens glimmered. The wind still shouted in the dim rafters. Mr Fisher began slowly to speak.

'I only hope she'll make you welcome. Very set against the church, she is, I gavver. 'Eard 'er taking on against the bells this morning. Quite carrying on, she was. Angry.'

18

Mrs Pearson suggested that Gladys should take Erika out to the Archway Road and show her how to shop in England, and Gladys eagerly agreed; company was company, and to be in the position of instructress, guide and patron to a young girl strongly suspected of being mental and with origins shrouded in interesting mystery, was an attractive prospect. To do Gladys justice, some real kindness also came into the matter.

Promising herself some interesting talk with her charge, she set out one morning through the dull streets, under the dull January sky, towards the Archway Road, accompanied by Erika, in a new bright red coat and spike heels.

Erika had a note in a red purse and, under Gladys's supervision, was to buy a large packet of fish fingers, a large packet of frozen peas, a white loaf, a large tin of peaches and some cream.

Gladys, while envying the lavishness in housekeeping implied in this list, for her part intended to keep her eyes open for a nice piece of stuffed rolled breast of lamb. Last you three days – if you was careful – and only twice the price of those fish fingers. She meant to instruct Erika in the craft of making every penny pull its weight, reduced to pathetically microscopic dimensions though that weight might be.

Archway Road was just another street to Erika, and streets,

for her, were associated with weary limbs and aching feet and the continual dreamlike drifting past of indifferent faces – faces – faces – the ever-increasing weight of her grandmother's bony arm leaning on hers, and the unrelenting cold. Hunger in the long streets, and the glare of sun on the bonnets of great pink or pale-blue cars; hunger and the doubt whether there would be food that night; hunger and cramped sleep in hovels or even rain-lashed doorways. Pain from hunger, icy-wet feet, fingers without feeling from the merciless cold. The wind's long howl.

'Cheer up for gawd's sake,' remarked Gladys, observing the reflection of these memories in her face. 'What say we have a cup of tea after we done our bit of shopping, warm us up, might go in one of those Wimpies, Mrs P. wouldn't mind I'm sure, ever so kind, gave you that coat, very smart those heels, wonder you can walk in them.'

But what Erika had suffered in dumb resentment from hard pavements and wrenched, weary muscles, she now suffered with something like cheerfulness because she was a girl, and over fifteen years old, and because the shoes were the first pretty ones she had ever owned.

Pretty was the word in English: Mrs Pearson said it often. Erika kept her face, still overcast with memories, bent down into the damp English wind so that she could look at the glossy brown plastic shoes and their little bows. Pretty.

They went briskly – that is, Gladys went briskly, dragging Erika in her wake – from shop to shop, and gradually Erika began to have the very rare sensation hitherto associated, for her, with cessation of cold, and a half-filled stomach: pleasure.

There was no painfully prolonged bargaining, no apprehension, no-one shouted at them or told them to be off. (Gladys would have had a good deal to say about the notion of anyone shouting 'Be off', at them, but Erika had not enough English

156

yet to breathe her vague thoughts aloud.) The fabulously expensive foods, wrapped in shiny stuff, went into Gladys's shopping bag. Oranges and carrots glowed through the grey air. Erika, as usual, felt hungry.

'There!' observed Gladys at last, poking a pound of bright green sprouts down into the capacious depths, 'nice sprouts, the frost's done 'em good, nothing like a bit of frost for livening up the sprouts, Annie'll like those, we'll just go over there and see'f we can see a nice bit of rolled breast, then we'll 'ave our tea. Won't we?' She suddenly squeezed Erika's stick-thin arm, her face beaming with companionship and the thought of boiling hot tea. 'And what say a bun?'

Erika nodded. Her lips quivered; it might have been hunger; it might have been a smile.

This large sugary plump bun floating in Gladys's fancy was due to a certain expansion in her ideas about housekeeping.

The repainting of the cottages, the arrival of central heating, a telephone, and grand furniture, and, finally Mrs Pearson, ever so kind and making no trouble, had given her a sensation of sharing in this prosperity; not as a conscious pensioner, or someone out to get what they could from a wealthy landlady, but more as a child might revel in the golden glow of a sunny day and feel itself enriched.

Gladys now felt that she could go to a better shop for a whole pound of sprouts, and treat poor Erika to a bun.

Erika was divided between voluptuous sensations centred on bun and tea, and a dim wonder that frost – one of the English words she did know – could be 'good' for anything.

Gladys, having exchanged some pleasurable back-chat with the butcher's young man and chosen a satisfactory piece of rolled and stuffed meat, battled her way through the shopping crowds and charged across the road in front of the impatiently throbbing traffic, monsters of ugliness and power briefly held in leash by the red light.

'What's your name?' she demanded suddenly, when the buns and teas had been ordered and they were sitting in the steamy, crowded, deliciously warm little café.

Erika, who had been slowly gazing about her, brought her eyes to rest on Gladys's face.

'Erika.'

''Course, I know that, silly, I mean your other name, like mine's Barnes. Erika what?'

After a longish pause, there was a shake of the head.

'Go on!' cried Gladys, registering unbelief with every note.

Another pause, filled this time by the arrival of the tea and buns, slapped down by a cross, pretty little Italian girl. Gladys fell upon hers, urging Erika to do likewise, but after a satisfying gulp and swallow she went back to her subject.

'Come on,' she urged, 'you must know it, girl.'

However, noticing that her companion's munching and sipping had ceased and that the usual shadow had returned to her face, she cried robustly – 'Oh well, ne'mind, Erika will do us all right, won't it?' and resumed her eating and drinking.

But faint new feelings were struggling in Erika. She set herself consciously to search, fishing confusedly about in memory, because she was grateful to Gladys for providing the treat of hot tea and bun.

'*Grössmutter*' – she said at last – 'Frau Hartig.'

'Hartig! There you are!' cried Gladys. 'You're Miss Erika Hartig! Got a whole name for you now, haven't we?' and Erika, after a long stare at her triumphant face, slowly nodded.

'Miss – Erika – Hartig,' repeated Gladys taking a huge bite of starch and sugar. 'Now we *are* all right, *Froline* Erika Hartig – Miss.'

It may be said that the slow upward climb of Erika began from that moment. Up till then, all her sensations had been negative ones; cessation of cold, absence of hunger's pain, the end of endless weary wandering. But here, with the gaining of *Fraulein* – *miss* in English – her stumbling foot struck rock. She was a person.

'Miss . . . Erika . . . Hartig,' she repeated softly. 'Miss . . .'

'Here, let's have another bun, eh?' cried Gladys recklessly, 'just to celebrate.'

The dull days of February went by. Mrs Corbett suddenly broke their quiet by calling Peggy into her bedroom one morning and announcing that she was going to Bermuda.

'For six weeks, dear. I cannot stand these grey skies of ours a minute longer. Don't you think it's a good idea?'

'Marvellous, Mrs Corbett. Wonderful to see blue skies again.'

'Oh I know, dear – and flowers – I've been keeping count, and do you know there hasn't been a break in the clouds, to my certain knowledge, for *ten days*. Ten days without a gleam of sun – I do really feel it's *more* than one ought to be asked to endure.' She rolled her kind, stupid eyes round on Peggy.

'I think you're absolutely right. If I could go, I'd be off tomorrow.'

It was not a hint. She had known from the first instant that she would not be going too; what arrangements had been made for herself, she would doubtless hear in a moment. But it amused her to make this kind of frank remark sometimes.

'Ah, that's the point – I wanted to talk to you about that (do sit down, dear – that's right). Now about you – I want *you* to look after my boys for me, in their own dear home, where they're comfortable. Everything will go on for them just the same as usual. I'm afraid they're going to miss me dreadfully. I was tempted to order *cream* for them, every day while I'm away, to make up a little. But I thought, *no*. Their health comes first, and it would be very bad for their little figures. Don't you agree?'

Peggy nodded. Mrs Corbett's way of talking to the dogs often irritated her, but she had to admit that her love for them was neither selfish nor unintelligent; their jet-bright eyes and satin coats and lively leapings proved that.

'And about Arnold, dear. I think it would be better if he stayed at the Club.'

Peggy nodded again; this time, her agreement was with all her heart. Her time was not worth much to her, but she did not want to spend it in fighting off Arnold Corbett: sulks so often ended in attack.

'The servants might be silly about – they might be silly,' Mrs Corbett explained. 'They've been with us for such a long time, you see, ever since my husband's early days, when he was starting his firm; Hobbs was one of his mechanics, and Mrs Hobbs got into the way of coming in to help from time to time, and Doris is her sister, and old Hetty was just a friend. I even got Frobisher through them. They've never been *trained*, of course, they just drifted into the job, and now I should never dream of getting rid of them. But they are crotchety; I admit it, and so jealous of everyone I have in the house. Arnold is always saying I ought to pension them off. But I'm used to them and they're used to me. Now, dear, I'm afraid to-day will be a busy one for you. I want you to arrange about my tickets and everything.'

'Are you going alone, Mrs Corbett?'

Yes, Mrs Corbett was going alone. In the hotel at Hamilton she would find other rich old men and women to gossip and play cards with. Peggy came out of her private world and went into that other, unreal one; of telephones, and routes, and times, and reservations. A week passed quickly in this bustle.

When she came down to her lunch, after Mrs Corbett had been gone some hours, she found Arnold there, returned from driving his mother to the airport. She lost no time in making her attitude plain.

'I expected you to be lunching at your club,' she said, as she seated herself; she was wearing a dark tweed suit, which made her appear very slender. She looked at him steadily; her fingers were keeping open the place in a book.

'All right, all right. I only want a bite of lunch. I do live here.'

Peggy employed herself with serving the dish which Doris was holding before her, and they began to eat.

'Aren't you going to read?' he asked presently.

'My manners aren't my strong point, but I do draw the line at reading at meals when someone else is there.'

'I don't mind, if you want to.'

'It isn't an interesting book,' said Peggy, and smiled, which caused him to exclaim:

'I say, I do wish you'd be a bit nice to me sometimes.'

She paused, as if thinking about an answer, then said indifferently:

'I suppose you mean let you kiss me.'

'Right first time,' he said, laughing. 'You're what my erks in the R.A.F. would have called a caution, aren't you? Care to make any further suggestions? I'm game if you are.'

'No thank you . . .'

'I'm clearing out this afternoon, so you can draw a deep breath.'

Peggy said nothing, but smiled once more; it was as if a stormy sunlight had touched her face.

He was staring at her miserably.

'You've absolutely landed me, you know,' he added suddenly. 'Hit me for six. You could do anything you liked with me – even marry me, and *that's* something I've never said to any woman yet. I don't know how you've managed it – you've been ruder to me than any girl I've ever known – and when you smile like that – I could die for you. That's exactly how I feel, and I've never felt like it in my life. Never. About any woman. I could die for you.'

'Ah,' said Peggy, getting up from the table, 'you should read Kipling on that – '*I am dying for you and you are dying for another*'. That's what he wrote about our situation – if it is a situation. He'd come across it before, perhaps.'

She went out of the room.

'But I love you,' he said, as if in astonishment, to the elegant disorder of the big table and the impersonal afternoon light, 'I love you.'

19

By tea-time, he had gone. Peggy settled herself into the routine of the house with cat-like satisfaction. The servants waited on her with obvious dislike and a curiosity about her comings and goings which amused her; she had the dogs for company.

She saw Arnold from time to time when he looked in for his letters; sometimes, he would telephone to ask if there were any for him and keep her for a few minutes in conversation – to listen to her voice, she supposed, indifferently.

She didn't believe that he had never spoken of marriage to any woman. In her experience, men of Arnold's type frequently spoke of marriage, but always in such a way that no definite proposal could be extracted from their remarks. They looked on themselves as glittering prizes, and enjoyed dangling themselves tantalizingly in front of women's noses. She sometimes gave a thought to poor Gwen Palmer, and she did not think it would kill Arnold Corbett to see that he and his money were not always wanted. Whether it would 'do him good' or not, she neither knew nor cared.

Once a week, she went over to see her mother. Her relationship with her father expressed its tensions in cool short exchanges, often with a sting in them, but his satisfaction in Mrs Pearson's improved health and spirits since her settling into

Lily Cottage was so strong that he could not keep it to himself, and it burst out in questions. 'Doesn't your mother look better? Haven't you noticed it too? She's livelier, isn't she? She enjoys her life, now.'

He spoke of enjoyment as a thing other people experienced. Bliss he knew, and cessation of suffering, but never ordinary simple enjoyment. His mother had laid the foundations of passion and pain in him both strong and four-square. Her dour nature, absorbed always in the moral problems looming beyond the practical ones of their poor life, had pressed like an iron clamp on the soft voluptuous one of a little half-Eastern boy; and Thomas's jokes, Thomas's joys, were not felt like those of ordinary men.

He went about his business during the day; meeting his managers or looking in at the fruit and vegetable shops in crowded Stratford or comfortable Ealing; sometimes taking a ten-shilling note or some silver and coppers from the hand of the derelict in charge of one of his junk shops as he walked past it; telephoning the rent-collectors who went round his dilapidated properties in Islington or Kennington.

All his projects were on a small scale . . . but his wiliness and persistence and his contempt for the law, blent with a natural dexterity in handling money, made him successful.

He owned solid *things*: houses, ship-loads of half-spoiled fruit, dilapidated little shops, collections of other people's battered and abandoned possessions. He could never wring from them enough money to buy the laughter and the security his mother had denied him when he was a child.

And in the evenings, when his crowded, yet curiously shapeless, day was over, he would go home to the small house with the bearded mask sneering by its door.

An Oriental's day; devious, and full of coffee-drinking and

long, apparently aimless conversations which caused blistering private comment among the enslaved creatures he employed. From these conversations, something solid always emerged which profited Thomas Pearson.

Mrs Geddes, a silent, calm, stout lady in her late seventies, began her régime at the Vicarage by a gesture which — had anyone there had the kind of imagination to see it as such — would have appeared symbolic.

She threw away the piece of rag that had been used for nearly a year to mop up burnt milk and spilled tea-leaves.

She also banished a pensioner known to Mr Geddes and Gerald simply as 'the cat', which for nearly as long had held insolent and unshakeable squatter's right over the kitchen.

But, where a lesser woman would have had it put to sleep and then suffered retrospective qualms of conscience, Mrs Geddes's triumph lay in her dispensation of justice with mercy; she banished it from the kitchen, indescribable saucers and all, but made for it a home in the ruined air-raid shelter at the end of the garden, where it had its saucers and its horrid old bed and was happier than it had ever been, and felt such gratitude towards Mrs Geddes that it haunted the back door in the hope of having her scratch its ears or call it Pussy, though all she ever said to it while doing so was: 'Go away, you know I don't like cats.'

She then began, naturally, to cook the kind of meals she had always cooked for her parson husband and the little only son who had also taken Orders; in the huge primitive kitchens of huge, icy rectories up and down England; potato soup and treacle tart, fruit cakes, kedgeree for breakfast and pot roasts.

Gerald Corliss, who had always taken this kind of food for granted, did not realize how much his system and spirits had been suffering from the lack of it until they began to revive on its return.

He had intended to mention old Mr Fisher's story about his new landlady's alleged trance. But, dazed with the reinstallation of comfort and eatable food at the Vicarage, he simply forgot.

One morning towards the end of February, when they were seated at lunch, Mrs Geddes said:

'A funny old man called to see you this morning, Robert. He had some little straw dolls on a tray that he wanted to show you.'

'Very old? With a face like a sheep?'

'He has, now you come to suggest it.'

'That's Mr Fisher . . . dolls on a tray?'

'Yes, rather nicely made. I don't think he was selling them.'

'I do know him – though he isn't a church-goer,' said the Vicar.

'I thought you'd want me to do something about it, so I gave him a shilling. He showed me the dolls, and then, though he didn't *say* anything, I think he expected me to give him something.'

'That was all right; remind me to give it to you.'

There was a pause, while Mrs Geddes served a perfect apple tart.

'Oh, by the way,' put in Gerald, 'I've been meaning to tell you only it completely slipped my memory – I found him asleep in the church – on – Christmas Night, it was.' He paused, looking guilty. 'Nearly six weeks ago – I'm so *very* sorry, I ought to have mentioned it before.'

'It doesn't matter, you know we get homeless people in there from time to time. It's part of our job to keep the church open, I expect he was just having a rest.'

'No, I didn't think you'd mind that. But he told me something about his landlady that was worrying him, and I said I'd tell you.'

'Trouble there, is there?' Mr Geddes said resignedly, 'well, it did strike me it was all a bit too rosy to last.' He checked an impulse to add that when people were all over each other in the first few days, it seldom did. 'Let's have it.'

'No, it isn't the usual kind of trouble these peop – that . . . er . . . seems to crop up with landladies. He said she – Mrs Pearson – suffers from trances.'

'*Suffers from trances*? What on earth . . .?'

'She had one on Christmas Night – if one can talk about someone "having" a trance – she fell into one, apparently, and "talked in another voice", he said. And he said she seemed like a lost soul.'

There was a silence. Cold February light looked in through the tall, shrub-darkened windows at the three faces; Mrs Geddes's calm as usual, the curate's earnest and a little disturbed, the Vicar's perplexed, with pursed lips.

'In one sense of course that's our business,' said Mr Geddes at last, 'because she is a parishioner. But in another it isn't at all. She hasn't asked for our help. This is just a report from a neighbour, isn't it?'

'Yes. And he's such an extraordinary old creature – a little unbalanced, wouldn't you say –'

'Eccentric. Eccentric, not unbalanced. He's like a child,' said the Vicar impatiently. He had to go to tea with his tiresome ex-parishioner in Hampstead, and had much in the way of deskwork to fit in before he left . . . 'What did you say he said – "*a lost soul*"? Extraordinary – he really is a queer old boy.'

'*A lost soul*. It made – an impression on me at the time. I don't know how . . . I came . . . to forget it for more than six weeks.'

'There's a lot on, here,' Mr Geddes said dryly. 'It isn't exciting, but there's always plenty of it. Lost souls don't often come our way. The small things smother the big ones, I suppose.'

'What C. S. Lewis called "the bustle, the notices, the umbrellas",' said Mrs Geddes in a low tone.

'Suppose you try to tell me exactly what he said,' Mr Geddes went on.

Gerald, now feeling thoroughly guilty, brought his excellent brain, which had found no difficulty in co-ordinating the minute details of exegesis or in mastering Greek, to bear on recalling what Mr Fisher had said.

Yet it was a version, rather than a report, because his own articulacy gave to the old man's vague phrases a clarity they had lacked. However, it left the Vicar with a strong feeling that something must be done, though all he said was, 'He may be exaggerating. Most people love a bit of drama.'

'Shall . . . do you think . . . ought I to go?' said Gerald hesitatingly. 'I suppose, that is . . . the thing to do is to visit her.'

'I'll go. It may be a case for a psychiatrist, though I have small confidence in *them*, as you know.'

'Yes, I thought that at the time.' Gerald let the matter drop, hoping his relief did not sound in his voice.

The Vicar went off to his study and the curate lingered for a moment, to see if Mrs Geddes needed help in the kitchen.

'Thank you, I'd be glad of it,' she said, and he busied himself with stacking plates on to the trolley while she went to the kitchen to see if the huge, wasteful boiler had hot water to offer.

Gerald carefully folded three starched white table napkins with a vague sensation of pleasure. He had noticed their appearance at the vicarage table without wondering how they came to be starched, accepting them as part of the general improvement under the Rule of the Vicar's mother.

Now he began to wheel the laden trolley out of the room and across the hall and down a paved corridor which echoed hollowly to its passing. He had spent all his childhood and boyhood in lofty, spacious places, and the heights and breadths of the vicarage's rooms provided one of the few familiar sensations in this new world.

'Put them in that drawer; thank you,' commanded Mrs Geddes, seeing out of the corner of her eye that he was moving the napkins absently up and down in one hand, 'and will you open the door to the cat; it wants its lunch.'

Gerald opened the door and the cat strolled in, glancing at him balefully.

'Go away,' Mrs Geddes observed, moving so that it could rub itself against her ankles. 'Gerald, give it its fish on the dresser, will you. Half will do.'

He shrinkingly obeyed, and the cat began to toy with the white wet flabby stuff in languid style. Some proud remark about its daintiness would have been called forth from any natural person; Mrs Geddes continued to clean plates with a mop and hand them to her helper in silence; presently the cat stopped assing about, and ate its portion with appetite.

'Let it out, Gerald, will you.'

He opened the door and stood expectant. The cat walked over to Mrs Geddes and gazed up at her passionately, waving its meagre tail and purring in a kind of croak.

'You know very well I don't like cats,' said Mrs Geddes, stooping to manipulate – the action does not merit the word fondle – its ears.

Gratified, and taking its time, the cat strolled past Gerald and out into the garden.

'That's all; thank you; that was a great help,' said Mrs Geddes, beginning to open a packet of old-fashioned starch, and, glad at heart, he followed the cat's example and went off on his own affairs.

20

Mr Geddes was cycling across Hampstead Heath.

Bicycling, at least, was better than hanging about for buses or stifling in the Underground, though – his practical eye considered the landscape as he wheeled swiftly along – the winter-bleached grass looked dirty and there was a dismal scatter of litter everywhere.

But the children of the age of affluence could not spoil the trees. Some forty feet above the marred earth there were bare silver branches, robust and thewed as the arms of giants, massive trunks, delicate tracery of leaf skeleton and twig.

He recalled his straying thoughts. What was to be done during the rest of the day?

Tea with Mrs Lysaght; Evensong; the list of his Lenten sermons to sketch out; the Men's Group at eight-fifteen; an hour or so after that with Sunday's sermon . . . what a waste of time these teas with poor Helen were.

Mrs Lysaght herself opened the door to him. Her flat was in a solid Edwardian block lifted up on one of Hampstead's numerous baby hillocks above the unceasing hell of noise in Heath Street. She was rather tall, and rather pretty. She was a widow, and she did not have to worry about money.

'How sweet of you to come early, Robert. Do come in, I've had some flowers sent me from the country, and I do so want you to see them before they go quite off. Let me take your coat – there!'

She laid the coat tenderly on a chair with one hand while with the other waving towards a bowl of wild daffodils, now well advanced in the process of 'going off'.

'I just wanted you to have one glimpse of them before I threw them away. You and I share a passion for flowers, don't we?'

Cheered by a glimpse of a laden tea-trolley lurking in a corner, he nodded, and expressed admiration of the daffodils, while being pressed into a chair near the fire – electric, and too hot; he always found Helen's rooms too hot.

'Now! What have you been doing since we last met?' Mrs Lysaght began, 'Do tell me about my dear old friends at Saint James's and all your news.'

'Well, everything's much the same as usual, I think. Mrs Peters is in hospital, had to have an operation.'

'Now which is Mrs Peters? Is she the old dear who always wears a blue and white spotted scarf?'

'No, I think you must mean Miss Cuthbert. Mrs Peters lives alone, in one of those houses on Hill Drive.'

'Of course, I remember now . . . And Miss Rogers – and Mrs – I forget her name but I know who I mean – she always brings a red shopping bag to church.'

'That's Mrs Miller. I'm glad she does – before she started doing that she left something in the pew after every service – gloves or specs or handkerchiefs or something.'

Mr Geddes spoke with firmness. He disliked Mrs Lysaght's habit of identifying the members of his faithful band of elderly ladies by their items of dress.

'I've really brought you here to make a confession,' said Mrs Lysaght suddenly, perhaps feeling some rebuke in his tone, and leaving the ladies of Saint James's, 'I hesitated about telling you – and then I thought – why not? He'll always be my spiritual guide – my *guru* – and – he'll . . . understand. I'm leaving the Church.'

Her large bright eyes beamed with pleasure, like a small girl giving someone a sweet. She gazed at him, upright and expectant. All Mr Geddes found to say was a mechanical, 'Oh, I'm sorry to hear that,' followed by the thought, *confound the woman*. Shocked at himself, he leant a little forward and said hastily:

'I'm sorry. But – er – what's happened? I always believed – hoped – you were settled at last, you know. Safe and sound in the Church of England.'

He uttered a short laugh. He hoped it did not sound irritable; at least it was a laugh. But with so much waiting to be done at home!

'I did think I was, for a few years, and I did try. But what finally defeated me, Robert, was the *narrowness*.'

'I'm not attacking Christianity,' Mrs Lysaght added with an access of energy, 'please never think that – *or* the character of Jesus. It's the Church I'm – well, not exactly attacking, but *accusing* – if you know what I mean –'

'I expect I do,' Mr Geddes said.

'– and particularly the Church of England – dear old 'C. of E.', as it's called – and I always think that's so significant – Rome doesn't invite that sort of nickname.'

'Are you thinking of "going over"?'

Mr Geddes experienced some satisfaction at the thought. Let her try on this kind of thing with a Roman Catholic priest and see what she got. He checked himself again.

'Of course not. Rome is even narrower, and dogmatic and superstitious into the bargain – that stuff about the Virgin

173

Birth – no, I could never join Rome. I'm afraid I'm *far* too fond of thinking for myself.'

I'm afraid you are very silly, Mr Geddes was thinking.

'What's suddenly brought you up to this?' he asked, feeling that he could not go on another moment without tea. 'I didn't hear anything about it last time we met.'

'No, I've been sitting on my little secret, I wanted to think it all out with absolute clearness and make up my mind quite coldly. Oh – half-past – excuse me – it's Gretl's free afternoon, I must just go and boil the kettle.'

She fluttered away, contriving somehow to do it in a sweater and skirt, returning shortly with the teapot and a silver kettle, the latter perilously poised over a live flame in a tiny silver lamp.

'I thought we'd use this old thing; isn't it pretty; it belonged to an aunt of mine; will you help me?'

In a few moments, the first sips of tea had refreshed Mr Geddes. He set down his cup, bit into an excellent piece of bread and butter, and began suavely:

'You haven't answered my question, you know; why are you leaving us?'

'Dear Robert, I thought I'd made it clear. The Church of England takes a very narrow view of the Cosmos. For the last three years I've read widely, very widely indeed, I've really *stretched my brains*, and oh what an inrush of knowledge and light –'

'Can you really call it knowledge?' pounced Mr Geddes, as his hostess paused to drink her tea.

'Well – not knowledge in the accepted sense –'

'In what sense, then?'

'In a higher sense, Robert. Much of what these very gifted people write is intuitive knowledge – revealed to them by spirits from other worlds who are guiding them and inspiring them.'

'But to get back to you leaving the Church of England,' said he, firmly, 'what do *you* suggest we should do about what you call our narrowness?'

'Well – I hadn't got as far as thinking what you should *do*, Robert . . . besides . . .'

'Suppose all of us – we parish priests – wrote up in a body to our Bishops suggesting we should abandon the forms of prayer and worship that we've used for five hundred years – some of them for close on two thousand years – because they had become "narrow" and "out-dated", what form of service do you suggest should replace them?'

'Well . . . something more universal . . . *I* think something about reincarnation and each person's *Karma*, their predestined life-pattern –'

'And what effect do you suppose that would have on old Miss Jones, who has been going to Saint James's for fifty years and looks after her ninety-year-old mother in a two-room flat? Is it going to help Miss Jones to hear about her *Karma*?'

'You're so hopelessly practical, Robert. Of course I'm not in a position to talk about details –'

'Suppose it's God's will that the Church of England should go on offering the "narrow path" that Jesus spoke of, the "straight and narrow way"? Straight, He said; *straight*, not wandering off in all directions. Most people just can't take the kind of thing *you've* been amusing yourself with.'

'Robert! That's not kind!'

'You're very happily placed for research into funny religions, you know, Helen – I'm speaking plainly now because I'm angry that you're deserting us – you've got leisure, and proper domestic

help, and friends, a pretty home – I know you're lonely sometimes – most people are – but on the whole you're one of the
lucky ones, aren't you. Well, aren't you?' as she sat looking at
him with obstinacy on her soft, unlined face.

'I don't like being told I'm deserting you,' she said at last.

'Well, I think you are. We need every soul we can get; every
living one of you, to bear witness! What are you going to do,
where will you go to worship God – I suppose you'll still need
to do that – when you've left us?'

'Oh I shall read and meditate.'

'If you haven't a church to go to that'll soon turn into
day-dreaming. You need a special type of mind to keep that
up, and you haven't got it.'

'Oh if you knew how I often long just to go into *permanent
retreat* – silence, and peace, and . . . prayer . . .'

'You could enjoy all that in a good hotel in Bournemouth,'
Mr Geddes said. '(May I have another cup, please.) I thought
you were rather worried about your prayers, by the way? (Thank
you.)'

'I don't find it easy,' Mrs Lysaght confessed, 'my mind wanders.
It seems worse lately.' The last words came out with a little
reluctance.

'Everybody's mind wanders. And yours will, while you're
stuffing your head with all this.' He tapped a pamphlet he had
taken up. 'You aren't a Hindu. *You aren't a Hindu*,' he repeated.
'You were born in England and you've taken in Western thought
all your life. It may not attract you as much as all this,' tapping
the booklet again, 'but it's moulded your way of thinking. Of
course your mind wanders worse than ever while you're trying
to pray.' He looked at the booklet inimically.

'Mrs Besant –'

'I really don't want to hear about Mrs Besant,' almost cried

Mr Geddes, snatching himself a biscuit, 'I hear enough about peculiar spiritual women from Gerald – my curate. I'm sorry, but I really can't stand them. I've been used to – the ordinary kind. Margery was the ordinary kind, and so is my mother. I dare say I should have disliked Saint Teresa very much. I can't help it; I can't stand them at any price.'

There was a pause. Mr Geddes angrily munched, and Mrs Lysaght stared into the fire with compressed lips. But perhaps the reference to his dead wife had turned her thought into softer and less exalted regions, for in a moment she said in another tone:

'Your mother is really with you at last, then? I'm sure it must be much more comfortable for you . . . how does she like London after Harrogate?'

Mr Geddes accepted the change of mood gratefully.

'Very much, I think,' he replied.

'Didn't she mind leaving that beautiful old vicarage?'

'She hasn't been living there for three years, you know. I think the idleness in the hotel got on her nerves.'

'But such a joy to have no cooking or catering or washing up!'

Mr Geddes merely said that his mother had always been very active.

'Oh – you make me feel so useless. I'm afraid I'm a very idle person. I try to excuse myself by thinking that I *am* more sensitive than most people, and I'm a dreamer, of course, too – always have been. Heigh-ho!' Mrs Lysaght sighed and looked at the electric fire with her head on one side; then went on in a more animated tone, 'I'm glad to hear my dear old Gladys still keeps up her church-going. *She's* a *simple* soul. I don't want to see *her* leaving the Church. She came to tea last week. Isn't it *thrilling* about Mrs Pearson!'

'Gladys? Oh – Miss Barnes, of course; yes. Yes, she comes to Sunday Evensong usually – can't manage the early service. I suppose she has to look after her sister.' (Mr Geddes braced himself; he foresaw more complications.)

'I can't wait to meet her – Mrs Pearson, I mean.'

'Mrs Pearson?' Mr Geddes asked, quietly stalling.

'Gladys's new landlady. Hasn't she told you about her? She's *a medium*.'

'I have heard of her,' he said unenthusiastically, 'though not through Gladys Barnes.'

'Oh *do* tell me what you heard. I'm so interested in her – a genuine psychic. My little plan is to get her to give me a sitting.'

'We were told about her by one of her tenants, an old man who lives next door to her – he described her as "looking like a lost soul".' Mr Geddes was feeling increasingly irritated and disturbed.

'"A lost soul" ! Oh that really *is* exciting! Did he mean she's *possessed*?'

'How can I possibly say, Helen? I suppose he meant she looks unusually depressed – despairing, perhaps – her looks seem to have made a deep impression on him, anyway. I imagine it might be . . . I don't know . . .' He decided, then and there, against telling Mrs Lysaght even the little that he did know.

'Do you know if she gives sittings?'

'No I do not.'

'Well don't sound so cross about it! I'm so excited – life's so awful in London in February when one hasn't much money – Ronald always used to send me to the South of France for three weeks – I miss that terribly (and him, of course) – and any little thrill is a godsend, this time of the year. Can you find out for me if she does?'

'Does what?' He glanced at the clock.

'Oh don't pretend you don't understand! Mrs Pearson. Give sittings. As a medium.'

'Helen, I really cannot undertake this – finding things out about her. The woman sounds as if she may be very ill. By far the best thing is to leave her alone.'

'But I might be able to help her . . . if she's hard up . . .'

'The whole thing's most undesirable, most unwise, I can't see a single reason for your having anything to do with her, except that it happens to be February, and you're feeling bored.'

He got up, and stood with an elbow on the mantelpiece, glaring at her. He knew her well enough to be certain that opposition from him would make her the more determined to get her own way.

'You needn't be mad about it,' she said, with an irritating ripple of 'naughty' laughter, 'why shouldn't I ? She needn't see me if she doesn't want to. You're *really* angry with me, aren't you?'

'I am really annoyed with you, yes. This is one of the times when I feel that one should . . . keep out. Keep away from her. I feel it very strongly. You need strong nerves, and a good brain, to tackle that sort of thing.'

'What sort of thing? You do believe there's something then?'

'Of course I believe there's "something", as you call it. There are – what I'd rather call mysteries, both holy and possibly unholy. I prefer to leave them alone. There's plenty to be done, God knows, without wading out into that kind of thing. I believe in Almighty God and I trust in Jesus Christ. That's enough for me.' Colour had come into his face; the crude avowal had not been easy to make.

Mrs Lysaght was shaking her head and sighing.

'There we are, you see, right back where we started from. Narrowness. You're a typical Anglican.'

'Thank you, that's a compliment,' Mr Geddes said forthrightly, and again looked at the clock. 'I must go, Helen. Now I hope, when I see you again, you'll have thought over this business of leaving the Church and decided not to. That's what really matters.'

'It's sweet of you to care, Robert. It really is. And I promise to think it over. But I *can't* promise to change my mind, so don't build on it.'

As he wheeled his bicycle across Heath Street, Mr Geddes was thinking that anyone who built anything on Mrs Lysaght's mind would need their head examining; the house built on sand was well-founded in comparison.

21

Mrs Corbett prolonged her holiday beyond the six weeks she had first mentioned. She had made pleasant acquaintances and was enjoying herself: she would not be home until after Easter. Arnold had the news first, and told Peggy when he telephoned her on the morning of Maundy Thursday.

'So how about coming for a drive with me on Sunday?' he went on.

'Are you mad? Easter Sunday? It will be absolute hell.'

'Not if you know the roads and aren't making for the coast.'

'I'll see.'

'I'll bring the car round about eleven, ma'am. That'll give everyone else time to be well on their way.'

'Don't be surprised if I'm not here.'

'I'd never be surprised at anything you did . . . righto, then. Eleven on Sunday.'

Mrs Pearson was content to let the hours drift by, eating her slight meals off trays and telling Erika to 'just make some tea, *schatz*,' six or seven times in a day. But Erika, perhaps impelled by some orderly ancestral instinct, painstakingly set a place for herself in the kitchen at meal times; cooked herself a mess of meat and vegetables; and sat in the chilly half-dusk slowly chewing, obstinately declining Mrs Pearson's invitations to share the warmth of her bedroom and the chocolates and nut-toffee that were always on her tray.

She would sit facing the dim light coming through the window overlooking the neglected garden, with her head lifted towards it like a flower tilted to the sun. A poor kind of flower, pallid and lacking bloom. But less pale, and less frozen in expression, than some weeks ago. And her hair was beginning to shine.

Gladys had firmly set her in the way of eating what she called proper meals.

'All that picking off of trays,' said Gladys, 'all right for im-balids, but a young girl needs to eat regular and hearty. Put a bit of flesh on your bones. Stews. I'll show you.'

She continued to teach Erika her own shopping-lore, learnt during more than seventy hard, impoverished years; Erika could take home that frozen stuff for Mrs P., but let her buy a nice bit of end of neck for herself, and some pot-herbs. 'What you used to get the lot for sixpence. That I should live to see turnips eightpence the pound. What we're coming to I don't know,' marvelled Gladys.

And then she taught her to cook.

Erika's dealings with turnips had heretofore been confined to clawing them out with frozen fingers from the edge of a frozen field, but she learned to approach them in their more civilized guise – 'washed, if you please,' as Gladys pointed out. She then added inconsequently, Lazy Sluts, and even Erika could not think that this remark applied to the turnips.

Mrs Pearson made no objections to Erika's shopping for her own meals. She agreed with Gladys, slowly moving her head up and down in a dreamy nodding motion, when the latter ventured to point out that young girls needed to eat proper; she agreed that it would be nice if Erika learned to cook.

Gladys had at the back of her mind a vague but splendid notion of Erika's one day becoming a cook in a posh restaurant, but she spoke of this to no-one except Annie.

There were other changes for the better, besides the fresh paint glowing in the strengthening sunlight and the clean white curtains; Annie often left her bed now to sit by the fire, putting on stockings and slippers to do so. Mrs Pearson's unforgettable appearance in their rooms on Christmas Day, holding out both hands and crying, 'You just hold on to me,' would never be forgotten by the sisters. It had marked a turning point, for Annie had even partly resumed former domestic habits, and sometimes had the meal almost ready for Gladys on the latter's return from work.

While loudly welcoming this, Gladys had been known to remark to acquaintances, met while shopping, that she never knew, nowadays, what Annie would be poking into during her absence.

But when the rackman visited his wife; when the car bumped gently to a standstill over the bomb-cracked road in the dusk; or when he walked noiselessly down between the rows of houses he owned, head bent and hands in his pockets, then a hush fell over the small, harmless lives in Rose Cottage. Gladys would start at the sound of his key in the adjacent hall, and look at Annie and nod, and they would become silent. The house, always quiet, would seem filled with a frozen air when he was in it; Mr Fisher would creep out on his walk, by daylight or dusk, noiselessly as a shadow.

Gladys was always ready to welcome kindness between people; it was in her nature to look for it. But though Pearson's manner towards his wife was loving, it never reassured her, and she spoke of it to Annie as *unnatural*, and *downright soppy*.

The few words he dropped, his glances, the sight of his

caressing touch, conveyed a burning-sweet, Eastern love that vaguely reminded her of certain films seen long ago; in her young womanhood, when the Orient was still a strange and romantic place and the Oriental lover was the ideal. His manner as a husband was so unlike the rough comradeship between married pairs that she was accustomed to; it increased her conviction that he was as false as he was dangerous.

Easter was at hand. The spring flowers were at the street-corners. Mr Geddes had of course been even more occupied than usual at Saint James's; he had not so much forgotten Miss Barnes's landlady as postponed thinking what to do about her until he should be less occupied.

But Mrs Lysaght had not forgotten.

One afternoon the telephone rang in Lily Cottage.

Erika, who was in the kitchen, tidying up, moved off slowly to answer it.

'Hullo,' she said cautiously. Mrs Pearson had explained to her that she must never be in a hurry to give their number; it might be someone whom Mr Pearson did not want to know it.

'Is that Highway 8741 – Mrs Pearson's house? I wondered if I might just speak to Miss Barnes?' cooed a voice. 'Miss Gladys Barnes. She lives next door to you, I believe.'

Gladys had gossiped about the door between the cottages, on her last visit to Hampstead.

Erika considered this, breathing oppressedly down the receiver.

'Hullo?' said the voice, tentatively.

'I ask,' almost whispered Erika, thereby adding more mystery to that already, in Mrs Lysaght's imagination, filling the house of the sorceress.

'Oh, thank you, I'll hold on –'

Mrs Pearson was lying on her bed as usual, pretty and wraithlike in one of her rose house-coats, and reading a woman's magazine.

'Hullo, *schatz*, what is it?'

'Der is a woman at der phone. She want to speak to Gladys.'

'Lady, dear – not *woman*. Always say "lady" and "gentleman" – you like to be called "a young lady" don't you? – Gladys is at work, isn't she? Just run up and see, love.'

By the time Erika had digested the lesson in social behaviour and nodded solemnly, and made her way down the stairs, and through the door, and up to the Barnes's quarters, and received from Annie an alarmed assurance that of course Glad was at work, where else should she be this time of day? Oh it wasn't the 'ospital, was it, Glad hadn't been knocked down, had she? She was that careless crossing the road; and Erika had in her turn assured Annie that it was only a lady, and Annie had said oh it wasn't one of those foreigners from where Glad worked, was it? because if it was something must be wrong, and Erika had looked at her in silent sympathy for a moment or two, unable to reassure her because, in her own lifelong experience, something had been perpetually wrong – nearly ten minutes had passed.

But Mrs Lysaght had nothing much to do.

She was still there when Erika, having returned to Mrs Pearson and reported what Annie had said, came back to the telephone.

'She is at vork,' she said, and, charmed by the usage of the instrument with which she had had no previous encounters, waited interestedly for the unknown lady's next remark.

'Oh dear, how tiresome of her. Aren't people tiresome? Now what am I going to do? Now wait a minute –'

Erika waited. During the next three or four minutes, Annie's remarks about hospitals and those foreigners finally reached a destination in her mind.

'Are you der 'ospital?' she asked at length, and there was a tinkling laugh. 'Of course I'm not the hospital – do I sound like the hospital? I'm just thinking –'

'Are you doze foreigners where Gladys vorks?' pursued Erika, with teutonic perseverance.

'No I am not – you funny girl, do I sound like a foreigner? Your English isn't very good, is it? Are you Mrs Pearson's *au pair* girl? How long have you been over here?' she went on chattily, 'I really think I'd better speak to Mrs Pearson.'

Erika did not know what an *au pair* girl might be. She announced, 'I ask Mrs Pearson,' and plodded away and up the stairs.

'But who is she? Didn't she say? Oh well – I'd better come down,' Mrs Pearson laid aside her magazine, 'it may be a message – something important for Gladys.'

She drifted down the stairs, too good-natured to feel irritation at the interruption. Her mind was busy with the story she had been reading; a suspense-story about multiple murder and hidden love in the Deep South of America.

'Hullo?' she murmured into the receiver, 'Miss Barnes is at work. Would you like to leave a message?'

'Oh –' said a voice, on an indrawn breath that might have been one of satisfaction, 'it's just that . . . I'm Mrs Lysaght, Miss Barnes used to work for me – and she was coming to tea with me to-morrow and now I find I have to go out of town on that very day – so tiresome – an old aunt of mine is ill (or thinks she is) – *would* you be very kind and explain to Miss Barnes – Gladys – it's difficult to think of her as "Miss Barnes", isn't it?' Then, suddenly, with a kind of cooing pounce in the voice, 'That *is* Mrs Pearson, isn't it?'

'Yes,' said Mrs Pearson, after a pause, with reluctance. She let the word drop flatly. The train of thought about the Deep South romance was interrupted; she looked blankly across the hall. Erika had gone back to the kitchen; she was alone. A plastic dog on the hall table, a pink dog with a pink bow, looked perkily back at her. The voice was speaking again.

'Oh I'm *so* delighted to have got *hold* of you – I've heard so much about you from dear old Gladys, such a character, isn't she? Mrs Pearson . . .'

'What?' Mrs Pearson said, weakly. It was almost a whisper; a sensation of helplessness was creeping over her. She knew what was going to be asked of her. Her eyes widened and stared into . . . somewhere . . .

'Mrs Pearson, I'm going to say something impertinent. (You must forgive me – I'm so *passionately* interested in the Occult.) Gladys has told me *a great deal* about you. You're a medium, aren't you?'

The question came out sharply, with a note of triumph; ah, I've tracked you down, this is what I was after. Mrs Pearson answered, faintly but instantly, 'I'm not well.'

'Oh dear, I'm so sorry . . . were you in bed? I hope I didn't disturb you, what's the trouble?' Decent regret only half concealed ravenous curiosity, and Mrs Pearson yielded, as she had done often before, to a superficially kindly tone. There was some innocent vanity, too, prompting her answer: ordinary people, non-sensitives, always took it for granted that you could see what you saw, and hear what you heard, and go on having nerves like whipped steel . . . let this woman hear the truth.

'I'm not well because being a medium takes it out of you,' she retorted, with feeble anger, 'that's why.'

'Oh – then – you *are still giving sittings*? I asked old Gladys but she seemed to think you weren't (it's rather difficult getting a straight answer to a straight question, with our Gladys, don't you agree?).'

'No, I'm not giving sittings . . . now.'

'Oh, how disappointing. I was wondering if you couldn't break your rule for once and give one for me.'

'I don't *give* them any more – I –'

'Just for once. I . . . would pay you, you understand. I don't want something for nothing.'

'I don't . . . take money now, I'm never going to give sittings again. My husband doesn't . . . he wouldn't like it.'

'But such a wonderful gift. So rare. Don't you ever feel it's your duty, Mrs Pearson, to use it? Like the talents? In the Bible, you know.'

'Not talk that . . . that . . . to me,' shrilled Mrs Pearson, in a voice like a bat's, and slammed back the receiver. She leaned over the table where the telephone stood, trembling, with both hands pressed over her eyes, and was still standing there, when Erika crept anxiously up to her.

'Mrs Pearson? You feeling bad?' she whispered. It was the first time she had heard a voice raised in anger in Lily Cottage; even the dread Mr Pearson never shouted.

'No, dear. I'm all right, I just had to send her away – she was worrying me – going on at me – bothering me – I'm all right now. Make me some tea, will you, *schatz*? and come up and have it with me.' She pulled out a packet of cigarettes from her pocket with a shaking hand, and went slowly upstairs.

Later that afternoon, some bunches of spring flowers arrived, with a note: 'To make my apologies. Hope you'll change your mind soon!'

Mrs Pearson tore the card into fragments over, and over again.

But she made Erika arrange the flowers all around her room;

she could resist flowers no more than she could resist a note of kindness in a voice. Her room was always full of them; her husband would not know that these irises and narcissi came from someone who wanted a sitting.

Alone, as twilight fell, she lay on her bed looking out across the room, so pretty in the pink light, with the faces of the flowers, trumpet-shaped, frill-shaped, horn-shaped, looking back at her from every side. It was completely quiet; the rich fresh colours glowed, the scents of daffodil and narcissi mingled with those from the bottles and jars on her dressing-table. Her grotesques, in glass and wood and plastic, smirked at her from the mantelpiece.

I wish Gladys hadn't gossiped, she thought. I wish she hadn't. Whatever happens, I mustn't let Tom know. He'd be . . . he might want me . . . no, I don't believe he would, now. We've got money, plenty of money . . . he wouldn't want . . .

Show them, the voice insisted, *show them. You're the only one who can do it, show them. I'll help you.*

Mrs Pearson moved her head deeper into the pillow, and let her eyes close. Oh the warmth, the silence, the lovely faces of the flowers. Any instant now, the green tunnel would be there; mossy, shaded by gentle boughs.

Show them, insisted the voice. *I'll help you. Show them.*

22

It was the afternoon of Easter Day. Peggy and Arnold Corbett were sitting after lunch in a silver birch coppice, surrounded by primroses. It had been raining lightly, but Peggy had sat with upturned face, the shower pouring down on her skin, while he sheltered under what protection there was, watching her with a wondering, feeble smile.

'We're between Slinfold and Sedgemere. If that means a thing to you?' he said now; he had been studying an AA map.

The rain had ceased. Peggy, who had wandered off to pick primroses, came towards him, moving silently between the tree trunks. There was a scent of wet moss. She was slowly wiping her face and brow with her handkerchief.

'Sedgemere's a pretty little place – three cottages and a church – we might go back that way?' Arnold suggested.

'If you like.' She was shockingly pale. Yet she did not seem ill; the brightness of her eyes was that of youth, not fever. She kept them fixed on Arnold's face, as if resigning the way that they should go home to him. All right, her brilliant eyes seemed to be saying, we'll go by way of Sedgemere. You decided, not me.

'Sedgemere it is, then.' He folded the map. 'And we'd better start now, if we want to avoid the lunatics.'

Peggy made him wait while she gathered up the smallest fragments of eggshell and paper and, amid his jeers, buried them under leaf-mould and moss. He watched her with the mocking smile that the slightest sign of gentleness in her always brought to his face. 'What's the point? Who the hell's going to see a bit of litter in here?'

'Nobody. If I can help it.' She wiped the moist earth off her hands and they went to the car.

Paler and paler grew Peggy as they approached Sedgemere in its narrow valley, and the stalks of the primroses were crushed in her hand and she stared unseeingly at the spring going by.

When they were passing through the little place with its three cottages covered in Sussex tiling and its square-towered, flint-set church, Arnold glanced at her. 'I'll slow down a bit, so's we can look at it – I say, are you car-sick?'

'Of course not. Do I look it?'

'You look a bit green.'

'I'm all right.'

There was silence again, while he drove slowly past the long cottage gardens and the duckpond. It was a heavy, slumbrous day; Sedgemere seemed asleep.

'Bet these little hovels'll sell for a nice price,' he said in a moment, 'when the inhabitants die off . . . but no-one seems to have got on to Sedgemere yet . . . oh, there is a riding-school.'

Rattray Riding School, said the notice above the white gate at the edge of the meadow, Rattray Riding School, *Rattray Riding School*.

A young woman on a horse was coming towards them down the unfenced track; she had the type of face once called sweet, and it was plain from the first sight of her that although she might try to fight for something she wanted, it would be hopeless; she was no fighter, and the battle would be lost from the start. *Fighting* and *battles* would mean little to that face. She glanced casually at the car.

'Do for God's sake get on, I'm bored with Sedgemere,' Peggy said, low but violently, and Arnold accelerated and they swept on, leaving Sedgemere asleep in the sun. The girl who lacked a fighting face turned her horse, and galloped back towards the buildings at the end of the meadow.

'That was a pretty girl,' said Arnold, 'notice?'

Peggy could not have spoken; she did not see the sweeps of green meadow or the hills crowned with white hedges of blackthorn or the silvery blue sky. All her spirit pursued, with hatred, the tiny figure receding at seventy miles an hour into the sunlit distance.

They reached home about five, having spent the last half hour of the journey running blithely along almost deserted suburban roads, while the cars on the main ones jerked and crept, jerked and crept, in the contemporary idiot rhythm. Peggy was still deadly pale and at last, to avoid further questions, had to say that her head ached.

'That's the first time I've heard you admit to a human weakness in six months,' he observed.

'Thank you,' said Peggy; if he would be quiet!

'Hullo!' added Arnold, 'there's the Rolls – my mother must be home.'

The Rolls was standing before the open garage with the old chauffeur, busy with a rag on the metalwork of the bonnet, looking distinctly sulky.

'Yes, that's mamma all right, all right, she's given him a rocket about the car being dirty, I did tell him, weeks ago, but the lazy old blighter hasn't touched it.' Having parked his own car, he went into the house.

Peggy followed slowly. She felt it as the last straw that her employer should have arrived back this evening; she had planned to go to her room and be on her bed until darkness came. She felt ill; shaken by jealousy and hatred.

Mrs Corbett spent the evening, naturally, in resuming control of MacLeod House and lamenting at intervals that she had put on ten pounds, that the car had not been cleaned, apparently, since she left, and the roses not pruned hard enough.

But, on the whole, she was satisfied with Peggy's stewardship, and the servants confided gloomily to one another in their sitting-room that it wasn't going to be no use complaining about *her*; she had 'wormed her way in', and would doubtless be left half – if not all – of Mrs Corbett's money.

It was, on the whole, a fine Easter. There were blue sky and warm sun and silver catkins and golden daffodils to be thankful for, as well as the alleged return from the dead of a gifted teacher with a messiah-complex. Gladys Barnes, one of millions made happy by the bright weather, confided an intention to Annie on the Saturday evening.

'I wouldn't. Not if I was you I wouldn't,' Annie said.

'If you was me you would, you soppy date. She's gone fifteen. She ought to go.'

'It's not your business, Glad. Now is it?'

'He's always going on about getting people to come.' ('He' was Mr Geddes.)

'Yes, but not if it means trouble, Glad. You know Mrs P. don't believe in the Church. You heard her, going on about the bells. We both 'eard.'

Gladys was silent. Her large eyes, innocent behind her glasses in their mended frame, were troubled.

'Now didn't we?' repeated Annie.

'Yes . . .' said Gladys doubtfully, 'but . . . I wouldn't be

193

surprised if it's not those turns of hers what make her go on like that. She hasn't never said a word to me against the Church not when I come in of a Sunday evening. Just smiles and says have a nice service? quite ordinary. I don't know . . .'

There was a pause, while they sat in their worn, comfortable old clothes in silence, enjoying the crackle and sparkle of a little coal fire, which replaced the greedy gas one in warmer weather. They were in the parlour.

''Course, she needn't know!' exclaimed Gladys at last, breaking into a sparkle bright as the fire's.

'Glad! That's downright deceitful!'

Gladys made a movement of her grey curls that took some sixty years off her age, and went on sparkling in silence.

'Erika's like her maid, Glad. She tells her what to do, and that . . . I know she don't pay her nothing but a pound a week and those opairs gets three, sometimes, but she gets all her board and Mrs P. buys her cloes – I'd have thought myself a regular queen, I can tell you, if Mrs Hunter or Mrs Ross'd bought me cloes like that when I first went out to service, and I was round about Erika's age, my first place.

'Remember those skirts? Didn't half pick up the muck . . . well. I'm going to ask her. 'Sides, it's as dull as ditchwater for a kid her age living here, she might get taken into that Youth Club, bit of jam for her, young company.'

'I wouldn't. Honest, Glad. We're all getting along so nice. I wouldn't.'

Gladys closed the argument by getting up and going down to the kitchen in search of Erika.

They walked to Saint James's through streets parked with pale-blue, scarlet or pink cars, like a mechanized age's version of the spring flowers. Such owners as had not started early for the coast were busy with hose and oil and rags, tending their treasures. Erika's thoughts were vaguely occupied by the new coat and hat she wore, Easter presents from Mrs Pearson.

Gladys marched them up to her usual seat, nice and near the front where they could see and hear all that was going on, and proceeded to instruct her charge; kneeling, clasping her hands and covering her closed eyes, praying.

'How what you mean, Glad, praying?' breathed Erika, looking sideways at her mentor under the coquettish hat with floating ribbons.

'Praying – good gracious, don't you know what that is? – here, where's the Ourfather –' Gladys grabbed at the prayer-book and pointed with a black-gloved finger. 'Read it. Then shut your eyes and say it, girl.'

Erika bent her head and tried to do what she was told. Her reading of English had so far been in the sheets of the *Daily Mirror*. Whether she felt any difference between the words therein, and those she was now studying, it is not possible to say. She was fully occupied with balancing her hat on top of her head and in admiring the church's festal white and gold, and the many flowers.

The service was interrupted occasionally, for her, by Gladys's hissing murmurs of explanation and comment. She pulled her down in awkward genuflexion when the cross was carried past in procession after the last hymn, and then they both knelt dutifully for a final private prayer.

'There!' beamed Gladys sitting up amidst the bustle and rustle of departure. 'Set us up for the week, won't it?'

'Who that boy?' whispered Erika.

The unexpectedness of it opened Gladys's mouth and kept her silent for quite two seconds.

Natural feminine interest in such a question from a young

girl struggled with her feeling that it should not have been asked here: 'Why was that boy carrying the cross?' yes; 'Who that boy?' no. Not in church.

'That? That's Barry Disher, very nice boy he is, good to his mum.' She shepherded her protegée out into the moving crowd. Erika could only have meant Barry Disher; he was more noticeable, somehow, than the other boys. 'She's got eight, just fancy, poor thing, only of course there's three grown up and married now,' Gladys went on.

Erika cautiously settled the hat, looking unseeingly at the ladies moving slowly ahead of her. Her face was beginning to fill out; a pear-shaped German face with white large cheeks and a narrow brow and small eyes blue as flax. That hat, thought Gladys, kind of comical on her. But looks all right, somehow. Wish she could get a bit of colour in her face.

'Enjoy it, did you? Like to come again?' she asked.

Erika silently nodded. Yes, she would like to come again. Gladys did not go on to ask why, and perhaps it was as well.

'Miss Barnes!' said Mr Geddes cordially, at the church door, 'nice to see you. How's your sister?'

'Getting on fine, thank you –' pause, and the usual steaming-up of glasses, as Gladys realized that she could neither remember his name nor find the rudeness to call him 'Vicar', 'walks about a bit sometimes now, well, I said, ever since Christmas Day, ever so kind she is. When I think what a state we was all in, we don't see much of him, I will say, but –'

'Don't go, I want a word with you,' Mr Geddes firmly motioned them towards a corner of the porch with one hand while he continued his farewells to his congregation with the other.

They waited for perhaps five minutes, Gladys looking with interest at the Easter clothes of the ladies, and Erika staring vaguely out into the April sunlight.

'Well,' said Mr Geddes at last, coming across to them, 'and who's this?' smiling at Erika.

'Miss Hartig, frorleen really, she's German, come over to help Mrs P. but more of a niece, in a way, had a very hard time,' lowering her voice and glancing significantly at the top of Erika's hat, 'grannie wasn't no more than a b-e-g-e-r-,' spelling tactfully, 'in an old-folk's home now, best place for them I said, now they're both old, but you could see it was from them, all in German, the rackman got a friend to make it out, so they're all right, and she's getting on nicely aren't you Erika?'

Erika looked up from under the hat brim, flat as a plate, and smiled. Her scarlet ribbons fluttered slightly in the spring wind.

'Well I'm pleased to see you both,' Mr Geddes said. 'Now what I wanted to ask you was this, Miss Barnes – would your Mrs Pearson like me to come and see her? I gathered – or rather Father Corliss gathered – from old Mr Fisher that she isn't at all well, and worried about herself, it seems. Is that so, do you think?'

'Oh I shouldn't if I was you, no I shouldn't,' Gladys burst out earnestly, 'very kind of you, means well, you can see that I said to Annie, but very against all that, well, I said, they have to ring them Christmas Day, no I shouldn't.'

Mr Geddes, recalling various shreds of information, gathered that Mrs Pearson was 'against the Church'.

'She wouldn't like it, then? I just wanted your opinion. I'm sorry. All the same, I shall come. When is the best time to see her?'

'Never goes out except in that car of a night with him, in her dressing gown all day but nice and tidy, ever so pretty really, all pink and gold and spotlessly clean, Erika and me do the shopping, don't we?'

'So I could find her at home most hours of the day, you think?'

'Sure to. Has her lunch on a tray, not a hearty eater, but smoke smoke all day I wonder she isn't afraid of that lung cancer and costs her pounds a week I reckon, shall I just mention it?'

'No. Please don't; I'll look in some afternoon and take my chance. Good-morning, Miss Barnes, good-morning, Miss Hartig, nice to have seen you and I hope you'll be coming regularly.'

'I'm not having no-one calling you Erika not without they know you better,' Gladys said, the instant they were out of earshot, 'Miss Hartig sounds more respectful – proper-like. That was the Vicar, the head of it all. But we don't want him round at ours, there'll only be trouble.'

She did not pursue this line of thought but at once began to enjoy their homeward walk.

She had forgotten – or it lingered only at the back of her mind – that Mrs Pearson did not know she had taken Erika to church. She thought, in a comfortable bustling way, oh well, where's the harm if it does come out, besides, all that going-on about the bells and that, it isn't right.

So, when she opened the front door; and they came into the hall of Rose Cottage just as Mrs Pearson was going past carrying a tray, she was unprepared for what happened.

23

'There you are, *schatz*,' Mrs Pearson exclaimed. 'Wherever have you been? I've been looking for you everywhere.'

She stood there in her pink dressing gown, holding the tray laden with cups and teapot, and smiling at them. There was no trace of annoyance in her tone.

'We've just been out –' Gladys was beginning, her voice loud with nervousness, as the implications of their excursion came suddenly upon her – when her words were cut across by Erika's slow voice:

'Gladys took me to the church.'

Instantly, Mrs Pearson's face became transformed. It was no longer her own, and Gladys stared in horror. A vile green light poured from her eyes, her mouth squared itself, and, fixing the fierce malice of those eyes on Erika, she squealed in a voice so high that the words seemed to keen past their ears like a narrowly tunnelled wind:

'No – no – keep away – never go there – you take her *there* and we tell him and he send her back and she die and – and – no – no – *NO*.'

The tray in her hands tilted dangerously, and Gladys, instinct startling her out of her terror, jerked forward and made to take it from her. But she clung to it with a passionate strength, as if her hands relished the contact with the wood, and for seconds, they almost struggled, in a hush that echoed with that other voice . . . Erika stood looking at them dully. Of course; sooner or later everyone quarrelled and fought. Suddenly, Mrs Pearson's hands relaxed their grasp, but gently; she almost settled the tray into Gladys's clasp, and said, in her usual voice but pitched higher:

'Sorry, dear — nearly dropped it. Take it, will you, I feel rather bad — dizzy — just sit down.' She groped her way to the stairs and sank on to them.

'Going to faint!' cried Gladys, putting the tray down anyhow on a table. Mrs Pearson, with closed eyes, moved her head weakly. 'Be all right in a minute.'

'Get the doctor,' and Gladys started for the front door.

'NO!' that other voice screamed thinly, and she stopped, gasping, and staring. Slowly, very slowly, the air in the hall, that reflected the sunlight in the street in a subdued yellow glow, seemed to unfreeze; to melt, and become the air of a spring day again. Gladys released her held breath; she was trembling. Mrs Pearson's eyes slowly opened, and fixed themselves on Erika.

'Been to church, dear? That's right — I don't like the bells, they go through my head, but it's nice to go. It's years since —' she began to get up, with feeble, groping movements, and Gladys, though still very frightened, hurried to help her. Erika stood motionless. A lowering sulkiness was creeping over her face.

Mrs Pearson began to mount the stairs, supported by Gladys's arm. Half-way up, she turned, and looked down at Erika.

'But I wouldn't go again, dear,' she said, in a higher voice, 'not if I were you . . . it upsets me, I don't know why,' pitifully, turning to look at Gladys, who held her firmly, though drawing now slightly away from her, 'it upsets me . . . and Mr Pearson won't like it. I might have to tell him, if you go again, dear. Because I must have my peace and my quiet. Just to enjoy my house . . . my house that can *touch* and *taste* and *smell* . . . I must have my house in quiet. So you remember, dear.'

She turned, leaning heavily on Gladys, and resumed her slow ascent. Then, as Gladys was opening the door of her room, she turned and whispered, staring at her, '*She* must have her way, you see. If she can't get it, she'll *set them on us*.'

When she was lying, shivering, under the eiderdown, Gladys remembered the tray of tea and said that she would go down and get it.

'Sure you be all right, Mrs Pearson?'

A nod, and a feeble smile. Lovely eyes, really, thought Gladys, bending over her, only . . . best go and see what young Erika's up to.

She bustled out. She felt, for all her bustling, shockingly weak, and her knees were not their usual sturdy selves and her heart kept on bang, bang, bang . . .

Erika was wandering about the kitchen, presumably occupied, though signs of occupation were absent.

'Well! There was an up and a downer for you,' said Gladys, sighing heavily. 'Never mind, she don't mean it – I expect. Eh?' glancing sharply.

Silence.

'Did you hear what I said?'

After a pause, that seemed insolent to Gladys, there was a slow movement of the head.

'Well, answer, can't you? Say something to a person. Sulks, now s-well's everythink else,' she added to herself. 'Oh come on, come on, talk about dwindlepin to wind the sun down . . . you'll be all right at that rate . . . let me do it for Gawd's sake,' snatching at the tea canister. Erika let go; Gladys missed it; and half a pound of tea showered on to the floor.

'Oh my *Gawd*!' shrieked Gladys and plumped down on the nearest chair and began to cry.

Erika looked at her in scared silence, then crossed over to her and, after a moment's wondering gaze at the blubbering face, put both arms around her and bestowed a small, inexperienced hug.

It was heartily returned, and Gladys fumbled for her clean, church-going handkerchief. She looked up and smiled waterily.

'Silly, aren't I? But that's fair put the wind up me. Ne' mind, all be the same in a hundred years, won't it? I don't expect she meant it – upset her, you going to church.'

'Mrs Pearson doesn't like I going to church . . .' said Erika, after an extended pause for thought.

'*Me* going to church, not *I* – you sound like that black what sweeps the road up the corner – don't want to sound like him, poor soul, do we? – no, she doesn't like it and now I sp'ose you can't go again . . . there's the kettle boiling now, it *would*, and the tea all over the floor . . . oh, my goodness, there's that tray waiting ready all this time in the hall! I'll forget my own name next. Here, we can take that up, and clear up the mess afterwards.'

Erika took the tray in; Gladys suddenly found herself unequal to facing Mrs Pearson.

Tiredly she climbed the stairs to their rooms, pausing for a moment on the landing.

It was not to collect her thoughts; she had never paused to do such a thing in her life. It was to put some cheerfulness on to her face and into her voice as she confronted Annie.

They had all been getting on so nicely. And now everything was upset. I can't never feel safe again, not after this, she thought.

'Glad – Glad! Oh do come on in, what *are* you up to, hanging about?' called Annie crossly. 'Something's up, isn't it?'

Slowly Gladys began to move across the landing, pulling off the brightly retrimmed little hat and gay scarf she had put on for church. Sunlight streamed in through their parlour window: the far-off slopes of the Heath were fresh and green. Parlour, thought Gladys, looks downright awful, full of old rubbish. Must be the sun, it always shows things up. There was not a thing fit to be seen.

Yet it was nice to be home. She didn't mind home being a lot of old rubbish.

She was unprepared for the presence of Mr Fisher seated in Annie's armchair, facing Annie's bed, with his feet very close together. He looked up mildly as she came in and said, 'Good-morning, Miss Gladys.'

''Morning . . . quite a surprise, seeing you, I thought *you'd* be off over the Heath, it being such a fine day,' she retorted; his presence was the last straw.

'Me and Mr Fisher's got the lunch on,' Annie said, 'I asked him to stay and have a bite with us, there's plenty.'

'There's crowds on the 'Eath this morning. I hates 'em,' said Mr Fisher, ignoring the reference to the invitation.

'Well what a thing to say! They've got a right to a bit of fresh air, same as what you 'ave,' said Gladys, scandalized moment-arily out of her perturbation by this frank statement.

'No doubt. No doubt. Just as you say, Miss Gladys. But the air they breathe isn't the same air as what I breathe, and I hates them. The litter, too. Ugly. Unharmonious – drives me mad.'

'Just as well to stay at home, then,' muttered Gladys. Faint sensations of comfort were creeping over her, caused by a savoury smell from the oven. 'You come and give me a 'and setting the cloth?'

'Glad –?' breathed Annie inquiringly as the old man obediently got up and shuffled towards the next room.

'A bit of trouble with Mrs P. – didn't like me taking young Erika,' whispered Gladys, with a warning glance at his back.

'I *told* you so!'

'Oh do give over, you're enough to give anyone the sick – it . . . wasn't nothing. She'll have forgotten by this evening . . . it's when she feels bad . . .' solemnly, with stilled face as memory swept over her, 'but my God, Annie, she *was* bad when we come in – not *like* herself – *not* herself – I was frightened, I don't mind telling you. Very frightened, I was, and you know that's not like me.'

Annie stared at her, awed.

'I'll tell you what –' Gladys burst out, but still in a subdued tone, after a pause, 'we're getting out.'

'*What?*'

'Out of 'ere. I don't like it. I've got the wind up and that's the truth. If she isn't mental . . . but . . . I don't know. I don't *know*. She's all right, been very nice to us, but I've got the wind up, and we're going.'

'Must be mental yourself!' Annie exclaimed, alarm giving her courage. 'Where'd we go?'

'We'll find somewhere. I'll write to Georgie . . .'

'Georgie! When we ain't heard a word for eighteen months –'

At this moment the appearance of Mr Fisher at the door, with mildly inquiring face, prevented further talk.

The Vicarage party were at tea on the afternoon of Easter Monday, in the cavernous drawing-room that Mrs Geddes had restored to use. They had decided against a fire, but the light pouring in through the tall windows came from a sky now clouded over, and had the cool, silvery quality of snowdrops. The cat had just strolled in, to a murmur of 'Well, I'm bothered' from Mrs Geddes.

The cat halted, purring, with its tail waving and lifted head, looking at her. Gerald absently took the milk jug and was pouring milk into his saucer, from which he had removed the cup, when Mrs Geddes's expression recalled him.

'I'm awfully sorry.' He began to laugh. 'I wasn't thinking – I do beg your pardon.'

'It's quite all right. But we really must not encourage it.'

'I'm afraid it is encouraged.' The cat had jumped on to his knees and was preparing itself for sleep.

'I know. But we mustn't encourage it *further*.'

The telephone bell rang in the Vicar's study.

When he returned, after some time, he looked rather concerned.

'Miss Barnes,' he said to Gerald, 'Mrs Pearson has been behaving oddly, very strangely indeed, and she's frightened. She wants me to go and see her this evening.'

'Mrs Pearson does?'

'No – no – Miss Barnes.' He took out his cigarette case.

'Shall you go?'

'Of course. But I'm not looking forward to it . . . if I hadn't such a mistrust of the psychiatric brotherhood I'd try and pass the whole thing on to one of them.'

'I'm inclined to agree with you – but don't you give them credit for anything?' asked Gerald.

'Arrogance,' said Mr Geddes tartly. 'Plenty of credit for that. They're the new Sanhedrin. You show me a wardful of happy, or even resigned and contented, people allegedly cured by psychiatrists and – I'll give credit where it's due. To Almighty God.'

Gerald laughed, gently kneading the dozing cat's ears.

'It's lack of time that's the trouble,' Mr Geddes went on. 'Each patient really needs the entire interest of one person concentrated entirely on him or herself. It just can't be done. It's cruel to pretend it can. They find themselves clinically pigeon-holed when they need to be loved . . . a perfect demonstration of "I asked for bread, and ye gave me a stone".'

'I know one chap – a psychiatrist – quite well, who's dedicated, highly-trained, skilled, charitably detached,' Gerald said musingly, 'but he has absolutely no *confidence* in anything, not even in psychiatry. If it were not a cheap expression I'd say – bloodless.'

'Say it, and blow the cheapness. Well, I'll get along there after Evensong. It will all depend on how she seems. If I think it is only nervous, I'll try recommending a doctor. Saunders is supposed to like nerve cases; I could try him.'

'Well, I shall be *most* interested to hear how it goes,' murmured Gerald – with perhaps too broad a shade of the Arsenal supporter in his voice for Mr Geddes snapped, 'I dare say . . . you can make the second visit,' as he went out of the room.

The weather was so dull that twilight seemed to have fallen earlier than was natural at this time of the year; clouds were trailing rain-banners over the roofs, in a sky lividly blue above the orange glare of the street lamps. The usual cars were darting restlessly about on their short evening journeys; discarded sweet-papers swirled in the dusty wind at the corners. Mr Geddes walked briskly along the empty pavement, away from well-lit streets, towards the darker districts.

His thoughts were not cheerful. They had ceased to be that since the death of his wife, and the errand he was on added its own shade. There might well be what his simpler parishioners called 'words', and it was never pleasant to know, without any doubt, that he was unwelcome. But the words *duty is duty and must be done* were there to be hung on to: if they did nothing else, they provided an anchor, and they saw to it that something got accomplished, every now and then, in this world.

He had some difficulty in again finding Rose Cottage, for his last visit had been long ago; wandering for nearly ten minutes up and down slight slopes that had once swelled gently beneath a carpet of turf and celandines; past boarded, ruinous houses faintly echoing to the almost inaudible rushing of a stream running below their foundations where willows had once looked at their reflection in the water and moorhens paddled and dived . . . ah (these were not the thoughts of Mr Geddes). Rose Walk – here we are.

And surely, yes, it was Mr Fisher approaching, shuffling towards him with his unmistakable gait along the dim, uneven pavement; the only person in sight.

'Hullo, Mr Fisher!' exclaimed the Vicar cheerfully. 'Off for your walk?'

Mr Fisher's reception of this was not reassuring. He paused some six or seven paces away, and, surveying Mr Geddes in silence for a moment, said, shaking his head:

'I'm sorry to see *you* 'ere, I am that.' His voice seemed fainter than ever and his appearance more frail.

'Yes, I'm going to call on your landlady, I expect you guessed.'

'I had. Yes, I 'ad guessed as much, and I says again I'm sorry to see you. An educated man – now don't you know better? It'll only mean trouble.'

'I can't help that, Mr Fisher. She needs help – you said yourself that she looks like a lost soul – and I want to help her.'

'There's been trouble since I larce saw you. Miss Gladys was

207

the cause. (The ladies mocely are, I finds.) Ups and takes young Erika to your church and Mrs Pearson was ever so upset, she threatened us.'

'Threatened you? How?'

'Sh'sh.' Mr Fisher glanced over his shoulder, then let his eyes wander over the silent, ruined façades stretching into the twilight. 'Don't speak so loud . . . the rackman. May be here any minute.'

'Oh nonsense – you mustn't let a little trouble get you down, you know. Tenants can get protection now, it isn't like it was a few years ago.'

'Not the kind of tenants what we are,' Mr Fisher retorted, with one of those thrusts based on unanswerable fact which occasionally struck out from his wandering talk, 'not when 'e's got all the money and don't care for the law . . . where'd we go? Into some 'Ome, that's where we'd go . . . me the age I am, and Miss Annie near bedridden and Miss Gladys – very nervous she is. Talks very fine and bold but very nervy. Where'd we go? No, best lie low and keep quiet; you're an educated man, you can understand. We like our 'omes and our bit o' things and our independence, where'd we go?'

'Yes. Yes, I can see it's all very difficult, but you mustn't be so – so down about it, Mr Fisher.'

'I ain't all that down. But I looks the facts in their face. Others don't. That's all.' His long sheeplike mask stared, with mild but immovable obstinacy.

'Yes. Well, I must get on . . . don't worry, I'll manage it, there won't be any trouble. Good-night.'

He nodded and smiled and walked quickly on. He felt that Mr Fisher was standing there, staring after him helplessly, but he ignored the fact. They could have gone on talking round the subject for an hour.

He stood on the steps of Rose Cottage, with his hand on the knob of the ancient pull-bell wondering which of the two was Mrs Pearson's house; he had not thought to ask the old man.

He glanced upwards, his attention drawn to something pale protruding from the wall above his head which he had not noticed on his previous visit; it was the mask of the man-goat; the thick lips and broad nose and stiff curls below the twin horns seemed to be played over by a peculiarly derisive smile.

Rather unpleasant, thought Mr Geddes, and rang the bell. I'd have that taken away.

A rich, melancholy jangling, with something that was not mechanical in its quality, echoed inside the house. He stood patiently, his eyes fixed on the block of Council flats across the railway gap, waiting. The eyes of the Pan, once god of stream and turf and celandines, stared out above him, with the smile that mocked at something.

The door opened, and there was the young German girl. She stared, with open mouth and startled eyes.

24

'Good-evening, Miss Hartig. Can I see Mrs Pearson, please?'

She hesitated, twisting her hands slowly together.

'I don't know . . .' she whispered at last. 'She . . . she not like me go . . . to dir church.'

'I'm sorry to hear that. Perhaps I can talk to her and make her feel differently. Is she in?'

Erika moved her head uneasily from side to side.

'Well, will you tell her I'm here, please? I've come quite a long way to see her,' smiling.

'I go . . . I go and ask Gladys . . .' she muttered, turning away but he broke in – 'No, we don't need Miss Barnes, just tell Mrs Pearson I would like to see her.'

How the child stared! Mr Geddes, putting manners aside, stepped quickly into the hall, and shut the door.

'Now.' He turned to her, while she looked, on this new development, as if she were about to run away. 'Go and tell her, please.'

A shake of the head. 'I tell her, and she shout, and tell me I away must go.'

'Nonsense,' Mr Geddes said, 'just go and *tell* her, like a good girl' – here he began to speak slowly in his rusty German – 'and I'll wait here.' He smiled again.

Erika was reassured by the words of her own tongue; the

well-known sounds, coming from this man associated with the church, where she had been blessed by the sight of such a boy as Barry Disher, conspired with these thoughts to soothe her fears.

She looked at him less fearfully, and he made a brisk movement. 'Off you go,' he said.

Mrs Pearson lay reading in the pink light of her bedside lamp. Suddenly, she lifted her eyes, in an unseeing stare.

'Erika?' she called, half raising herself, '*schatz*?' There was no answer. In the hall, Erika turned to look at Mr Geddes with widened eyes.

'Erika? Who are you talking to? Who's there?' Mrs Pearson called, her voice sounding faintly behind her door.

'I come,' Erika called, 'now, I come, Mrs Pearson.' Ignoring Mr Geddes, she made some attempt at speed up the stairs.

'That's someone at the door. Who is it down there? You know Mr Pearson doesn't like visitors, *schatz*. Who is it?' Mrs Pearson demanded, as she came into the room.

The faint voice, commonplace in its lower-middle-class timbre, floated down to Mr Geddes, reassuring him. Here was no deep-toned Witch of Endor or shrill psychopath.

'Mrs Pearson? It's the Vicar – Mr Geddes. May I come up?' he called at length. He thought that the owner of that voice would find it hard to tell anyone that they could not see her. He went quickly up the stairs.

The pinkness and plumpness of the bed could have hinted at voluptuousness, and offended his modesty. But one sight of the face on the pillow banished every such suggestion; it was impossible for any man to look at that face, and its large eyes of pansy blue, and not want to protect and help its owner. A girl's face, a good girl, he thought . . . but how shockingly ill.

'Mrs Pearson?' he said gently. 'I'm afraid you aren't at all well. It's good of you to see me.'

She made a movement with one hand towards a low chair beside the bed, and he sat down.

'It's nice of you to come . . . I expect you get rather fed up, visiting round to a lot of strangers, don't you?' A delightful smile, aged about thirteen, just looked out, and Mr Geddes was surprised into a laugh.

'You're quite right − I do − but it's part of my work, you know; you and . . .' he glanced at Erika, who had wandered up to the bed and was standing staring at them . . . 'your household are part of my family − the Church's family, and we have to keep in touch with you all.'

'*Schatz*, give the Vicar a cigarette,' said Mrs Pearson and then shook out one for herself, while Erika found, and extended to him, the gold case that was never used; there followed the small ceremony of lighting up. But he wished that she had not immediately begun to cough. The rose-petal quality of her looks was instantly shattered; it was, in any case, poised on the extreme edge between prettiness and its ghost.

'Oh, I'm a bad one −' she gasped, laughing, when the paroxysm had passed. 'I smoke all day and all night too, don't I, Erika? I thought . . .' the great eyes wheeled sweetly on to his face . . . 'you'd come to scold me about her not going to church again, p'raps?'

'Naturally, I'd be very pleased if she came regularly.'

'Oh, I know. I know one should . . . go . . . regularly.' She was quiet, for an odd little moment, and he thought that she was still getting her breath back from coughing. 'And . . . only you see Gladys Barnes took her along and I didn't know . . . and . . . they ought to have asked my permission. Yes, that's it. They ought to have asked *my permission*,' she ended, on a higher note, turning her eyes away. How their colour changed in the light! They were certainly unusually beautiful. 'But I don't mind.

She can go, if she likes,' and she held out her hand to Erika, 'do you like to go, *schatz*?'

'I think *you* did not lak, Mrs Pearson,' Erika said, looking straight out from under lumpy white brows.

'Me!' Mrs Pearson turned her head away quickly and restlessly. 'I don't mind . . . it's only the bells I mind. They go through my head somehow and . . . I just like to be very quiet, you see,' she confided, turning to him again and fixing her eyes pleadingly on his face, 'because I'm not . . . well.'

'What is your trouble?' he asked and, behind the bluntness of the question, every curious story and hint that had been repeated to him, and every fear that had been expressed by the other people in the house, seemed to pass in warning procession. The sweetness, the gentleness seemed real; he would have been prepared to swear they were – but there was *something else as well*. He could feel it, unseen, in the silent, pink-lit room. The extraordinary sentence suddenly sprang to his mind: *This room is a battlefield.*

'Oh . . . nerves.' Mrs Pearson smiled. 'My nerves are dreadful – have been for some years. I can't go out or lead a . . . lead a . . . a normal life,' she whispered, and away went her head again; and he saw a tear run down from one lucid eye.

'And you're having treatment, I suppose,' he pursued. Let's find out if anything's being done for her medically, first, he thought, before we take any peculiar plunges.

'Oh no. My husband agrees with me – we both can't bear doctors – all I need is peace and quiet. Peace and quiet, that's all . . . I . . . I am getting better. Aren't I, Erika *schatz*, aren't I getting better?' Erika still stared, louringly, in silence. 'Later on I'll go out – see the lights – *touch the pavements with my feet* – to the pictures and . . . and everything . . . just like I used to.'

213

He thought it better, at this moment, to look away. What an extraordinary phrase. It would not leave his inward ear. *Touch the pavements* . . . she was wiping her eyes with a fragile handkerchief now, scented by one of the too-sweet fragrances of the shops.

'Well I'm glad to hear that, anyway . . . Tell me about yourself, now. We like to know our people . . . have you any family?'

'Oh yes. A daughter. Just the one girl. She's away from home, in a job at Hampstead. She's a funny girl – she doesn't seem to want to get married. She's mad . . . mad on animals. That's what she's there for really, to help this lady with her four little dogs. Sweet little things they are. So lively. I used to see them when we were all at the seaside (that was where we met this lady). She's very wealthy, a widow. It's a great big house, Peggy says, more like a little palace. Old-fashioned but very *stately*. She's a lovely girl to look at, my Peggy. Dark, like her father. "She walks in beauty, like the night",' Mrs Pearson ended in a murmur. 'That's exactly Peggy.'

Mr Geddes stared for an instant; he had expected to hear some unusual things, but not Byron.

'It was under a picture in some magazine . . .' Mrs Pearson added in explanation, 'I saw it and I thought: "That's Peggy".' Her eyes came round to him again. 'Now if you could get *her* to go to church . . . she frightens me sometimes, she's so obstinate . . . (Erika, *schatz*, go and get me my tea – you'll have some, won't you, Mr Geddes? – no? Then you don't mind if I do, do you?) I can't live without my tea, can I, *schatz*?'

'Does she like her job?' Mr Geddes inquired; keep the simplest kind of chat going, he thought, just so that I get a foot in . . . she knows my name . . . perhaps Gladys or Mr Fisher told her.

'Oh I suppose so . . . she doesn't *seem* to like anything much, except dogs and the country and horses . . . she's horse-crazy.'

Mrs Pearson brooded for a moment, her face all sadness. 'She was at this riding-school in Sussex . . . I'm sure something went badly wrong there for her.' She paused again. 'A man,' she said, with a soft rueful smile. 'Girls . . . you know what they are.'

In fact, beyond a few bracing jokes, Mr Geddes didn't know; the girls in his set having jumped straight from the awkwardness of an unattached 'spooniness' – it was the precise word – into life-long happy wifehood.

'Oh dear,' he said ineptly, 'I'm sorry to hear that.'

'You can't stop them. She must just go her own way. She has to learn, and she's going to learn.' Mrs Pearson's voice trailed off, and she took another cigarette. He lit it for her, glad to let the subject slide away.

'I wish –' he began deliberately, when she was lying back on the pillows again, 'you *would* see a doctor. If I may say so, you do look . . . not at all strong. They do marvellous things for nervous cases now – (I'm not speaking of psychotherapy, only of medicine). Surely your husband . . .'

He had not wanted to introduce this name. The man's reputation was as bad as it could be. Yet, so far, according to Gladys Barnes, no actual harm had been done to his tenants, and the woman looked cherished as some sultana in a harem.

She shook her head, smiling. 'Tom would never have it, Mr Geddes. He doesn't trust them.'

'But surely –'

'He got through so many illnesses when he was a little boy, in Tashkent, he thinks you can cure anything, now, with hot whisky and water. I could tell you some stories –!' Her eyes were laughing, challenging him.

'Tashkent? But that's down near Samarkand – right down near the Pamirs – don't tell me you were born there, Mrs Pearson?'

'Me? Good lord, no, I was born just round the corner, in Margrave Road.'

'Your husband, then –?'

'Oh yes, he was born in Tashkent – "in the sloms of Tashkent", as he always says; his mother was a Scottish lady, governess to a Russian family, and she married an Armenian out there.'

'Quite a romance,' said Mr Geddes, not absolutely certain that he believed in the romance.

'It's romantic all right . . . I s'pose so. But I often think to myself – it's the quiet, happy things that are the really romantic ones, not the queer foreign ones . . . I've had enough of them.'

'Yes . . . well . . . perhaps, yes.' Mrs Pearson was undoubtedly a character, thought Mr Geddes. Unusual. And quite unlike what he had expected.

'Of course, I didn't mean that about getting Peggy to go to church. She never would . . . you . . . you wouldn't ask her or ever mention it, would you? She'd be so furious – and with me, too.'

'If ever I try, I will choose my time carefully,' he promised.

'I shouldn't like you to see my Peggy in a temper.'

'An alarming young lady.' Mr Geddes smiled stiffly.

'Yes, she is. That's just what she is.' Mrs Pearson spoke earnestly, raising herself on her elbow. 'She's like her grandmother, my husband's mother. She was like iron. A *terrible* old lady, I've sometimes thought. Very quiet, never raised her voice to you. But you could feel it – like iron. I was just nineteen. I can tell you, I nearly turned and ran, when I saw her.' A faint laugh. 'But there was Tom' – she actually breathed a soft, amorous sigh – 'oh, my Tom. I thought I'd risk it.'

'You were very young,' Mr Geddes said, with an effect of indulgence for some half-forgotten folly. He would have strongly disliked such a conversation; hints about the men in a girl's life, sighing about a husband (really!) and so forth – had it been outlined in advance. But in Mrs Pearson, vulgarity simply did not exist. It was changed, in some way, into something merely amusing, pleasing. He found his lips smiling.

'Where did you meet your husband?' he pursued. 'In Tashkent? Were you working out there?'

'Me?' Again the innocent suburban cry. 'No – I was on holiday. A whole gang of us was on holiday, just after the war. Government temps, we were – under twenty, all of us – me and Vera Coe and Iris Sutter and Linda – Linda – I forget her name (fancy my forgetting Linda's name!) and Elaine Ward and Lily Bott – six of us. All in this party. In Venice, for two weeks.'

'In Venice!' exclaimed Mr Geddes. 'How . . . surprising.'

Venice seemed a million miles away from this room. But even farther away, in some other world, were the young faces of Vera, Lily, Iris, Linda, Elaine and Mrs Pearson in Venice, on holiday, just after the war. They were all laughing; their laughter was reflected now, like the ghost of old sunlight, on Mrs Pearson's haggard face.

She was sitting up to take the tea-tray, which Erika carried into the room.

'Sure you won't change your mind?' she babbled, smiling, drawing the folds of her robe closer about her neck, 'then if you'll excuse me . . .' She drank thirstily. There were some superior-looking cakes on the tray, and Mrs Pearson pointed.

'Excuse me pointing . . . Gladys made those . . . now I know you'll try one.'

'I mak dem,' interrupted Erika gloomily.

'Did you, *schatz*?' Mrs Pearson cried. 'Well, you *are* getting on, aren't you?'

'Dey was for a zurprise,' explained Erika, with ever-deepening *Götterdämmerung*.

'Surprise, were they? and I thought Gladys made them, well, I *am* sorry. They're lovely, dear. Delicious.'

Mr Geddes thought he had better take one, to assist in healing Erika's pride, and did so.

'Delicious,' he pronounced in turn.

'Dey better dan Glad's,' pronounced Erika, sitting down by the fire with the plate, and the *sturm-und-drang* beginning to lighten.

'. . . there were all these boys, you see,' Mrs Pearson was explaining, 'after us girls. We were so blonde – all blondes (those that weren't to begin with soon were, when they saw how the Eye-ties liked blondes), and we used to go and walk round those gorgeous shops in that big square at night. Under the arcades. (Things were just getting back into the shops in those days, you know, just after the war.) Tom was with them. He was the quiet one. They used to walk round behind us, calling remarks. But he always used to look at me, and – oh, I *did* like him. Lovely dark eyes, he had (still has, for that matter). All on his own in Venice, in one room, but he'd got one or two irons in the fire – only twenty-one, but started out on his own already.'

She paused, with her cup suspended, looking down. When she spoke again, her babble had been replaced by a more deliberate speech.

'Some people will tell you,' she said, stirring her tea, 'that Tom's hard. Well, you have to be, to get on in this world, and a hard woman brought him up. All I know is, he's never been hard to me. Never. He's the best husband in the world.'

She looked defiantly and sadly at Mr Geddes; as if awaiting some verdict.

'It's always good to hear a wife say that,' he said gently, at last, 'and now, do you know, I'm afraid I must be going.' He got up from his chair. 'I've got a lot to do this evening when I get home.'

'Yes, I expect you're awfully busy . . . it was kind of you to come. Oh, I have enjoyed our chat about old times.'

'I hope you'll let me come again soon, or my curate, and hear some more about that holiday in Venice.' He took her hot, sweet-scented fingers for a second in his. It was like touching damp petals.

'Erika, dear, you take the gentleman downstairs . . . good-bye, then . . . *au revoir*!'

He left her lying on the pillows, smiling, moving her fingers towards him with a fluttering childish movement, and shut the door.

When Erika returned, after seeing him out and performing one or two small tasks in the kitchen, she did not see Mrs Pearson for a moment. The bedside lamp was out, and the room in shadow. A lump, smooth and curved, lay under the eiderdown. Erika paused in the doorway, staring.

'You sleep, Mrs Pairson?'

'Gone,' keened a high voice she had heard before, after a silence, 'and gl –' There followed some tentative squeaking sounds, more animal-like than anything else; exploratory, ending in a tearing-silk noise of disgust. 'Can't! Can't! . . . stopped . . . not come again . . . never . . .' – then, in a rush of words – '*put my feet on the pavement like* –'

The words broke off. Erika cautiously began to pick up the tray with the cakes, groping forward in the shadows and the now heatless glare cast by the electric fire.

'Keep him away!' burst out a thin, minute squeak. 'Keep him away!' Glancing incuriously towards the bed, she saw two small steady lights, of a reddish-brown colour and very bright, shining out from the darkness. The hump outlined against the pale wall stirred.

Balancing the tray, Erika shut the door behind her with her foot, and went downstairs: she was afraid only of hunger and cold and homelessness, nothing else. If Mrs Pearson had had one of her 'bad turns', as Gladys called them, it was sad, when the room had been so warm and there had been laughing. But she had the cakes, and she would take them away and eat them in the kitchen.

25

The little street was deserted. Mr Geddes had nearly reached the corner, and was about to turn into the wider one, when he saw a man coming down towards him through the dim lamplight, a short stout figure in a dark overcoat. When they drew level he received such a threatening look from the eyes under the brim of the dark hat that he was horribly startled.

His muscles drew themselves together in a kind of readiness, and he walked on, listening, waiting . . .

The expected thing happened. The footsteps stopped.

'Here . . . you . . .' called a voice behind him, 'where've you been? You been to my house, worrying Mrs Pearson?'

Mr Geddes turned. The man was almost on top of him! He must move like a cat . . .

'I've been to see her, yes. I went to try and help her,' he said, raising his voice, speaking firmly, looking full into the dark melancholy eyes. 'I'm a priest, and that's my work in the world.'

'We don't want your help. Keep out.' A clenched fist began to swing at his side, as if driven by the force of his anger. 'Or I'll teach you.'

'If you love her you'll want –' Mr Geddes was beginning, when the man spat at him.

It struck his coat, and with it there came into him the controlled impersonal rage which had been useful forty years ago, when he boxed at Cambridge. The spring followed, but he stepped lightly sideways, and, as Pearson lunged at him, landed an uppercut to the left jaw; not hard, not vicious, just enough to stop him. The force of his own movement carried Pearson beyond the blow, and he lost his balance and fell into the gutter. His hat fell off, into some rubbish.

'Sorry,' Mr Geddes said, 'had to stop you somehow,' and held out his hand.

The evening's most surprising event then occurred; Pearson let himself be helped up. He stood silent, while Mr Geddes brushed him down; then gave him his hat, and turned his attention and a handkerchief to the spittle on his coat. All this was done in silence.

At length he turned to his motionless assailant.

'I'm not going to keep away,' he said firmly. 'You both need help.'

'Keep away. Leave us alone. I can take care of her,' Pearson repeated, but without spirit.

'Not alone, Mr Pearson. You must have help. She would never have got into this state if you'd been able to take care of her alone. She says you won't let her see a doctor . . .'

'She doesn't want a doctor.'

'But she may need one.'

Pearson turned away, repeating in a voice of hollow bravado – 'Go away. We don't want you. Leave us alone.' He walked slowly on towards Lily Cottage.

'I'm going to help you,' Mr Geddes called after him. 'I shall come again. I . . . I warn you.' The wind seemed to blow his words away.

Shaken, ashamed, and also exultant, he retained enough consciousness of the outside world, during the walk home, to pause at the busier crossings.

'Dear! You looked downright battered,' his mother exclaimed, coming into the hall at the sound of his key in the lock, '. . . coffee or chocolate?'

'Chocolate, please. Yes, I've been in a punch-up – I think that's what they call it nowadays.'

Mrs Geddes neither asked whether he was all right or any other questions, but did slightly show some disturbance in her feelings by muttering, as she turned to the kitchen, 'He's been in a punch-up,' to Gerald, who came loping down the stairs at that moment with some question about Saint Gregory of Nizam.

'I say! Are you all right? I say,' as Mrs Geddes disappeared through a door, 'are you all right, sir?' Saint Gregory of Nizam was forgotten.

'Oh yes. It wasn't much – a man spat at me and I hit him.' Mr Geddes smiled. 'Quite a neat uppercut, in fact, knocked him down.'

'Good for you!' cried Gerald, all admiration. 'Really – I mean, at your age, that was pretty good . . . (I beg your pardon). How did he take it?'

'Oh – meekly. I was relieved, I don't mind telling you, I thought a knife would be the next thing. No, it wasn't much, really. He soon cooled down – poor brute.'

'You'd better let me come with you the next time you go out at night – I'll take my alpenstock.' Gerald's eyes were sparkling.

'Of course not, don't be absurd – I can take care of myself – besides, trotting round with a bodyguard – and by the way, Gerald, you will keep this absolutely to yourself, please. It isn't to go an inch further.'

'Yes of course – have you any idea who it was?'

'I know who it was. Mrs Pearson's husband.'

'The rackman, as Miss Barnes calls him?'

'Yes.'

He felt that his curate's next remark was going to be, 'I say, how exciting,' and though he made allowances for youth, and even for his own satisfaction over that neat uppercut, he did not intend the situation to become a kind of dramatic comic-strip.

'I beg your pardon,' Gerald said. 'I just wanted to say I'm . . . so glad you're all right . . . did you manage to see her first?'

'I did. We had a long chat and I'm going again – or you can.'

'I'd like to,' Gerald assured him at once. 'Do you think he'll go for me with the knife?'

'Of course not. (I said I *expected* a knife, not *saw* one – and that was only at first.) He's a cowardly creature, I should think – and miserable, certainly. Very unhappy. Worried about her, I expect – she seems fond of him anyway. She's certainly very ill. Written all over her.'

His mother came in at this point. 'Gerald, supper is on the table. Will you very kindly go and see Cat doesn't get it? I'll be there in a minute . . . dear, here's yours.' It was on a tray; the events of the last hour conspired to make it seem even more appetizing and beautifully arranged than usual.

'Really, Mother . . . what a blessing you are.' Mr Geddes's voice trailed off in a grateful mutter.

She smiled, and went out of the room.

He sat beside the fire in his study, looking into the flames for a long moment.

What he remembered most vividly out of the events of the evening were not the spittle on his coat, nor the cool timing of the uppercut, nor the feel of his knuckles against Pearson's flabby cheek, nor the lost girl looking out of Mrs Pearson's face; what continued to pursue a mysterious, twisting dance in and out of his tired mind was a sentence.

Put my feet down on the pavement. Not *walk*, as everybody else said. *Put my feet down on the pavement.* As a foreigner speaks; as a newcomer to . . . some unfamiliar country.

The lives led by the rich fascinated Mrs Lysaght.

She herself enjoyed the sort of income that is called *comfortable*, in that she need not think once about taking a taxi or hiring a car. But to winter in Bermuda, to spend four or five hundred guineas on a brooch, to 'run' a big car and a chauffeur – the size of the income implied in such luxurious expenditure was irresistibly interesting to her.

She happened to be in the High Street one bright afternoon, and as she was coming out of Boots', she met an old acquaintance.

They were exchanging news as they left the shop when her companion's eye was caught by an ancient Rolls, temporarily halted just opposite in the flow of traffic.

'There's Mrs Corbett – J. H. Corbett's widow – the aircraft designer, you know – enormously rich – I met her once at a party – what a hat – she must be nearly eighty. I *beg* your pardon' – cannoning off the hips of a ripe, trousered intellectual who was manoeuvring a laden pram. 'Do look, Helen. And *four* dogs . . . I do think . . .'

Mrs Lysaght looked, and felt mingled emotions; envy at the enormous car and the air of being in some way Somebody, which surrounded Mrs Corbett; curiosity as to how she might spend her days; satisfaction at the unbecoming lines of the twenty-guinea hat.

Having parted from her acquaintance, she went for a stroll, and was making her way homewards, about four o'clock, with thoughts of Transcendence and Immanence mingled with those of tea in her mind. These subjects, and others equally incongruous, frequently shared shelter there.

Barking, growling, and cries of alarm fell upon her ear as she emerged from a path leading up to the Spaniards Walk, and there, almost on top of her, was the stout mink-clad shape of Mrs Corbett, the Rolls parked near by, the chauffeur hastily clambering out of it, and the four little dogs barking frenziedly, and snarling and swirling about their mistress.

The aggressor was an unusually large Alsatian, and in the midst of the agitated group, shouting and waving her arms, was its owner, the very kind of owner that every other dog-owner dreads being involved with; a huge war-like woman belonging to the newly affluent class, whose stony eye challenged every object, living or inanimate, which it encountered.

'That's right, Billy, you go for them, nasty little brutes, ought to be ashamed of yourself, taking up half the pavement —'

'Cee! *Cee!* Come here *at once* . . . Dee! Frobisher — can't you do something — oh dear . . . oh *dear* . . . *Bee* . . . come here . . . oh dear, now it's all round my leg . . . *Frobisher* . . .'

'If you could just grasp his neck, madam . . . Dee! Sir! Down, you ugly beast, sit!' to the Alsatian.

Frobisher was keeping well outside the combat area.

'I'll sue you, setting your dirty little beasts on my dog, think you own the place, I s'pose . . . bloody dogs all over the pavement . . .'

'*Bee! Oh*,' as the Alsatian sank its teeth in Bee's neck, 'oh, oh my boy — oh help —'

Mrs Lysaght had a recurring fantasy of herself interfering in a dog-fight. Unhesitatingly, though with suddenly accelerated heart-beats, she walked into the struggling, hovering, swaying shouting group, gripped the Alsatian by its collar, and began to pull.

'You leave my dog alone,' bellowed the huge woman, touched in the agonizingly tender spot of possession, 'leave him alone. My husband'll *do* you, he will —'

The Alsatian took no notice of Mrs Lysaght's action, but A. unhesitatingly flew at her and bit her in the leg. She shrieked; the pain was shockingly keen, and the surging, furry sensation of the great dog pushing and struggling under her hands was frightening. But it was also exhilarating.

She hung on. She could see blood streaming down her stocking, and she set her teeth – a thing she had always read about and wanted to do. I set my teeth, she thought exultantly, just set my teeth and hung on. I didn't give in . . . I'll master you, I thought . . .

But when Cee, perhaps maddened like a shark by the sight of blood, launched himself at her and bit her other leg she shrieked again, and dropped the Alsatian – which flew at Mrs Corbett, who screamed piercingly, as well she might. Mrs Lysaght struck at the dog's behind with her bag. Frobisher, surrounded by shrieking women, snarling dogs, and gore – for the pavement was now scattered with dark drops – looked distractedly over everybody's head in search of men.

'Oh – *oh*,' shrieked Mrs Corbett, also swiping wildly at the Alsatian with her bag, 'call him off – oh call him off . . . how can you . . . help . . .'

Her mink coat had so far protected her. The huge woman was yelling, 'Serve you right, your dogs started it,' and Mrs Lysaght, bleeding copiously now, but with re-set teeth, had her bag in both hands and was banging it up and down with all her force on the Alsatian's rump. In for a penny, thought Mrs Lysaght, weirdly enjoying herself, in for a pound.

At this point three young men ran up. They were not civilians, they were sailors, and therefore, instead of standing about and watching to see what would happen, one of them gripped the Alsatian by its muzzle and another took it by the throat, while the third with a series of swift light kicks that suggested practice on the football field, scattered, A., Bee, Cee and Dee, like the leaves of autumn. Their outraged yelps brought a shriek of a different quality from Mrs Corbett.

'Oh – oh – my boys – my poor boys,' while Frobisher, to whom the newcomers looked like avenging angels, seized her and hustled her towards the car. Mrs Lysaght, still belabouring, was left to face the huge woman.

'Bits of boys, now,' screamed the huge woman, 'you leave my dog alone or I'll –'

'Belt up, ma, the Navy's here,' said one, without a smile, almost absently, and caught at Mrs Lysaght's wrist and gripped it, 'here, lay off – he's all right now – get out, you,' with another lifting kick, not hard, that checked A. in mid-spring, 'let's break up this here little party, shall we.'

The Alsatian had a wound in the neck, inflicted by Dee, which was now attracting his attention; he had expended some energy, and he was prepared to calm down. His growls rumbled off into silence. The huge woman continued to shout threats. Mrs Lysaght suddenly felt sick. Mrs Corbett was exclaiming:

'Oh do come into the car – I'm afraid you're dreadfully bitten – so brave of you – really, I don't know *what* I should have . . . I can't thank you enough . . . *do* come in, *all* of you, please.' Mrs Lysaght hurried towards the car.

They left the huge woman explaining her wrongs to a small crowd of mildly interested strollers, and Frobisher drove away, the young sailors having grinningly but politely declined a lift.

Mrs Corbett, after a struggle with maternal feeling, told Frobisher to drive to New End Hospital rather than to the nearest vet's.

'So wonderfully brave of you – *really* the bravest thing I've ever seen – I'm afraid you must be in shocking pain . . .'

'Oh, it was nothing, really. We always had dogs at home . . . I'm used to them . . .'

'We'll go straight to the Casualty Department . . . just like Emergency-Ward Ten, isn't it? I am afraid you must be in great pain.'

'I do begin to feel it now, yes.'

'Here we are,' as the car slid to a stop. 'I'll come in with you . . .'

'Oh please don't trouble . . .'

'But of course I will . . . and Frobisher will help you to get out. No, boys, no more walkies, bad little boys to fight that great big Alsatie, but brave little boys too . . . come along . . .' to Mrs Lysaght.

It was early evening when they at last got away, Mrs Lysaght walking stiffly on her disinfected and bandaged legs and Mrs Corbett worried about the bite in sulky Cee's neck.

She insisted that Helen – it had been Mrs Lysaght's suggestion that Christian names should be used between them – must come back with her for a drink, 'Unless you're dying to get back to your own nest at once,' she added.

'Oh no, I should love it . . . a drink is just what I need.'

Sitting back in one of Mrs Corbett's great brocade-covered chairs, with a strong pink gin in her hand, Mrs Lysaght felt that the expenditure of energy in pain and fright had been worth it. The luxury here was of just the old-fashioned, comfortable kind that she liked; and there were even glimpses of *servants*; all very old, of course, and in a kind of shirt-and-jacket-white-apron-overall contemporary uniform (you could not expect *caps*, of course), but there must be three or four of them, and she was also introduced to a dark girl who was Mrs Corbett's companion, and to a middle-aged man who was her son.

Her enjoyment was only spoilt by the thought that the incident would all too soon be ended.

But Mrs Corbett's heart, never hard or ungrateful, had been touched, and she also recalled that, lately, she had been thinking about the desirability of making new friends: Dorry and Madge and Cis, thought Mrs Corbett, get me down sometimes. I'll ask her to tea, she decided.

'Now Arnold will drive you home, of course –' she announced, when Mrs Lysaght, getting up carefully and testing her throbbing legs, at last said that she must go.

'Oh that's terribly sweet of you but I'm sure Mr Corbett won't want to turn out again.'

'Oh he'd love to, wouldn't you?' to Arnold.

He said that it would be an honour.

'As if we'd let you go home by taxi! And Frobisher will be there punctually to-morrow to take you to Emergency–Ward Ten.'

26

Mrs Lysaght settled herself with a sigh of satisfaction; it was pleasant to ride in a car with a personable, prosperous man.

Arnold really detested elderly women, and the sweeter they were the more he hated them. They thrust at him the fact that young women were sweet in a different way; and that in seven more years he would be fifty, and compelled to spend even more money and skill on attaching them to himself.

'How strange life is,' began the specimen at his side, in a musing tone, 'really weird . . . isn't it, Mr Corbett? Don't *you* find life weird?'

'Oh . . . I don't know.' He half-smiled at her, running the car too fast up the hilly road, 'Is it? Sure you're quite comfortable? That thing not too tight?' That thing was the safety belt.

'It's *perfect*, thank you . . . for instance, in the last week, after really months of just nothing happening at all, I've been in a dog-fight, and talked to a medium.'

'Yes . . . well? . . .' he said vaguely. He could feel his sorrow waxing, and, as he glanced out of the window he knew why; some trees on the other side of the road, with their leaves blanched to colourless sprays in the chemical light, brought Peggy to his mind; Peggy, walking beneath them with the dogs.

'I have a dear friend – a parson; I call him my *guru*, you know, like the Hindus have, a spiritual guide, philosopher and friend – and of course he's very against my having anything to do with this Mrs Pearson – the medium.'

'Pearson?' He was edging the car into the beginning of the High Street and did not glance at her, but she caught the note of interest.

'That's her name – and such a pretty, unusual address for the dreadful part she lives in – Lily Cottage, Rose Walk. Isn't it charming? – and in the heart of a slum. All bomb-ruins.'

'My mother's companion is a Miss Pearson,' Arnold explained; some reason must be given for his obviously awakened interest.

'Oh yes, of course – I remember now – I'm so bad at names. (*I* always look at people's faces.) Rather a nice-looking girl, I thought. But not warm. I do like *warmth* in a face,' enlarged Mrs Lysaght, who in fact did not mind what was in a face so long as it promised some form of entertainment 'Has she been with you long?'

'About four months . . . she's very good with the dogs. My mother's had some trouble getting the right girl; foreigners don't understand them, she says.'

'Well, I agree with her. It takes an English person to understand a dog . . . I wonder if they're related? But how absurd I'm being . . . it's a common name.' Arnold murmured something in answer.

So her mother told fortunes. He wondered in what the 'invalidism' consisted? It might be mental; it might be drugs. We'll cultivate Mrs Lysaght, anyway, he thought, she can probably tell us more . . . and if Peggy doesn't want my mother to know about all this, that might come in useful too.

Poor kid. The words floated up, unexpected and pure, from somewhere, and he put them angrily aside.

★

Some weeks later, in the lengthening twilight, Mr Geddes was locking the door of the vestry. It was after a service ill-attended but for the church's faithful ladies, and the Vicar had remained in the vestry after it to attend to one or two small tasks.

The side door of the vestry opened on to a narrow slip of turf, set with old elder bushes, that faced the Vicarage, and led into its garden; there was one of those false impressions of rural solitude here that linger in London, and Mr Geddes was always reminded, on crossing the turf, of more congenial days in another parish.

He tried the door, slipped the key into the pocket of his cassock and turned away, then started violently.

A dark, silent figure stood beside him in the dusk. 'What do you want?' Mr Geddes demanded loudly, with thoughts of that evening's collection darting through his mind.

'I came to . . . You remember me . . . Pearson. Thomas Pearson . . .' the man answered in a low tone.

'Is your wife worse?' Mr Geddes asked instantly.

'No. Not this evening, but . . . I came –' he hesitated, then went on, 'I came to talk about it.' The words were spoken so quietly that Mr Geddes hardly caught them.

He hesitated.

But then he realized that the creature's usual aura of menace was lacking. What came forth from Thomas Pearson into this clouded, lingering spring dusk was only sadness. Mr Geddes turned back to the vestry, drawing out the key from his pocket.

'We'll talk in here . . .' he said, unlocking and pushing open the small heavy door, and switching the lights on again. Pearson followed him in, and, uninvited, sat down in the chair that faced the larger one, used by successive Vicars, drawn up to the wide old table.

Mr Geddes settled himself, leant back, felt in a drawer for

cigarettes, and held out the packet. His companion silently shook his head.

'Then I will . . .' said the Vicar, 'if you don't object.' Thomas Pearson neither moved nor spoke while he lit the cigarette, drew in smoke, and dropped the blackened match carefully into the wastepaper basket under the table.

The visitor sat in a huddled posture, with both small, dark-skinned hands resting, with a curious suggestion of helplessness, open-palmed and upwards on his knees. He was looking down, and seemed lost in dejected reflection. Mr Geddes allowed him to remain thus; he thought that he should be given time to collect his thoughts.

In a little while, Pearson slowly raised his head and stared at him, with miserable eyes. His lips moved once or twice, and at last he said in a low tone:

'I am − I am − in despair. Have you ever been like that?'

'Oh yes.' Mr Geddes nodded, 'I've been in despair. Most people have, at some time in their lives.'

'So I came,' Pearson went on slowly, as if he had not spoken, 'I came because I am in despair, and because − to ask you something.' He paused.

'Yes?'

'It is a question for a priest. I thought you would know about such things. I thought − if I go to a doctor or a psychiatrist they'll treat me as if I were a sick man. But I'm not sick, I'm well and strong −' He uttered a loud sigh, uncontrolled as a child's, settling himself wearily in his chair. 'Yes, a question for a priest . . .'

Then he was silent again. Mr Geddes neither moved nor spoke. Traffic rushed unceasingly past in the main road and the old clock high on the vestry wall sent out its message against the distant roar, like the voice of eternity behind the voice of the temporal world.

'You will think me a fool. Unprogressive.'

Mr Geddes gently moved his head. 'No.'

'But when these questions . . . when . . . I come to you to ask this one question, there is no such thing as unprogressive, or being a fool. Such things aren't important.'

'No.'

'But perhaps you don't know the answer. Why should you? Priests are men. Perhaps you don't know any more than I do.'

'If it's a question about God, priests are trained to answer that kind of question, you see.'

'Oh, I know that. They were told, as young men, and as old men they tell other young men, and these young men grow old, and so it goes – but are their answers true?'

'Yes,' Mr Geddes said, looking steadily at him. He himself had never doubted; that, at least, he could give to the wracked creature.

'Yes, they are true,' he said again, and was silent, neither amplifying nor qualifying the statement. The clock spoke its message and the traffic rushed past.

'I wish I knew –' said Thomas Pearson, grinding his hands together, 'if only I knew. Then I could – I wouldn't be in so much despair.'

'Tell me.'

Instinct told Mr Geddes, imperiously, to say very little, but that with absolute conviction.

27

Pearson made a sniffing, choking noise and to his dismay began to weep; loudly, almost wailingly, so that the lofty little room echoed.

'Steady!' Mr Geddes said sharply, 'someone will hear you – you'll frighten my mother,' (who was likely, in that event, he knew, to walk straight in to investigate).

'I can't.' Pearson's hands were clasped above his head now, and his face uplifted, in the immemorial pose of Oriental grief. Tears were running down.

'Pull yourself together,' said Mr Geddes, looking on in momentary helplessness, 'be a man.'

'It's because I'm a man . . .' Pearson sobbed.

Mr Geddes was silenced. Born to sorrow as the sparks fly upwards, he thought. But, accustomed to the shamed mutters and averted face of English mourners, he could not help feeling this noisy grief to be theatrical, and it irritated, as well as embarrassed, him.

'What's the matter, exactly?' he asked, 'is your wife worse?'

A nod. 'Not to-night. But she's been very bad. That night you . . . hit me, I got home and she was . . . she was . . .' grief choked him. '*You* made her ill, *you* made her bad,' he said fiercely at last, wiping his eyes with a large gaudy handkerchief, and glaring above it.

'You mean she had an attack immediately I'd gone?'

Pearson nodded again.

'She seemed perfectly well when I left – better than when I came, I thought.' Mr Geddes hesitated, and Pearson put in roughly, 'That thing was in her.'

For a moment Mr Geddes did not take in the meaning of what had been said. Confused thoughts of some weapon or growth, came to him.

Then, in one wave, that seemed to swell downwards and break over him, he felt for the second time the force of every hint and rumour that had loomed about her ever since he had first heard of Mrs Pearson.

The atmosphere of the familiar, homely vestry changed; chilled; shut itself off from the world of the rushing traffic beyond its door; and was ominous. The man's extraordinary words had locked it into terror. Mr Geddes stared at him.

'What do you mean?' he demanded; then, as Pearson continued to rock and mutter, with his eyes half-shut, he broke out, 'Oh, for the love of God, man, pull yourself together . . . we'll never get anywhere like this.'

Pearson leant forward across the table, sniffing, drawing in short exhausted breaths, staring out of drowned eyes. 'This thing comes into her. Something that isn't Nora. It drives her out. It was there when I got home, I tell you. The light was out, and it was there.'

'Well, she was delirious, I suppose – though how . . . these attacks must come on very suddenly? I do wish you'd be sensible people, and see a doctor.'

'Doctors are fools.' Pearson slowly wiped his eyes again. No shame, thought Mr Geddes. Foreigners . . .

'Well, a psychiatrist, then.'

'Doctors, psychiatrists, priests – all of you. Fools. But . . .' he stopped, looking sullenly at him, '. . . she likes you.'

'I liked her,' Mr Geddes said at once, 'a sweet woman, I thought.' Instinct, conquering social habit, prompted him to say aloud what he would never have dreamt of saying to a less pitiable creature. Yes, the dreaded rackman was pitiable. He looked with new eyes at the plump, ravaged face.

'And so . . .' Pearson was hurrying on, 'that's why I came to you. *She* said, go to him. She said, perhaps he'll pray . . . or do something like that . . . yes, she is sweet. I tell you,' he leaned forward, fixing his moist eyes on Mr Geddes, 'when I saw her first, in Venice, I believed that God had sent a *peri* – an angel – in a woman's body to make up to me for what I'd been through. She wore a blue dress. She was eighteen. She was like a spring morning.' He wiped his eyes again.

Mr Geddes looked down at the table. He knew these thoughts; they were his own, though he had never put them into words. He had known a girl of eighteen who had been like a spring morning. But the dress had been yellow.

'When I was a boy,' Pearson was saying excitedly, 'my mother beat me. I stole because I was hungry, and she beat me. She sent me out to work for money when I was seven years old. I ran away when I was thirteen . . .'

'Yes . . . yes . . .' said Mr Geddes, 'I'm sure you've suffered greatly. But what you and I have to do now is to help your wife.'

He paused. Pearson was staring at him, with an expression best described as suspended; his attention had been caught.

'This . . .' Mr Geddes was feeling his way, '. . . these attacks . . . you say they are as if . . .'

'A thing gets into her,' Pearson interrupted impatiently, 'a . . . something. She goes away, and it comes instead. It isn't *as if*. It happens. My wife goes away and this thing comes.'

'And is she conscious of what's happening?'

'She knows there is something. Once she said: this thing is wandering about, and it wants a body. *It wants to live.*'

Silence fell. The pitch pine walls of the room looked solid and warm in the bright light, and all the Victorian furnishings – the heavy chairs, the clumsy cupboard where the choir surplices hung and the church's records were kept, the old pieces of brass and china that had drifted, in the course of a century, into the deep window-sills, the massive table at which the two men sat – stood out coloured and shaped by the light and air of Earth. They seemed friendly; they were familiar, and the heart could rest on them.

When Mr Geddes next spoke he had to make an effort to keep his voice at its normal pitch; his instinct had been to lower it.

'Do you believe this?' he asked.

'My God, my God,' Pearson shouted at the top of his voice, springing up, 'of course I believe it – I've seen it – I've seen the thing – its eyes, and heard it speak – can you imagine that, seeing and hearing it in your wife's body, the body you . . . you . . .' He sank slowly back again.

'No.' Mr Geddes shook his head. 'I can't, I haven't much imagination. But that doesn't matter. What matters is that I want to help you and I will.'

'You can help? You believe you can help us?'

'Not I but Christ in me,' said the priest, 'I will try.' It was said with an effort.

'All that . . .' Pearson said gloomily, 'Christ, praying, all that – my mother believed. But, very soon, I didn't. Would it be better –?'

His eyes had a calculating look, under his surprisingly delicate black eyebrows, as he fixed them on the other's face.

'Of course it would, it's always better if people believe. But if you don't – God is very merciful. You must just trust in that. And now . . .'

'If He lets her die – or go away, and this thing gets hold of her body and comes instead – I'm going after her,' Pearson said, almost casually. Then, as Mr Geddes, once more prevented from attempting to make plans, was betrayed through irritation into a contemptuous exclamation, he began to work himself up again.

He raised his voice. 'I swear it. I shall go. I'll kill myself. And then, I suppose' – he bent forward, and brought out the words with an air in which there was something pettish, almost feminine – 'your merciful God will keep me from her for ever?'

'That I don't *know*,' Mr Geddes answered coolly, 'but the evidence points to its being likely.'

'I don't care – I don't care – I defy Him.' And he shook both fists upwards at the ceiling. Mr Geddes uttered a short laugh.

'Really, Mr Pearson. Sit down, there's a good chap, and let's see what we can work out.'

Once more, Pearson slowly resumed his seat. 'That's what I came to ask you, if He would keep me from her for ever.'

'Well now I've told you. I don't *know*, of course, but I think it's quite likely. Only – it isn't God Who will keep you from her. You'll do that yourself, by committing suicide.'

'So I can't win,' said Pearson, after a pause. 'Or you say I can't.'

'No. I'm afraid you can't – not in that sense. But look here, Mr Pearson. Your wife is still alive. These moods – fits of –'

'It's an evil spirit.'

'Very well, evil spirit. This thing – as you call it – isn't there all the time, is it?' She has longish stretches when she's all right; normal; she was when I saw her the other day. That means there's hope.'

'It'll get her body in the end. Then I'm going after her.' He was looking down as he spoke, and his tone was unemphatic. Mr Geddes felt more alarmed than he had done throughout the histrionics. He made a swift, very urgent silent prayer.

'Yes, well, never mind that now. Put it out of your mind. I know it's hard, but you must try to bear your troubles and look on the bright side.'

The platitude, apparently so helpless and smug in face of the situation, was suddenly immeasurably strengthened, for him, by a conviction that pierced through to him like a ray of dazzling starlight. There *was* a bright side – oh, bright beyond human dreaming. Its smugness and inadequacy did not matter; the little phrase faithfully reflected that unimaginable radiance.

'How can I? You've got your God. You can hope. I was made to hate Him by my mother. You know what my mother did? Married an Armenian servant, and hated him, and took it out on me because I was his son. Even my mother,' bitterly, 'so clever, so strong, had her sex. She was at the time in a woman's life when that goes away – you understand me?'

'Of course I – Mr Pearson, we really *must* try and work out something practical. We may not have much time.'

'Oh God – oh God, don't I know it?' He put his face in his hands, shaking his head in a sort of frenzy, 'but what can we do? . . . I was telling you . . . this man, my father, was a servant in the house where she was governess, a noble Russian house – pigs, swine, bastards – and they were all shot. They were refugees, in their great palace, in Tashkent, and . . .'

'*Mr Pearson*,' Mr Geddes put his hand across the table and caught at his arm and shook it, 'you *must* control yourself. Now. Be quiet. Think of how much you love your wife and want to help her, and be quiet.'

He kept his grip on the plump arm, waiting. In a moment, Pearson threw it off, looking at him almost with hatred.

'I tell you, we can't do anything. We're both . . .'

'We can at least try,' Mr Geddes said curtly; he was tired. 'Now. To begin with, I will pray for her; pray every day, and I will ask two or three others to do the same. Then I will visit her – every day, too, if you want me to (I think it should be every day). What I shall try to do –'

'*You'll* try to do! What can you do? What can either of us do? What help have we got?'

'Christ is our help,' Mr Geddes said.

After a silence, which seemed to him full of nothing but depression and nullity, he went on, with the irritation born of exhaustion. 'And for pity's sake can't you do something to make her life a little more normal? Open the windows – I'm sure all that stuffiness is bad for her nervous system – and pack that German child off to an orphanage or somewhere (I mean somewhere suitable, of course) and let Miss Barnes look after her. Pay her, if necessary; she's a splendid woman, Miss Barnes. A tonic in herself.'

'Old fool,' said Pearson sitting listlessly, with a hopeless expression, half-listening.

'That doesn't matter . . . she's a good woman and a kind one.'

'Nora is fond of her,' Pearson said grudgingly.

'Of course she is. They're both nice women . . . what I shall try to do –'

'She's fond of Erika, too – the little bitch, she's starting to go after boys – I've had to stop her.'

Mr Geddes made a gesture dismissing Erika and her boys. 'What I shall try to do,' he repeated with a kind of gritty patience, 'is to fill your wife's spirit with . . . things . . . that *this* . . . whatever it is – can't bear. Holy things. Then it will go away.'

It gave him a curious sensation to speak of what was afflicting Mrs Pearson. He disliked it. It was as if, by doing so, he allowed it to edge over into his own mind. He had never had cause to think of Possession before; not with deliberation; not for any length of time.

Pearson startled him by a loud laugh. 'And you think that's going to drive it out? It doesn't want her soul; you and your Christ can have that; it wants her body.'

'Her soul lives in her body. There won't be room in there for this thing and a soul filled with Christ. It will go away,' Mr Geddes said stubbornly.

'You think so? Open the windows, and drive this thing away with your fresh air – this thing that lives – only it doesn't live – in a place where *it's always misty and cold and the wind never stops blowing*? It wants to *come here*; I've heard it say so.'

'You've –' Mr Geddes could only stare. An irrepressible shudder snaked along his spine.

'Oh yes,' Pearson said, beginning to button his coat as if preparing to go, 'when we were young, first married, we used to – play with it. It told the future for us, and when we had no money at all I brought people to the house and Nora told their fortunes. *We three were friends, in those days.* We played with it, as if it were our child. But later on . . . it began to want to come here. My daughter was born, and Nora only cared about her.' He got up, and stood staring at Mr Geddes with sad, quenched eyes. 'Perhaps it was jealous.'

'Mr Pearson, you . . . you've let your imagination . . . I think you need praying for, as well,' was all Mr Geddes could say, and as he spoke he was very aware of the stout old cupboard that contained the choir surplices. Its glossy bulk was comforting.

'Perhaps we all do,' Pearson sneered. 'Well, I asked you the question and you told me.' He lingered, showing those unmistakable signs of wanting to begin a discussion all over again after it has been satisfactorily ended. 'Perhaps . . .' he hesitated.

'I'll come and see Mrs Pearson again to-morrow. In the afternoon, if that's convenient,' Mr Geddes said decidedly. 'Or my curate will. It will do her good to see as many people as possible.'

'In those days, perhaps, *it* wasn't like it is now . . . I don't know. Or perhaps the one we played with was driven away by this one . . . I don't know.'

'Well I'm sure I don't,' Mr Geddes muttered. 'About three, then.'

'Nora says she told lies to people about their fortunes. Sometimes – she says – she lied.'

'Mr Pearson, these small sins . . . we can't really . . .' Mr Geddes had opened the vestry's thick little ogive door, and was standing beside it.

'But Nora is always talking about it. It worries her,' Pearson insisted. He seemed unwilling to go out into the restless night.

'Yes . . . well, of course, any meddling with this kind of thing, unless it's with the purest possible motives, *is* terribly dangerous. And people can deceive themselves. I've always thought and said so. Even when the motives *are* pure. I'm a hundred per cent with the more conservative members of the Church about that. It's dreadfully, frighteningly dangerous. Does she – blame herself, then, do you think, for the present situation?'

But Pearson seemed to have gone back into his usual taciturn, faintly menacing self. He shrugged.

'Nora is very gentle,' he muttered, pulling his hat over his eyes, and made a vague gesture and turned away. The uneasy night, broken with the screech of brakes and throb of engines and the roar of pleasure-seeking traffic on its way into London, received him.

Mr Geddes stood for a moment among the dim elder bushes, looking up at the spire outlined against the stars; then went slowly into the house.

28

He was sitting with Gerald Corliss, taking half an hour from the crowded business of the following day to explain to him the situation at Mrs Pearson's, and what they must try to do, when the telephone rang.

He snatched off the receiver and told Mrs Lysaght that he was busy.

'Oh you're always busy, Robert, surely you can spare five minutes for an old friend. I've got so much to tell you . . . life's been really hectic lately . . .'

'Helen, I'm . . . I'm *very* busy . . . I'll . . .'

'Oh. Oh, I see. Well, call me back, then. I'll be in all afternoon.'

Of course you will; what else have you to do? And I wish people wouldn't Americanize the language, I'm too old to put up with it, Mr Geddes thought, gathering his scattered thoughts.

Gerald's own thoughts had come back, on being summoned from his room where he was presumably working on next Sunday evening's sermon, from Peru and England, in the 1860s.

He had found, on one of the more remote shelves of the London Library, the biography of a Miss Eliza Dewer of Santa Rosita in Peru, daughter of an English merchant living there. Miss Dewer had lived a life of unusual piety, combined with devoted work among the Peruvian Indians, but this had not lessened her sense of her sinfulness and general worthlessness. Dying at forty-one, she had found her biographer in one Agnes Pettey and the latter revealed, in a footnote half-way through the small volume, that she had devoted her life to persuading Authority to include her friend among the English Saints.

Gerald had been playing with the idea of writing a joint biography of this forgotten pair, in the style of Lytton Strachey; with hardly any adjectives, and occasional tiny, dry etchings of the Peruvian and Victorian English scenes. What fun it would be.

It was this dream that had been broken into by an impatient summons from Mr Geddes.

'So,' the Vicar concluded, 'that's the plan. We pray, and we get one or two others to pray, and we visit regularly.'

He paused, studying his curate's long face, where the heavily-lidded eyes seemed half-asleep. What female ecstatic was holding his attention now? 'Well?' he said.

'I suppose . . .' Gerald began hesitatingly, 'he can't be persuaded to consult someone professional?'

'We are professionals,' Mr Geddes snapped.

'Yes, of course, but I meant . . . it's difficult to express . . . professional in the contemporary . . . I meant, more likely to suggest authority and competence to unbelievers. Yes,' (relieved) 'that's what I meant.'

'No he can't. He was absolutely definite. He mistrusts them. He isn't educated, he has no self-control, and I should think, apart from the low cunning that's made him his money, he's stupid. And so much feeling! Quite embarrassing.'

'Well, it is rather a . . .' Gerald murmured.

'Yes, yes, quite. But you can take it from me that doctors and psychiatrists are out. It's up to the Church, and the Church must act through me and you. You'd better go along there this afternoon.'

Gerald looked down, to hide an instant's panic.

'Whatever it is – secondary personality, mental trouble, evil spirit – our way is perfectly clear,' Mr Geddes added, getting up from his chair, 'and we must follow it. About three, I told Pearson. I said I might ask you to go; it'll be a fresh face for her.'

'Very well,' said Gerald.

'You'll like her,' Mr Geddes added, 'she's a nice woman. Apart from all this extraordinary business, a sweet woman. Easy to talk to. Just chat, any ordinary gossip will do, the more ordinary the better.'

And now, I suppose, Mr Geddes thought, as his curate strode off with cassock and silky forelock floating, I'd better ring up poor Helen. Checking an exasperated sigh, he lifted the receiver.

Mrs Lysaght told him all about the dog-fight, and exactly where the bites were on her legs, and knew that he would be pleased to hear she had made a *new friend*.

He would be pleased for her sake but *also for his own*; oh yes, he needn't deny it, she had been rather possessive lately and once or twice he had let her know it. Of course, a woman friend wasn't like a man friend, but she was *better than nothing*.

'Now Helen – don't – really, there's nothing to cry about . . .'

'I'm not exactly crying. I'm only weak, it's the reaction from all this excitement. And I thought I'd lost you.'

'Now – now, you mustn't talk nonsense,' said Mr Geddes, alarmed.

'I'll try not to be silly – it's just that it's so nice to hear your voice again . . . I never realized that someone enormously wealthy could be a simple person – she showed me her collection of souvenirs – she's kept all the programmes of the flying displays at Hendon for years back – one of them's for 1913 – and the Victory Aerial Derby in 1919 – after the First World War, you know, and she spends a lot of her time sitting in a window overlooking what used to be Hendon fields. Just brooding, I suppose *you'd* call it.'

'Helen, I really must go, I have so much to do this morning.'

'You always have. But I won't be naughty. Give my love to your mother. See you soon, I hope. Bye-bye.'

Mr Geddes replaced the receiver. The mention of his mother reminded him that even she had been giving her moiety of trouble lately; small indeed, compared with that offered by everyone else, but there, and irritating.

He had briefly outlined to her the situation in Lily Cottage, trusting in her good sense and propriety not to make a wonder out of it. But she ignored the plight of the Pearsons, and the secondary one of those old people depending upon the Pearsons for their home, and seemed to be interested only in that German teenager.

'My dear Mum, I really don't know,' had been his mildly annoyed retort to her 'And what about that child?' when Gerald returned from his visit. 'Did you see her, Gerald?'

'It must have been she who opened the door . . . yes, I did.'

'What did she say?' put in Mrs Geddes (the three were in the kitchen, washing up). 'No, Robert, don't snort, I have my reasons for asking.'

'Oh . . .' Gerald paused, with the tea-towel drooping dispirit-edly, and began to dredge in his memory, where Eliza Dewer and Agnes Pettey were fighting a losing battle with Nora Pearson.

'Was she polite?' Mrs Geddes went on.

'Oh very. I remember now, she said, "Good-evening. How can I 'halp' you,"' he said, with a smile at the sudden recollec-tion of a face like a fat young pear.

'Good,' said Mrs Geddes oracularly, almost snatching the tea-towel from him, 'I'll finish those.'

'Why "good"?' he asked curiously. Mr Geddes had fled to his study, in irritation at the number of human beings there are in this world.

'Oh – well – because everybody else in that place is middle-aged or old. They've had their chance. But she's at the precise age when the right chance and a bit of the right influence can set a life into the right pattern.' Mrs Geddes ranged plates along the dresser with a series of gentle clashes. 'I'm going to see she gets it.' She nodded at him, in dismissal.

But in spite of Mr Geddes's tiredness, and his difficulty in believing with his reason in the existence of Mrs Pearson's invader, to say nothing of the practical difficulty of fitting the visits into the crowded programme of parish work, there began to be, after a while, a growing comfort.

He had enlisted the help of three people of devout life who attended the church, and their prayers were going out in an unbroken flow. He could trust Gerald Corliss to pray with every resource he possessed; he might fail in friendliness to some simple soul, but Mr Geddes had never doubted his spiritual dedication; and, when the daily visits and the silent concentration had been going on without pause for nearly two weeks, Pearson, coming noiselessly upon him late one afternoon as he was descending the stairs at Lily Cottage after his visit, said grudgingly, 'It's better.'

'Thank God,' Mr Geddes said, and waited.

'That thing hasn't come now for nearly three days. Before, it was coming several times a day.'

'I'm more thankful than I can say, Mr Pearson.'

'I suppose you think you're working what you'd call a miracle?' Pearson said jeeringly.

'Oh no. Don't let's exaggerate. Just thank God.'

'"Thank God"! It's my right, isn't it? to have her safe, in her own body, not sharing her with a devil? God is only giving me my rights.'

It should have sounded impressive. It sounded pathetic; Mr Geddes looked at the dark face, made to mirror the delights of voluptuous tenderness, in a kind of testy despair.

'Thank you,' said Pearson suddenly in a low tone, and turned away.

Arnold Corbett had delayed for some time in speaking to Peggy about her supposedly disreputable mother.

It was so pleasurable, to feel that he had this secret power over her! He played with the thought, watching her as she sat with them at meals or in the evenings; and, naturally, grew to believe the power stronger than it was in fact.

He began, too, to feel that if he was to *get any benefit* from his knowledge, he must speak soon. She had changed, since the spring weeks came in; he could feel restlessness breathing from her dark body and sometimes see it glittering in her eyes and throbbing in her quiet, harsh voice. He was certain that she meant to leave them.

It was true that the whole of Peggy's inner life was changing. The beauty of those weeks of spring, with the awakening of the sap in the leaves and the strong, ever-increasing light, had seemed to awaken some positive force within herself; something that protested against the negativity of pride and pain; and the glimpse of his wife, on Easter Sunday at Sedgemere, had worked with the pressures exerted by the blossoming year to overthrow the barriers of pride that she had set up.

She had begun to ask herself why she should suffer as she did, shutting herself away from the delight that was offered?

It was only because he would not promise to cut himself

off, completely, from Janey and his children. She had told him that if she could not have this, have him utterly and finally for herself, she would have nothing. His every thought and feeling must belong to her alone.

But suddenly her pride was crumbling, and, what mattered more to Peggy, her belief in it. She was beginning to suspect that she had behaved like a fool. She felt herself – poor Peggy – to be years older than the furiously angry girl who had parted from Fred Rattray a year ago, after laying down that immovable condition. Inwardly, more and more often as the summer advanced, she would burn and tremble at the know-ledge that complete happiness, utter rapture, were awaiting her, without doubt, as the result of a telephone call. She would give his number – charged and laden with its weight of meaning – and then – she would hear his voice.

Peggy would get up from her chair, here, and walk restlessly across the room and lean out of the open window and stare fiercely into the dusk. Nothing stood between her and this happiness, this perfect happiness, but her own pride.

With these thoughts and sensations, it was not surprising that she replied as she did to a suggestion made one morning by Mrs Corbett that she should accompany herself and the four dogs to stay at the home of a friend in Ireland, during the following month.

'Oh I don't know, Mrs Corbett – I can't possibly say now – I don't know yet what my plans are,' and she hurried out of the room.

'Well!' Mrs Corbett stared after her. 'That wasn't very polite, was it, boys?' Then her expression became depressed. 'Going to leave, I suppose . . . just as we were all so comfortable.' She sighed.

Arnold was coming up the stairs towards his own room. Peggy gave him barely a smile, and was hurrying past.

He paused in front of her: he looked excited and triumphant, as if a flood of words was banked up behind his face.

'Don't be in such a hurry. I've been wanting to speak to you. Come on, come in here a minute.' He held open the door of the room known as his 'den'. 'Come on,' he repeated excitedly, then, as she did not move and looked at him coldly, 'it's all right – I only want a word with you.'

She shrugged, and went into the room, and he followed.

'Look here,' he began at once, as he shut the door on them, 'does my mother know about your mother being a medium?'

'How did you know?' she exclaimed, too taken by surprise to conceal dismay.

'Mrs Lysaght let it out: I drove her home, that first evening . . . she wants a "sitting", or whatever it's called . . . Does she know, Peggy? My mother, I mean.'

For a minute, she said nothing, only stared, expressionlessly now, at his red triumphant face. Her eyes looked unusually beautiful, he thought; dark as some animal's suddenly alarmed, with the star deep in them.

'I didn't see any reason why she should,' she said at last. 'It isn't a crime.'

'No, but it's all a bit funny, isn't it? and she lives in a funny kind of neighbourhood, too. My mother hates anything she calls "creepy".'

She shrugged again. 'Mrs Lysaght may have told her by now, if she's after a sitting (I don't think she'll get one, my mother gave it all up some years ago). What's all this about, anyway? You doing a little blackmail – or hoping to? If you are, you can stop hoping. I don't care a damn whether she knows or not – she met my mother and my father too, when we were staying at Hove – she knows my mother's an invalid –'

'An invalid! Why not admit she's mental?' He laughed unpleasantly.

'Because she isn't. She *is* psychic. But she hasn't used what she calls her gifts for years. I've just said so. Here, can we break this up now? – I want to take the dogs out.'

'Oh all right. If you could manage to be a bit nicer to me I'd drop the whole thing. Can't you, Peggy?'

'*No – I – can – not*. Leave me alone – I'm sick of it here – I'll get out, I think – I've been meaning to.'

She went towards the door, and he stood aside, unwilling to touch her, because the detestation of him, and the contempt that came from her, made him profoundly sad. Sadness held him in a kind of paralysis.

'I'll go to my mother at once, now,' he said dejectedly as she went past him, 'and we'll see . . . it is all pretty shady, you must admit . . .'

'Oh go to hell.' She ran downstairs, and in a minute he heard her talking to the dogs in the hall as she buckled them on to their leads. He thought that her voice sounded different; there was hysteria in it, under the cheerful words.

29

He lunched in London, and did not see her again. Late in the afternoon he returned to MacLeod House to find his mother sitting in her favourite place overlooking Hendon in its valley. With her was Mrs Lysaght, also enjoying a martini among the house plants. Arnold came into the room to overhear his mother complaining about the ingratitude of the servants, which, she was saying, had been worse than usual lately. Mrs Lysaght was agreeing and sympathizing though in fact she was so satisfied with her new Crimplene suit that she could not feel anything was very unpleasant: the skirt, thought Mrs Lysaght, hangs like a dream.

'What *I* cannot get over is your Miss Pearson's mother and my medium being the same person . . . I do wish you would change your mind about coming for a sitting . . . it would be such fun!' she attempted, feeling the lament gone on long enough.

'Oh I couldn't, dear . . . I hate anything creepy,' Mrs Corbett said absently, 'and just now I'm too worried about all this to enjoy *anything*. Doris and Frobisher have never got on well, as I told you, but downright quarrelling . . . I cannot *stand* it. And Peggy's been so funny to-day.'

'Where is she this evening?' said Mrs Lysaght.

'It's her free evening; she can go out any time, of course, but Tuesday is a fixture. I wish,' plaintively, to Arnold, who was sitting in silence with his hands hanging between his knees and an empty glass beside him, 'you hadn't gone for her like that this morning. I'm sure you've upset her. I can't imagine what you were thinking about.'

'I didn't "go for" her. I simply thought you ought to know her mother was mental and lived in a slum, and I told her so.'

'Well of course it isn't nice, dear, and as I said just now, I do hate anything creepy, or anything shady either . . . I always thought her people were comfortably off – she only gets five guineas a week here – nothing nowadays, with secretaries getting twelve and fourteen – but she's always seemed satisfied – why her mother has to live in what you call a slum I don't know. But I don't care; Peggy suits me, and it really isn't my business. I do wish you'd left well alone.'

Arnold shrugged, and Mrs Lysaght said that she thought Peggy had the look of a medium's daughter; you could tell; she had thought then something was queer there the first time she saw her.

'Well I only hope you haven't upset her badly, that's all. I've never had anyone so good with the dogs since dear Alice,' said his mother, 'I don't want her leaving . . . yes, do draw them, please, Doris,' (as the old woman came into the room), 'it's getting chilly.' The dogs, disturbed, got up and rearranged themselves, turning in circles, at her feet.

Doris waited until she had performed half her task before she sent up her rocket. Pausing precisely between the drawn curtain and the undrawn, and looking full at Mrs Corbett, she said, in her primmest voice:

'I beg your pardon, Madam, but I think there's something you ought to know.'

'Oh. Well I hope it's something pleasant for I've heard enough unpleasant things for one day . . . what is it?'

'Miss Pearson's took her cases off with her, Madam. And the

drawers is all anyhow, and her room upside-down. I've just been in to turn the bed down.'

Arnold started. Mrs Lysaght exclaimed, 'Well!' Mrs Corbett said, 'There, Arnold, that's *your* fault. She's gone off now – I knew it – I knew she would.'

'Shall I see if there's anything missing, Madam?' Doris asked, no muscle of her face reflecting her triumph in this moment of kitchen-prophecy fulfilled.

'Of course not – don't be silly,' said Mrs Corbett, distractedly, 'I expect she's taken some things over to her mother's. Now don't go telling everyone she's run off, Doris.'

Doris compressed her lips and went out of the room.

'Would you like me to telephone her mother, and see if she's there?' said Mrs Lysaght. 'I do have her number.'

'Oh no, no – leave it alone, please – I'm not running after her – if she can walk out as calm as you please, leaving me and the dogs, after all my kindness – let her go.' Mrs Corbett was almost crying. 'I'm not surprised – I told you I thought you'd upset her, Arnold.'

'Oh nonsense,' said Arnold. 'I'll go up and have a look – there may be a note or something – the whole thing's probably a scare – Doris always hated her, anyway (I don't know why you can't sack that bunch and get in some human beings) . . . She'll be back. She knows which side her bread is buttered.' He hurried out.

Mrs Corbett and Mrs Lysaght sat in silence, Mrs Corbett gently moving her toe among the curled-up, silky mass that was the dogs. Once, Cee barked a gruff little ghost-bark, as he hunted some flying cat through his dreams.

Peggy had gone to the nearest Underground station, and the telephone boxes.

They were all occupied, the one outside which she took up her place by two laughing, very young girls, their faces sparkling with sexual mischief as they took it in turns to speak, feeding the box again from a mass of coppers in the pocket of one as fast as a call was concluded. After a few seconds, Peggy tapped sharply on the window.

The faces turned to her, amused and defiant; then they went back to their fun. She rapped again, furiously this time; her heart was beating painfully and her eyes seemed to burn; her throat ached.

'Coo – look at 'er! I can't remember his number, where's the book?' The young voice sounded sharp and fresh through the closed door.

Peggy wrenched it open, gripped each child by a shoulder and, amid shrill cries of anger, pulled them out of the box and went in and slammed it. At once, the noises of the station and their voices were shut off; she was alone with her purpose.

She had the right money; she had made all her plans. She gave a number, seeing, out of the corner of her eye, a coloured woman ticket-collector good-naturedly shepherding the protesting children, with their spike heels and tight black trousers and mermaid hair, towards one of the exits. Then she gave a great, harsh, breath –

'Fred? I . . . I . . .'

'Where are you?' said his voice instantly, 'where are you, Peggy?'

She told him, hearing with furious impatience the sound of another voice, fainter, that was saying something in the background. ('*Don't talk to her, Fred, please don't talk to her, please –*' it was saying. Gabbling, thought Peggy. Shut up. You're done for.)

'I'll come and get you to-night? Where will you be? (*Don't, Janey, it's no use.*) Yes? I can't hear?'

She gave him the name of a railway station in London, and a place.

'I'll be there . . .'

'*Please, Fred, please – please,*' said the voice of his wife.

'*Leave me alone, can't you . . . I'm sorry, God knows, but leave me alone* . . . Peggy? Yes, right. I'll be there as soon as I can.'

'All right. I'll wait.'

She thought that his wife had dragged away the receiver. She heard his voice shouting, then the line went dead. She replaced the receiver and stood for a moment, drawing in breaths that were sweet with triumph. The rapture was almost unbearable; the release from pain too exquisite. She was going to see him, to be with him, and for ever. She had given in; her battle was over. She had surrendered.

Presently she found herself sitting in a taxi that she did not remember entering, going down into London. Janey Rattray and her brats, who had held Fred back from her for nearly a year, were defeated.

She had won.

When the taxi reached the station, she paid off the driver, and picked up her case and went to the appointed place: to wait for her life to begin.

The daily visits from the clergy of Saint James's were welcomed by the Barnes sisters, just as soon as Gladys realized that neither Mr Geddes nor the curate were going to take advantage of them to plead with her and Annie to go more often to church.

Gladys felt herself responsible for this incursion of respectability, in its highest form, into life at the cottages, and the feeling was accompanied by a sensation of being protected. Someone, she felt, was now keeping a daily eye, so to speak, on the more helpless inhabitants.

Too much of an eye, she was soon saying, so far as Erika was concerned; for Mrs Geddes had had the latter to a buffet-supper at the Vicarage, introducing her on that occasion to some members of the Youth Club; and was now talking about 'training'; this, looming ever larger on Erika's small horizon, seemed to be connected with 'being a nurse', and, as it threatened those vague but splendid plans of being a cook that Gladys had in mind for her protégée, it was suspect.

Gladys had loudly pointed out that nowadays nurses had to be ever so clever and 'go into a lot of those examinations', whereupon Erika had announced that examinations would not frighten her; Mrs Geddes had said she was 'bright as a botton'.

'Oh you are, are you?' retorted Gladys, jealousy wrestling with affection and pride in her heart, 'well that's nice to hear – p'raps she'll tell you how you can smoke smoke smoke all day without drying up the poor souls you're nursing like so many kippers? We'd just like to know, wouldn't we, Miss Gallagher?'

The three were standing outside a small greengrocery shop in one of the back streets near the cottages; Gladys had suggested going to old Mrs Watson's that afternoon, as it was 'that blowy, sure to rain again any minute, we won't go up the Archway.' The use of her old acquaintance's surname, rather than the usual 'Violet', was intended to make Erika feel her present behaviour was more or less shutting her off from familiar intercourse with approving friends.

Miss Gallagher, having named her requirements to Mrs Watson while the latter moved slowly around a kind of cave in the wall piled up with potatoes and carrots, felt that something pleasant might usefully be said.

'Going to the dance next week?' she asked of the silent Erika. 'In the church hall.'

'Never knew there was one!' cried Gladys, eager, as always, for news, 'never heard about no dance, did we, Erika?' Erika slowly shook her head. She had progressed to lipstick; it was called *Way-Out Melon*.

'You ought to go,' Miss Gallagher said; she, for her part, was always eager to send someone off to somewhere nice, and, for that matter, to go herself, when her very exiguous means would permit.

'I would lak,' pronounced Erika, after some, but not much, reflection.

'Oh Mrs P. would never let her, no, can't be done, it's the Church, see?' Gladys accompanied this with meaning nods and more than one wink at her friend. 'Very funny about Church she is, isn't she, Erika?'

'I would lak,' Erika slowly repeated, her eyes fixed on distance.

'Oh she ought to go. It's going to be lovely. They're having The Spacemen and refreshments. Only three and six. You ought to go,' said Miss Gallagher earnestly.

'Well, best forget it,' said Gladys. 'Don't want no more trouble – Vicar knocked him over, don't want any more of that, do we? I was just looking out of the window, drawing the blackout – blackout! hark at me!' (a cackle of laughter in which Miss Gallagher more gently joined) – 'and there they were, just down the street. Called out at him and the Vicar stopped and they had a word and he hit him. Never so surprised in my life – gave me quite a turn.'

'The Vicar did? Hit who?' Miss Gallagher exclaimed, stupefied. 'The *Vicar*?'

'Shouldn't have said that, no, don't tell a soul, Violet, never do if it got round, no it wouldn't, yes he did. Fell over. I nearly hollered out loud. The rackman. Fell over. Good thing it wasn't raining.'

Many years' acquaintance with Gladys Barnes had taught Miss Gallagher that incidents related by her had a colouring of drama which they did not, if you happened afterwards to hear the facts from someone else, actually possess. She now dismissed the account as 'one of Glad's tales' and turned the conversation once more to a matter about which she might afterwards hear something interesting that was also true.

'Oh you ought to go,' she said to Erika, 'oughtn't she?'

Gladys earnestly repeated that it wouldn't never do; the dance was 'got up' by the Church.

'Let her go up to that buffy-supper at the Vicarage but I s'pose that's different, p'raps she might, as it's that Youth Club, I don't know, reckon all your money's gone on cigarettes, hasn't it?' to Erika, 'spends I don't know what, don't you?'

'I zmoke Mrs P.'s cigarettes,' explained Erika with dignity, 'all der time.'

'Oh . . . well. I s'pose it's all right then,' said Gladys, righteous indignation collapsing under the calm enormity of this state-ment, 'so long as she don't mind . . . 'ow many a day do you reckon, for mercy's sake?'

'You heard from your nephew lately?' put in Miss Gallagher; not hastily, but slid in on a gliding note, bred of long practice in diverting the course of situations created by Gladys Barnes. The stratagem was successful.

'Only yesterday!' cried Gladys dramatically, 'well, how strange you should ask. Only a p.c. but ever such a pretty little place, Osney, regular village it is and got a job in the old Guard House. Under the National Trust it is, got a little bungalow right next door to it and a good bit of garden, has to show people round it, there's a kind of museum, old guns and things, says we must go down in the summer and see it. Fancy you should ask.'

'And how's the old gentleman these days?' pursued Miss Gallagher, seeing that the subject of Georgie Barnes must be limited, unless they delved into his past life, to what had been on the postcard.

'Not himself,' announced Gladys, with equal drama but in another key, 'not himself at all. Very frail. Doesn't have his walk every day now, and don't go far afield with those rubbishing dolls. Hasn't given himself another name not for weeks now. Used to go right up as far as Harringay this time last year, but none of that these days. Up in his room most of the time. Comes down to us for lunch most Sundays. Annie will have her way. Don't smell no fish and chips, neither.'

Miss Gallagher looked mild inquiry.

'Sometimes of a Saturday,' explained Gladys, 'very arbitary about what he eats, always going on about brown bread, nasty old cardboard I say, but likes his fish and chips every now and then, we always smell it, been looking deffly pale too. Well so long we must be toddling.'

Summer's getting along – if you can call it summer, she thought vaguely, as they hurried homewards before the threatening rain; a wet, cloudy, hushed summer, reluctant and brooding. The green leaves hung limp in the soaked air. June: seems more like September, thought Gladys.

At tea-time, when she accompanied Erika with the tray on a visit to Mrs Pearson, she found the latter looking disturbed.

'Anything the matter?' asked Gladys bluntly, after the tray had been settled and the first cup poured, '*he* been upsetting you?' The Reverend Gerald Corliss had just left, and Gladys had not quite the respect and liking for him that she had for the Vicar.

'No, oh no, dear. But I am upset – there's going to be a phone call and it's going to bring trouble.' Erika, who had been about to launch a request that she might go to the Spacemen's dance, lowered her curtain of sulks and instantly determined that *go she would*, no matter what 'trouble'.

'Oh don't say that!' cried Gladys, dismayed and excited.

'It's true, dear. It's coming. Later this afternoon. You'll see.'

'But who'll it be? Who from? Can you tell that, too?' Gladys asked, almost whispering, as she approached closer to the subject of her landlady's mysterious powers. She stood by the bed, with folded arms, looking fearfully down on the skeletal form.

'Something to do with Peggy. I dread it – oh, I do dread it,' Mrs Pearson whispered.

'I'll go,' said Gladys, in spite of a sudden fear that the antici-pated call might be from 'another world than this', 'I'll answer it. Give them a bit of my mind, too, if we have any sauce. You leave it to me.'

'It's kind of you, dear. All right, if you like. But Erika could do it, couldn't you, *schatz*?' turning to her. Erika parted lips well coated with *Way-Out Melon*.

'I would lak,' she announced, 'go to that dance with the Zpacemen.'

'With – what *is* she talking about?' demanded Mrs Pearson, turning wearily to Gladys.

'Some dance at the church my friend was telling us three and six quite enough too nothing but washy lemon powder and bang bang bang enough to deafen you on those drums and they like doing it anyway – *Oh my goodness there it is!*'

The telephone bell's shrillness seemed to leap out into the silence of the house; urgent, insistent, frightening.

'I'll go – I'll go,' Gladys babbled, not moving.

Mrs Pearson gave her a loving smile. 'You're a dear soul, Glad Barnes. Off you go, then; it's nothing to frighten you – only bad news for me. Bad news about my Peggy.'

30

'H-hullo? Who's there?'

Gladys half-expected to hear some ghastly tones from the vaults or haunted seashore of a horror-film.

'Oh is that you, Gladys? How nice to hear your voice,' said Mrs Lysaght. 'I just —'

'Oh — oh — it's you! Oh, I'm not half glad — very pleased to hear you speak — I was —'

'Why, is something wrong? I hope Mrs Pearson hasn't been very much upset by all this business?'

'No — she's all right — a bit better, I'd say, with them calling regular every day but keeps ever so thin — what business, excuse me?'

'Why — but you don't mean to tell me she hasn't heard? It's hardly believable — the girl's own mother. Have they quarrelled?'

'Not so far as I know — but what's 'appened? We never heard a thing.'

'That girl has simply *gone off*,' proclaimed Mrs Lysaght. 'About a week ago. Left half her clothes and her room upside-down and never said a word to anyone . . . she worked for a great friend of mine, I know her quite well, I used to see her almost every time I went there — and my friend is so upset. The dogs miss her dreadfully, you see.'

'Poor little things. Well I never,' marvelled Gladys, enjoying all this the more because it was so unlike the eerie communication from comic-book-land which she had anticipated. ''Ave you told the pleece?'

'No. My friend, Mrs Corbett, won't hear of that. She says Peggy's of age (and more than capable of taking *very* good care of herself, if you ask *me*) – and it's up to her people. But I did think my friend ought just to *get in touch* with Mrs Pearson, to see if she had any news. However – she won't, so that's why *I* called up.'

'She won't half be upset,' murmured Gladys.

'She hasn't heard from her, then?'

'Not for days, I don't think. She did say, though – only this afternoon, it was ever so queer –' Gladys paused, hesitating and blundering.

'Queer? How?' Mrs Lysaght pounced.

'Said there was going to be a phone call with news. Said it not fifteen minutes ago.'

'News about Peggy?'

'That's the funny part.'

A pause followed. Both were wondering what to say next. Into the silence came a faint imploring call from upstairs:

'Glad!'

Gladys started. 'There she is! Calling out. I'll just run up and tell her – shan't be a tick.'

'Yes, do – oh – and, Gladys, see if you can't persuade her to give me a sitting. You know – tell my fortune – I would so adore it – I'm thrilled by all that kind of thing.'

Gladys toiled up the stairs. A conviction that Mrs Lysaght was a bit soft was in her mind, so firmly lodged behind the barriers set up by habit, loyalty, and gratitude for those pound notes sent off every Christmas, that it never rose beyond them.

But she did feel that this was hardly the moment to make a suggestion about telling fortunes.

Mrs Pearson was sitting upright, a listening look on her white face framed in the burden of princess-like hair. She heard the news, given by Gladys with a conscious attempt at softening it, in silence; then lay back on the pillows.

'All right, Gladys. Thank you, dear.'

'She said would you tell her fortune,' added Gladys, 'but don't you do it, not if you don't want to − I'll tell her, shall I?' She lingered, troubled by this silence, this weary falling back on to the bed. Mrs Pearson shook her head. 'Oh − I don't know. I can't say now. Tell her . . .' her voice changed slightly 'ask her to ring up again.'

Gladys gave the message and heard her old employer's eager promise to do so. When, she asked, when? Gladys said she didn't know, and hung up the receiver.

A week passed. The evening of the dance at Saint James's church hall approached. Mrs Pearson had not mentioned Peggy's name again. She lay quiet for most of the day, smoking without pause, her eyes fixed on the glimpses of summer sky visible through the window.

Gradually, a fear for Mrs Pearson, mingled with a vague grief, began to diffuse itself through the cottages; a cloud, a whisper, rising from the hearts of the three old people. She was so changed − and still changing. Gladys said nothing; but, sometimes, she shook her head.

Erika had not bothered herself by asking Mrs Pearson a second time if she might go to the dance. She was collecting, with teutonic thoroughness, her equipment. Dress, shoes, stockings, and a hair-band that was to clasp the narrow end of the pear lay neatly displayed along the top of her chest-of-drawers, together with a new *Way-Out Melon* (the original was used up), a tiny plastic box of sapphire eye-shadow, and a bottle of scent named *Brazilian Night*.

Her room shone, gleamed, and smelt fresh. Every object was in place to a hair's-breadth. The bed might have been made under the eye of a sergeant-major. The old book of German fairy tales, placed beside her bed by Mrs Pearson's order, had gone into the dust-bin: Erika did not like torn, shabby things; also, all that – the Märchen – was nonsense.

After a few weeks of staring, eating to stupefaction, and learning her surroundings, she had suddenly fallen, like a quintessence of all German housewives, on the dusty, disorderly room. When she had brought home a bunch of flowers, and arranged it in a vase and put it, after consideration, now here and now there, and finally on the mantelpiece, and taken a slow stare round the fresh orderly place, a broad, gnome's smile of satisfaction split her queer face. *Gut*, thought Erika, *sehr gut*.

She felt grateful to Mrs Pearson for giving her this room for her very own, and sorry, in a preoccupied way, that she was ill all the time, now, and hardly spoke. But she went calmly on with her preparations.

The dance was announced by a placard, tacked to one of the ancient wooden posts that still marked where a gate had once protected the cobbled lane beside the church from intruders. It was drawn by Barry Disher, whose gifts, varying from one for lettering to one for religious enthusiasm, suggested the riches poured forth by Michelangelo or Lord Bacon; it had a picture of *The Spacemen*, with blown-out cheeks and hair wantoning over their collars. (Barry's own hair was of a temperate length, and perhaps the pictured locks indicated some degree of humorous disapproval.)

The distant but still horrible noise made by the four, hard

at work, echoed down the quiet, elder-shaded, litter-scattered lane, sounding like sweetest Chaminade or Chopin to Erika as she approached.

Mrs Geddes was sitting in the door of the hall at a table where the tickets were given out, looking absently into the summer evening. She smiled at Erika: the scarlet coat over a skimpy red dolly-rocker, the eyes glittering with anticipatory joy, and the *Way-Out Melon*, gave the old woman a happiness and tenderness that must not overflow. (You must never comment; nearly all of them resented comment.)

'Good evenink, Mrs Geddes,' said Erika correctly, holding out three and sixpence in a white-gloved paw, while her eyes struck past her into the hall, where flags and coloured decorations could be glimpsed, 'Der boy Barry Disher is he here?'

'Yes, he's here. Thank you. You can put your coat in there, look.'

She watched while Erika peeled it off; she could almost see the powerful young woman emerging from the chrysalis of a terrible childhood; the wings were powdered, not with gold dust, but with strong, coarse bronze.

'I can't make der dance,' Erika confided cheerfully. She looked across at Mrs Geddes and her smile flashed. 'But I learn quick.'

She launched herself into the crowd, and began to move through the tossing, gyrating groups, toughly inserting herself under flying limbs and past whirling legs until she was level with Barry and the tower-headed girl he was partnering. Mrs Geddes saw him stop, in the midst of a particularly violent contortion of his thin young self, and turn to her. Mrs Geddes nodded in satisfaction.

'All right – you don't mind, do you, Bunny?' Barry said to the tower-headed one, who blithely shook her head and continued to stomp and sway by herself. 'Come on – give us your hand – like this . . .'

When Mrs Geddes next glanced towards them, Erika was whirling and stamping like a dollyrock'd dervish, her skimpy skirt sliding up and down to reveal flashes of white frill and lively knees; her hair had shaken down from its confining scarlet band and was flying about her face.

Four hours passed like one. She found partners all the time; the gnome's smile and the abundant energy drew them without effort on her part; she was a success. The members of the Youth Club whom she had met at the Vicarage were present, and had spread the rumour that 'that chick had had a deprived childhood'; fortunately, the other girls present this evening had enough success themselves to prevent their saying more than 'She doesn't act deprived'. There were some murmurs of 'You can say that again'.

As she drew near to the cottages, midnight was striking from the steeple among the crowded television masts on the old roofs.

She ran the last hundred yards, keeping in the shadow of the ruinous doorways to avoid a group of boys that was attacking, almost silently, a man at the end of the Walk. She waited until they were all concentrated over his fallen body, kicking and smiting in hushed fury, then shot lightly past, on the other side of the street and gained her own front door.

She rang the bell imperiously; she had not yet been promoted to a latchkey. After a prolonged interval, it was opened by Mr Fisher. Erika did not turn at once from her silent contemplation of the group still busy at the corner. He peered out, past her.

'What? – t-t – my Gawd. Shocking, innit.' His long mask hung beside her, horrified and sad. Erika shrugged.

'In Germany,' she said, almost whispering, not turning her head, 'I haf seen shootings. Witz blood.'

'I dare say you have . . . and you aren't the only one. Now come on in, you don't want to get mixed up with that . . . Where you been? Some dance?'

She nodded, and turned a face glowing with remembered pleasure. 'I dance. Oh, I did dance, Mr Fisher!'

He was shutting the door, having gently motioned her inside. 'Now I wonder,' he mused, 'should I phone up the rozzers?'

He paused, listening, holding the door ajar. The street was empty now, save for a dark object lying on the pavement; not moving. Everything was quiet. The old man shook his head. 'Poor soul,' he said. 'Lying there.'

Erika yawned suddenly. 'I go to bed,' she announced. 'Goodnight, Mr Fisher.'

'That's right. Best place for you.' She ran off, swinging her head-band blithely.

He lingered in the hall. It was absolutely silent; the pink light shone down on the prettiness everywhere, giving a false calm. 'Chances are,' muttered Mr Fisher, 'by the time they get 'ere it'll be all over bar the shoutin' . . . best leave well alone.'

He looked after Erika, as she vigorously mounted the last stair. 'Flyin' around everywhere now, and couldn't hardly creep when you first come – it's all this food they give them nowadays, I don't hold with it. They can say what they like, I don't hold with it.'

When the soft mumble of his words ended, the silence came forward again. The peaceful stairs beckoned him up to his bed. The absolute stillness always characteristic of the cottage was, if possible, deepened by the hour, but from outside the thick, closely shut old door came the myriad murmurs of a London summer night, indistinguishable from one another in the vast, coarse hum rising from all over the city's sleepless miles, but unmistakably sinister. The old man's eyes were fixed on the door, as if trusting in its age and thickness, yet seeing beyond it the dusty pavement, and the battered head, cooling, perhaps, on the stone.

He moved a little towards the stairs, then hesitated, turning back towards the telephone on the table. It was more a twisting, hesitant movement of his body than of his feet; he swayed, as if caught in conflicting currents, and all the time he murmured disconnectedly. At last, as if bracing himself, he almost snatched the receiver in his firmest clasp, and dialled the frightening, yet comforting, signal that meant help would come.

In his firmest voice, too, he gave the details, and the place, and his name. A voice, calm and authoritative, instructed him. When he replaced the receiver, he passed his pale tongue over his dry lips and sighed dreadfully; his heart shook against his rib-cage as if it were an animal bounding from side to side and trying to get out; he had never been so aware of it, and he felt, too, what power it had, how he relied upon it, how it sent the blood that kept him alive running along his veins. It was dreadfully moved to-night, it wanted to take him creeping upstairs, and make him lie down quietly in his room in the dark.

But – 'Might juss make that difference,' he muttered. 'Curse the lot of them. Beasts and pigs. Don't suppose he's no better than the rest. But it might make all the difference.' He shook his head, compressing his lips, shutting his eyes.

'Gawd –' said Mr Fisher, 'don't You think I'm doing this for You. You and me parted brass-rags when Minnie . . . It's on'y that it might juss make all the difference. You never know. It juss might.'

He shuffled to the door, and, with difficulty because his hands were shaking so and because every pore and cell in his body was shrieking to him to keep it shut, he turned the catch and slid it open.

The warm blue night looked mildly in, and a whisper of wind cooled his face. The colossal murmur of the streets, indifferent yet threatening, flowed against his ear-drums. He shuffled quickly down the steps, under the eyes of the horned, smiling head, and down the Walk, between the silent and boarded houses, towards the bundle lying on the pavement. There was not a soul about; not a car; not a footstep or a sound; only the night and the distant roar of the wakeful streets.

It was very dreadful to see. Mr Fisher, the lover of green grass and leaves, felt sickness begin to rise in him as he looked at it. He made his trembling knees bend until he knelt beside it, and he put out his clean, ancient hands to feel the heart. Don't touch anything – it always said – but . . . feel . . . there were buttons to undo, and while he was fumbling helplessly, almost senselessly with them and muttering through shaking lips – 'If we was all . . . all of us . . . everyone . . . might juss make the difference . . .' someone crept up behind him and a shadow fell across him.

He started round and looked up; in time to see a face, ripe and smooth, with a frightened boy's grin, and young muscles lifting leather-clad arms above rich, flowing hair, before he was struck with enough force to kill him: more than enough indeed; a quarter of it would have sufficed.

31

The Police and the Church, between them, managed it all, and got Mr Fisher's body put tidily, and even with a brief reverence, into the earth; on a morning of steady sunlight, beating down out of the bluest of skies.

When the sisters were at home again, Gladys could not resist the temptation to speak of what had been in her mind ever since the shocking early hours, three days ago, when they had been aroused with the news of his death.

'What about his things, Annie?' she burst out, with a glance towards the ceiling.

'Oh Glad! It wouldn't be right.'

'Oo says so? Give me his key, didn't she – "You do it, Glad dear," she says, "I'm so tired". Might be mice in there or anything . . .'

But what Gladys was thinking might be 'in there' was money; savings; a *hoard*, like you read about sometimes in *The People* or the *Hornsey Journal*.

'But all his things, Glad. He always kept himself so private.'

'Too private, I'd say . . . there's a mystery there, I often thought to myself. Got a fortune hidden away, I shouldn't wonder.'

'A fortune! Why, he couldn't hardly afford a bit of fish and chips not more than once a munf!'

'There was that man in Hornsey Lane, lived in that 'ouse opposite those new flats, regular recluse, all over spiders everythink was, the paper said, and two hundred pounds up the chimney!'

'Silly place to put it,' was Annie's comment.

'Well, 'oo *is* to go, if I don't?' Gladys demanded as her sister was silent. '*She* won't, and I s'pose *you* won't, seeing the way you're carrying on, and I'm not having Erika up there.'

'Then I s'pose it'll have to be you,' muttered Annie, defeated.

'I s'pose it will. And don't go creating about it afterwards, *if* you please.'

'Oh do leave me alone, Glad, there's a dear,' and Annie, weeping, retreated into the ghost of a long-discarded balaclava.

A few days passed. Gladys, after the day's holiday given her with willing sympathy by the Cypriots to attend the funeral, went back to her work, and life continued: yet it was greatly changed; she felt the change so strongly that her cheerfulness deserted her.

In the cottage the hush, always noticeable, was now oppressive; it weighed upon her so that she had not even the spirit to grumble at everyone – Annie, herself, Mrs Pearson, the rackman – for being 'so down'.

The man, of course, was not grieving for Mr Fisher; *his* heart was not likely to be touched by the murder of a tenant paying eight and sixpence a week. She knew this; and she expected to return from work any afternoon and hear that Mr Fisher's attic was to be let; at ten times the rent.

No; it was Mrs Pearson the rackman was worrying about; her increasing thinness, her silence. Gladys had glimpsed, and overheard as she went about her occupations, his low-toned arguments in the hall and on the landing with Mr Geddes or the curate, in which Pearson's obstinacy and growing anguish struggled against accepting their advice to consult a doctor.

Yet Gladys thought that Mrs Pearson, 'in herself', as the slightly mysterious phrase has it, seemed what she thought of as brighter. She had had no more, so far as Gladys knew, of those frightening attacks and the clergy went away from their daily visits with faces that were grave but not sad.

It was mid-June; the big poppies were out in the parks, and the evenings were long, long, and lingering into a crystal dusk.

Mrs Corbett had been brought as near to stubborn resentment as her nature could come, by Peggy's flight. She would not talk about her, and even reproved the dogs for missing her; she was tart with Arnold for obviously missing her too, and when, on one of the long evenings, when he had returned early from an engagement in London and they were sitting in the bay window over-looking the valley, he confessed that he had 'thought about marrying' her, anger and astonishment and shock exploded into a bitter sentence about gold-diggers.

'No, Mamma, you can't accuse her of that. She's lazy and likes her comforts, that's all. (They aren't like most people's, either.) But she wouldn't marry for money, and she dislikes me, if anything.'

'I suppose she'd marry for these "comforts" whatever they may be – she's such a *peculiar* girl – why you had to choose . . . and there's poor Gwen . . .'

'Oh nonsense about poor Gwen. She's been tied up for years with Arthur Bennett.'

'Arnold! No! How *dreadful*!'

He shrugged. 'Now keep it dark, will you? I didn't mean to tell you, only . . .'

'But *poor* Elsie. Such a devoted couple . . . I always thought . . .'

'That's just it,' Arnold said darkly.

He had hoped that the revelation might have deflected her thoughts, but realized that the first confidence naturally possessed staying-power over the second: she returned immediately to his confession.

'I never imagined it for an *instant*. I thought you got on quite well, of course, not like you were with Alice – and even Peggy, splendid though she was with the dogs, wasn't like dear Alice – well, if all this has been going on, I wonder you haven't done something about finding out where she is.'

'I know where she is.' He leant forward to stub out a cigarette. 'Or I'm almost certain I do.'

'Arnold! You're quite extraordinary to-night! Where is she, then?'

He told her, briefly, about the excursion to Sussex on Easter Sunday and the girl who had turned her horse and galloped away in terror.

'There's a man there,' he concluded, 'runs the school, I expect. That's where Peggy will be.'

Mrs Corbett was nearly eighty-four years old; a cherished, healthy, placid eighty-four, and supported on a plinth of years that had been of almost unclouded pleasantness. Yet there *had* been eighty-four of them – and she suddenly felt that she did not want, after this last piece of information that hinted at a scandal, this evening, to hear anything more that was surprising and unpleasant.

She looked across at her son through the contact lenses that allowed her eyes to shine almost as blue and clear as they had at sixty, and said, grumpily:

'I suppose you'll be off down there any day, then,' and his answer was, 'Yes; I'm just giving the thing time to pack up, and then I'm going.'

She said no more. It was a stranger, crueller world than the one she remembered. There was a favourite television programme due in five minutes, and she turned, with a sensation of comfort, to that. He left her; sitting in the bay overlooking the meadows now hemmed in by houses, where the propellers of aeroplanes sent to the scrap heap half a century ago roared silently behind the noise and glitter of a main road.

Peggy had been gone three weeks. He did nothing more about his plan; he waited.

An instinct, vague yet strong, prompted him to let a month elapse before he went to Sedgemere. It was so imperious that he did not even trouble to find out if she were staying near there; it let him take the risk of ignoring the house in the bomb-broken slum where her mother might tell him where she was. It compelled him to wait, passively, until next week would bring the month to an end.

One evening towards the middle of June, while her sister had ventured out to Joneses, Gladys suddenly marched out on to the landing and stood, arms akimbo, looking challengingly up Mr Fisher's stairs.

Ever so queer to think he had gone . . . and *where*? Gladys turned her thoughts away from *that*, and ran them rapidly over the situation in the cottages.

Mrs Pearson asleep; she had made certain by a cautious peep round the door . . . Annie chin-wagging round at Joneses (not that I grudge her, thought Gladys . . . making up for lost time) . . . Erika off out somewhere . . . been more like herself since the old gentleman went . . . so long as she don't take up with some beast in a caff. However, reflection assured her that Erika was dowered with that mysterious capacity for 'looking after herself' which could handle even a beast in a caff. The rackman . . .

Gladys actually shivered. Lord send the rackman didn't choose this evening to come nosing up to Mr Fisher's room. Oh well, she thought, take my chance, that's all. She felt the key in her overall pocket.

The calm evening light covered ancient woodwork and grimed paint with its benison. A faded pearl sky looked in through the landing's one window. The house was quite quiet. Gladys, rather slowly, began the short ascent.

Eight stairs; carpetless; splintered at the treads. They ended, abruptly, before the comfortably-shaped broad door of an old house, yet its filthy brown paint made it seem forlorn. A heavy lock, with black paint rusting off. Gladys put the clumsy key into the keyhole, and briskly turned it. It moved easily – 'Oil,' muttered Gladys and pushed open the door, and went straight in.

'Well I never,' she muttered in a moment, after a standing survey, the key dangling from her fingers, 'ever so bare . . .'

It was the only word she had to express the stripped, dedicated poverty of the attic.

The bed was a pile of old blankets, their coverlet Mr Fisher's dressing-gown. There was no bed-linen, no pillow. A row of nails held a few thick old clothes. The floor was carpetless, the grate overflowing with the peculiarly white ash that is left by a wood fire. There was a large cupboard, and a big old zinc tub in one corner with a chipped jug standing in it; one of those that used to go with a basin when there were wash-stands, wreathed with poppies in a pallid red, and in front of the uncurtained window, where the stars must look in, winter and summer, a kitchen table.

On it a large old suitcase, shut.

Gladys went straight across to it, and, nodding to herself in triumph, tried the catches.

Ah! The second one slid back. She lifted the lid – and her eyes leapt, burrowed, darted, into the contents.

It was a full minute before she could take in the fact that they were nothing but piles of used envelopes; all kinds; their torn edges meticulously trimmed and the original addresses carefully scratched out. Evidently a pair of scissors, so tiny, so spidery, so rusted that they must have been at least a hundred years old, had been used, and the Biro, which lay beside them in one of the small compartments in the lining, had readdressed them.

There were also many odd sheets of paper, apparently torn from magazines or paperbacks with a blank half or quarter sheet; these were stacked, as neatly as their irregular shape permitted, with the envelopes.

It was an address on one of the latter that caught Gladys's eye as she was slamming the lid shut with a violence that expressed her bitter disappointment.

'His Excellency the Prime Minister of Eire' – what on earth . . .?

She snatched up another from the pile. 'The Hon. Mrs Eyles, 53 Brogan Street, W.4.' And another, 'Sir John Formby, The Sheridan Theatre, Birmingham.'

Gladys had heard of begging-letter writers. She instantly decided that this was how Mr Fisher had 'kept himself going'.

She had never believed that his sale of the straw dolls in their beads could bring in enough money, added to his pension and money from the Assistants, for even an old man to live on in these days, and here, in the case, was the proof of his real source of income.

The discovery made up, in a little, for her disappointment. And there was still the cupboard!

She had just started to rummage enjoyably through the mass, when there was a step outside, and a man's voice said, 'Hullo, Miss Barnes.'

Gladys, as she afterwards described it to Annie, jumped almost out of her skin. She added that just for a minute she had thought it was *him* come back again – a thought not pleasant to one engaged as she was. But it was that curate from up the church; a visitor hardly more welcome.

'Oh . . . hullo . . . good-evening, ever so nice now, isn't it, I was just . . .' she said, with false welcome gleaming in teeth and eye.

Gerald said nothing. He was not yet capable of rebuking someone, of background different from his own, whom he found in suspicious circumstance; also – he must be fair to her – she might have been deputed to go through the old man's possessions, though her manner did not suggest it.

'Mrs Pearson give me the key,' said Gladys, as if thought-reading, 'poorly to-day, nerves I suppose but what good do you do lying up, I often ask myself, suppose we all did, many's the time, you keeping well?'

'Yes, thank you . . . er . . . I came to see if I could be of any help . . . er . . . use?'

'Help me go through this here old rubbish if you'd be so kind,' cried Gladys merrily, having decided at lightning speed that there really were no notes concealed in the envelopes, 'day's work here, if you ask me, won't keep you long not if you're busy, always plenty to do isn't there?'

She ruffled her hands in the suitcase, as if rinsing clothes, while Gerald cautiously approached.

Together, standing side by side in the bare, haunted, room, they turned over the envelopes, commenting on the addresses in tones touched with a curiosity that grew ever stronger.

'Her . . . Majesty . . . Queen . . . Elizabeth . . . the . . . Second, Buckingham . . . Palace . . .' read out Gladys slowly, 'whatever next! Begging off of the Queen. Cheek . . . not that I ought to say it, him being passed over, but did you ever?'

Gerald gently lifted the now confused mass of papers until the bottom of the suitcase was revealed, and as gently, after a survey, set it down again.

'I'm . . . not sure . . . it is – was – begging,' he said absently. 'Have you looked in the cupboard?'

Gladys had been hoping he might overlook the cupboard. While that remained unexplored, there was hope.

'Haven't not only just got up here,' she stated sunnily.

'Well . . . let's look, shall we?' and he crossed towards it and turned the catch on its door.

There was some crockery, and a brown teapot and half a loaf of wholemeal bread on a plate, under a ragged scrap of gauze. But all the other shelves (six of them, for the cupboard ran the height of the room) were filled with those same carefully trimmed and readdressed envelopes; hundreds and hundreds and hundreds of them, stacked with exquisite neatness, filling every niche except about a square foot of the floor, which was occupied by an old wooden box containing bundles of straw and reels of thread and some small transparent packets that glittered.

'Stuff for making them rubbishing dolls,' said Gladys, pointing. But Gerald did not answer. He was looking at something else.

It was a card, tacked on to the inner side of the door, bordered by hand-drawn wreaths of flowers painted in delicate colours and gilt, which surrounded some words written in copperplate:

'My Life's Work' he read in a low voice, and stepped back, slipping his thumbs into the leather belt confining his cassock. 'How . . . Miss Barnes, how strange.'

He put out a finger, as if to touch the card, then withdrew it. 'How *very* strange.'

They stood in silence, staring.

The fading light fell into the attic; the dreadful roar from shaken houses and streets came up to them faintly and without cease; there was a sensation of someone's absence that was strong as a presence. For once, Gladys Barnes had nothing to say.

'Look . . .' Gerald said at last, lifting out some envelopes and ruffling through them, 'they're all addressed to people in one street – right along, from 1 to 102 – in every house, too – he must have walked thousands of miles, over the years, collecting the names, and then delivering the envelopes . . . and here, look, these are all for another street – and here – the streets are in alphabetical order . . . what *can* it all be?'

'Must have brought him in a regular fortune,' Gladys cried, willingly shaking off the silence and the feeling of that absence strong as a presence, 'question is, *where's he hidden it?*'

Gerald rather energetically shook his head; as if defending something from the crass stupidity of the world.

'No, no, it isn't that, of course it isn't that, Miss Barnes, it isn't *getting money* – "My Life's Work", how could that be –' he broke off. He was silent.

'Must have been mental, then,' suggested Gladys who, in the pause, had also had her thoughts about money, 'never would believe it, always said he wasn't. But writing envelopes all round the place, must have been.'

'What was in them?' Gerald was muttering, as he knelt before the lowest shelf and carefully lifted and replaced each pile, after glancing beneath, 'that's the answer, what was in them?'

''Ullo, 'ere's something,' and Gladys, who had been using her eyes while he used his hands, pounced on a piece of folded paper lying half-hidden at the end of a shelf, 'that's been through a bit of wear, hasn't it?'

The paper was almost cracked in two with use; it fell open limply in Gerald's scrupulous hands.

'Well, tell us,' said Gladys impatiently, as he continued to study it without speaking, 'does it say where it is?'

Still Gerald made no reply, and when he did at last hand it to her, he had not spoken. Gladys studied the paper impatiently, while he, slowly rocking on his heels, stared out of the window into the fading light.

'Kind of a letter,' Gladys said finally, spelling out under her breath the ceremonious copperplate:

'Dear, Missus, Mister – I beg you never to give thoughts to war, in no way, not to work for it, not by writing nor by reading about it nor by looking at the pictures nor on the television about it. Not in any way ever, at all. Not by being a soldier, sailor, airman, work in factory or above all at atom bombs. *Above all* atom bombs. No obligation for this, dear fellow creature. Signed Your Fellow Creature.'

'P.S.,' said Gerald slowly, without turning from the window, '*If we all do this, we shall succeed.*'

The last of the silences that had fallen between them that afternoon fell between them now.

'Funny . . .' Gladys said at last, '*must* have been mental. Going on about war and atom bombs. Must have been. Oh well, it's all a lot of rubbish, the dustman'll create if he sees it, ever so arbitrary they are if there's a bit extra, get the place cleaned up quick then Mrs P. can let it, hope we get someone nice that's all, not much room except for one, is there, what say we take it all downstairs and burn it in the yard?'

'What?' he asked, slowly turning, 'I'm sorry, Miss Barnes – what were you saying?'

'Take it down, burn it in the yard,' Gladys repeated impatiently; her lowish opinion of Gerald Corliss, formed on that first afternoon when she had called at the Vicarage to ask for advice about the rackman, had been strengthened by this evening's work. 'Best thing to do.'

'No – not yet,' he exclaimed, 'look, Miss Barnes, I'd just like to look over these papers, it won't take long, if you'll give me twenty minutes? They're – interesting.'

Gladys dismissed a suspicion that he might have found a clue to the hiding-place of Mr Fisher's fortune which she had overlooked. He wouldn't be likely to do that, not a curate – might want it for the church, though, but then – no. She rapidly decided in his favour.

'All right, then. What say I make us a cup of tea? You could do with one, I expect and I'm sure I can.'

'Thank you . . . er . . . what a splendid idea.'

Gladys went off, not with her usual haste. Suspicion lingered.

In the dusk that had now crept into the room Gerald found candles, lit several, and began to turn over the envelopes stacked along the shelves. They were in perfect order: every house in two streets named Waterman and Ellis, lying next to one another in the south-eastern part of the Borough of Camden, were covered; and apparently every family living in them had its letter; in the same earnest formula.

The words of Mr Fisher's letter seemed to sound silently through the twilight and the silence as he read.

'Is it nothing to you, all ye that pass by?' and the answer, as it always had been and always would be, was *nothing*.

Yet, for a Christian, despair was a sin.

The finish of the enormous, dotty, noble dream was there; in the old suitcase on the table.

Gerald shut the case and went away, leaving behind him a

fortune indeed, but not of the kind to be recognized by Gladys Barnes.

If he had trusted God, he thought, as he went down the stairs, if only he could have trusted.

But God did not give to everyone the gift of trusting in Him, and what had to be said was, 'Though Thou slay me, yet will I trust Thee.'

That was what had to be choked out somehow, from the human heart and in the human voice.

32

Arnold's memory for landmarks was excellent. He recalled, as he approached Sedgemere in its small valley, having noticed on the Easter Day visit a large, smart public house, lying back from the road, perhaps a mile on the London side of the village. He made towards it.

The saloon bar was full. It was a prosperous-looking crowd of commuters, known to each other, exhausted after the day spent in London's pressures, and noisy with nervous tension. Arnold ordered a pink gin, and, by a stroke of luck, caught the barman's further attention amidst the loud voices and the smooth red necks.

'Any chance of a bed here. Do you let rooms?'

'We do, sir; but the place is smaller than you'd think. We've only got three rooms, and they're occupied.' He was hovering, almost on the wing, as he spoke.

'Do you happen to have a Miss Pearson staying here?'

It would be too much to say that the man leered or brightened; but there was a change in his expression, a kind of masking of suddenly aroused interest.

'Yes, sir, Room Three.' He added, 'But she's out this evening . . . three double whiskies, yes, sir, thank you,' to a face, larger, smoother and more carmine than the surrounding ones, that suddenly loomed between them.

This face, too, had showed a change as its owner caught Peggy's name. He looked with concentration at Arnold, who noticed the look, and afterwards saw him rejoin a group near the door, which, after he had said something, turned as one man to stare. The expressions were something less than amiable.

'No idea where she might have gone, I suppose?' Arnold went on, unhurriedly and ignoring the row of faces, and the voices clamouring for same-agains along the curve of the bar. The voices now faltered, unmistakably, and died off into a noticeable hush.

'Couldn't say, sir,' answered the barman, into what was certainly an interested and hostile silence – yes, it was hostile – 'but she may be up at Rattrays'. The riding-school in the village. Understand she used to work there, sir. Good-evening, Mr Burroughs, the usual?' He turned away.

'Thanks,' Arnold said.

He strolled out into the dusk – through the crowd that did not quite make room for him to pass and did not quite stare at him. The stares were furtive. The atmosphere was like a strong smell.

So Peggy's been making herself unpopular, he mused, setting out along a dim white lane between poisoned hedges in the direction of the riding-school. It's that little girl. She looked sweet. I bet they're on her side. Oh well, all the better. I can do with some local support. He wondered if he ought to have brought the car; it must be less than a mile to the riding-school but she might be upset, and need transport . . . if he found her.

But he did not doubt that he would find her; he did not even wonder if he would have to go up to the school itself or how he should approach the people there if he did. My star's guiding me, he thought wryly, casting a cynical glance up at a particularly brilliant one; he had once or twice thought of his strong sensation of guidance as his star. It was almost dark; the line between downs and sky was barely visible. The stars were the 'isles of light' that Byron once called them.

Suddenly, coming round a sharp turn in the lane, he saw her coming slowly towards him; a tall figure in a white coat, moving slowly in the dusk, and crying quietly as she came. Crying! Women! Oh yes, twenty years of loneliness made you cry sometimes, whisky or not, but you didn't cry out loud. He began to walk more quickly. Soundlessly, save for the muffled noise of her sobbing, they approached one another. In a moment he saw the lights of a car, approaching fast, and as it passed him, caught a glimpse of the furious, gesticulating, backward-glancing occupants; they had just missed killing her, and naturally this had irritated them.

After the noise of the engine and the reek of petrol fumes and the impression of anger and resentment had passed, silence and night flowed back into what had formerly been a lonely lane. She was still coming towards him, unshaken, apparently, by her escape, a white moving shape, weeping but more softly now, with her face lifted to the stars. He quickened his step.

'Peggy?'

She let out a full shriek – but almost instantly it stopped. 'Oh – it's you –' She stood, arms hanging, limply, staring at him. He could see her face clearly by the light of the stars, and it was swollen, ravaged, wild.

'Did you think I was going to murder you?'

'Oh – I don't know – a car just nearly knocked me down – there is a man on the run somewhere, they want him for murdering a girl in Brighton yesterday – for a minute I did think –'

'Well, it's only me,' he answered, keeping his voice quiet and normal.

He felt neither. The sight of her face, and the spectacle of Peggy babbling like an ordinary girl – *Peggy* – had shaken him out of his carefully-prepared state of mind. If she was really broken, if she really had had it, then this was his chance, and he might never get another, and he was frightened, because he wanted nothing but Peggy; nothing in the world.

'I saw something on the placards, coming down,' he said indifferently.

'How did you know I was . . . how did you . . . where I was?'

'Guessed.' He firmly took her arm, and, turning her, began to walk back in the direction of the public house. His confidence faltered for an instant; established, as it was, over so much longing and so much fear. 'How . . . are you? Long time no see . . .'

The silly question and the cliché died off into silence. It was a warm night; over a gate in the hedge to the right he noticed a field of long grass, silvery in the starlight. The whole field suddenly shivered towards them, under a caressing wind. He wanted to press her arm.

'You can see how I am, can't you?' Her voice quivered. 'I should think . . . anyone could . . .'

'You needn't mind me. You know I love you.' He had not meant to say it, and he broke into a sweat of fear.

'Oh shut up – shut up, can't you? I don't want anyone to love me . . .' she began to sob again, dragging her arm away and standing still, in the middle of the road, pushing her hands down into her coat pockets. 'It's all . . . you don't know what it's like . . . you don't know . . . I never dreamt . . . I didn't imagine, not for a second, that he'd . . .'

Quite an effort, that, from our Peggy, he thought wryly; I don't suppose she's ever talked to anyone before – except that chap. The warm wind, gathering strength, poured itself against him, laden with the scent of dry grass.

'I suppose he's let you down,' he said bluntly, but almost holding his breath.

'That's it – that's it – he would come back here, and I was to stay here while he settled things up and he's gone back to her – the bitch –' she went on into a maze of what used to be called obscenities; he listened with disgust, with satisfaction, with pity. But the pity was stronger than the satisfaction and the disgust, and slowly, from the depths into which he had thrust them, there rose up the words *poor kid*. She was twenty-two. Not, thought, Arnold, a great age.

'Take it easy,' he said suddenly, taking her arm again, 'this kind of thing's happening all over the world, all the time –'

'She's pregnant. I couldn't *believe* it – she – she – I thought –'

She wrenched herself free and flung herself down into the dust and loose flints of the road, and lay there writhing, uttering choked sounds. Arnold stooped and gripped her and shook her. He was suddenly frightened almost out of his wits.

'Peggy! A car's coming – *get up.*'

The sound of the engine had grown upon his ear even through the shocking sounds that came from her. He wrenched her body aside as the car swept past, after fully revealing the two of them for a second in its powerful headlights. (The occupants, already late for a television programme specializing in scenes of violence, preferred to indulge their taste without risk of involvement, and ignored the girl lying in the road and the man stooping over her.)

He wanted to wipe his face. He was streaming with sweat. He pulled her up, so that she crouched beside him, moaning, 'It's my life. It's my life. You don't understand.'

'I understand absolutely. You had an affair with a chap who's married and he went back to his wife. It's always happening. Didn't you know that – dear?'

'I *knew* we'd be different – he said – he *said* – I *knew* it would be different – at least, I didn't even think about that – I just knew – he said –' Arnold shrugged.

'You mustn't take any notice of what we say. When we want you, we'll say anything. You really didn't know that?' She shook her head (at least, he thought, *something's* getting through to her) as he pulled her to her feet.

'Now, pull yourself together,' he commanded. 'You used to be pretty good at the stiff-upper-lip. Let's see a bit of it . . . it seems to have slipped up somewhat.'

'Shut up and leave me alone.' But she let him take her arm; she let him begin to lead her steadily along the road. They walked in silence for some time; then, as the lights of the public house were seen some hundred yards ahead, she pulled away from him, and stopped.

'I'm not going into that hole. They're all on . . . her . . . side . . . she's lived here ever since she was born or something, and they had the bloody nerve to *disapprove* . . . I didn't notice, at first . . . but then . . . I'm not going in, I won't.'

'There's no need to. The car's outside. All we've got to do is to get into it.'

She said nothing, but let him lead her to it, and stood, motionless, hands in her pockets, staring sullenly at the lights and the regulars coming and going all around them, while he unlocked the doors and opened them.

'I suppose you don't want your things?' he asked, as she slid into the seat beside him. 'Do you owe them anything?'

'No, I don't. I took bloody good care not to.'

'What about your things?'

'It was only a suitcase – nothing much.'

Her tone was indifferent, harsh with crying, and exhausted. But it was undoubtedly more like her usual one, and he began to feel some relaxation of anxiety and fear. If only he could play upon these signs of ordinary humanity in Peggy! Even the monotonously recurring 'bloody', he felt, was reassuring in its school-girlishness.

She was a woman – a girl – and therefore she was not as strong as a man. And he could manage her. Because he was a man, and she was not. It was as simple as that.

It was a black day for you, dear, when you let the upper lip slip, he thought. Or was it? Perhaps – he let the thought shine out for an instant – she needed, and wanted, a master.

'Any plans?' he asked presently.

She shook her head.

'Want to come to Morocco?'

She turned to look at him. The beauty of her eyes was familiar, and struck him with the old, accustomed pain. The stars were bright in their drowned dark depths, glittering between her swollen lids.

'Not particularly. Why? Are you going?'

'I could be. Not to any luxury hotels, I don't mean that kind of trip. I'd camp in the desert, spend five or six months out there, wander about.'

As he spoke, he thought how much he would dislike it; the lack of mildly congenial male society, the solitude, the intrusive and omnipresent sense of Nature uncurbed by the hand of man. Yet what had been his aim in life for over thirty years? To find, and frequent, smart bars, where there were men he could grouse with. To play golf; to drink; to want, and lack, wonderful women.

In the desert there would be Peggy.

'We might go to Brazil,' he said presently, 'see some of those blank spaces on the map they talk about.'

She said nothing. Rather sadly, he offered what he had not wanted to offer. 'I've got plenty of money. We could do things – in style. If you liked,' he added.

'I know that,' she answered crossly. He welcomed the crossness; it suggested that the emotional temperature was sinking.

'All right,' she said grudgingly, at last, and at once hurried on, 'but I'm not sleeping with you. We'd better get that clear from the start.'

'I haven't asked you to,' he said mildly. 'We'd better get married, though; it's better, for all sorts of reasons – I'm not thinking only about what people'll say.'

If Peggy was looking into the cage, testing the strength of its bars with her eye, and measuring the length of the space prescribed for her walking, none of this showed in her face, where there was only sullenness and exhaustion. But perhaps some warning of what this would mean did penetrate her numb, inward anguish. She turned to look at him.

'You *must* get it clear – ' she said, forcing the words out, 'I hardly care whether you're alive or dead. I won't sleep with you. If ever . . . he . . . wants me back I'll go . . . though we're in the middle of Brazil.'

'Oh, it would take a long time from there; long enough for you to change your mind,' said Arnold almost jocosely. And added, 'You may change your mind about a lot of things, before we're through.' He took one hand off the wheel to give her arm a friendly pat. 'You did say "hardly". I shall keep on hoping.'

She turned away, and for the rest of their journey to London looked at the meaningless traffic and houses going by. But presently, as they were passing through the outskirts of the city, she spoke slowly.

'You were right. I've changed my mind already.'

'What?' he exclaimed, unable to control a note of alarm.

'Not about that . . . I mean about going back. I wouldn't now. I hate him.'

Oh, then we're all right, Arnold thought, more hopeful than he had been throughout the crisis. If you hate him, it was just a pash, and from now on I can begin to move in. Deathless adoration, eternal whatsit – and you hate him. Well, well. That isn't the way I love you, and it's not the way you're going to love me. One of these fine days. Some enchanted evening.

33

Mrs Lysaght was sitting in her drawing-room, a week later. It was ten minutes past eleven, and she was sipping her coffee and reflecting that Gretl did not make it as well as a Continental girl should. Gretl was sitting in the kitchen, sipping hers and reflecting with complacence that it tasted just like that served in the London coffee-bars.

Mrs Lysaght's chair commanded a view over the quiet tree-lined road at the back of the flats. Suddenly she uttered an exclamation. Could that be the Rolls, Cora's car? gliding between the parked ranks of lesser machines? Yes, and Frobisher looking more glum than usual. She got up from her chair.

'Gretl! Gretl! Mrs Corbett will be here in a minute. Listen for the bell, dear,' she called musically, at the opened door.

'Ollright.'

'And *don't* say that, dear. "Yes, Mrs Lysaght".' Her employer sat down again, and glanced round the room. Yes: charming. One did not try to *compete* . . .

The bell. Gretl's voice, Frobisher's voice, not a word from Mrs Corbett? Mrs Lysaght thought it more graceful to get up and move towards the door as it opened.

'Cora! What a lovely surprise.'

'All right, Frobisher, wait, will you, please,' her friend said heavily. Face, voice, expression, her summer suit and stole of pale brown ermine, all seemed burdened; her elaborate white hat had no airiness. She turned lifelessly to Mrs Lysaght, who was staring.

'Helen, I felt I must have someone to talk to. Dorry and Madge and Cis can be so unkind about Arnold . . .'

'Of course, dear, of course. Come and sit down, let me take your fur . . .' Mrs Lysaght was so full of thrilled anticipation that she omitted to calculate, as she gently removed it, what it must have cost. 'Is something wrong? Is it Arnold? Not an accident? He isn't—?' She broke off, in hushed, staring alarm.

'Oh no,' Mrs Corbett said bitterly. 'He's perfectly well. I heard from him this morning. By phone, from a hotel in Fez. He's there with . . . Peggy. They were married last Tuesday.'

'Cora! I can't believe it!'

'Well, it's true. I couldn't believe it either at first. I hardly know where I am, I'm so shocked, so hurt, so . . .'

'Here dear, you must have . . .' Mrs Lysaght found enough kindness and pity in herself to forgo the spread feast, and hasten to the door and command Gretl, in carefully controlled tones, to bring another cup. 'And biscuits, Gretl. Hurry, please.'

'Packet finish,' reported Gretl, leisurely, through the crumbs of the last three.

'Open *another*, then.' Mrs Lysaght shut the door and hurried back to Mrs Corbett, who was slumped in her chair and staring at the carpet, and sat down close to her.

'Hadn't you any idea at all?' she asked gently.

'I knew he wanted to marry her. He broke down and told me one evening. I could hardly believe that, either. The last type of girl . . . and he said he knew where she was and was going to find her. I ought to have been prepared, I suppose. He did warn me. (I keep on telling myself that.) But – so sudden. No engagement – nothing. I used to look forward to – to having . . . having . . .' she began to cry, hopelessly, '. . . *grandchildren*,' she ended, crying with bent head, into her tightly-gloved hands.

Mrs Lysaght sat gently patting her. It spoilt the excitement to have her taking it like this. Why couldn't they have talked about Peggy's slyness, and the couple's future plans, and what they would do in Fez, and money?

Gretl came in with biscuits and cup, and, on Mrs Lysaght's mimed instructions, put them down and went out again. Mrs Lysaght muttered. 'Tt-tt.'

'What is it, Helen?' Her friend looked up, a little relieved by tears.

'Oh nothing – she's brought the *packet* in – really, these girls . . . go on, dear.'

'There's nothing more to say, really.' Mrs Corbett wiped her eyes. 'It's all so . . . I don't know . . . I shall just have to put up with it, that's all, I suppose. One thing, I can't have many more years to suffer.'

'Now – now,' Mrs Lysaght gave her a playful shake which Mrs Corbett disliked extremely but was too miserable to shrink from. 'You mustn't talk like that – next year you might have a lovely little grandson.'

'What – with that girl? Don't you believe it,' cried Mrs Corbett, roused, 'she's as hard as nails – dreadfully, dreadfully hard. I'm sure she'll never have children. She won't *want* them.'

'"With God",' pronounced Mrs Lysaght, '"all things are possible".' To which Mrs Corbett muttered 'Oh . . . *God* –' and a silence fell which Mrs Lysaght felt might be preliminary to the resumption of the dyed ermine stole, and departure – before the juice had all been squeezed from the situation. A dazzling notion burst upon her.

'Cora!' she cried. '*I* know. Now's the time. You're coming

along with me – to Mrs Pearson for a sitting. No –' as Mrs Corbett began to speak. 'I won't hear a word. It will take your mind off it. I'll ring her up now.' She started from her chair.

'Don't be silly, Helen – how can I? Peggy's mother.'

'Oh . . . yes, of course . . . do you know, I'd *forgotten*! But you'll have to meet her some time –'

'Why should I? horrid spooky woman – oh dear, why did you remind me? – and living in a slum –'

'Frobisher can drive us!'

'Oh Helen, do be quiet – my head's splitting – there's all that to think about, too. I wish I was dead,' she wailed.

'That's easy to say. We've all felt like that. Why, when Ronald died –' She broke off. No, we had not all felt like that. She never had. Mourned, missed, regretted, yes; but not beyond the bounds of commonsense. 'You must be brave,' she advised.

'I hate being brave. I've always hated it. Charlie took care of me. When he was alive I didn't have to be brave. And now I shan't even have Arnold. He did at least see about super-tax and things . . . and I can't bear Mr Truscott, he's so *blunt*.'

'Well, I'm going,' said Mrs Lysaght, undeterred. 'I shall ring her up now. Oh come on, Cora,' catching girlishly at her hand, and just stopping herself from adding 'be a sport'. 'It'll cheer us both up.'

'Helen, I can't. You know how I hate creepiness. I don't know how you can suggest such a thing. All I wanted was . . . a little sympathy . . .' She turned away, looking desolately around for her stole. She no longer wanted to go on pouring out her troubles to Helen.

Mrs Lysaght, seeing that the last drops were unforthcoming, lifted the two yards of ermine reverently from a chair-back and draped it about her. 'I didn't mean to be cross,' Mrs Corbett added, 'but you must see how difficult it all is. Comes of marrying the wrong type of girl – all sorts of things crop up.'

'There's her father, too,' said Mrs Lysaght, as they moved towards the door; she could not resist this sentence, which brought a fresh burst of alarm, tears, and lamentation before Mrs Corbett was packed into the Rolls and, waving weakly and mouthing promises to meet again soon, was driven away. Mrs Lysaght had not suggested prolonging the visit; she was already moving, in spirit, towards further pleasures.

She had come down to the car with her friend. She returned to her flat with light and purposeful step. The news had stimulated her and lifted her spirits, as well as giving her the perfect excuse (one almost coloured by duty) for telephoning Mrs Pearson.

Mrs Pearson lay looking out at the summer weather. The splendour of the morning had soothed even her wearing anxiety about Peggy. She could see a few feet of sky, its vivid blue delicately tempered by the net across the windows, and the chimneys on the roof of the house opposite, glowing in the sun's rays to wallflower-red. Her mind was empty; her soul dreamt; only her heart carried its burden, and that seemed remote this morning; her heart was numb.

She was thinking that a drive into the country would be nice – it was years since she had seen open fields – when the telephone bell in the hall rang. The faint insistent noise penetrated the shut door and her passive dreaming. She did not move but turned her eyes questioningly towards it, frowning.

It went on and on.

Erika must be still asleep. Resolved to ignore it, Mrs Pearson let her thoughts dwell on the child: she had been different since the death of Mr Fisher, giving up her excursions to buy stockings, or to meet a girl friend who knew plenty of boys, to be with Mrs Pearson; hardly leaving her room and sitting up with her all night. Her broken sleep had to be made up by late rising. She had bought flowers and taken them to the old man's grave too, and she was more silent. At least, thought Mrs Pearson, turning her eyes again to the blue sky and the red chimneys, most of that worry with Tom about boys seems to have stopped. Not that I grudge her, it's natural, but . . .

She could almost put aside all frightening thoughts, on this calm sunlit morning. Fear had retreated to the dimmest depths of her mind. She was not even touched by a suspicion that her own illness bore, in its slow secret current, the occasional sign, like a dark rock seen for an instant in the sweep of a grey stream, that pointed towards death; that Erika had seen these signs, and was awed.

The ringing had stopped. Thank goodness, thought Mrs Pearson luxuriously. But, even as the thought arose, she became aware of something crouching on her body's threshold, waiting and intent, as it had not done for many days; not since the prayers of those kind people had, as you might say, begun to work . . . Her large eyes widened as if she saw the approach of something dreaded, and then she turned them towards the blank pink surface of the door, on which a faint knock had sounded.

'Who's that? Come in.'

Annie's small old face peeped round the crack. Mrs Pearson raised herself on one elbow. 'What is it, dear? Is something wrong?'

She asked this because of Annie's expression.

'Not as I know of. I'm sure I hope not. But it's a lady. Says she must speak to you. It's very important, she says.' She paused, staring in vague alarm.

'Didn't you say I'm ill, dear? Not that it's true, really, this morning, I feel almost my old self.' She laughed, a little laugh. But as she laughed she felt the watching, waiting thing move very slightly nearer. One part of her could laugh, but another felt unmistakably, on some unnamed threshold, the stealthy, almost imperceptible, advance.

'I said you was better, Mrs Pearson.'

'Oh. Oh, then perhaps . . .' She hesitated, still resting on her elbow, veiled in rosy nylon and lace. How pretty her room was. Her little plastic and glass creatures gleamed and glowed in the reflection of the outside world's sunlight, and the many vases of summer flowers breathed their scents into the quiet, warm air.

'All right, Annie. Will you ask her to hold on? I'll . . .'

'She said to say it's about Peggy,' Annie blurted, and at once Mrs Pearson sat upright, her smitten heart pumping blood in a rush to all the drowsing cells in the delicate skin of her face.

'I wasn't goin' to upset you. But she did say . . .'

'All right, all right, go and tell her I'm coming.' She scrambled from the bed, pushed her thin, pretty feet into slippers, tied her girdle, distractedly moved her heavy hair about as if to gather it into order, then let it fall again and hurried, moving unsteadily, out of the room. Annie had just finished giving the message when she reached the telephone. Mrs Pearson snatched it.

'Hullo? Who is it?'

'Oh, Mrs Pearson. I'm so glad to hear you're better. This lovely weather is enough to make us all feel better, isn't it? I really rang up to congratulate you – it's Mrs Lysaght speaking. You remember me, don't you? Dear old Gladys used to work for me. I sent you some flowers.'

'Congratulate . . .? Yes, I remember . . . but . . .'

'Haven't you heard?' Mrs Lysaght could hardly keep the note

congratulating herself out of her voice. 'About . . . but you must have.'

'I haven't – I haven't – heard anything. What do you mean?'

'What a naughty girl she is. About Peggy –'

'Oh do *please* tell me. I haven't heard from her for five weeks. I don't know where she is –'

'My dear, she's in Fez. In Morocco. And she's married.'

'Who to?' said Mrs Pearson, after a pause just long enough to lessen Mrs Lysaght's enjoyment slightly. Her voice was exhausted and quiet.

'To Arnold Corbett. Mrs Corbett's son. He – hasn't she told you about him?'

'She hasn't told me anything,' said the mother. 'She never did, not from a little thing.'

'Well, he's in the middle forties and really very nice. Quiet, you know, and plays a lot of golf. And – though of course, I hope dear Mrs Corbett will be with us for *many* years yet – one day he will be a rich man. Very, very rich. He's more than comfortably off now . . . I'm astonished you hadn't heard. Really astonished. But it's *good* news, isn't it? Such a comfort to think of one's girl being settled. One doesn't want to be material-minded but money is always useful. And the cost of living nowadays . . . I'm so glad you're feeling stronger.'

'Do you think she loves him?' Mrs Pearson asked pitifully, and received in answer a tinkling laugh.

'Oh I'm sure I don't know. I only knew them both very slightly. Of course, all that wealth – a girl wouldn't be human if she didn't find that tempting. One thing I must warn you about, Mrs Pearson – *his* mother isn't at all pleased.'

'Isn't she?'

'No. (I don't think I'm telling tales.) I thought it only kind to tell you.'

'Yes. Thank you.'

Shock, and the special pain reserved for mothers, now overwhelmed Mrs Pearson, throwing down the slight barriers built up by peace and hope. Peggy had not told her; she never told her anything. What was the use of a blue sky and a sunny morning, with their whispers of some far-off happiness that should last for ever? They were only a blue sky, only a sunny morning.

The invader, pushing apart the cracked barriers, crept in agilely over their fragments, spurning them, smiling in triumph. *I'll help you. I always have, haven't I? Don't you remember the old days? I'll help you. I'll give you my strength and help you.*

'Now that you're feeling so much better,' Mrs Lysaght was saying brightly, 'how about keeping your promise and giving me a sitting?'

34

It had been arranged that Gerald should come one evening and burn what Gladys had begun by calling 'Mr Fisher's papers' and speedily came to referring to as 'all that old rubbish'; a bonfire was to be made in the yard at Lily Cottage. Gerald was glad of the plan: he wanted to see Mr Fisher's life-work turned into pure red and yellow flame. The card with its earnest legend was in his pocket-book, and he meant to find some private occasion and give it to Annie Barnes, whose quiet grief had not gone unobserved.

The sisters had been cheered by the postcard from their nephew, inviting them to spend a day with him and see his new bungalow at Osney.

There had been a suggestion that they might spend the night, but this of course was unthinkable, though it was discussed at such length that anyone might have been excused for supposing it wasn't; the discussion added to their pleasure, giving a sensation of luxurious freedom and power of choice. There had been the stimulating surprise of discovering that the coaches didn't go there; it was all trains; and the wondering whether it would be fine, and the two-day examination of the question whether Annie could make the journey.

It had all ended in unflawed enjoyment; the train-ride, the meeting with Georgie, after eighteen months, at the station in his car; the drive through the countryside shimmering in June's brilliant green under a smiling sun; and then, best of all, the bungalow and its comforts. The museum had been ever so interesting, too, when they could take their minds off the gas cooker and the television. And Georgie in charge of it all!

But on this evening Gladys opened the door to Gerald and looked at him in scared silence, every trace of the cheerfulness bestowed by the memory of their visit gone from her face.

'I'm glad you've come,' she said quietly.

'Is Mrs Pearson worse?' he exclaimed, alarmed.

He went into the hall, and she shut the door. It was a very beautiful evening; Midsummer Eve, he suddenly recalled, as if the reflected light in the hall, neither pink nor gold, and the silence, had brought the fact into his mind.

The light came in through the small curved transom of the door, barred with a lead device; a falling light, and soft. The silence, he noticed, the characteristic silence of Lily Cottage, seemed deeper this evening.

Gladys was standing staring at him, in a most unwonted quiet, twisting her hands about in the flowered stuff of her overall.

'Oh yes, dreadfully bad this evening. There's been ever such an upset. He . . . he's . . . upstairs now, he is. With her. I was wondering . . . I don't like young Erika being here, I don't, straight. I wondered would Mrs Geddes have her?' The words came out in a kind of slow distracted way, so unlike her usual manner that he began to feel a faint alarm; her hands continued to twist, twist, among the gaudy flowers.

'But she was so much better! Do you think she'll want to see me? Or perhaps Mr Pearson . . .' He paused, with a foot on the first stair, also speaking very quietly. A hush at the top of the stairs seemed to flow down to them.

'Oh I know – I know. She was getting on ever so nicely, we all said so. The praying, I reckon. And then that Peggy getting married so sudden and not telling her – and then Mrs Lysaght come along this afternoon, and would have her fortune told. I opened the door. Came in a taxi, with a lovely bunch of roses. I used to work for her.' She paused. A little of her usual manner was returning.

'Had a bit of a chat but wild to get upstairs and see Mrs P. Erika and me helped Mrs P. get ready, wasn't like herself, I noticed. Didn't seem the same at all. Ever so sharp with us. (I don't mind telling you, I had a bit of a cry. Annie said I was soft.)'

Gerald murmured something. He was beginning to feel disagreeably disturbed. The atmosphere in the house was insistent; he was not imagining it; the divine steady light pouring in through the transom seemed outside and apart from the cold silence snaking down from the landing. He compelled himself to listen.

'So I took her up . . . we thought we'd made sure *he* was out. My Gawd, you ought to have seen Annie's face when he walked into the kitchen. I was just making Mrs P.'s tea and young Erika was going to take it up. Put two cups, and a bit of a cake I'd made, hasn't been so mad lately on boys and that, let's hope . . . didn't shout at us or anything. But such a face! You never saw anythink like it. I was that upset I couldn't say a word. Grabbed hold of my arm, if you please, and then I did speak up. Said I'd have the police on him if he laid his dirty hands on me. Didn't take a bit of notice. Kep' on saying who's in there with her, who is it, as if he'd gone mental. So I told him. Off he goes, like something had stung him, flying off with not a word of beg your pardon and the next thing there was him shouting and banging the door upstairs enough to bring the house down and Mrs Lysaght hollering out, "Gladys, Gladys, get me a taxi, quick," and I says to Erika and Annie, "Now don't you stir one step from this kitchen," and runs out and there she is, in the hall, crying and carrying on and saying she was frightened and I don't know what, and there was an evil spirit in the bedroom and we must get a priest – as if she'd gone mental as well. As if I knew where to get a taxi!'

She paused. Her voice had been running on in a hushed current, rapid as usual, but exhausted; even the small bursts of indignation lacked force.

Gerald had listened with sensations that were quite unfamiliar to him. It was the chill emanating from the shut door on the landing that reinforced each word of Gladys's, loading them; colouring them ominously. He could feel it on his face and hands now, and through the thick old clothes he had put on for the burning of the papers. It was as if he were standing in a steady wind that was streaming off a glacier.

'I made *her* get the taxi. Looked it up in the phone book, and then it took ages coming and she was carrying on all the while – crying and saying she'd never seen anything so horrible in her life and praying to God to protect her – she made me downright wild. Only . . . when . . .'

Gladys paused, looking downwards as if in some strange kind of shame at confessing what she had seen.

'See, I went and had a peep round the door, after she'd gone, it was so dead quiet and I thought . . . and . . . and . . . *he* was lying on the bed. Holding her hand. And crying. Crying he was. Didn't see me. She did, though. Looked right at me – and her eyes – I can't tell you – and says somethink. Spitting – like. I don't mind telling you, I fair ran. It's . . . it's awful, sir . . . hadn't we better get the Vicar?'

'I don't know . . . I'd better go up.' He thought of putting his hand comfortingly on her shoulder, but did not; his alarm, and the desire to help, and the feeling that a climax was approaching, were not yet strong enough to overcome his dislike of making gestures. 'Now try not to worry,' he said, 'we're here – the Church, I mean – and we'll see to things. It will . . . be all right.' He smiled, briefly and stiffly.

'Thank God, someone's 'ere,' said Gladys. She turned away.

Shivering in the cold, Gerald knocked. There was no answering voice, and in a moment he knocked again; then, after another pause, opened the door.

The room looked as usual: the colours and the prettiness were as they had always been; the cheap wood of the furniture, shaped into debased contemporary curves, had its usual chemical sheen and the grotesques on mantelpiece and dressing table smiled their pert smiles. The electric fire glared, the glow of pink walls and ceiling mastered the more delicate pink of the sunset. And it was all stilled: checked: a mask, covering the real room. It was a room reflected in a looking-glass.

His eyes went straight to the figures on the bed. Mrs Pearson's body was lying with open eyes, the mass of her hair spread on the pillow. It was only her body; that was the one thing he knew. Her spirit had gone somewhere else, and something, another, was smiling out of her eyes, and their colour had changed to iridescent green, and their shape had lengthened, and slitted, and tilted at the corners. The smile on the lips and in the eyes was not mad or in any way linked, even distortedly, with the smiles of the race of man; it could only be called a smile because there was no other word that could be used for it. Somewhere else, perhaps, there was a word, or a sound, that was used.

Pearson lay sprawled across the foot of the bed, face downwards, with one palm flat against the curve under the bedclothes.

Gerald drew back, with an indrawn breath, and shut the door slowly to give himself time to force his courage and his thoughts back into control. The desire to do the right thing, the thing that should succeed, was overwhelming; it was stronger than horror or fear and it instantly replaced them. He prayed, as he raced down the stairs.

The sisters were in the kitchen, talking subduedly together; Erika was sitting by the table, with bent head, in silence. All three turned pale faces to him as he came in.

'She's very ill indeed,' he said quietly, 'and we must get Mr Geddes – no –' as Gladys began to say, 'There's the phone' – 'no, that'll make a noise. I want to keep things absolutely quiet. Go along, all three of you, it's better you should be out of the way. Go on, Gladys, there's . . . a dear . . .' for she was hesitating, and again starting to speak, 'you see, I don't know what's going to happen.' He broke off. 'You'd better take night things. And tell Mr Geddes to come at once – at once.'

He hardly thought of them from that moment, but raced back up the stairs, pausing again at the door to pull himself together.

He thought, vaguely, that until this moment he had always thrust anyone thought of as being deadly ill in body or mind into the hands of the experts. Now, he was the expert. Thank God, another would soon be on the way. He opened the door.

The two had not moved. He shut the door and went across to a chair beside the fire and sat down – to wait.

At first, he tried to pray, and then to fix his thoughts upon something holy – a line from the Psalms, some remembered painting of the Crucifixion – but it was useless; he could hear the words and see in his mind's eye every detail of the painting, but he did not possess enough spiritual technique necessary for keeping them in his thoughts.

He began to experience nothing but a detached curiosity. His moral sense told him that it was evil; yet he could feel nothing else, and the cold, crawling out from somewhere beyond the warmth of the summer evening, slowly burned into his flesh inside his clothes and began to seep inwards, in the form of this passionless curiosity, threatening his spirit.

There had never been any clock in the room, he realized, and he glanced at his wrist-watch, seeing, without thoughts, that it was . . . The glow was fading to a clear yellow; he watched the seemingly interminable change through the net veils at the window, and saw the colour die off the slate of the roofs, leaving them a dull warm grey; it was early yet . . . and it was Midsummer Eve, of course, Midsummer Eve . . . he gave a violent start.

Pearson was weeping, without lifting his face from the surface of the bed, moving his shoulders shudderingly. A shock of horror struck Gerald, like a sudden blaze of heat: the creature beside Pearson on the bed had started up, Mrs Pearson's beautiful hair falling about the face it had usurped, and was silently laughing.

He could bear no more. He too sprang up, as the door opened, quickly but silently, and Mr Geddes came in, his pale face one question. Instantly, the triumphing creature, awkwardly turning Mrs Pearson's head towards him, became quiet. It sank back, coiling into its hollow in the bedclothes.

35

Mr Geddes looked across at Gerald and beckoned, and Gerald got up and went over to the bed; on another gesture, he stationed himself on the other side.

Stillness began to creep into the air. Pearson's lamentations had ceased. Gerald noticed that Mr Geddes's veined hands, clasped about a small Bible in a red cover, were trembling.

It was a shock when he spoke: Pearson lifted his face, swollen and wet, from his arms to stare; and yet the sound was not impressive; Mr Geddes's attempt to put sternness into it only emphasized a lack of strength in his ageing vocal chords.

Gerald had expected a prayer, or some invocation. But he asked:

'What is your name?'

Silence. The thing neither moved nor made any sound. Pearson remained motionless, staring at Mr Geddes across his outflung arms; once he swallowed a sob, but did not move his eyes from the priest's face.

'What is your name?' Mr Geddes repeated in a moment, in the same tone, with its note of compelled severity. Gerald suddenly drew in the chilled, still air with a gasp; he had been holding his breath.

Again, Mrs Pearson's body did not move nor any voice come from it. Gerald, from his height, could look down on the slits of the eyes; his thoughts began to wander, and he recalled the glistening green surface of a pond near his home; brilliant as gems, suggesting some marvellous Byzantine or Hindu pavement, that would part and reveal darkness and slime beneath.

The patient question, and the silence that answered it, proceeded without pause.

His wandering thoughts were recalled to the enclosed circle that was the room after what seemed a very long time; there had occurred, he realized, a change in the sensation that had held his body interminably; the faintest lessening in the grip of the cold.

Another fifty or so repetitions of Mr Geddes's question into that furious silence, and Gerald was certain. He moved the muscles of his chilled shoulders cautiously. Something was building up in the room that was driving back the cold. It was invisible and it was silent. But he felt it.

It, whatever it might be, was beginning to fill the space about the bed where they stood. They were surrounded, lapped, bathed in it. Freshets of power, Gerald thought, that will swell to a river, to a flood, and at last to the colossal strength of the sea.

His dreaming stare, fixed unseeingly on Mr Geddes, was disturbed by a sudden gesture. Mr Geddes had wiped his forehead. He took his own stare from the creature coiled in the bed and looked across at Gerald and nodded.

Gerald parted his lips. They parted stickily and with difficulty.

'What is your name?' he began.

The last light was beginning to wane down into the west, and the roofs were darkening against the sky; the confused roar of returning traffic had subsided into its usual ominous drone. A window opposite sprang suddenly into yellow light. Gerald heard his own voice, sounding gentle, almost casual.

'What is your name?'

Into the silence. A brief pause; the voice of twenty-seven years moves more quickly than that of sixty-odd.

'What is your name?' And silence, and no movement, and Pearson's head lifted, listening, and again 'What is your name?' into the rebutting, furious, fighting silence.

Gerald felt that his quiet voice could not be of any use, it was weak and inept. But at the same time he could feel himself drawing upon the power that was building up, and instinct told him strongly not to force any change into his level, almost relaxed, tone. He could feel the power; there was no human word for it, nor any picture of it in his mind's eye; but it was strength, and he could draw from it, and when he drew from it, it was not lessened but increased. Knowing nothing of its nature, suspecting all, he feared to change even the position of his hands, that he had begun by clasping tightly, feeling them slippery with sweat and trembling, and presently found linked, and unmoving, and cool.

At some moment in time – it may have been just after nine, for he seemed to remember having heard chimes striking from some church in the world outside the room – he came, as it were, back into consciousness and heard himself ask, 'What is your name?' It was the sixth-hundredth time, because he was young and strong, but the remote sound of the hour striking threw him off his balance, and his concentration faltered for an instant. He looked across at Mr Geddes, who, lifting his head slightly, at once began.

'What is your name?'

They had not moved from their places. Sweat poured down under their clothes, draining away energy from their bodies. But, precisely as a stream replaces the water pouring through its bed with an endless benison of more from the source, so

Power poured through them, channels that they were; that they had allowed themselves to become.

All this time they had not looked at Pearson. He had remained half-lying beside the bed, from which he had slid on to his knees, motionless except for an occasional twitch of his limbs, while his eyes unmovingly watched the face on the pillows.

But, in a moment when Mr Geddes was passing the task over to Gerald, he did glance down at Pearson, and he experienced a second's dismay. The man's face expressed an unmistakable fierce hope. It's too soon to hope, Mr Geddes thought dimly, and then thought – all thought – faded again as he rested (he could rest now) on the Rest in the room. And the hours passed.

It was at the two thousandth asking that the change came. Mr Geddes had spoken the question; he did not know that now his voice was as if rock itself had been given vocal chords, or steel could speak.

'What is your name?' he demanded.

Then the head on the pillow rolled right round and the eyes stared at him and the thing behind their slits, struggling like an impaled snake, shrieked, 'No – no!'

The protest whistled through the air, unstirred for hours by any sounds except those of the question, seeming to cut it; it was thinner, higher, shriller than the keenest audible sound; indeed, it was only just audible.

Mr Geddes started forward.

'Your name – tell me your name!' he thundered, transformed, towering. 'In the Name of Jesus of Nazareth the Christ – *your name!*'

'Your name . . .' Gerald repeated softly and almost dreamily; he was a channel worn down to its bed, too exhausted to produce more than echo of the older priest's words. Years of experience and of unquestioning, unfaltering, unself-conscious giving, had enabled Mr Geddes to lay himself open more completely to the Power on which they were drawing.

'Your name!' Mr Geddes called again. The room, the streets lying beyond, the sky with its bright risen stars, were held and locked and cradled within the Power.

The green eyes rolled upwards, almost disappearing into the head and displaying whites milky and flecked with emerald; Mrs Pearson's lips parted and out into the room fled a single sound.

It was almost visible; so dry and glittering with malice was it; but it made no syllables recognizable by human ears. It was kin, in its un-humanity, to the snake's voice and the hissing of sand blown along by the wind. Yet it came through from a world belonging to neither. Instantly, on the rustling past of this sound that was a name into the presence of the Power, there followed a new sound.

It was a voice, human, yet not human, coming to their ears with a sense of exquisite refreshment because, for the first time since the exorcism had begun, they heard a sound that was beautiful. This voice, also, came from the lips of Mrs Pearson; and neither of them ever spoke, afterwards, to the other of their mutual astounding conviction that there had been in it a note of holy triumphant laughter.

'Peace,' it said to them, 'be at peace, I have her now. Come with me' – and it uttered the sound that was the creature's name – 'come. Out of her.'

And that was all. When that voice ceased, a silence began that was different. Something was beginning to withdraw from the room, whence the paralysing cold had already retreated. Gerald became aware that he was stiflingly hot; of course, the electric fire was full on, and it was a summer night – Midsummer Eve . . . he wrenched his thoughts back, with an effort.

Mrs Pearson's body lay on the bed, empty. The mask-like and shell-like change had taken place. She had gone, and the temple was void. There was not a shred or shadow of hope about that going and that emptiness. The shell, inhabited, had been so pretty, and one man had loved it so much, and now it was a white peace.

That man was edging himself along the bed towards it.

The two watched, breathing heavily in silence, too tired to move, for a moment; then Mr Geddes lurched stiffly forward, holding out a hand in protest.

But Pearson had wrapped his arms around the body, in frenzy, calling her name. Gerald's strength was returning. He gripped him by the shoulders, trying to lift him away, speaking quietly because of the presence of the dead.

'Don't, don't do that – leave her alone – it's all right – it's all right now, I tell you, it's all right.' But Pearson neither ceased his writhing nor his frantic cries.

A current of cool air suddenly flowed over Gerald; Mr Geddes had staggered to the window and with an effort hauled down the heavy sash. He stood, gaspingly breathing in the air's refreshment, then came back to the bed.

Gerald, taking away his hands from Pearson's shoulders, turned to him helplessly.

Suddenly, Pearson was quiet. They watched him, surprised, their thoughts suspended for an instant; then Gerald sprang forward to catch his hand.

But he was not in time; it had been crawling to his pocket and then to his mouth while they were only hearing his cries and seeing his writhing body.

There followed a time so dreadful that their nerves were

not capable of responding, and they felt nothing and could do no more than hold his arching body between their feeble, horrified hands, their eyes fixed upon his face, where a desperate eagerness struggled with the appalling agony.

They heard him gasp something in another language through the foam on his lips, and then they saw the spirit shoot out of him – *go*, in a kind of leap, a frenetic haste, as if it had literally sprung away after her.

They lowered the body on to the bed. 'Thank God in His mercy,' Mr Geddes said weakly, in a moment, 'much the best thing. Much the best.'

He wiped his forehead.

'That's right,' as Gerald drew something over the awful face, 'cover him up, poor chap. Poor chap. I – poor chap.' There was a pause. 'Upon my word I – will you go down and telephone the police? I'll be with you in a moment . . . Tell them – I'll be with you in a moment. Tell them to hold on – I'll speak to them. I'll be with you in a moment.'

He lowered himself to his knees, beside the bed, pressing with both hands to support his trembling body. But nothing, no words, came. He merely knelt there, shaking violently and feeling, through the darkness between the palms covering his face, the presence of the two deserted shells lying side by side, a few inches from his bent head.

When, after some minutes, he looked up, and out at the world again, the first sight that met his eyes was a mighty star, flashing in the darkness through the open window.

It had not the five needle-points which man's imagination has given to the star, but was a great blur of light, a finger-shaped burning, lying along the blue cavern made in space by its own sovereign flame.

36

The suicide of Pearson attracted little attention.

There was a third of a column in the local paper, and that was all.

Gerald reproached himself, afterwards, for enjoying his caricature of a 'pale young curate', with his 'shocking' and his 'very sad', and his apparently simple-hearted rejoicing over the happy settlement of the two old ladies left in Rose Cottage: they were to keep house for a nephew living in the country. And had the young reporter heard that Rose Walk and the two cottages were coming down? Camden Council was to make an Adventure Playground on the site.

He wondered, fantastically, while he was seeing the reporter out of the Vicarage door, whether any of the black and white and brown children who would play there would ever meet with another kind of adventure, from a haunter lingering starvedly by that levelled ground? But he did not think so; he could hear the voice that had rescued her yet; it rang in his inward ear, and he felt certain that she would not again come through to Earth.

Some weeks went quietly past for the Barnes sisters.

Gladys had been reduced to saying at intervals that it never rained but it poured. Shock upon shock! And now the Walk coming down. But that, stupendous event though it was, would not, thank God, affect them. They were going to live with Georgie.

Though Gladys was always loyal to the past and a great repeater of old saws and songs and reminiscences, she also lived for something to look forward to, an attitude not affected by her passionate relish for, and enjoyment in, what was happening now. She was thus suspended, most enviably, in three worlds all equally pleasurable. She was also unendurably irritating to people whose feelings were deeper.

So lively was her talk and manner, on the evening six weeks later when they were sitting on Osney station, awaiting Georgie and the car, that Annie told her for goodness' sake to be a bit quiet.

'What for?' Gladys stared. 'No-one to hear me, is there?'

The surprisingly large station was, indeed, deserted. No-one had got off the train except themselves. Osney station was due for closure; it lay at the end of a branch-line that was the middle of a satisfactory chain leading to off-the-mapness, and it was four miles from Osney village. It could have just as well been called Clinton-by-Bede.

'I should think they was glad to see the last of us,' said Annie.

'Who was, I should like to know?'

'Them in the train.'

'Oh – them.' Gladys looked joyfully round at the dim sweep of platform, the afterglow touching the white chimneys of an intimidatingly large hotel looking aloofly down at them in their hollow, and finally at their collection of shabby bundles. 'Lot of miseries. What say we go up and wait outside?'

'Up all them stairs? Oh Glad, I can't. I'm that tired.'

'Tired? You been sitting down two hours.'

'Well, I am. And all that stuff to carry.'

'Oh come on. I'll help you. We don't want to bring Georgie down all this way.'

Collecting their carrier-bags, and Annie's old friends the coats, and their small ancient suitcases and their paper parcels, they made their way slowly along the platform and across a bridge that offered them a view of quiet fields, fading into a twilight misty with heat, below a cloudy sky flooded with rose-red. Annie paused, partly to ease her aching arms and partly to consider the prospect. But she said nothing: she was thinking vaguely that it looked lonely but not sad. A distant scream recalled her. 'Not a sign of him!'

She found Gladys in not quite amiable conversation with the elderly ticket collector in charge at the exit.

'What — no caff, not even a refreshment room?' she was exclaiming; on their previous visit they had been carried off so briskly by Georgie that they had had no opportunity to investigate the resources of Osney station. 'I couldn't half do with a cuppa and my sister's wore out.'

'There's the Ladies. On the platform,' said the collector, lingering at the open door of a little office where a storage-heater, turned off for the summer months, offered its sole and sullen company in the long twilight. There was also the scent of hay and dew, but that was not company.

'Thank you for nothing — I should think so,' said Gladys. 'We just come all that way up.'

'There's a waiting-room, I meant,' and he returned into his cell.

Gladys marched out through the dusky little entrance, past the ticket office, and piled her parcels on a melancholy old seat with a damaged back. The hotel, glowing with discreet lights and hung with flowery window baskets, still stared aloofly. A pale road, lampless, bordered by a dusty tall hedge, wandered off into the unknown under the fading pink sky. The air was silent and very warm.

'Can't go in there, cost the earth,' said Gladys, studying the hotel with a stare as critical as its own. 'Don't expect he'll be long.' She sat down.

'Had a breakdown, p'raps,' suggested Annie.

'Go on, be cheerful,' said Gladys mechanically. She turned to her sister, 'Best put one of them round you, catch your death,' and she snatched a coat from her unresisting arm and draped it carefully round her shoulders, in spite of Annie's protest that she was 'boiling alive now'.

They sat beside their bulging parcels and composed themselves for a wait. At intervals, Gladys got up, explored the outside of the station, peered in through the window, not without mutters, at the collector reading his paper by the dim yellow light of a gas lamp beside the unsympathetic person of the storage heater, and returned to her seat.

''Ere he is!' cried Annie, as a car approached, announcing its arrival moments in advance by the comet of its headlights flaring some miles down the road. But it dwindled into the distance, with an appearance of heartlessness.

'I can't get over it all,' Annie murmured presently, 'seems like a dream. I keep thinking about young Erika. Going to be a nurse. Paying for her and everything (not what Government won't help). She'll make a fine little nurse.'

'If she don't stifle the poor souls smoking,' was Gladys's detached comment, without removing her severe gaze from the view, growing ever more lost in twilight, down the road. 'What I can't get over is Mrs L. coming back to our church – used to tell me she was fed up with it. Always saying so. Keeping on about it. Used to say she *envied* me. A bit soft, I always thought.'

'She 'ad a fright, Glad. A bad fright.'

Indeed, the fright had been bad; it was quite a year before Mrs Lysaght recovered herself sufficiently to resume her picking of ecclesiastical holes and her badgering of Mr Geddes and her alleged study of esoteric religions.

'That Mrs Geddes was ever so kind, I will say,' Gladys said presently, 'it's a draughty old place, I wouldn't live there for keeps not if you was to pay me, and there wasn't never enough tea –'

'You was everlasting saying so.'

'– and *they* got you down, going off to pray and that, and those *black robes*. I didn't half want to laugh the first time they come in the kitchen wearing them things.'

'But they was ever so nice to us, Glad.'

'And that old rackman. Doing himself in. Best thing for him, wasn't it – poor Mrs P. But it's all for the best,' she ended vaguely, and added a comment which, in this case, was true, 'merciful release, really. Send Mrs Geddes a card at Christmas.'

'I'm that thirsty,' Annie was beginning, then broke off with a pleased cry as a biggish car, driven at a reassuringly sane pace, bumped gently round a corner from a lane, which they had not observed, at the side of the station. Both got up, peering anxiously.

It stopped, and there, smiling at them from the driver's seat, was a large rosy face.

'Georgie!' cried Gladys, all affection.

'There you are, Auntie – hullo, Auntie Annie – sorry I kept you waiting, had a bit of trouble getting her to start, she does that sometimes. Your box has come all safe,' Georgie went on, referring to a large ruinous theatrical basket containing those of their possessions not contained in the carrier bags and little suitcases. 'I got your rooms all nice and ready. Come along.'

They bustled about in the owl-light, helping him to stow away their bundles and Annie's coats. The ticket collector came out to watch and assumed a new (and slightly embarrassing, in view of Gladys's previous talk with him) identity for them by being called Mr Skeggs and being familiarly known to Georgie.

A gentle sensation of home-coming pervaded the occasion, particularly for Gladys, whose 'own boy' Georgie had always been. There was, too, a feeling of wonder that it should be Georgie, whom they remembered with a comforter settled immovably in the middle of his large rosy face, and sitting in his pram in the charge of their two proud fourteen-and-twelve-year-old selves, who should be giving them a home in their old age. All be together, Gladys was thinking comfortably, as she climbed into the car.

'There is a rug, Auntie,' he now said mildly to Annie, 'look . . . on the seat.' He eyed the coats expressionlessly: his aunts wouldn't want those old things now they was living with him. But there was plenty of time for the disposal of them.

Georgie had been born with the assumption that there was plenty of time, and, as a result, looked forty when he was sixty. As he was also uncursed with ambition or any overwhelming amorous drive, and was by nature secretive and rather good at using what brains he had, he had succeeded in getting exactly what he wanted from life; his fair share, and comfort. This had been George Barnes's war aim. He had also, to his surprise, neatly killed two men.

'Not thinking of getting married, Georgie?' asked Annie unexpectedly, when they had been driving for a little while along the twilit road. A rabbit, its fur gleaming silvery in the headlights, dashed across in front of the car and they all exclaimed and laughed; even Annie, who had suddenly been struck by the thought of some bit of a girl intruding on their new comforts. But Georgie's laugh came again, on a shy, but also sly, note.

'Not me, Auntie,' he said, in the tone with which he had greeted this question for the past forty-seven years, 'I know when I'm well off. You and Auntie Glad are all the wives I want.'

There was more enjoyable laughter, followed by the agreeable revelation that a toad-in-the-hole was keeping hot for them in the oven; Georgie was a good cook. They would be in time, too, for an exciting telly programme.

They could see the house lights of Osney now; two modest rows of gold curving along a village street between dim fields where mist was rising. It was quite quiet, but of course they could not hear the quiet because of the noise the car was making, and there was nothing notable in sight except that lovely curve of the street, unexpected as the flick of a quiet personal will, meandering past a few lightless shops, where the colours of cotton dresses and packets of processed foods and cartons of chips all glowed gently in the benevolence of the almost-faded afterglow.

Soft and clear they glowed, in their unpleasing shapes, and a stout old church, looking down on Osney from its place on a little rise at the beginning of the village, caught just the very last ghost of the light on its stones, and glowed faintly too.

They had seen all this before. It was like coming home, knowing the place already.

Gladys wondered what time the shops opened in the morning and which was the best place for stockings, and who the butcher would be and if there would be real country vegetables. She thought for an instant of the shops in the Archway, and of Joneses, then forgot them.

The last prospect before the shops and cottages closed in on either side caught her eye, on the left; a field of pale stubble leading on to woodland, dark against the almost vanished pink. A big bird flew up leisurely from the field as the car went past, and winged off to the distant trees. Gladys's eye watched it go. It wasn't hurrying itself. Well, in the country things didn't. She spoke, but something in the view held her memory, and she did not turn her head.

'Looks just the same, doesn't it?' she observed, 'like when we used to be little. The country,' and Annie, her eyes already fixed on the white front of Georgie's bungalow, next to the fantastically carved wooden façade of the Old Guard House, echoed her in the same tone.

'Just the same. Not changed a bit. Eh, Georgie? Just like when we was all little.'